ONLY
with the
HEART

ALSO BY SHERRI SZEMAN

The Kommandant's Mistress

ONLY
with the
HEART

A *NOVEL*

SHERRI SZEMAN

ARCADE PUBLISHING • NEW YORK

FIRST EDITION

This is a work of fiction. Names, places, characters, and incidents are either products of the author's imagination or are used fictitiously.

Library of Congress Cataloging-in-Publication Data
Szeman, Sherri.
    Only with the heart : a novel / Sherri Szeman.
        p. cm.
    ISBN 1-55970-538-8
        1. Alzheimer's disease — Fiction.   2. Mothers and daughters — Fiction.   3. Terminally ill — Family relationships — Fiction. I. Title.
    PS3569.Z39 O55 2000
    813'.54—dc21   00-36272

Published in the United States by Arcade Publishing, Inc., New York
Distributed by Time Warner Trade Publishing.

Visit our Web site at www.arcadepub.com

10 9 8 7 6 5 4 3 2 1

Designed by API

EB

For Judy Pistilli,

Blessèd be thy advice,
and blessèd be thou.

I Samuel 25:33

For Barbara Walker, Mary McGuire, Sharon Brown,
Becky Keller, Connie Post, Christopher Williams,
Terrence Glass, Evelyn Schott, and Kelly Wingo,

Blessèd are they who have not seen,
and yet have believed.

John 20:29

And for my husband, Tom Gannon,

For I am my belovèd's,
and my belovèd is mine.

Song of Songs 6:3

$\mathcal{A}$CKNOWLEDGMENTS

Grateful acknowledgment is made to Dr. Judy Pistilli; Judy Turner, director of the Miami Valley Alzheimer's Association; Tom Gannon, Mary McGuire, Christopher Williams, Dr. Sharon Brown, Dr. Terrence Glass, Evelyn Schott, Becky Keller, Geri Thoma, and Dr. Donald Swanson, all of whom read the novel in draft and provided valuable criticism; Dr. Sherry Wheaton; the speakers of the Miami Valley Alzheimer's Association Caregiver Series; the Miami Valley Regional Crime Laboratory; attorney Don Brezine, pharmacist Carl Johnson, and Officer John Winks, who generously answered all my questions.

To Rose Carrano, who shared her personal stories with me.

To my agent, Jennifer Hengen, whose faith and optimism were a source of great encouragement. To my editors, Dick Seaver and Webb Younce, for their excellent critical feedback.

To Linda VanArsdall and Sonja Bond-Clark, for all their support.

And special acknowledgment to my husband, Tom, who patiently read three different versions of the manuscript, and to Spike, Zoë, Zeke, Vinnie, and Hannah, who keep me company while I write:

> *For thy sweet love rememb'red such wealth brings*
> *That then I scorn to change my state with kings.*

Shakespeare,
Sonnet 29

It is only with the heart that one can see rightly;
what is essential is invisible to the eye.

Antoine de Saint-Exupéry
The Little Prince

Claudia

Doubts are more cruel
than the worst of truths.

Molière

CHAPTER ONE

*T*HEY GOT THERE SOONER THAN I EXPECTED. I was waiting at the upstairs window, so I saw them when they arrived, their lights flashing, their sirens silent. There were two policemen, in two separate cars, and the paramedics in the ambulance. As they got out of the vehicles, the emergency lights turned everything a strange, pulsing red: the snow, the ice at the edge of the window, the bedroom where I stood. They slipped across the yard on their way to the front porch, their breath hanging white in the air. As they rushed up the front steps and disappeared from my view, I let go of the lace curtain and turned around to look at the body. I suppose I should have gone over to the bed and closed its eyes or covered its face, but I couldn't make myself do it.

The squad stopped at all the other bedrooms on the floor before they found the right one. When they saw me and the body, they rushed in, plying stethoscope, oxygen mask, and blood pressure cuff, calling out to each other in their own telegraphic language. Their hands rushed as quickly as their words, but none of that made any difference. There was no life left in that body. There hadn't been for ages.

All that time, I didn't move or make a sound. When the policeman came over to me, he had to put his hand on my arm to get me to look at him. It was almost as if I were the one who was dead.

And to think that was only the beginning.

No, that couldn't have been the beginning. Everything must have started long before I found the body, even if it seems like it all started that day. Dr. Daniels says it doesn't matter when it started because it's time for me to let go of the past. But it's the past that won't let go of me. You see, I have to know if I'm responsible for everything that happened. I have to know if it was my fault.

Sometimes I think the beginning was over thirty years ago, on the morning of my thirteenth birthday. When I finally woke up and went to the bathroom to brush my teeth, I found a note from foster mother Grace taped to the mirror over the bathroom sink: "Claudia — Get dressed before you come downstairs." After I ran a wet comb through my hair and bundled it into a ponytail, I rubbed a damp washcloth over my face. I stood on my tiptoes and moved closer to the mirror, looking for a new outbreak of freckles across my nose and cheeks, then pulled on my jeans and sweatshirt and went downstairs. But my breakfast wasn't on the table, and no one was in the kitchen. When I opened the oven door, there wasn't any French toast with cinnamon waiting for me, not even cold French toast. My heart lurched against my ribs.

Oh, no, I thought. It's happened again. I raced through the dining room, through the living room, and back to the kitchen. I scrambled halfway down the basement stairs, leaned over the railing, and called out. I ran upstairs, to the second floor. By the time I'd gone from Roger's room to Mother Grace's room and back again, I knew it was true: it had happened again. I went halfway down the stairs and sat, trying to think of a plan. That's when they pulled into the driveway. After Mother Grace got out of her car, I saw the two of them in the car behind. Mother Grace stood in the brown grass at the edge of the driveway while the two of them got their briefcases and paperwork out of the car. She kept turning around, looking toward the house, her hand shading her eyes since all the leaves had fallen from the trees. I grabbed hold of the banister and pulled myself up to my feet as they came up the walk. I knew that when they got to the porch and the front door opened, my life would be over — again. So when that front door opened, I ran.

At least open your mind to the possibility that you're not responsible for everything that happened, says Dr. Daniels during one of our sessions. I must have done something, I tell her, shaking my head. *What makes you say that?* I shrug my shoulders. I feel so guilty, I say. *Because of something you've done or because other people say you're guilty?* It's all my fault, I tell her, pulling my bare feet up onto the couch and hugging my legs against my chest. It's my fault for thinking I could be happy. She goes over to the window and adjusts the heat. When the fan comes on, a fabric butterfly hanging from the ceiling twists slowly. If only I had a chance to do everything over, I say as she sits back down. *What would you do differently?* Being with Sam in the first place, I tell her. That's the first thing I'd change.

After that first night, after everything had happened, we lay in each other's arms, without talking, our clothes scattered on the apartment floor. The countertop, stove, and table were covered with saucers and cups, each filled with a candle, but all the candles had gone out. Though the early morning sun came through the icy windows, the apartment was still mostly in shadows. I raised myself up and leaned on my elbow. Hannah was on the other side of Sam, on her back, her paws sticking up in the air. When I reached over to pet her stomach, her purring vibrated her body. I untangled the blanket and sheets so I could lie next to Sam again, our skin touching. His chest rose and fell slowly under my cheek, his heartbeat under my ear. Lying there with him like that, I felt things I'd never felt before, and suddenly I was afraid it had all been a dream. I held my breath, closed my eyes as tight as I could, then slowly opened them. Yes, everything was just the same as before. I was still there, and he was still there with me. So it wasn't a dream after all. Sam shifted his position, hugging Hannah closer and kissing her before he opened his eyes and looked at me.

"Claudia," he said as I touched his face with the back of my hand.

5

He took my wrist and kissed it.

"Where'd you get that bruise?" he said.

I didn't care about the bruise. I didn't care about anything in the world but his mouth on mine, his arms around me, his heart beating in the same rhythm as mine. When he moved under the covers, Hannah jumped off the sofa bed, went over to the pile of cushions, and curled up on top of them. The sun slanted through the windows over the sink, shining on Sam's dark hair and eyes. He held my face in his hands as he kissed me, and my heart pounded as I stretched my body against his. I kept my eyes open the whole time, saying his name over and over. Everything about him excited me: his unshaved cheek, the weight of his body, the pressure of his thighs. When I tangled my fingers in his thinning hair, when he lifted my hips so my body fit his, when he moved deep in me, I knew I belonged with him, no matter what, for the rest of my life. God, I was so happy. I was so unbelievably happy.

Aren't you allowed to be happy? says Dr. Daniels. Every single time I've ever been happy, something terrible has happened. *And you think there's a connection?* There has to be, I tell her. It's just like when I was a child. She takes a sip of her coffee before setting the mug back onto her desk. *If it makes you feel better to believe it started in your childhood,* she says, *then go all the way back.* To my memories of Mother Esther? *You tell me,* she says. *You're the one who says it all started in your childhood.* I don't think it started with Mother Esther, I tell her, though I suppose it could have.

"There, isn't this nice?" said Mother Esther as we settled ourselves in the living room in front of the television. "Here we are, just the two of us. My, Claudia, you're getting to be such a big girl. I remember when you used to go down for your nap right after lunch."

But not that day. I climbed into Father Jacob's chair as she sat on the couch. When I stretched out my legs, my feet almost reached over the edge of the chair seat. I put my hands on the armrests, on top of the crocheted doilies, just like Father Jacob did. My half glass of soda, surrounded by porcelain figurines, was on the table beside the chair. As Mother Esther drank her soda from the bottle, I turned to her.

"You're my mommy, right?"

"Not your real mommy, honey," she said, putting her bottle down on the coaster on the floor at her feet. "Remember? We told you. We're like Mother Ruth and her husband. Daddy Jacob and I couldn't have any babies of our own, so we're your mommy and daddy till . . ."

"Till I'm all growed up."

"No, honey, till the judge finds you a new mommy and daddy. Don't, Claudia," she said, frowning as she got up from the couch. "You don't want to hurt yourself again."

She hurried over to the chair and held me tight, trapping my hands and arms against my body. I twisted and turned, but she wouldn't let me go. I couldn't speak, I couldn't breathe, I couldn't get away from her voice in my ears.

What was she saying to you? says Dr. Daniels, but I don't want to remember. I get up from the couch and go to the window. The sun is finally shining, and it glints off the heaps of icy snow. It's so bright it hurts my eyes, so I go back to the couch and sit down. *That's one of your gifts, your memory,* says Dr. Daniels. *You should be grateful for it.* Why don't I just be grateful for all the suffering and the deceit and the persecution? I say, yanking some tissues out of the box sitting next to me on the couch. Why don't I just be grateful for all the people who've betrayed me? After I've emptied the box and crumpled the last tissue and added it to the pile beside me, she gets another box out of her file cabinet drawer. She sits down in her rocking chair and waits until I'm quiet. *Do you want to tell me about all this anger?* she says.

"If there were ever anything you wanted to tell me," said Roger, standing behind me, "you could."

"Are you cold?" I said, turning around to look at him. "You don't think it's cold in here?"

He shook his head. Sam was outside shoveling again, heaping the snow into waist-high piles along either side of the driveway. All around him, the snow continued to fall, dense and thick, swirling around in great gusts each time the wind rattled the windows. When I went down the hall, Roger followed me. I turned the thermostat up another few degrees. On the way back to the living room, I took one of Sam's wool sweaters off the coat tree and pulled it on over my own.

"I'd never tell anyone," said Roger.

I went to the window, putting my hands around all the edges, checking for cold air, but I didn't feel any. The shovel scraped loudly against the driveway. When he finished, Sam leaned on the upright shovel and looked out across the deserted street, snow whirling around his head, ice crystals clinging to the scarf over his mouth and nose. Before he'd made it back to the house, the driveway was covered with white again.

"You can trust me," said Roger, touching me on the back. "No matter what."

"What about Eve?" I said.

"I wouldn't tell her."

"And Sam?"

"Not him either. Especially not him."

Sam came up onto the porch, stamping his boots to free them of snow, leaning the shovel against the house. When he opened the front door, Roger moved away from me fast.

"No matter what," he said. "Remember that."

Why does that memory make you angry? says Dr. Daniels. Why does it make me angry? Don't you realize what he meant? *What do you think he meant, Claudia?* He thought I was guilty. *Did he?* He thought I was going to confess to him, for Christ's sake. *And that makes you angry?* How could he think that? Roger, of all people? *Are you sure that's what he meant? Did you ask him?* I know what he meant. God, I'm so sick of all this. Why can't I just forget it all? *Repressing memories is not*

8

the way to be happy, says Dr. Daniels, but I'm not repressing anything. Sam says none of it matters anyway. He says it didn't all start on the day I found the body or in my childhood — not on my thirteenth birthday or on that day with Mother Esther. He says everything started the day I became his fiancée.

The night we were going to tell his parents about our engagement, we left for the restaurant forty-five minutes early. I was so nervous, my hands were cold on my wineglass. His parents didn't even know we'd moved in together, so every time the restaurant door opened, my mouth went completely dry. Then Sam stood up, straightening his tie, and his parents were there. Sam shook Harold's hand. Eleanor kissed me on the cheek and sat beside me, moving her chair closer to mine. She took my hand and held it tightly. She was so close that I breathed in her perfume.

"At last," she said, "I'm going to have a daughter."

When she said that, the noise of the other diners was pushed into the background. Sam's laughter and Harold's chatter became a blur. Everything in the world faded — all those years making Mother's Day cards in school then shoving them into my dresser drawers, all those nights staring into mirrors looking for my real mother, all those days following happy children around school yards wishing I could trade places with them — all of it, in that one single moment, disappeared. Everything disappeared. Except Eleanor. "At last," she said, "I'm going to have a daughter," and something in me stirred.

That night, if you'd told me everything I know now, I don't think it would have made any difference. "At last," said Eleanor, "I'm going to have a daughter." From that very moment, I loved her.

Eleanor loved you, too, says Dr. Daniels, but I'm not sure it was love that Eleanor felt for me all those years ago. I sit in Dr. Daniels' office, with its pastel walls and its butterfly mobile, and it's hard to sort out what I know now from what I knew then. *It doesn't matter, Claudia,* she says, *because it's time to let go.* She makes it sound so easy. Like closing your eyes and opening them up to a new life. I want to do that, but I keep wondering if I'm responsible for what happened. Everyone said I was. *Everyone?* That's what they said after I found the body, and even if that's not when things started, that's when things got worse. *After you found it? Not before?* No, it was only after I found the body that my life really deteriorated.

After I found it, I went to the phone upstairs to call for help. While they were on their way, I went back into the bedroom, but I didn't go near the bed: I stood by the window. After the police and the paramedics got there, after they tried to force life back into the body, after the older paramedic finally took the stethoscope out of his ears and rolled up the blood pressure cuff, all of them turned toward me, but no one said anything. The emergency lights kept flashing their red against the walls. While the younger paramedic left the room and went downstairs, one of the policemen bent closer to the nightstand to look at the prescription bottles. Then he got down on one knee to look at the bottles on the floor. I swear I don't remember seeing them at all till he knelt down. All I saw was the body.

The younger paramedic returned, unrolling a dark bag, which he laid out on the bed. I hugged myself and looked out the window. Roger and Eve pulled into the driveway. Mrs. Adams from across the street stumbled through the snowdrifts to talk to them. Roger nodded to Mrs. Adams, but Eve kept walking toward the house. When Mrs. Adams looked up at the bedroom window, I stepped back behind the curtains. I was still that scared little girl who hid behind Mother Grace's curtains thirty years before.

I stood behind those velvet curtains, the hem of my sweatshirt pulled up and stuffed in my mouth, the cold air from the windows piercing my bare back, and listened to what they said about me. As Mother Grace's footsteps went upstairs, I peeked out. The man and woman stood in the entry hall. The woman, even in her high heels, was much smaller than the man. He bounced his briefcase against his leg as she rifled through the stack of papers she held. When Mother

Grace came back down the stairs, leaning heavily on the banister, they both looked up at her.

"I can't find Claudia anywhere."

"She didn't run away again, did she?" said the man.

"Of course not."

"Why would she?"

"Could she be with your son?"

"No. Roger's at work."

"Maybe he took her someplace before he went to work," said the woman, leaving her fingers in the stack of papers while Mother Grace crossed the entry hall.

"She's probably outside in the backyard. I'll call her."

"We don't have a lot of time, Grace."

"It won't take a minute."

"I don't understand why you don't want to tell her yourself."

"After everything that poor child's been through . . ."

"That's exactly why we think she'd rather hear it from you."

I let the velvet curtain slip back in front of my face as Mother Grace went through the kitchen to the back door. She called and called for me.

"How do you think she'll take it?" said the woman in the hall.

"The same as they all take it."

"Don't you think she'll be surprised?"

"After what she's been through, nothing would surprise her."

No, it wasn't surprise I felt as I hid behind those curtains. I thought of my backpack — filled with my books and some clothes — upstairs under my bed, and I cursed myself for not having hidden it out in the garage. I'd have to leave without it: I couldn't risk letting them find me. After Mother Grace returned and the three of them went out onto the front porch to look for me, I ran as fast as I could through the house, out the back door, to the garage, and I didn't look back.

I didn't run when I found the body, though I wanted to. I stayed right there and watched it all. I saw Dr. Barnett shake his head and put his stethoscope away, I saw the policeman using his pen to roll the prescription bottles toward him, I saw the paramedics wrap the sheet around the body, lift it, and center it on the dark bag. The policeman beside the bed tapped Dr. Barnett, then pointed to the prescription bottles on the nightstand and on the floor. Dr. Barnett glanced down and shook his head before he continued writing, the emergency lights splashing red on the walls, on the bed, on their faces. Roger came into the bedroom, still wearing his uniform, with Eve right behind him, and crossed the room to put his arms around me. Eve stood near us, hugging herself, staring at the bed. The bag crackled as the paramedics closed it. When they covered the face, I looked away.

"Close your eyes, Claudia," said Harold on my first Christmas with Sam's family. "You're not peeking, are you?"

"I already know what it looks like."

"It's not the same without the lights," said Harold.

"Besides, I have one more ornament to hang up," said Eleanor. "A special ornament. So don't look yet."

"Put your hands over your eyes, so we can be sure you're not cheating."

There was more rustling of paper and whispering. I tried to see between my fingers, but their backs blocked the tree.

"Ready?"

"Not yet."

"How much longer?"

"Just a second."

"Wait: turn off the other lights."

"Okay. Now."

God, it was beautiful. The lights twinkled and blinked, the tinsel glittered and sparkled, the boughs drooped with ornaments. I walked toward the tree, its branches covering the entire width of the front room window and its top grazing the ceiling. In the center front of the tree was a crystal ornament engraved with my name and the year. It was lovely. Eleanor hugged me. At last, I thought, I've finally found what I've been searching for. The tree from my childhood.

Every Christmas Eve, Mother Anne bundled us foster children up in our coats, hats, scarves, and mittens, then piled us all into the backseat of the car. While Mother Anne's new husband and her father put up the tree, she drove the rest of us around so we could look at all the Christmas lights and decorations. We rated the trees as if we were Olympic judges. Only one tree ever achieved a perfect score, the tree we always saved for last — Iris Tristan's.

We drove up the long, icy hill that led to Iris Tristan's house and sat in the cul-de-sac, our breath fogging the windows as we gazed at her tree. No tree on earth was as wonderful as hers. We sat there in the dark, surrounded by glittering snow, imagining the most fantastic presents underneath her tree. I would have given anything to be one of Iris Tristan's grandchildren and to wake up Christmas morning to the presents under that tree, even if it meant I had to be chubby and wear thick, dark eyeglasses. We sat there looking at her tree till the cold forced us home. On the way back, I didn't feel like singing, but I moved my mouth to the songs anyway. When we got to Mother Anne's house, our fingers and toes numb with cold, the oohs and aahs of the others blended with the sound of coats and gloves and boots dropped in the rush to see the completely decorated tree. I stood by the doorway, looking at the lights and decorations, but every year, the tree disappointed me.

Every year, every tree disappointed me in some way. Christmas disappointed me. Until that first Christmas as part of Sam's family. It was more than the engraved crystal ornament, more than the gold bracelet Harold and Eleanor gave me, more than the pearl earrings Sam gave me. That night, standing there with Sam and Harold and Eleanor, Christmas carols playing in the background, I gazed up at the star on the tree's top and thought it was the most beautiful light in the world.

Yet in thy dark streets shineth,
The everlasting light.
The hopes and fears of all the years
Are met in thee tonight.

After I found the body, my life turned to darkness again. *Only your life?* says Dr. Daniels during our next session. *What about Sam's life? Didn't he suffer, too?* Not in the same way. *Tell me how his suffering was different from yours.* I have told her — many, many times, right here, in this very office, but no matter how often I explain it, she still says she doesn't understand. I don't know how to make her see the difference. It's absolutely hopeless.

"It's hopeless finding a wedding dress I can afford," I said to Eleanor the third time we went shopping.

"This brocade one's darling," she said, holding it up.

I shrugged.

"What about this one?"

I shook my head.

"You know, dear, it would've been fine with me if Eve had come with us," she said as she put the dress back.

"I thought it would be nice, just the two of us," I said. "We never get to spend any time alone together."

"I don't like hurting Eve's feelings," said Eleanor.

The salesclerk brought out a pale blue dress, but as soon as she saw the look on my face, she turned around and took it back. Chiffon, satin, lace. Beige, almond, blush. Beads, embroidery, seed pearls. Each dress was lovely in its own way, but none was the dress I'd dreamed of. I sat down on the love seat next to Eleanor, took off my shoe, and massaged my foot.

"I just thought of one more place we could look," she said. "Put your shoe back on."

Instead of going to the mall or to a dress shop, though, Eleanor drove to her house. She pulled into the driveway, stopped the car, and got out, motioning for me to follow. We went upstairs, all the way to the third floor, to the finished attic. After she opened the curtains of the window in the eaves, she went to an armoire and rummaged around in it. I bent down at the window that overlooked the backyard and saw the tree where Sam and Roger had built their tree house: there were still a couple of boards in the lower branches. From behind me, the crinkling of tissue paper and plastic stopped, so I turned around. The discarded wrappings were on the floor at Eleanor's feet, and there, hanging inside the open armoire door, was the most beautiful wedding dress I'd ever seen.

"It was my mother's," said Eleanor. "I wore it, too."

I moved toward the dress like I was sleepwalking. I was almost afraid to touch it, it looked so delicate, with all its lace and intricately sewn seed pearls. As my fingers slid over the gorgeous material, Eleanor lifted the veil and draped it over my hair. She took the dress from the hook, held it up in front of me, and turned me around in front of a full-length mirror.

"Claudia, dear," she said, "would you like to wear this dress?"

At that moment, I loved her more than anyone else I'd ever known. I thought she loved me, too. I thought she could give me everything I'd ever missed in my life, everything I'd ever longed for, everything I'd ever lost. How could I have been so wrong?

"Don't get me wrong, Claudia," said Harold. "I'd be happy to help out with your bookstore . . ."

"But you don't think this building will work?"

"It's been neglected for years."

"The underlying structure's sound," said Sam.

Harold walked around the room, tapping on the walls, rocking on his heels on the floor. Near the back wall, he took out his tape measure to check the distance between the doorframe and the corner.

"What are you planning to do with the kitchen?" said Harold.

"Keep it the way it is. It might come in handy having a kitchen here."

"You're sure you can run a bookstore by yourself, Claudia?"

"Eve will help out."

"Is she going to be your partner?"

"No, this is going to be my bookstore."

"Is she okay with that?"

"Eve just wants to work till she has the baby. And she wants to sell some of her jewelry here. Sam's going to make her a glass display case."

"Her jewelry?" said Harold. "You mean she makes that stuff she wears?"

"Yes."

"Did she make that necklace you gave Eleanor for her birthday?"

"Why? Don't you like it?"

He shrugged before he took out his pocketknife to unscrew one of the switchplates. He put his glasses on to examine the wires, then replaced the plate. He went back to the front windows and looked out at the street.

"Prime frontage," he said.

"The best of any place we've seen," said Sam.

"How much do they want down?"

"Ten percent."

"You mean, you got enough inheritance from Mother Grace to cover the whole down payment?"

"Sam and Roger each gave me a loan," I said. "I'd want to hire you and Sam to build the shelves. . . ."

"You've got a lot of work to do before you get to any shelves."

"You won't hurt my feelings if you don't want to do it, Harold."

"He'll do it."

"Sam, I told you not to pressure him."

"Who said I didn't want to do it?"

"You see?" said Sam.

"How much?" I said.

"How much what?" said Harold.

"How much do you think it'll cost?"

"Jesus, Claudia, I'm not going to let you pay for this."

"You can't do it for nothing, Harold. You just said it'll be a lot of work. I have to pay you."

"You're buying the materials, Claudia."

"Harold . . ."

"All right. Give me a discount on books."

"You can have books for free," I said, kissing him on the cheek. "For the rest of your life."

While he and Sam took measurements and discussed materials, I stood in that neglected building and saw my dream. I didn't see the holes in the plaster or the cracks in the wood floor or the dangling electrical wires. All I saw was what I wanted to see.

The eyes couldn't see by the time they closed that bag over its face, but it wrenched me anyway. When they lifted the body to set it on the stretcher, it felt like something was tugging me along with it. As they maneuvered the stretcher, it hit the doorframe, so they had to wrestle the stretcher back into the room several times before they got it into the hallway. It was as if, even in death, it didn't want to leave me. It was as if, even in death, I'd never be free.

As we followed the paramedics, Roger took my hand and whispered something. On the stairs, we had to wait while they fought the stretcher around the turn. Suddenly, I was hot and cold all over. Nausea overwhelmed me, and I couldn't breathe. It felt like it was me in that black bag, like it was my eyes in that darkness, like it was me who'd stepped into another world and could never go back. I reached out before I remembered that Sam wasn't there. Then Eve cried out and Roger grabbed my arm as the darkness swallowed me.

CHAPTER TWO

*A*FTER I OPENED MY EYES, the darkness scattered. I lay on the living room floor, with Eve wiping my face and Roger waving smelling salts under my nose. When I jerked my head to the side, I saw the body bag on the stretcher, abandoned in the entry hall, and the pulsing red lights of the emergency vehicles through the windows on the front door. As Dr. Barnett listened to my heart, the paramedic checked my blood pressure. The policeman stood over us.

"I knew something like this would happen," said Roger, brushing the hair from my forehead.

"She's exhausted herself," said Eve.

"These situations are always so difficult," said Dr. Barnett.

He wrote on his clipboard as the policeman who'd looked at the prescription bottles frowned at me. The red lights from outside swept across the body bag. I closed my eyes. Eve's fingers were cool on my face. Dr. Barnett's pen scratched and scratched.

It seems like we haven't even scratched the surface of my life, I tell Dr. Daniels. *Not even scratched it?* she says with a laugh. *We've excavated it, cataloged it, mourned it, then started over again from the beginning.* It doesn't feel like that to me, I tell her. It feels like I'm trapped. *You are trapped, Claudia. By choice.* I want to get up and walk out, but of course I can't, so I go over to the window instead. On the windowsill, next to a picture of Dr. Daniels' two children, there's a figurine of a white-bearded wizard wearing a purple robe. Next to him is a kneeling angel, her white wings fanning out behind her shoulders. *You can live in the past with your wounds,* says Dr. Daniels, *or you can heal yourself and live the rest of your life.* Oh, God, I am trying, I tell her, but it's not as easy as it sounds. Sometimes I go for days without thinking about everything that happened, but then someone in the grocery store will look at me over the display of tomatoes, nudge her friend, and . . . *And that's when you're thirteen again, fumbling frantically with your bike chain in the garage.*

The garage door was open, but since it faced the alley behind the yard, no one from the house could see me. I knelt on the concrete floor of the garage, wrestling with my bike chain. Every time I had it almost completely on, it slipped off, and I had to start over. After the fifth or sixth time, Roger's car pulled in behind me. I wiped my eyes and nose on the sleeve of my sweatshirt as he opened the car door and got out.

"Hey, Claude," he said. "Kinda chilly for a bike ride, ain't it? Did the chain fall off again? I'll do it."

"Let go. Get off."

"What's wrong with you, Claude?"

"Nothing. And stop calling me that."

"Okay, Claude-ski. You don't have to yell. I thought you'd be in a good mood today, seeing how it's your birthday and all," he said as I struggled with the chain. "So, don't I get a hug or something? The present was my idea, you know."

"Thanks a lot, Marble-head."

"Whoa — what's that for? What's going on, Claude?"

"Stop calling me that. How many times do I have to tell you?"

"What's the matter with you? I thought after you got your present you'd be . . . Hey, wait a minute: you don't think that . . . No, you can't believe that we'd . . . Geez, Claude, you are so stupid."

When he yanked me away from my bike, it clattered over onto the garage floor. I yelled at him as he lifted me over his shoulder and carried me toward the house. All the leaves had fallen from the trees, and they rustled loudly as Roger marched across the yard.

"Put me down. Put me down, you jerk."

"Not till you get your birthday present."

"Let go of me. Put me down, you big, stupid, ugly —"

"Hey, quit scratching, Claude."

"I hate you, you Marble-head."

"Heavens, what's all that screaming? Roger, what are you doing? Put her down," said Mother Grace as the back door swung open. "Put her down, I said. Claudia, dear, where have you been? We've been looking everywhere for you. Roger, let go of her."

"Not till she gets her present. You won't believe what she thinks it is, Mom."

"She was running away," said the man with the briefcase.

"No, she wasn't," said Mother Grace.

"I knew this wasn't a good idea," said the woman.

Roger pushed me into the living room ahead of him and sat me down on the couch, across from everyone else, who remained standing. Mother Grace wrung her hands, her eyes filling with tears.

"I never dreamed it'd be like this," she said. "I wanted her to be happy. That's all I wanted. For her to be happy."

"It's like a bad dream," said foster mother Ruth that first time in court. "Tell me this isn't really happening."

"Mrs. Irving, please, you're not supposed to say anything," said the lawyer.

I tried to sit still between them, but the lace on my socks was stiff and scratchy, and my new shoes pinched my toes. The judge, sitting far away and high above us at his bench, shuffled papers back and forth. There were two flags on poles behind him, and one of the poles had a gold eagle on top. There were curtains behind him but no window. When the judge closed the folder and spoke, he didn't even glance at us.

"Due to the marital status of the applicant," he said, "the motion for adoption is denied."

Mother Ruth's breath went in so sharply that I looked up at her.

"The court hereby rules that the minor child be placed in the children's home until a suitable family can be found."

He hit his gavel once before the lawyer rose and started piling his papers and folders into his briefcase. Mother Ruth caught hold of his jacket while the caseworker tried to take my hand in hers.

"What if my husband and I don't get divorced?" said Mother Ruth as the lawyer snapped his briefcase closed. "What if we get back together? Can I have her then?"

"Once you've reestablished a secure and stable environment for the child, Mrs. Irving, you can always reapply."

"It's more secure and stable without him. You've seen the police reports. You know how he gets when he drinks."

The lawyer nodded to the next group of people coming to the table. When the caseworker tried to take my hand again, Mother Ruth pulled me closer to her side.

"Why can't Claudia stay with me," she said, "at least until they find her a new place?"

"The judge denied that motion, Mrs. Irving," said the lawyer, opening the door to the hall.

"I don't understand why."

"He doesn't feel it's in the child's best interest."

"He didn't even talk to me. Why didn't he talk to me? You said he'd ask me some questions."

"I said he might."

"Why didn't he? You said he would."

The lawyer stopped and turned around, sighing loudly.

"Apparently, Mrs. Irving, he didn't feel it was necessary."

"But that's not fair."

"I have another appointment, Mrs. Irving," said the caseworker. "You'll have to say good-bye now."

Mother Ruth knelt in front of me and hugged me hard. There were people all around us, going in and out of courtrooms. When I put my arms around Mother Ruth's neck, she said something in my ear, but she was trembling so hard that I couldn't understand her.

"Now look what you've done, Mrs. Irving: you've upset her," said the caseworker. "Come here, Claudia. Come here, honey. That's a girl. Don't cry. Really, Mrs. Irving, you didn't have to do it like this."

Mother Ruth stood up quickly, her handkerchief covering her nose and mouth. She didn't look at me as she stumbled down the marble hallway, as she put her hand on the doorframe to get her balance, as she went out the courthouse door. I pulled and tugged, trying to get free of the caseworker. I kicked and screamed and bit, but the caseworker didn't let go. She held me so tight, my stomach hurt. She held me so tight, I thought I died.

But I didn't die that day. I didn't die the day I found the body, either, though sometimes I wished I had. After I'd fainted and was lying on the living room floor, Roger held my hand so tight it hurt, but I was glad for the pain. When I looked up at Roger and Eve, Roger put his hand against my face.

"If you cried," he said, "it might make you feel better."

"Shock," said the paramedic as he rolled up the blood pressure cuff.

"Shock, huh?" said the policeman.

"Undoubtedly," said Dr. Barnett.

"That's what you think it is, huh? Shock?"

"What else could it be?"

Roger and Eve stayed with me after they took the body away. Roger wanted to stay all night, but I told him to go home with Eve and not to come back after dinner. All alone, I wandered from room to room. The house was so quiet. So empty. I sat on the stairs, at the bottom, for a long time. I sat there, all by myself, all alone in that emptied house, and I thought, At last, it's over. After all these years, it's finally over. Then I wept.

There were no tears left on my thirteenth birthday after Roger dragged me back into the house. Even after we were inside and sitting on the couch, he wouldn't let go of my wrist. He was afraid I'd run, but there was no point in running then: it only worked if you did it before they found you. Afterward, it was best to get it over with. I sat there on the couch, with Roger's fingers around my wrist like a manacle, and I made myself a statue — deaf, dumb, blind — safe.

"Pay attention, Claude."

"Roger, please don't call her that. You know she doesn't like it."

"But she's doing that zombie thing again, Mom."

"Roger, don't. Claudia, dear, did you hear what they just told you?"

"She can't hear you, Mom. I told you — she's a zombie."

"Grace, what's he talking about?" said the man.

"Nothing. It's a game they play. Claudia, dear . . ."

"Claude, listen up."

"The court has approved a family who wants to adopt you," said the woman in the high heels, perching on the edge of the overstuffed chair across from me. "Unfortunately, the father has passed away."

"But the mother is very healthy," said Mother Grace.

"She's not listening to a word we're saying," said the man, dropping his briefcase on the floor beside the flowered love seat as he sat down.

"Due to the family's keen interest in you and to its relative financial stability," said the woman, "the court has decided to award permanent custody to the family."

"If you agree to the adoption," said Mother Grace.

Suddenly they were all staring at me. It was so quiet, I could hear the grandfather clock ticking in the dining room. Roger elbowed me, but I didn't move.

"You're old enough to have some say in the decision, Claudia."

"Aren't you going to answer us?"

"Say something."

"This must be a terrible shock for her."

"What she needs is to be turned over somebody's knee."

"Claudia," said Mother Grace, "do you want to stay with us, dear?"

"Yeah, Claude, do you want to be my kid sister permanent or don't you?"

Roger let go of my wrist then, but my hand and arm lay there, cold and still, like I really was a statue. When Mother Grace came and sat beside me on the couch, when she touched my arm, her fingers warm and soft against my skin, I did the only thing I could do.

"Christ, you'd think she'd be happy," said the man.

"I knew we shouldn't have done it this way, Grace," said the woman.

"My sweet baby girl," said Mother Grace, taking me in her arms.

"Hey, now we're stuck with you for good," said Roger, and he punched me in the back.

"Don't put your hand over your glass," said Sam after he came up to me at the table.

"Don't hit my hand," I said.

"I didn't hit you. I was just moving your hand."

"I don't want any more to drink, Sam. I've already had enough."

"It's a wedding. There's no such thing as enough champagne."

"Sam, stop."

"Oh, shit, sorry. Did that get on your dress? Sorry. I told you not to put your hand over your glass."

I blotted the front of my gown with a napkin as Sam, his arms full of champagne bottles, sat down in the chair beside me. Two flower girls, chased by the ring bearer, darted around the table, giggling when Sam reached out for them, squealing with laughter as they eluded his grasp and raced back onto the dance floor, disappearing among the long gowns and tuxedos. Sam pushed my hands away when I tried to take the champagne bottles off the table.

"Hey, there you are, Claude," he said suddenly. "Where've you been? I've been looking all over for you. Jesus, Claude, something terrible's happened. I gotta tell you."

"You haven't called me Claude since we were kids."

"I call you Claude all the time. Listen, Claude . . . Here, have some more champagne," he said, pouring from the second bottle. "You'll want some when you hear what I gotta tell you."

I moved my glass, so he filled the one next to it, then drank that one along with his own.

"Claude, listen: I've got something to tell you. You should wear pastels more often."

"That's what you wanted to tell me?"

"And you look really good in that dress. Did I tell you that?"

"Quite a few times."

"Well, you look really, really good in it. I really think you should have some more to drink, Claude."

"Where's Angela?" I said as Sam emptied another glass without pausing for breath.

He put down the champagne flute and sat there for a few seconds without saying anything. Then he gripped my hand in his.

"She's gone, Claude."

"She's going to have to drive you home."

"She's not here, Claude. Jesus, how many times do I have to tell you?"

He ran his fingers roughly through his hair, making some of it stick out. I leaned toward him and smoothed it down.

"You don't have to raise your voice. I was just asking where Angela was."

"Sorry, Claude. I didn't mean to yell. Are you sure you don't want

25

some more champagne? 'Cause I think you're gonna need some. Just as soon as you ask me where Jerry is."

"Who's Jerry?"

"Jesus, Claude, don't you even remember your own boyfriend's name?"

"His name's Gary."

"Oh, yeah, Gary. Okay, so ask me where Gary is."

"Where's Gary?"

"He left. With Angela. Wow, you think that's funny? I never thought you'd laugh about it."

"Where are they, Sam? Really?"

"They left, Claude. D'you see them anywhere?"

I glanced around the reception hall, crowded with people in their best clothes. Everyone was laughing, dancing, eating, drinking. Everyone except Angela and Gary.

"Maybe they went out for . . . cigarettes."

"They left in a state of partial undress," said Sam, "so I don't think they went out for cigarettes. Besides, Angela quit smoking. But ask me if I care if she left with Dildo. Sorry, I mean, Jerry. Go ahead: ask me. No, I do not. And you wanna know why I don't care? 'Cause I was going to break up with her anyway. The only reason I brought her with me tonight was so I'd have a date for the wedding. But right after the reception: 'hit the road, Jack, and don't you come back no more, no more, no more, no . . .' Aw, come on, Claude, don't start crying on me. Wait. Where are you going?"

"To find Gary."

"He's not here, Claude. Christ, d'you think I'd make something like that up?"

"Let go of my wrist, Sam."

"I told you: he's not here."

"Let go, Sam. You're hurting me."

"Hey, Claude, d'you wannna dance?"

"You're joking, right?"

"Come on. Best man's supposed to dance with the maid of honor."

"You must be really drunk to think I'd want to dance after —"

"Who you calling drunk? You stand up if you're going to call me that. I don't care if you're already standing. Okay, then I'll stand up. Hey, don't go. Come on, Claude. I didn't mean it. You know I didn't. Come on, don't leave me all alone."

After I sat back down, he picked up a piece of ham and a portion of deviled egg from one of the abandoned plates and shoved them into his mouth.

"Hey, Claude, did I tell you that dress looks really, really good on you?"

The flower girls came running back, this time without the ring bearer, their organdy dresses rustling as they leaned against Sam, their hands sticky with sugared almonds. Each time Sam opened his mouth, one of them popped another candy in. When there were none left, they licked the sugar off their empty palms. Then they dashed back into the crowd of dancers. While Sam was watching them, I took the extra champagne bottles off the table. Roger and Eve were waltzing in the center of the group, and the chandelier's light sparkled on the silver embroidery on Eve's gown. When Roger said something, she smiled up at him, and he kissed her on the forehead. Lots of people were dancing, but Gary and Angela weren't among them. Sam stood up, taking his keys out of his pants pocket.

"Hey, where's my champagne? Somebody took it. Quick, Claude, call the police. Call Roger. No, don't call Roger. Not today. Call the other police. The ones who aren't here. Nobody leaves till we find my champagne. Hey, what are you doing? Gimme my keys."

"I'd better take you home."

"Okay, but quit pulling on my arm like that. I'm not the one who left with somebody else. Hey, Claude, you look really, really good in that dress. Did I tell you that? You're the greatest, Claude. Don't let anybody ever tell you you're not the greatest. In the whole wide world. The absolute greatest. Jerry's an absolute, complete, and total jerk. And Gary's a jerk, too. Jerry and Gary and Angela — they're all jerks. They deserve each other, as far as I'm concerned. 'Cause you're the best, Claude. Really, the greatest."

Just as I pulled my shawl around my shoulders, Sam leaned forward and kissed me. Just like that. He took my face in his hands and kissed me. Right there at the reception, with everyone dancing and eating and laughing around us, he kissed me. After what he'd just told me, he kissed me.

He wasn't trying to hurt you, says Dr. Daniels. But that's what he did. And then he wanted me to comfort him. Just like always. *Hasn't Sam ever comforted you? Or protected you?* In the last twenty years? I say. Or are you talking about a time before that? *Can you let go of the anger just long enough to consider the possibility that everything that happened was because Sam was trying to protect you?* What does that mean? *It means that, in his own way, Sam could have been trying to take care of you.* And? *It might have been Sam.* Sam? *It could have been him,* says Dr. Daniels. I can't believe that you'd say something like that. *Why does the idea upset you so much?* she says. After everything I've done for him, after everything I've sacrificed . . . *Maybe Sam made an even greater sacrifice. For you.* You don't know what you're talking about, I tell her. You're wrong. It was Eleanor who ruined things. Everything bad that happened, it was all because of her. *In the beginning, even Eleanor made you feel loved,* says Dr. Daniels. *In fact, the closer you got to the wedding, the more loved Eleanor made you feel. Like the time she sent you the card.*

I recognized Eleanor's handwriting as soon as I saw the envelope. "Congratulations On Your Engagement," said the card, in letters made of pink ribbons and lace, surrounded by doves and bells. After I opened the card, a sheet of paper fluttered to the floor. I picked it up and turned it over: it was a check, from Harold and Eleanor, made out to me. I went to the kitchen, where Sam was eating lunch, and laid the check on the table in front of him.

"Wow," he said, putting down his grilled cheese sandwich. "What's that for?"

"I don't know yet," I said, then read the card aloud.

Dearest Claudia,

Traditionally, the parents of the bride pay for the wedding. Roger mentioned to us that he's helping you and Mother Grace pay for everything. Since we'll never have the joy of contributing to a daughter's wedding, we hope you'll allow us to share in your happiness by accepting this gift from us, for wedding expenses. Harold and I want you to have some of the things you've always dreamed of. With all our love and best wishes for your future happiness.

"I'll be damned," said Sam, wiping his hands on the leg of his jeans so he could take the card.

"Did you know they were going to do this?"

"I'm as surprised as you are."

I sat at the table, staring at the check in my hands. This time, instead of packing my suitcase and setting it out on the curb, someone was opening her door. This time, instead of my standing on the outside, where it was cold and dark, I was being invited inside, where it was warm and loving and bright. Finally.

"Time to meet the family, Claude," said Roger.

He ambushed me in the hallway, dragging me into his bedroom. I was going to hit him with my softball mitt until I saw what he'd done to his room: all over the floor, all over the bed, all over the dresser and the desk, there were photographs. Hundreds and hundreds of photographs. Roger pulled me along a path to his bed, where a space was cleared, just big enough for the two of us to sit next to each other.

He took my softball and mitt, laid them on the bed, and handed me a picture.

"This is Uncle Kenny, Mom's brother," he said. "When you meet him, ask him to sing his song."

"What's his song?"

> *They grabbed Mr. Frog and began to fight,*
> *King Kong Kitchie Kitchie Ky-Me-O,*
> *In the holler tree, 'twas a terrible night,*
> *King Kong Kitchie Kitchie Ky-Me-O.*

"That's dumb," I said.

> *Ky-Mo, Kee-Mo, Ky-Mo-Kee,*
> *Way down yonder in a holler tree,*
> *An owl and a bat and a bumblebee,*
> *King Kong Kitchie Kitchie Ky-Me-O.*

"Don't laugh, Claude. That's Uncle Kenny's song. He sings it to us kids at holidays."

"What's it mean?"

"Nobody knows but Uncle Kenny. Ask him when you meet him."

He put down the picture of Uncle Kenny and passed me a photograph of two boys. Both had rifles, wore hunting clothes, and held up birds they'd shot.

"Oh, sick," I said. "Did you kill them?"

"Me and Sam did. His dad takes us duck hunting."

"Did they bleed?"

"Not much."

Roger replaced the picture with another from the pile. In the next photograph, they stood in front of a wedge tent, smiling broadly. Roger pressed his forefinger to each one.

"Me, Dad, Sam, his dad."

"Your dad?"

"He's dead."

"I know that, Marble-head."

Roger slipped that picture out of my hand and put another one in.

"Cousin Oscar. Everybody calls him Dutch, like his dad, but Mom doesn't like it, so don't call him Dutch in front of her. Here, cousin Mary's wedding. I'm the ring bearer. I have my arms crossed over my chest and that look on my face because I had to give the pillow back. Did you know that ring bearers and flower girls have to give the pillows and flower baskets back? Man, that's so unfair. Here, that's Dutch again, hanging upside down on the swing set. This is Aunt Margie-Lou with her husband — I think he's her fourth. That's Uncle Fred's convertible, and that's me as a kid, washing the tires: I thought I was pretty hot stuff. Here's Cousin Dottie with both sets of twins. Can you believe she had two sets? One right after the other. Oh, and this is Cousin Rita with her parrots. This one's Binky, and that one's Booper. Hey, I'm not the one who picked the names, okay? But the birds are really cool. They talk and everything. I'm teaching them to cuss."

The whole family was there — on the bed, on the dresser, on the floor — all of them there just for me. I stood in the middle of the room, turning around and around, looking at them all. Roger put on my mitt, tossed the softball up, caught it, and tossed it up again. The late afternoon sun slanted through the Venetian blinds, and dust floated in its light. They were all so beautiful. I'd never seen so many beautiful people before. I dropped the photographs I was holding, put my hands over my face, and wept.

I didn't cry when I found the body. Not while everyone was there. But afterward, when I was alone, I cried. Roger says it would have been better for all of us if I'd cried when the police were there. Sam says it wouldn't have changed a thing. He says the witch hunt had already started, so crying wouldn't have made any difference. But I did cry. After they left the house, I cried so hard, I thought it would finish me. Then I dragged myself up from the bottom stair where I'd been sitting and went to the chair by the living room window. Then I waited.

I didn't move from that chair. I didn't turn on any lights. The streetlights shone on the snow outside and on the occasional car that moved slowly down the empty street. The phone rang a couple of times. Early in the morning, just when the sky was changing to a lighter shade of purplish blue, a few lights went on in houses across the street. But still I sat there, my legs hugged to my chest, Sam's sweater over me like a blanket. The only thing that moved me was the sound of Sam's truck pulling into the driveway. The sweater fell to the floor as I rushed to the front door. The snow on the porch wet my socks as Sam ran up the steps. Then his arms were around me and he was holding me so tight, he lifted me off my feet, his cheek against my face.

"I should've been here with you," he said.

My face was buried in the mound of stuffed animals, so it took a while before I heard the knocking at my bedroom door. I pulled my head out from under the covers.

"Who is it?"

"Sam."

"Don't come in."

I pushed the stuffed animals away and got up. The light from the hallway made a line across the floor, from the doorway to the bed. When I got to the door and leaned against it, the wood was cool, then warm. With my hand on the knob, I could hear Sam's breathing.

"I just wanted to see how you were doing," he said.

"I'm okay."

"Do you need anything? A Coke? Tissues? Anything?"

"Roger told me what you guys did to Mike."

"Yeah."

"How's your hand?"

"Okay."

"Roger said you busted your finger."

"It's just bruised."

Sam's feet shuffled on the carpet in the hall. He cleared his throat.

"Mike wasn't really my boyfriend anyway," I said.

"He still should've been a man about it. Geez, taping a note to your locker."

I could hear the television from downstairs, but I couldn't hear what Mother Grace was watching. Roger's stereo was playing in his room. I ran my finger down the inset panel in the door. The wood floor was cold against my feet whenever I moved them to a new spot. The music in Roger's room stopped, then started again, on the same song. Sam coughed.

"Grace is real mad at Roger," I said. "His new jacket was all messed up."

"Roger didn't even touch him: I told her that already."

We stood there a little longer, the door between us, the band of light steady and bright across the floor. When I stared at the light, I couldn't see anything else in the room. My toe edged closer to it.

"Well, that's all I wanted," said Sam. "If you need anything . . ."

"Okay," I said.

After he went to Roger's room, I closed the bedroom door. I stood there until my eyes got used to the dark, then went over and knelt on the bed. When I put my ear to the wall, I could feel it vibrating to the music. Roger's and Sam's voices were a low hum. I lay down, re-settled all the stuffed animals around me, and pulled up the blankets, but I didn't bury my head under the pillow.

He's always tried to protect you, says Dr. Daniels. I never said he didn't. I take my sweater off and put it on the chair next to the couch. In the next room, the phone rings until the answering machine turns on. The closed door muffles the sound of both. There's no music playing today, but on Dr. Daniels' desk, a small fountain spills water over a bronze bowl of pebbles. It was Eleanor who ruined everything, I say. *It wasn't Eleanor's fault, Claudia.* She betrayed me. *How did she do that?* You already know how. *Tell me again.* She was supposed to love me forever. *She did love you, even at the end.* Not the way she loved me in the beginning, not the way she loved me when she gave me the ring.

"I thought it was your engagement ring, Eleanor."

"No, it was my grandmother Rose's ring."

I touched the gold ring in the red velvet box on the plate in front of me. Eleanor passed me a cup of tea. The table was covered with a lace tablecloth and set with Eleanor's gold-rimmed wedding china. A quiche and a green salad were on one side of a vase full of wildflowers, and a plate of small, decorated cakes was on the other.

"Grandmother Rose wore that ring till my mother's wedding day, when she passed it on to my mother, who wore it till I married Harold, when she gave it to me. And now that I'm going to have a daughter . . ."

Eleanor slipped the ring on my finger and kissed me on the cheek.

"I'm so happy, Claudia," she said. "So very, very happy."

Maybe Eleanor loved you even more at the end, says Dr. Daniels. *And maybe she gave you a great gift.* What do you mean? *Maybe Eleanor did it. Maybe she did it for you.* You mean you think that she . . . As a gift to me? No, I don't believe it. *You're not comfortable with the idea that she was trying to give you a gift?* That gift damaged my life. *Eleanor may have been trying to show you how much she loved you.* No, I tell her, shaking my head. Love doesn't destroy your life. *If it wasn't Eleanor giving you the gift, was it Sam?* My God, no, not Sam. *Why not?* Because he knows how I feel about it. He wouldn't do it. *Not even to protect you?* I couldn't stay with him if I thought that he . . . I'd have to leave him. *Even if he did it out of love for you?* He didn't do it. I know he didn't. *Can't you even consider that possibility?* No, it's too painful. It hurts more than I can bear. It would mean I'd lost everything.

It hurt when I found the body. It hurt being alone in that house. It hurt when Sam came home, too. Everything hurt. Maybe that's how it feels when something like that happens. We stood in the bedroom doorway for a while, not talking, not touching, just staring at the empty room. After Sam went over to the bed and sat down, I crossed the room to close the curtains.

Sam turned on the light beside the bed, then adjusted its shade so it was level. He moved the picture of the family so he could see it from where he sat. He ran his palms over the sheet, folded down over the blanket, and straightened the pillows. He picked the rag doll up from the floor and laid it carefully on the pillow, next to the other doll. He reached down and put the faded terry-cloth slippers side by side, in front of the nightstand. He smoothed the sheet again. When I came over, he held out his hand, and I sat beside him on the bed.

"You changed the sheets," he said.

We sat there, side by side, holding hands, and all I kept thinking was, "Now, it's really over." After all those years of praying and pleading and bargaining with God, I finally had what I'd wanted.

Why didn't it feel like I thought it would?

Why didn't anything feel like it was supposed to?

CHAPTER THREE

$\mathcal{F}$OR A LONG TIME AFTER I FOUND THE BODY, I didn't feel a thing. Every morning, still wearing my nightgown, I sat at the table with the dishes from the past night's dinner, poking at the dried and shriveled pieces of meat, the crust of gravy over the mashed potatoes, the hard heels of bread. Outside the kitchen window, sparrows and finches squabbled on the feeders, their feathers a shock of color against the grey of the snowy yard. Out in the street, the neighborhood children had snowball fights, their laughter and shouts reverberating against the closed windows until the school bus lumbered down the street. But still, I didn't clean up the table or do the dishes, I didn't take a shower or get dressed, I didn't go down to the bookstore, not even the day Eve came to the house and insisted I go. I didn't do anything but sit there, morning after morning. I might have spent the rest of my life like that if it hadn't been for what happened next, if it hadn't been for what the police did.

"I know this is an inconvenient time, Mrs. Sloane," said Detective Mitchell when he called, "but we'd like to discuss a few things with you."

"What kind of things?" I said.

"Everything that happened. It's procedure."

"When someone dies at home instead of in the hospital?"

"You might say that. Can you come down to the station?"

"Can't we talk right now?"

"Not over the phone. We need you to come down to the station."

If I'd realized why they wanted to talk to me, maybe I could have prevented all the terrible things that followed. I would have seen all the warning signs that fell into my path, instead of blithely stepping over them.

"Don't walk away from me," said Eleanor as I went toward the kitchen. "I'm talking to you."

"I can't believe you're accusing me of having a bracelet I've never even seen."

"You wore it when you and Sam went out to dinner on your anniversary," she said.

"I don't have it, Eleanor. I borrowed your pearl necklace when we went out."

"You borrowed my bracelet, Claudia."

"You're not talking about the one you gave me for Christmas, are you?"

"No, not that one. My bracelet. Grandmother Rose's bracelet."

"I've never borrowed Grandmother Rose's bracelet," I said. "I'm not even sure what it looks like."

She marched over to the entry hall closet, grumbling as she yanked out her coat. While she pulled on her gloves and picked up her purse, I went to the bedroom and got the Christmas bracelet. As I walked back to the foyer, I pulled Grandmother Rose's ring off my finger. Eleanor was still standing in the entry hall, buttoning up her coat, and I held the Christmas bracelet and the ring out to her. She acted like she didn't even see me. When she opened her purse to get her car keys, I shoved the jewelry into it. She stood there, glaring at me, her purse gaping.

"Now that you have them," she said, "you might as well keep them."

Don't keep holding on to the past, Claudia, says Dr. Daniels. *You're not that person anymore.* The sun, shining through the window and across the couch where I'm sitting, is so warm and bright that I want to lie down and go to sleep. But if you don't remember the past, I say, aren't you condemned to repeat it? *There's a difference between remembering the past and being obsessed with it,* she says, and though I hear what she's telling me, I don't understand what it has to do with me.

"I'm telling you, Claude, it's mine," said Sam. "Give it to me."

"And I'm telling you, it's not yours."

"Yes, it is, Claude," he said, yanking the coat away from me and trying to force his arm into the sleeve. "Oh, man, look what happened. It shrunk."

"It didn't shrink, Sam. It's Gary's coat."

"Gary's? Are you sure?"

"I'm sure," I said, taking it away from him and putting it back on the hanger.

"Let's rip it up," said Sam.

"Don't be ridiculous."

"Why not? Don't you want to get even?"

"It's snowing."

"So what? I hope he freezes his ass off. And I hope Angela freezes her . . ."

"Shhh. Someone will hear you," I said, trying to hand him his own coat.

"I'm not the one who left with somebody else's date."

"Jesus, Sam, why don't you say it a little louder? There must be some people up at the North Pole who didn't hear you."

"I'm not the one who . . ."

"Jesus, Sam, stop it," I said, pulling him away from the doorway. "God, you must be drunk."

"Why'd you close the door?"

"Do you want everyone in the whole world to know what happened?"

"I'm not the one who left, Claude."

He tried to get to the door, but I braced myself against it. He struggled with me for a few seconds, then suddenly stopped. He put his hands flat on the door, on either side of me, while he leaned forward, smiling.

"Hey, I got an idea," he said. "How about if we pay them back?"

Then he was hugging me close to him, his mouth open on mine, his tongue insistent. I dug my nails into his back, but that only made him press against me harder. From the other side of the closed coatroom door, I could hear the laughter and the music of the wedding reception. Someone rattled the doorknob several times, but I couldn't move. Sam held me by the hips, my back against the door, his body crushed to mine, his breath hot on my face and throat. When he forced his leg between mine, up against the bone, when he moved his body against mine, hard and slow, then harder and faster, I kissed him back. I opened my mouth and kissed him back so fiercely that one of us moaned. Then I shoved him away. We stood there, the two of us, staring at each other, our breath loud and ragged in the heavy heat of that tiny room.

"Wake up," said Sam.

I pushed him away.

"Wake up, Claude," he said. "They're here."

As soon as Sam touched the children, Matthew and the twins scrambled out of their sleeping bags, lying on the cabin floor. It was just getting light outside, and we could hear birds through the open windows.

"Can we come on vacation with you and Aunt Claudia every summer?" said Matthew, tucking in his shirt.

"Every year your mom and dad go on a second honeymoon," said Sam, gathering up the loaves of bread.

"How come we're not using the tent?" said Laura.

"Yeah, you're supposed to be in a tent if you're camping," said Matthew.

"We need the cabin with all of us here," I said, combing Sarah's hair.

"I wish Hannah could've come," she said as I bundled her hair into a ponytail.

"She'd be scared. She's better off at home," said Sam. "Okay — is everybody ready?"

After the children shoved their feet into their sneakers, we ran out the backdoor, off the porch, and through the field of wildflowers. The sun, low and close to the horizon, winked at us through the trees as we ran. The lake was on the other side of the field, and the water was covered with ducks and geese. Sam held up his hand to stop us. The children and I hunched down near him as he crushed his bag of bread. When he opened it and moved slowly toward the water, we tiptoed after him. The ducks and geese gobbled up the pieces of bread. After a few of the ducks came out of the water, more followed, and the children hurriedly cast down their own bread.

Then Sam held out his hand, palm up, filled with bread crumbs. He stayed very still. As the children watched with wide eyes, one of the ducks came up and ate the bread out of Sam's hand. Matthew grinned and imitated him. Soon we were surrounded by birds, their honking and quacking loud in the early morning air. The twins giggled and jerked back their hands, dropping their bread. The ducks wandered from open hand to open hand, even after all the bread was gone, before they made their way back to the lake, their noisy calls punctuated by the sound of the splashing water. The children huddled around Sam, their sweet faces gazing up at him. And Sam, his sun-darkened hands resting on their fair hair, smiled back down at them.

Maybe Sam was trying to be your savior that last time, too, says Dr. Daniels. Savior? He didn't save me from anything. It's being with him that caused it all in the first place. That's why I'd change it if I could go back. *What if it was Sam who saved you at the end?* No. Don't say that. *Does it upset you that much to think that Sam might have had something to do with what happened?* I'm not upset about that. I just don't feel like we're making any progress. *All right, then let's just imagine that Sam might have done it.* I couldn't stay with him if I thought that. *Even now?* No, I couldn't. But I know he didn't do it. *How do you know?* He wouldn't do that to me. *Does he know how you feel about it?* Of course, he knows. *You mean, you told him? You didn't expect him to read your mind?* Why do we have to keep going over the same things all the time? I thought you were supposed to help me get through all this. *I'm trying,* she says, *but you keep pushing me away.*

I shoved him away from me and we stood there, staring at each other, the coats from the other wedding guests hanging all around us, the heat from that small room pressing in on us.

"Don't," I said.

"Don't you want me to?"

"What about Gary and Angela?"

"They deserve each other."

"You don't love me."

"Yes, I do."

"Don't say that."

"I do love you."

"Don't say that. Not tonight."

"What if I mean it?"

"You're hurt, that's all."

"No, that's not it. I've always loved you."

Then we were in each other's arms, our mouths open, our fingers fumbling with zippers and buttons and snaps, our breath loud in our ears. Sam shoved me back against the door, yanking up the gauzy layers of my gown till he touched my bare thighs. I tried to touch him, but his hands were faster and stronger than mine, fast and strong as his fingers wrenched the lace aside and shoved themselves into me, fast and strong and deep inside me as his thumb moved firmly outside. I tried to touch him when he lifted me by the hips, but he pushed my hands away and thrust himself into me, my lace panties straining against my skin, his zipper scraping me, my head spinning, my back slamming against the door. From the other side of the locked door, in the reception hall, came the sound of music and laughter, but all I could hear was the pounding of my own heart as he plunged into me, as he said my name against my cheek and throat, over and over and over, like some incredibly beautiful song.

Look at everything we lost, I say to Dr. Daniels, and it was all my fault. *You told me you didn't do anything,* she says as she hands me a box of tissues, *so how is it your fault?* I sit there on the couch, my head throbbing. On the desk, the water from the small fountain runs over the pebbles in its brass base. In the corner, on the lateral file cabinet, the aromatherapy diffuser fills the room with the smell of lavender. I look up at Dr. Daniels, my eyelids sore from wiping them with the tissues. I must have been guilty of something, I tell her. *I think that's the nuns and priest from your childhood talking,* she says, smiling, but I don't see what's funny at all.

"We're not making any accusations, Mrs. Sloane," said Detective Mitchell.

He closed the door to the small room. The walls were dirty grey, and they looked like they'd been made out of the same tiles that were on the ceiling. A couple of the tiles in the corner were missing, and there were dark water stains around the hole. A small table was in the center of the room, with a few chairs around it, and heavy metal screening was over the window. Detective Mitchell pulled out the chair opposite me and sat down.

"Why did you want to talk to me?" I said.

"We just want to discuss a few things," he said.

"Would you like some coffee, Claudia?" said Officer Troy, still standing by the door.

"Yes, thank you, Troy."

"Cream and sugar?"

"Yes, please."

As Troy went out for the coffee, Detective Mitchell pulled out a pack of cigarettes and offered me one. After I shook my head, he laid the pack on the table. He didn't say anything until he'd taken a few drags on the cigarette, turning his head when he exhaled so the smoke blew away from me.

"It's pretty rough, what you've been through," he said. "My wife's in the same spot, with her dad, almost eight years now. How long was it for you? More than eight years?"

I nodded.

"Whew," he said. "That's real rough."

When Troy came back with the coffee, he joined us at the table. The coffee was too hot to drink, so I let it sit there while I waited.

"You shouldn't be smoking," said Troy.

"I didn't say I was quitting," said Mitchell. "I said I was thinking about it."

"No, I mean because of her," said Troy, jerking his head in my direction.

"Oh, yeah, sorry, I forgot," said Mitchell, putting the cigarette out in the ashtray on the table. "So, Troy tells me he was an usher at your wedding."

I nodded.

"Me and Roger and Sam, we go back to when we were kids," said Troy.

"How long had you and the deceased lived together, Mrs. Sloane?" said Mitchell.

"A long time," I said.

"But things started happening before you moved in together, didn't they?" said Troy.

"We didn't notice," I said.

"It's easy to miss the beginning," said Mitchell. "You think you're imagining things. Other people think you're imagining things, too."

I wished Sam or Roger were there with me. The coffee had too much sugar and not enough cream. I put the cup down. Detective Mitchell picked up his packet of cigarettes and turned it repeatedly, end to end, between his thumb and fingers.

"Mitch and me, we got to talking," said Troy, "and we started wondering about the pills."

"What pills?"

"The pills in the bedroom, on the nightstand."

"Those were empty bottles."

"But they held a lot of pills at some time. What were they all for?"

"Anxiety, insomnia, depression . . ."

"Did you get all those prescriptions from the same doctor?"

"Yes."

"From Dr. Barnett?"

"Yes."

"Listen, Claudia — here's the problem we're having," said Troy as he frowned, first at his coffee mug, then at me. "Sam says there weren't any pills."

Sam swears he never said anything like that. He says the police were lying, to confuse me. Roger says the police were looking for in-consistencies in my story, but there aren't any inconsistencies in the truth. Dr. Daniels says I might have misunderstood or made a mis-take. But I didn't make a mistake. Not the kind of mistake that leaves a dead body.

"Are you sure you didn't make a mistake about the night?" said Mother Grace as she stood in the middle of my room.

"The dance is tonight, Mom," said Roger from the doorway as I threw myself on the bed.

"Be careful, dear, you'll mess up your dress," said Mother Grace.

"Who cares?" I said. "No one'll ever see me in it anyway."

"Hey, Claude, you want me to go beat the guy up for you? You want me to slash his bike tires or break his spokes or something?"

"Now, Roger, there's no need for any of that."

"But he stood her up, Mom."

"He didn't stand her up, Roger. I'm sure he just confused it with some other night. I'm sure that once Claudia talks to him, they'll get it all straightened out."

"He's not home, Mom," said Roger. "I already called his house and checked."

"You see? He might be on his way over."

"No, Mom, he's down at the Turnabout Dance already. With Amy."

"That's not fair," I said, pounding my pillow. "She gets all the boys."

"That's 'cause she's a tramp."

"Roger . . ."

"It's the truth, Mom. She even goes out with guys my age."

"Everybody knows I asked him. Everybody knows I made the dress and everything."

"If only Roger didn't have to work," said Mother Grace, "he could take you to the dance."

"He's my brother."

"There are worse things in life than going to a dance with your brother, dear."

"My life is ruined. Completely and totally ruined."

"Don't worry, Claude," said Roger. "I just thought of something."

Then he dashed out of the room, singing "Here I come to save the day," leaving me and Mother Grace staring after him.

I could have done something to save Roger if I'd known what the police were thinking, if I'd known what they were looking for. Sam says it's too late to think about it now. Eve says I couldn't have done anything without changing who I am. But I could have destroyed that plastic bag I found in the garage.

As soon as I lifted the trash can lid, I saw the bag. It was right on top, not pushed down or hidden underneath anything. It was just lying there on top of everything. It was a plastic food storage bag, a large one, and it was empty except for a powdery white residue coating its sides. I put down the bag of kitchen garbage on the floor, next to the trash can, and picked up the plastic bag. Outside it was raining so hard, it sounded like stones were falling on the garage roof. I opened the plastic bag and touched my finger to the white powder to taste it. It was bitter. So bitter. I gagged. Of course, that white residue wasn't nearly as bitter as what happened next, and it's not as bitter as some of my memories. Oh, God, if only I'd known what was in that bag . . . I never would have taken it up to the kitchen. I would have burned it, or buried it, or something. Anything to have saved us from what happened afterward.

"Claudia, dear, what happened?" said Eleanor as soon as I came into the bookstore. "What are you doing here? I thought you were taking the day off. For your anniversary."

"Eleanor, have you been having any problems with the customers?"

"None that I can think of. Why?"

"Three customers called me this afternoon complaining that you gave them the wrong change."

"You're talking about that Ruby Redfield, aren't you?"

"She's one of them."

"I counted out her change several times, Claudia. I don't know what she's so upset about."

"She says you gave her the wrong change every time."

"That Ruby has never been very clever, you know, and ever since she's started reading those tarot and palm-reading books, she hasn't gotten any smarter."

"Just give me her receipt, Eleanor."

Instead of opening the desk drawer where the money and the receipts were kept, she got up and went to the bookstore's kitchen, where her purse was sitting on the counter. She opened her purse, rummaged around in it, then pulled out some pieces of paper and handed them to me.

"You put the receipts in your purse? Jesus, Eleanor, are you crazy?"

"You don't have to snatch them out of my hand like that, Claudia."

"This is a bookstore, Eleanor, not a lending library. You can't put the receipts in your purse."

"I wasn't going to keep them in there. I just couldn't remember where you told me to put them."

"The same place you put them last time."

"Where did I put them last time?"

"In the middle drawer."

"Oh, that's right," she said as the bell on the outer door rang.

She followed me back out to the main room, chattering the whole way.

"And about the receipts, I know you told me to write out their names, dear," she said, "but I don't know if Ruby still spells her name that funny way or if she's gone back to the normal spelling."

The customer picked up the magazine she wanted and brought it over to the desk. I wrote out her receipt. After she left, I turned back to Eleanor.

"Mrs. Redfield says she gave you twenty dollars, and the book was twelve ninety-five. How much change did you give her?"

"Now, Claudia, you know I'm not good at math."

"That's why the calculator's sitting right there, Eleanor."

"You don't have to raise your voice, dear. I may be getting on in years, but I can still hear perfectly well. And if I'd known about the calculator, I would've given them the right change. Not that I gave anybody the wrong change. I mean, I suppose I might have given somebody a nickel too much. . . ."

She was lying, to cover up what was happening. Who knows how many other lies she told? *She wasn't lying,* says Dr. Daniels. How can you defend her? Especially after what she did to us? *Don't dwell on the pain, Claudia. Focus on the happy moments.* How can I do that when they're ruined because of everything that happened afterward? *Eleanor can't be blamed for any of that. It wasn't her fault.* Why couldn't things just stay like they were in the beginning, when all of us were happy, when we still loved each other? *You mean, when none of you knew what was happening?* I mean, when we were happy.

It was the happiest day of my life. The lace veil was in front of my face, the candles flickered all around the church. On Sam's right, Roger smiled at me. Eve stood behind me to my left. The priest sprinkled the rings with holy water in the form of a cross.

"Bless, O Lord, these rings, that they who wear them shall keep true faith unto each other."

Over Sam's shoulder, I could see Eleanor smiling at me, and Harold, his shoulders back. Across from them, holding Roger's and Eve's baby, Mother Grace dabbed her eyes with her handkerchief. Mother Ruth and her son sat next to Mother Grace. Incense and the scent of roses filled the air.

"May they abide in Your peace and in obedience to Your will, and ever live in mutual love."

Sam took my hand, slipped the wedding band on, and repeated the vow. After I put Sam's ring on him, we knelt at the altar rail. The ring on my finger glowed silver in the candlelight, and my tears slipped down behind the veil.

"O God, by whom woman is joined to man," said the priest, "look graciously down upon this Your handmaid, now about to be joined in marriage. May Your protection be to her a yoke of love and peace. Faithful and chaste, may she be pleasing to her husband like Rachel, wise like Rebecca, long-lived and faithful like Sarah. In none of her deeds may that first author of transgression have any share. May she be fruitful in offspring; may she be approved and blameless, and attain unto the rest of the Blessèd in Your heavenly kingdom."

He made the sign of the cross in the air over us.

"May they both see their children's children unto the third and fourth generation and arrive at a happy old age. Through our blessèd Lord and Savior, Jesus Christ."

But God didn't protect us. He was the one who cursed us. All my life, Sam was the only one I could depend on. And Roger. From the time I was a teenager. From the time of my first high school Turnabout Dance. Sam and Roger were the ones who saved me.

"I still think Randy just confused the date of the dance, Claudia," said Mother Grace as I splashed my face with cold water. "When you see him in school on Monday . . ."

"Hey, Claude," said Roger, knocking and opening the bathroom door. "You got about five minutes till your date gets here."

"Oh, my God, you didn't call him down at the school, did you, Roger?" I said, water dripping from my chin as I looked up at him. "I'll just die if you called him there."

"I wouldn't call that jerk for anything. Now, do something with your face before your date gets here."

He was out the door before either of us could say anything else. Mother Grace and I looked at each other a few moments before I glanced in the mirror. When I saw my red nose and puffy eyes, I covered my face with the towel.

"We'll fix you up in no time," said Mother Grace, tugging the towel away. "Here, let me get to my side of the medicine cabinet."

"Mascara? I thought I wasn't allowed to wear mascara till I was sixteen."

"This is a special situation."

"Blush, too? But you said . . ."

"I know what I said, but this is a special occasion. Now hold still. There. You look lovely."

"I look like a freak. Oh, my God — the doorbell. I thought he said 'five minutes.'"

"Don't run, Claudia. You'll tear your dress."

Mother Grace followed me downstairs. There, in the entry hall, wearing a suit and tie, was Roger's best friend.

"Sam?"

"Hey, Claude," he said, and Roger elbowed him. "Sorry. I mean, Claudia."

"What's this, Roger?"

"It's her date, Mom."

"Her date? But . . ."

"Everybody knows I asked Randy."

"You sure fooled them, didn't you? Didn't she fool them, Sammy?"

"She fooled them, Rodge."

"But I asked Randy."

"She doesn't get it, Sammy."

"That's what it looks like, Rodge."

"Okay, Claude, picture this," said Roger. "From the very beginning, you planned to invite a senior to the Freshman Turnabout Dance, but you wanted to keep it a secret, see?"

"Why?"

"So no one else would invite a senior," said Sam.

"Right. So no one else would ask a senior. You pretended you asked . . . what's his name again?"

"Randy."

"Yeah, Rando. You tell everybody you're going with Rando, but then," said Roger, putting his hand on Sam's shoulder, "you show up with Sammy here."

"The handsomest senior in the school," said Sam.

"Second handsomest," said Roger. "Ah, I can see the headlines of the school paper now: 'Claudia Page Goes to Freshman Dance with Senior.' They'll be talking about it for months."

"Is Sam allowed to go to the Freshman Dance with her?"

"Mom, just a little while ago, you wanted me to take her."

"You're her brother."

"Well, she's not going with me. She's going with Sam."

Roger moved me till I stood next to Sam, who was taller than I was. His dark hair was brushed back from his face, and his tie was almost the same blue as my dress.

"You've got cat hair on you."

"Sorry. I was kissing Mudball good-bye. There. Did I get it all?" he said, and I nodded. "We'll get some flowers on the way to the dance."

"You better get going, Sammy, and don't stay out too late, you two."

"Oh, Roger, stop teasing them. Have a good time, dear. Stay at the dance as long as you want."

"Don't do anything I wouldn't . . . I mean, have a good time with my little baby sister, Sammy."

"Yeah. Later, Rodge."

You got what you needed, says Dr. Daniels. I got what I needed that night. *You always have, Claudia, even when you found the body.* I didn't need to have my life turned upside down and twisted inside out. I didn't need to have every dream I've ever had smashed and shattered. And I certainly did not need to be the one who found the body. *Yes, I think you did,* she says, and I'm so surprised that I don't know what to say. *It may have been an accident of circumstance that you found the body, but I think you needed to find it.*

"It must've been an accident," I said to the funeral director over the phone. "Well, then it's a mistake."

Sam came into the kitchen and sat down at the table. He picked up the newspaper as he drank his coffee.

"But we already have the plot," I said, still on the phone. "No, I wouldn't expect you to know that, but . . . well, who was it that changed the arrangements? Mr. Sloane? Which one?"

Sam buttered his toast and dipped it into the yolk of his fried eggs. He folded the newspaper and propped it between his glass of orange juice and his plate. After I hung up the phone, I stood there without moving. Sam didn't look at me until I sat down at the table. Even then, he didn't ask me any questions. He just sat there, eating his bacon and eggs, like it was the same as every other morning.

"They cremated the body," I said, but he never said a word.

"Just a few more questions, Mrs. Sloane," said Detective Mitchell. "What about that plastic bag you found in the garage trash can? What was in that bag?"

"Some leftover crushed pills."

"Why did it have crushed pills in it?" said Officer Troy.

"We had to crush her pills to put them in her food," I said.

"Why?"

"Sometimes she didn't want to take them."

"Why not?"

"I don't know."

"So you crushed them?"

"And mixed them with her food. To keep her from having a catastrophic reaction."

"Catastrophic reaction?"

"That's what they call it," I said.

"Yeah, I heard that before," said Troy, getting out of his chair and going to the far side of the room.

"So you put them in the plastic bag to crush the pills? How many pills did you crush at a time?"

"One or two. Sometimes three."

"You used a gallon plastic bag to crush two or three pills?" said Troy, frowning.

"No, I used a small one."

"Did you ever use a large one?"

"I don't think so."

"What size would you consider this bag?"

"A large one."

"And you didn't use a large one like this to crush her pills?"

"Not that I remember."

"Were there any circumstances under which you'd use a large bag like this to crush up her pills?"

"Only if we were out of small ones," I said.

"How about the week before her death?" said Mitchell as Troy came back to the table and sat down. "Did you run out of small bags then?"

"I don't remember."

"Maybe you ran out of small bags and used a large one," said Troy. "Is that possible?"

"I really don't remember."

"What did you use to crush the pills, Claudia?"

"The first time, I did it with a mortar and pestle. After that, I used a rolling pin."

"When was the last time you got the prescriptions refilled, Mrs. Sloane?"

"I'd have to look in the checkbook."

"What if I told you that you got all the prescriptions refilled the week before the death?" said Mitchell. "Does that sound about right to you?"

"I don't know."

"We checked the pharmacy records," said Troy, opening a folder. "You had all the prescriptions refilled at the end of the month. This is a copy of the refill order."

I glanced at the sheet before I handed it back to him. My head was aching by that time. When I looked at my watch, I was surprised at the time. It felt like I'd been there for days.

"How many pills a day were you supposed to give her?"

"Whatever it said on the bottle," I said.

"But roughly, how many a day did you give her?"

"One or two of each kind."

"Then you should've had lots of pills left, since you just got them refilled a week before the death."

"Do you know if there are any small plastic food storage bags in your pantry right now?" said Troy.

"I'd have to look."

"We already looked," said Mitchell, "and we found a whole box of the small bags. Right next to the large ones."

Mitchell stood, holding his coffee cup. Troy sat with his hands on the folder of paperwork in front of him. Neither one said anything. I picked up my cup, but it was empty. Troy leaned back in his chair, his eyes on me as Mitchell opened the door.

"We'd like you to take a polygraph test," he said.

CHAPTER FOUR

*D*O YOU UNDERSTAND HOW THE POLYGRAPH WORKS, Mrs. Sloane?"

I nodded, staying as still as I could. The blood pressure cuff was on my left arm, the rubber tubing around my chest, the electrodes on my fingers. Behind me, the examiner did something with the machine. My hands were cold, the chair was hard, and my leg had a cramp in it, but I was afraid to move. I felt like a criminal.

"All right, Mrs. Sloane. Now, you recall the areas the questions will cover, correct? Good. I'm ready to begin. Answer the questions with either a yes or no. Is your name Claudia Sloane?"

"Yes."

"Do you reside at 1312 Maple Avenue?"

"Yes."

"Have you lived there more than five years?"

"Yes."

"Was Eleanor Sloane your mother-in-law?"

"Yes."

"Did she reside with you and your husband?"

"Yes."

"Did your mother-in-law's illness cause problems between you and your husband?"

"Not really."

"Just yes or no, please. Did her illness cause problems between you and your husband?"

"No."

"Did her illness affect your own health? Mrs. Sloane?"

"No."

"Did her illness cause your miscarriages? Mrs. Sloane, did her illness cause your . . ."

"No."

"Did you kill your mother-in-law?"

"No."

"Did your husband kill her?"

"No, of course not."

"Did you want her to die?"

That's what I did wrong. I told them the truth about my feelings, and they condemned me for it. Roger says they looked at the circumstances, too. At the fact that I was alone when I found the body. But it wouldn't have mattered if Sam had been home. The police wanted to believe I was guilty, so they did.

"I can't believe it. No one ever showed you this before?" said Mother Ruth. "Your own baby picture."

Eve was in the bookstore, waiting on customers, while Mother Ruth and I went upstairs, to the spare room beside the office. The sofa bed from Sam's old apartment was there, along with a couple of chairs and end tables that Mother Grace had left me, so we called it our second living room. Mother Ruth and I sat down on the couch. On the coffee table, there was a plate of brownies I'd made, along with a carafe of fresh coffee. As Mother Ruth took off her gloves, I looked at the photograph. It was an old, black-and-white picture, faded and cracked, with one of the upper corners torn off. On the back, in black ink, someone had written "Claudia, 3 months, 1953." I turned it over. The baby's eyes were so wide they looked perfectly round, and her mouth was opened in a circle.

"Where did you find this?" I said.

"In the attic, when we were packing," she said, leaning closer to look at the picture with me. "You know I'm moving in with my son and his wife. Al's the one who found it, actually. We thought you'd like to have it."

"And you didn't take this picture?"

"Oh, no, you were older than that when I got you."

"Then who took it?"

"I don't know, dear, but I'm quite sure I didn't. I remember putting it away after I lost you. I knew you'd want it one day, so I kept it for you."

I looked at the picture again. The baby's hair was curly, but she'd been too young for any freckles. If it had been a color picture, we could have seen the color of the baby's hair and eyes. I put the picture down to pour us both some coffee. When I slid the cup and saucer over to Mother Ruth, she smiled at me and tapped the photograph with her forefinger.

"That picture is exactly how I remember you," she said. "You were always such a happy baby."

Mother Ruth remembers you as a happy baby? says Dr. Daniels. You're just as surprised as I was, I tell her, because I don't remember being happy. In fact, when I remember all those courtrooms and judges and adoption motions — *What do you mean, "all those adoption motions"?* she says, almost getting out of her chair. *Mother Ruth tried to adopt you more than once?* Several times. *Why didn't you ever tell me that?* What difference does it make? They turned her down every time, so all the courtrooms of my life meant the same thing: pain and suffering and injustice. *Injustice? Even now?* What happened to us wasn't justice. And when I think back to all the injustices Eleanor inflicted . . . *Like what?* Like how long she must have known that something was wrong but didn't tell us. *It makes you angry at her.* Yes, of course. *It makes you so angry you want her to die all over again.*

No one was thinking of death that first picnic of the summer. No one but Eleanor. Sam and I had just bought our first house, and that was our first cookout. We were all out back, at the picnic table: Harold and Eleanor, Roger and Eve, me and Sam. That house had a beautiful yard, with tall bushes on each side and a line of cedars across the back. Nestled against the trees at the back of the yard was a swing set from the family before us, and next to that was a sandbox. Sam and I thought our baby would be playing there within a few years.

"How are you feeling, Claudia?" said Harold after I set the salt and pepper on the picnic table. "You want me to get you anything?"

"She's pregnant, Harold, not an invalid."

"I'm just watching out for her, Eleanor," he said, tucking his napkin in at his collar. "I hope the first one's a girl, with Claudia's red hair."

"I hope her hair's dark and straight, like Sam's," I said.

"How do you know it's going to be a girl?" said Sam, standing at the grill. "It might be a boy."

"I hope it's twins," said Harold. "A boy and a girl."

"Oh, no, not twins," said Eve, groaning loudly. "Then she'll look like I do."

"You look wonderful, dear," said Eleanor, patting Eve on the hand. "Pregnancy agrees with you."

"You look like you're going to have them any day now, Eve."

"Three more weeks," said Roger.

"I bet they'll be here sooner than that," said Harold. "Then at Christmas, we'll have our own grandbaby."

"We shouldn't be talking about it," said Eleanor, passing around the bowl of potato salad. "It's bad luck."

"We do have almost six more months to get through, Dad," said Sam as he brought the plate of hamburgers and bratwurst to the table.

"Claudia, I started the rocking horse," said Harold. "I glued the eye- and earpieces to the head."

"It doesn't even look like a horse yet," said Eleanor.

"It will by the time the baby gets here."

"The baby won't be able to ride it for years."

"But it'll be in her room, waiting for her."

"In *his* room," said Sam, squirting ketchup on his open bun, "waiting for *him*."

Everyone laughed, and I crossed my fingers under the table. For a few minutes, no one said anything. Everyone was filling his plate with potato salad, macaroni salad, hamburgers, potato chips, and pickles. A cool breeze rustled the bushes and trees, while from somewhere in the neighborhood came the sound of children playing. Once, Roger put his hand on Eve's belly, down low, so no one else would notice. It made me want the months to fly away so Sam and I could have those looks on our faces. We were all thinking of life then. All of us but Eleanor.

"Our neighborhood doesn't have many young people anymore," she said as she put down her fork. "Just a few. Some teenagers. And one less of them now. Sam, do you remember the Robinsons, over on Minster Street? Their son shot himself. In the basement."

"Jesus. You mean Eddie?" said Sam, almost choking on his food. "When did that happen?"

"Roger's the one who had to go down there."

"Oh, please, let's not talk about it," said Eve.

"When we were young," said Eleanor, "we never heard of people killing themselves, especially not young people."

"Old Man Jensen did it. Next door. In the house where the Whitmans live," said Harold, his mouth full. "He did it right after we moved in. And he wasn't even sick."

"His wife died of cancer," said Eleanor. "He was depressed."

"He was still alive."

"Wouldn't you kill yourself, Harold, if you were that depressed?"

"Hell, no. Too much to live for."

"What if you were sick, or dying anyway?"

"Still too much to live for."

"I'd do it," said Eleanor. "If I were going to die anyway."

"You would not," said Harold.

"Yes, I would."

"The hell you say. I've lived with you over half my life, and I know you wouldn't."

"If I had an inoperable brain tumor, I might. Or . . . or if I were going . . . crazy."

"You'd be crazy if you killed yourself," said Harold. "No doubt about that."

"Roger, would you ever commit suicide?" said Eleanor.

"Jesus, Mom, this is a picnic," said Sam, reaching for more potato chips. "What kind of talk is this?"

"She's been morbid for months now. I told you."

"Harold calls me 'morbid' every time I want to have a serious discussion."

"Only when she gets obsessed with it. Like abortion. Or the pope."

"God, don't get her started on the pope," said Roger as he picked up the jar of mayonnaise.

"Don't make fun of the pope," said Eve.

"Hey, you got any more hamburgers on that grill?" said Harold, shoving his plate toward Sam. "I'm ready for a second. And give me a bratwurst, too."

"Yes or no, would you ever kill yourself?" said Eleanor. "That's all you have to say, Sam."

"You know he's going to agree with Harold," said Roger. "They agree on everything."

"Not since Sam was old enough to shave."

"So would you or wouldn't you, Sam?"

"I really don't want to talk about this right now, Mom."

"Well, then, tell me this — would you help someone you know kill himself?"

"I wouldn't," I said.

"We know you wouldn't, dear," said Eleanor, "but I was asking Sam."

"How well do I know this person?" said Sam.

"You wouldn't help anybody commit suicide," I said.

"I might, if the person was dying anyway."

"No, you wouldn't," I said.

"I don't know," said Sam. "I might."

"Not if you wanted to stay married to me," I said, and everyone laughed.

Sam was so depressed after Eleanor's death, he stayed in bed till noon every day, and when he got up, he didn't shave or bathe or get dressed. He walked around in his T-shirt and shorts, his bare feet getting dirtier and dirtier, carrying the silver box with Eleanor's cremains around with him. The house was deathly quiet: he didn't listen to his music, and he didn't say a word to me, even when I asked him a question. At mealtimes, he sat at the table without eating, the box of cremains next to his plate. Then, one Sunday, when I got back from the bookstore, I heard his music all the way out in the driveway.

> *I can't feel,*
> *feel a thing.*
> *I can't shout.*
> *I can't scream.*

The music vibrated through the walls of the garage and up through the floor when I went into the house. I called out to him, but he didn't answer.

> *All this pain*
> *from within.*
> *And I just can't pour my heart out*
> *to another living thing.*

I found him sitting on the couch, his bare feet on the coffee table, the silver box in his lap. When I tried to take it away from him, he wouldn't let go.

I won't cry when you say good-bye.
I'm out of tears.
I won't die when you wave good-bye.
I'm out of tears.

I couldn't feel a thing after I found the body. After they'd taken it away, and even later, when Sam came home, I felt nothing. When Sam touched me, pressing me back on the bed with its clean sheets, slipping his hands under my shirt to take it off, I didn't feel anything. I wanted to, but I didn't. He wrapped his arms around me, his head resting against my breasts. He stroked my arms, my shoulders, my back, but the only thing I felt was empty. I wanted him to fill me up, to wipe out all that was dead in me, to make me feel something again. He touched my breasts, my belly, my thighs, but still, it was nothing. He kissed my face and throat, whispered my name, forced himself into me. I dug my nails into his back so hard that he cried out. But I still didn't feel anything. Afterward, he untangled himself from me and lay beside me on that bed. When I sat up, he reached up and touched me.

"We'll make it through this," he said.

You did make it through, says Dr. Daniels. *I know you don't believe it, but you did.* On the table next to the couch, there's a new fountain, its stones forming a four-tiered pyramid in a grey ceramic base, the water tumbling down the tiers. If I close my eyes, I can imagine I'm at a lake or by a waterfall. *I want you to start concentrating on the good things in your life.* Like what? *Like what Eleanor did for you in the bookstore before it opened.* That doesn't count. *Of course, it does,* she says, and she laughs.

"Sam, I really don't feel good enough to be here today," I said as we got out of the car and walked toward the back door of the store. "I'm still not over this flu, and the car made my morning sickness worse."

"You don't have to stay very long, Claudia. Just a couple of minutes."

He took my arm as he slipped the key into the lock, wiggled the doorknob, and opened it. I put my hand over my nose and mouth after we entered the dim kitchen. I wanted to turn around right then and go back home, but Sam led me to the main room. Just as I thought I was going to gag from the smell of the paint, he flipped on the lights, and people jumped out at me, shouting.

"Surprise."

"Surprise."

I looked around the bookstore in amazement. The shelves were built, the floors polished, the window frames refinished. The stuffed easy chairs from Sam's old apartment and the love seat from Mother Grace's were arranged in front of the bookshelves. Some of Eve's artwork was hanging on the walls, and her jewelry was in the display case. Everyone was there: Eleanor, Harold, Roger, Eve, one of Eleanor's friends, Mother Grace. Every one of them was splattered with paint and grinning with the whole bottom half of his face.

"You got it all done," I said, moving around in a daze. "How did you do it?"

"We've been here this week while you were sick."

"And most of us stayed here all weekend."

"It was Eleanor's idea. She organized everything."

"We wanted to surprise you."

"Did we surprise you, Claudia?"

"She's surprised."

I sat down at the new desk. Its cherry wood gleamed under the lights. A two-layer cake decorated with books made of icing sat in the center.

"Sam and Harold made the desk. They've been working on it in the basement for months. Isn't it lovely?"

"Grace made the cake."

"Roger and Eve bought the fig tree and the hanging plants."

"And we'll all help unpack the books."

"Do you like it, Claudia?" they said, crowding around me, touching me. "Is it how you thought it'd be?"

"It's everything I've ever dreamed of," I said.

"I can't believe you're really here," said Sam, coming up behind me in his apartment and putting his arms around me. "It's like a dream, Claude."

"Don't call me that. Not now. Not like this."

He undid the pearl buttons of my gown — slowly, so slowly — kissing my bare back after he'd undone each button. When the dress was completely open, I slipped it from my shoulders and arms. Sam unsnapped my bra and slid it off, putting his arms around me to cup my breasts in his hands. His skin was darker than mine, from all his work outdoors in the sun, and his ruffled shirt was stiff against my back. I eased the gown over my hips and let it fall to the floor. I turned around to place my palms on his chest, smooth and tanned, then slipped my arms around him, under his shirt. I kissed him. I kissed him again. Dragging his arms down around me, he lowered himself to his knees, his lips and tongue sliding across my belly and thighs. He teased me with his tongue until I ached for him. When he slipped his hands between my legs, my fingers tightened themselves in his hair, then plunged behind the collar of his open shirt. All around us, the candles flickered in the darkened room, but we were the ones who burned.

"Someone's got a fire going already," said Eleanor.

"I love the smell of burning wood," I said.

We were walking every day then, even in the fall when the weather got cooler, the orange and yellow leaves all around us. Eleanor pumped her arms as she walked, so her cheeks were rosy. At the wooden bridge, we stopped for a few moments, looking down at the stream. Beneath the bridge, the water swirled around rocks and broken branches.

"Do you remember my friend Lois McDonnell?" said Eleanor.

"No."

"Yes, you do. She's the one who helped Grace sew the slipcovers for the bookstore love seat."

"Oh, is that Lois? The one with the cat-eye glasses?"

"Yes, I knew you remembered her. Anyway, I was thinking of asking Lois to come walking with us in the mornings. She's not feeling like herself these days."

I kicked a pebble off the edge of the bridge before I pulled my jacket closed, buttoned it, and put my hands in my pockets.

". . . she's pretty sure that's what happened to her grandfather," said Eleanor. "Of course, we can't be certain, but about ten years ago, Lois' mother told her . . ."

I kicked more pebbles into the water. Some of them made plopping sounds, some of them made ripples that spread farther away from each other. I pulled my collar up. When I walked back to the road, Eleanor followed me.

". . . it's dreadful, her husband Fred saying she's the same when Lois knows perfectly well she's not. She might've had a little stroke or something. I told her she should go to her own doctor. Then she'd find out the truth. I told her she should start walking with us, too. It's made me feel years younger . . ."

I bent my head against the wind as the rain started. Our morning walks were the only times I didn't have to share Eleanor with Harold or Sam or Holy Angels Church, and it hurt that she wanted Lois there. It still hurts, even after all these years. She was supposed to be my mother. She was supposed to love me.

Mother Esther never scolded or complained when chocolate chips disappeared from the cookie dough. I stood on a chair at the table stirring the dough, and she just poured a few more chips in, then spilled some beside the bowl. While the first batch of cookies baked, I hovered near the stove, the oven mitts covering my arms almost to my shoulders. I was so excited when the cookies came out that I couldn't wait till they cooled: I always burnt my tongue on the first bite. The snow piled up outside as the warm cookies piled up inside, and some of those cookies actually managed to escape me and get wrapped up as presents for Mother Esther's grandchildren. The kitchen windows were etched with ice, the kitchen was steamy, the chocolate cookies were gooey and warm. Everything was perfect. Everything.

All your life, you've been trying to make things perfect, says Dr. Daniels, *but the real world rarely is.* That's because people don't try hard enough. On the windowsill of her office, there's a clay jar between the statues of the wizard and the angel. On the clay jar, in gold lettering, are the words "Fairy Dust." I pick it up and open it. The fairy dust sparkles silver and gold. *If you're always looking for perfection, Claudia, you'll never enjoy the things you have,* says Dr. Daniels as I put the lid back on the fairy dust. *Nothing will ever be perfect enough for you.* But if everyone tried just a little harder, I tell her, things would be the way they're supposed to be. *You mean, if everyone tried as hard as you did with the ashes?*

I had to do something about the ashes. I had to. I waited till Sam fell asleep on the couch, the silver box with the cremains pressed to his chest. In the dark, the only sound was the steady ticking of the grandfather clock in the living room. He didn't wake up when I freed the box from his grasp. Clutching it tightly, I went through the house to the backyard. I opened the box and walked slowly around the garden, spilling the ashes. The empty box glowed pale in the moonlight, and against the dark soil, the ashes glowed, too. I stood there for a while. All by myself. Then I went back into the house.

After her house was sold, we helped Eleanor pack. I was doing the kitchen while Sam and Roger carried the furniture out to the truck.

Eleanor was in the living room. When Sam came in the kitchen to get a drink of water, I turned to him.

"Did you get all the guns moved?" I said, and he nodded. "Did you remember the one in our bedroom?"

"I just told you I got them all moved, didn't I?"

"I don't want to fight."

"Who's fighting?"

He turned on the faucet, bent over the sink, and splashed his face with water.

"You can go over to Roger's any time you want to shoot," I said. "I know you don't like to think that your mother was trying to —"

"She wasn't."

"I don't think it was an accident, and neither does —"

"What do I care what Dr. Daniels thinks? It was an accident, and that's all it was."

He tore off some paper towels to dry his face and neck.

"We need to protect Eleanor from the guns, Sam, more than we need the guns to protect us."

He went out without saying another word. I put a few more things from the cupboard into the box before I pushed it aside and went into the living room, where Eleanor was sitting on a footstool, in the midst of dozens of boxes, holding one of the porcelain figurines in her lap. The cassette tape Sam bought her was playing, and she was crying.

> *Here is the moment of parting,*
> *I can feel all the fear in your hand,*
> *Leaving a home full of memories,*
> *On the verge of a strange new land.*

"Do you know what it's like to see your whole life in boxes?" she said.

No, not in boxes. But I knew what it was like to have your whole life in a single, tattered suitcase. I knew what it was like to leave your favorite blanket and your roller skates behind. I knew what it was like to lose Teddy or Bunny or Kitty, whom you loved more than anything else in the world. I knew what it was like to stare out the back window of a car as the house you lived in got smaller and smaller and smaller. I took a tissue out of my pocket and handed it to Eleanor, but she wouldn't take it. She just sat there, crying and crying. There was nothing I could do for her. Nothing at all.

"What can I do for you, dear?" said Mother Constance after she eased herself into the rocker across from me and put her feet up on the needlepoint stool. "You know, you're even prettier than you were as a little girl. And your hair's just as red as ever."

The vinyl covering on the sofa crackled when I sat down. The tables were covered with crocheted lace doilies, and the lampshades were covered with plastic. I set my purse on the floor.

"You knew they put a mall across from my old house, didn't you?" she said. "The traffic was terrible. So was the noise. My son-in-law found this nice house for me. You don't remember my old house, do you? No, you were too little. Well, this house is exactly like my old one, only smaller. Would you like some iced tea, Claudia, or some cookies? Do you still like sugar cookies? I made a batch for my great-granddaughters just the other day and there's some left."

"No, thank you, Mother Constance. I came to ask you something," I said, and she sat back down. "Do you know anything about my real mother?"

"Your real mother? You mean the one who gave birth to you? What about her?"

"I know I was sick in the hospital: Mother Esther told me that. But I don't know why my mother never came to get me."

"Well, first of all, dear, you were in the hospital, but you weren't sick. You were there because of what she did to you. My, oh, my, it still breaks my heart to think of it," she said, shaking her head as she took an embroidered handkerchief out of her apron pocket. "You were covered with bruises, poor thing, all over your little body, and both your legs were broken."

"Broken?"

"That's why they took you away from her in the first place, dear. I thought you knew that. You didn't? Of course, nobody talked about child abuse in those days, but everybody knew what happened to you wasn't any accident. That's why they wouldn't let her see you when she came to the hospital."

"My mother came to the hospital?"

"Oh, yes. I saw her. They'd already called me by then. Well, there she was, in the hallway, as close to me as you are now, with a policeman holding onto her arm. She was crying and yelling and trying to get past him into your room. But every time she moved, the doctors and nurses circled around her. They weren't taking any chances letting her near you again."

Mother Constance sighed as she dabbed at her eyes with the handkerchief.

"Then I saw you, with those terrible bruises all over your body and those dreadful casts on your legs. And you so tiny and delicate anyway."

"Did you ever see my real mother again?"

"My goodness, no. Why would I want to?"

Did you ever find your birth mother? says Dr. Daniels. No, I never found her. *Did you check the hospital records?* I couldn't: the hospital ceiling collapsed during a storm and the records were destroyed by the water. *Did you contact the county records office for a replacement of the birth certificate?* No, I didn't. I take one of the pieces of Halloween candy from the orange and black basket on the table. Candles in the shape of a ghost and a pumpkin are beside the basket. Dr. Daniels leans forward, looking at me intently. *You mean, you made a conscious decision not to find your birth mother?* I don't understand why she has to ask me that after what I've just told her, so I don't say anything. We sit there for a long time, each of us waiting for the other to speak, but there's nothing else to say.

Eleanor didn't talk much at the end, but I think she heard me, and so does Eve. Sam doesn't believe it, but if babies in the womb can hear, and persons in comas can hear, then why couldn't Eleanor have heard me?

> *Sleep, my love, and peace attend thee,*
> *All through the night.*
> *Guardian angels God will lend thee,*
> *All through the night.*

Mother Ruth sang that to me when I was a little girl. I sat in her lap in the rocker in front of the living room windows. As she sang, I leaned my head against her and looked out at the yard. Sometimes the yard glittered with fireflies, and sometimes it sparkled with snow. I liked the ice on the windows, I liked Mother Ruth's arms around me, I liked the angels watching over me.

Sometimes, as I sang that song to Eleanor, she began to sing with me, even after she didn't talk much. When she pressed her body closer, I put my arms around her and kept singing. She settled her head against my breast and wrapped her arms around my waist. At times, she sang an entire line before falling silent again.

> *Soft the drowsy hours are creeping,*
> *Hill and dale in slumber steeping.*
> *I my loving vigil keeping,*
> *All through the night.*

She never let go of me — not while I was singing — and I held onto her with all my might.

CHAPTER FIVE

"Where's Eleanor?" I said when I came into the kitchen.

"Asleep," said Sam.

He was bending over the table, his back to me, his arms moving rhythmically in front of him.

"What are you doing? I thought you were carrying your stuff out to the car. Aren't you going to be late?"

"I've got plenty of time," he said.

The table was dusted with white. It was covered with bowls, measuring spoons, and Eleanor's bottles of prescription medicine. Sam was holding the rolling pin over a large plastic bag filled with white powder.

"What's all that?" I said.

"I was going to give Mom some pudding before I left."

"What's in the bag?"

"Her medicine."

"That's an awfully big bag, Sam."

"I was crushing some extra so you wouldn't have to do it by yourself this weekend."

"How many did you put in?" I said, uncapping one of the bottles. "Oh, no, don't tell me you put the whole thing in."

"Don't you do it that way?"

"Jesus, Sam, how are we supposed to know how much is one pill?"

"Can't we just measure it?"

"Did you crush one pill and measure it before you did all the rest?" I said, putting down that bottle and picking up another. "Oh, no, don't tell me. Sam, you didn't. You put two different kinds of pills in?"

"I was trying to help."

"You call this helping?"

"You're always saying I don't help out enough with Mom."

"Putting all her medicines in a bag and crushing them all together — that's helping?"

"I'm sorry."

"God damn it, why didn't you ask me first?"

"You were taking a nap and . . ."

"I just got them refilled Saturday, and now we have to throw it all away."

But you didn't see him throw that bag away, says Dr. Daniels. I found it, though, in the trash can in the garage. *Was there enough powdery white residue in that bag to account for all the bottles of pills Sam crushed?* I look away from Dr. Daniels, at the pictures of her children, on the table beside the couch. In one picture, the boy is running, dragging a kite through the air behind him. In the other, the girl is peeking out from under a blanket, a sleepy smile on her face. *If Sam did it, he would have been doing it out of love.* You know I couldn't stay with him if I thought he'd done it, I say. *Why does it upset you so much to think he might have been responsible?* Why are you trying to make me believe that he could have done something like that? *What I'm trying to do,* she says, *is to make you stop being a victim.*

"Don't you ever get tired of being the victim?" said Eve.

"What's that supposed to mean?"

"She's Sam's mother, Claudia. Let him take care of her."

"Sam has to run the business, Eve."

"So do you, Claudia: BookLovers. Remember?"

"Sam takes care of all the accounting, Eve, and I do all the ordering."

"But you're never here, Claudia."

"I'm here now."

Two customers came into the store. I flipped through the cash receipts a couple of times as Eve helped them find a book. She called them by name and asked if they liked the book they'd bought previously. They nodded and started to explain the plot. She got the new novel for them, did the paperwork, and waved good-bye as they left the store. Then she looked at me.

"I want to be a partner."

"Just because I'm staying home more?"

"I'm the only one working here."

"Jesus, Eve, you act like it's my fault Eleanor got sick."

"No one's forcing you to stay home and take care of her."

"She needs me."

"No, Claudia, you're the one who needs her."

Eve said something you didn't want to hear, and that made you angry. She'd been my best friend since junior high school. What I needed from her was support and understanding, not additional demands and stress. *So you wanted Eve to validate your perception of the situation, but you didn't want to validate hers.* I thought you were supposed to be on my side. *Do you want me to be on your side,* says Dr. Daniels, *or do you want me to tell you the truth?*

"Oh, my, someone needs to tell that young lady the truth," said Eleanor after a teenage girl came out of the store's dressing room. "That'll never pass."

I looked up from the rack of sweaters. Eleanor was shaking her head at two teenagers, one of whom modeled a green-and-black plaid skirt for the other.

"Girlfriend, that skirt's so perfect on you, it's bad."

"It's the baddest, ain't it?"

"The baddest I've ever seen. It's definitely you, girl."

The girl in the skirt squealed, twirling around in front of the mirror, the short, pleated skirt flaring out, showing everything underneath.

"Oh, dear," said Eleanor.

She walked over to the girls and tapped the one in the skirt on her shoulder.

"If Sister Mary Margaret sees that skirt, she won't like it," said Eleanor.

"Huh?"

"What'd you say?"

"That skirt will never pass."

"What're you looking at my skirt for, Granny? Are you a lesbian?"

"It won't pass."

The two girls looked at each other, their eyes and mouths opened wide in laughter.

"What's wrong with her, girl?"

"She's living in the Zone, girlfriend. Sister Margarine-something. Shoo, don't pay her no mind."

Eleanor put both hands on the girl's shoulders.

"Hey, Granny, don't you be putting no hands on me," said the girl. "Get off me, Granny."

"Kneel down. I'm trying to prove that it won't pass the test."

"Get outta my face, you nasty old —"

"Come on, girl. She's crazy," said the other girl, trying to tug her friend out of Eleanor's grip and back toward the dressing room.

"But I wanna know why she's in my business."

" 'Cause she escaped outta the loony bin," she said.

She shoved her friend into the dressing room and barred the door with her body. Holding Eleanor off with both hands, the girl called out to me.

"Hey, you. Yeah, you. You know we're talking to you. You better come get your mama."

"If she'll just kneel down, you'll see that — Claudia, what are you doing? Let go of my arm. I'm trying to help her. Claudia, stop it this minute. Let go of me, I said."

I didn't let go of her till we were out of the store. Then I walked as fast as I could to the car. Eleanor hurried after me, blabbering the whole time about Sister Mary-Margery-something-or-other and some test on knees. I looked at the ground the whole time. When we reached the car, I unlocked it and got in.

"I thought you wanted to get a sweater," said Eleanor. "My God, Claudia, you didn't even wait for me to close my door. Are you trying to take my leg off? What's the matter with you?"

"What's the matter with me? Are you kidding?" I said, pulling out into traffic. "You just accosted two strangers and tried to force one of them to kneel down in front of you, and you're asking what's wrong with me?"

"And that was extremely rude of you to interrupt me while I was talking to them. Claudia, slow down. I don't want to be in an accident. My God, you almost hit that car. Will you please slow down? I'm not going to be able to go anywhere with you if you're going to drive like this. Claudia, watch out. For heaven's sake, will you please slow down? You went right through that stop sign. You didn't even take your foot off the gas. Claudia, look out —"

Look how long it's been, says Dr. Daniels, *and you're still holding it against her.* The stained-glass hummingbirds hanging in her office window flash color over the walls of the office: violet, rose, faint yellow. *When are you going to forgive Eleanor?* she says. *When are you going to let her back into your heart?*

"It broke my heart to see you like that," said Mother Ruth. "Your legs all bruised and . . ."

"Broken?" I said.

"Broken?" she said, folding back the netting on her hat. "I never heard anything about broken legs."

"Mother Constance told me."

"I guess she'd know more about that than I would. You were two years old by the time you came to me, and by then you had those hideous braces on your legs," said Mother Ruth, shaking her head. "The things they did to children back then. It was just dreadful."

"I don't remember any braces."

"Oh, you wouldn't, dear. You stopped wearing them by the time you were three years old. But they were the most awful things. Some doctor got it into his head that your feet turned in too much — as if all babies' feet don't just naturally turn in like that — and he put braces on your feet."

I laid the baby photograph on the coffee table. Downstairs, the bell on the door of the bookstore jingled as customers went in and out. I heard Eve greet them. Mother Ruth stirred more sugar into her coffee before she put another brownie onto her plate. She picked the walnuts out of her brownie before she took a bite.

"Tell me about the braces."

"They had shoes on them," she said. "Bolted to a steel bar to keep your feet turned out. Heels touching. Like ballerinas do. That's why you can still turn your feet out so far. We had to cut the toes out of the shoes because your feet kept growing. I thought Esther showed those braces to you. She didn't? Well, they were heavy, I can tell you that. They were the heaviest things I ever felt. And to think you wore those things until you were three years old."

I poured some sweetener into my own coffee as I looked at the photograph. It was only a picture of a baby, not a child with broken legs or heavy braces.

"Oh, my, you were a dangerous weapon wearing those braces," said Mother Ruth, wiping her mouth with her napkin and laughing. "You knocked out an entire section of the bedroom wall slamming your feet and braces into it. And Lord knows how many mattresses you destroyed. If we didn't get you out of bed as soon as you woke up from your nap, you let everyone know how angry you were."

After the bookstore phone rang downstairs, the music stopped. A few minutes later, after Eve had changed the disc, the music drifted up again. I poured Mother Ruth more coffee as she wiped powdered sugar off her dark skirt.

"We lived in absolute terror that you'd hurt one of the neighborhood children with those braces," she said. "When you got angry, you'd throw yourself onto your back on the ground and swing those braces at them. My, it was lucky you never hurt anyone."

I put the coffee carafe down and picked up the picture again, but I still couldn't see the little girl she was describing.

"One day when I came home from the store, Frank — that was my first husband; you wouldn't remember him — well, there he was, standing at the bottom of the stairs, laughing his fool head off. It seems you'd taught yourself how to go down the stairs. I mean, your feet were bolted together with those braces, for heaven's sake, but that didn't stop you. No, it didn't. You made yourself rigid, stiff as a board, then slid right down the stairs. Like you were a sled on snow. It scared me to death, I can tell you, and there was Frank, laughing away, getting you to do it over and over. It's no wonder I left that man."

She folded her napkin and put it on her plate. Her hair was as grey as the netting on her hat, but other than that, she still looked like I remembered her. She picked up the picture of me and smiled at it. The baby in the photograph didn't look like a dangerous weapon or like a sled on snow. She didn't look like anything except a baby.

"When Esther brought you over to visit, after we were finally allowed to see each other again, the first thing I did was look at your legs. I watched you walk and run."

"I remember," I said.

"You do? I thought you were too young."

"I didn't understand why you wanted to see me walk."

"I was so glad to see you walking normally. Those braces could have crippled you. Thank God, they didn't."

"But you don't know if my legs were broken or not."

"All I know is that doctor was trying some new fad to buy himself a bigger house or a new car," she said, shaking her head. "Just thinking of it makes me so mad, I want to go to that doctor's grave and spit. To do such a terrible thing to such a sweet little girl. Are you sure you never saw those braces?"

"No, never."

"How strange that no one ever showed them to you. Well, for the life of me, dear, I don't know what ever happened to them."

I do, says Dr. Daniels, and I look up at her. You do? I say, and she nods. *You're still wearing them.* I shake my head, but suddenly I can feel those braces, chafing my skin, grinding against my bones, dragging me down, down, so far down. I put my arms around myself, hugging tight, as Dr. Daniels' voice softens. *When did you stop fighting?* she says. *When did you become a victim?*

"We're not going to have this fight again, are we, Claudia?"

"I told you we needed locks at the top of the door, Sam. Now look what's happened."

"Did you leave the door unlocked?"

"Of course I didn't. How can you just stand there drinking water?"

"I'm thirsty."

"Your mother's missing, for Christ's sake."

"Is that why you wanted me to rush right home?" he said, putting the glass upside down in the drainer. "So you could yell at me?"

"It's pouring down rain outside, and she's been lost for an hour already. Don't you even care?"

"I'm not having this fight again, Claudia," he said, and I had to hold his sleeve to keep him from leaving the room.

"You want her to die."

"If I wanted her to die, I'd get my gun and shoot her," he said, shaking off my hand. "Jesus, Claudia, what's wrong with you?"

"I told you we couldn't keep her at home anymore. But Harold was right: you never listen."

"Why don't you go upstairs and take one of your tranquilizers?"

"How many times do I have to tell you? They're not tranquilizers: they're sleeping pills."

"I'm in the same room with you, Claudia. You don't have to scream for me to hear you."

"I told you I couldn't take care of her by myself anymore. I told you —"

He strode past me, out of the kitchen, through the entry hall to the front door, slamming it when he left the house. I paced back and forth, praying that someone would find her and call, but the phone didn't ring. I went down to the basement again, to see if I'd missed any of her hiding places. I checked the garage and the shed again, too, but she wasn't anywhere. She was wandering around lost in the unfamiliar neighborhood, and it was all my fault. If I hadn't locked myself in the bathroom to get away from Eleanor, if I hadn't yelled at her, if I hadn't said the terrible things I'd said, she never would have left. I'd never forgive myself if something happened to her. Never.

You still haven't forgiven yourself, says Dr. Daniels. *Even after all these years.* You don't know what I said to her. *You're not a saint, Claudia. You're allowed to be human.* I run my index finger over my left thumb, over the raised white scar on the top knuckle, where I'd cut it, years ago. The skin over the knuckle had been sheared clean away, like a slice of onion. It happened so quickly I didn't feel the cut, but there was blood everywhere. Sitting there in that office, with Dr. Daniels watching me, I rub my finger over that scar, until finally she speaks. *Do you want to tell me what you said to Eleanor the day she ran away?* I can't. Even now, after all this time, after everything else I've told her, I still can't tell her that. I can't tell anyone.

We didn't tell anyone where we were going. When we got out of the car and went up the walk, Eleanor took my arm, holding it tightly as we went up the stairs, as we pushed open the heavy wooden doors, as we entered the hushed twilight of the church. I dipped my fingers into the holy water and made the sign of the cross before I followed Eleanor up the aisle, genuflected, and joined her in the pew. Candles were burning in front of a white marble Mary holding baby Jesus in her lap. Eleanor's lips moved slightly as she prayed, and the flame in the red lamp above the altar flickered beside the crucifix. The light from the stained-glass windows glowed blue, rose, and violet on the grey marble floor. Gradually, the hush and the flickering candlelight made me feel quiet again. Quiet and peaceful and calm.

"I like to think she's at peace," said Eve.

The old woman lay on her side in the nursing home bed, her eyes staring straight ahead at the wall. The sun was shining, but the room, shaded by the trees outside the window, was cool. I put my sweater back on.

"You know, Claudia, the waiting list here is a year and a half long. If you think you'd like to —"

"We don't want to put her in a home, Eve."

"She'll be well taken care of, Claudia. Not only are there nurses and nurses' aides, but there are volunteers, like me and the twins."

I buttoned my sweater as I looked out the window, at the riot of tulips and irises in bloom. Eve took the woman's limp hand and held it while she talked to her.

"My little boy Tommy has his first tooth. He's chewing everything he can, including kitty-cat tails, but Zoë didn't scratch him. She just ran and hid under the bed. Sarah and Laura are going to their first dance tonight, at the junior high, did I tell you? That's why they're not here today. They absolutely refused to get matching dresses for the dance. Roger and I both thought it would be so sweet if they wore the same color, at least, but they didn't want to. Sarah's dress is long and mint green; Laura's dress is short and pink. They're so excited. Matthew volunteered to drive them. Now that he has his license, he wants to drive everyone everywhere. Oh, look who came with me today: my friend, Claudia. Her mother-in-law's ill, and Claudia's the one taking care of her, so I wanted her to meet you."

The old woman didn't know that I was there, or that the sun was shining, or that Eve was holding her hand. When the nurse came in, she smiled at us before she went over to the bed, took the old woman's wrist, and placed her fingers there. As soon as she noted the pulse, she began to rearrange the woman in the bed, gently unbending her from her rigid pose, talking all the while.

"Mona, it's your nurse, Janet. I didn't even know Eve and her friend were here, they were talking so quietly. There you go, Mona, nice and easy. Here, let me fix this pillow for you, Mona. There, that's better," she said, turning to face Eve. "I hope I'll have such loving volunteers if I ever need them."

"You know what comforts me the most?" said Eve. "To think that she's already up in heaven, with God, even though her body's still here."

"Yes," said the nurse. "To know she's at peace. And happy."

It made me happy to work on the memory book with Eleanor, and we worked on it almost every day after she first moved in. Each time we made another collage of things from Eleanor's past, it was like she was giving me some of her life. One day, she laid a yellowed handkerchief on the table and carefully unfolded it. Inside was Sam's baby tooth, a lock of his dark hair, and his hospital identification bracelet. Eleanor hummed along with the music and watched me as I pasted the items on the page.

> *Oh, Danny boy, the pipes, the pipes are calling*
> *From glen to glen, and down the mountainside.*
> *The summer's gone, and all the roses fallen.*
> *It's you, it's you must go, and I must bide.*

After the page was completed, I eased it into the clear vinyl protector — so she could look at it as much as she wanted without damaging it — then opened the binder and put that page in the book. Eleanor rummaged through the box until she pulled out a photograph. In it she wore a formal dress with ruffles around the neckline and on the skirt. On her left wrist was a corsage of rosebuds. On her right wrist she wore a thin gold bracelet. The boy beside her wore a suit and tie.

"Homecoming," she said.

"Is that Harold?"

"Jack," said Eleanor. "He died."

But come ye back
When summer's in the meadow,
Or when the valley's hushed
And white with snow.

Eleanor laid a piece of pale blue satin ribbon and a dried rosebud next to the photograph. She pulled a faded, blue-tipped carnation from the box and laid it on the page. I pasted everything down, then slid the page into its protective cover. After I put the Homecoming page into the binder, Eleanor took the memory book from me, her fingers tracing the outline of the ribbon, the dried rosebud, the blue-tipped carnation. Outside, the rain had started, and the drops tapped against the window. As I cleaned up, Eleanor sat with her memory book in her lap, looking at the Homecoming page. She glanced up once, when the rain pounded harder, but then she looked back down at her book, opened to that same page the whole afternoon.

Yes, I'll be here,
In sunshine
Or in sha-a-dow.
Oh, Danny boy,
Oh, Danny bo-oy,
I love you so.

Hold on to what you felt when you worked on the memory book with Eleanor. But what about all the other things that happened? *Let them go.* How? How do I forget the bad things that happened? *Lean back against the couch and close your eyes,* says Dr. Daniels as she turns on a cassette and soft music plays. *Now, imagine those painful memories are balloons, floating away from you, farther and farther away. Just keep thinking of them, big and round with all the painful memories, floating away from you till you can't see them anymore.* I do see them — balloons so big and dark and heavy that I don't believe they could get off the ground, but somehow, as I'm listening to her voice, they do. They rise up and float away. I keep watching them until they've become so small they're like little pinpricks against the blue of my imagined sky. Dr. Daniels' voice is soft and soothing as she tells me how small those balloons are getting, how far away from me they are. Then we both sit there, with the music that sounds like bells and rain and music all at the same time. When I finally open my eyes, it feels like the weight that's been crushing me for years has been lifted. She smiles at me. Is that all there is to it? I say to her. Is it really that easy? *Now that you've dealt with the pain,* she says. What do I do when the bad memories come back? *Image the bad-memory-balloons leaving you. In fact, why don't you image them every day,* she says, *whether or not you're remembering sad things.*

I image those balloons leaving me all the way home, at every red light, at every stop sign, and when I pull into the driveway, that crushing weight is still missing, and I can still breathe. After I go into the house, I go into each room and look at it, as if for the first time. How different it all looks that day: the rose bedroom with its flowered wallpaper and ceiling fan, the pastel blue bedroom with its playful wallpaper, the living and dining rooms with their restored woodwork. When I pick up the cat and kiss him, he purrs. I kiss him again and again. He licks my face. How lovely everything in that house looks. How safe. The whole time I'm making dinner, I can still breathe. My chest doesn't hurt, and neither does my head. When the cat rubs against my legs, for one brief moment I feel happy. For no reason at all. When Sam comes home from work, without saying anything to him at all, I throw my arms around him and hold him as close as I can.

"Let go, Mom. Don't hold it like that," said Sam. "Aim the water at the car."

Instead, Eleanor turned the hose on Sam, blasting him with the water. After she turned away, he stood there, dripping wet. When she turned again, aiming the spray toward the soapy car, she drenched him a second time.

"Ha, ha, Mom. Very funny. Go ahead and laugh, Claude. You're supposed to get the car wet, Mom."

Sam shook his head so that his hair splashed around like a wet dog's. I was still laughing when I picked up my sponge and heard Sam say something to Eleanor. I looked up just in time to see them grinning as the water crashed toward me, hitting me right in the face. Sam and Eleanor were the ones who laughed that time. I took off my sunglasses and dried them. Eleanor turned the water back onto the car. As I picked up my soapy sponge, water ran from my hair down the back of my neck and under my shirt. That's when I threw my sponge at Sam. Eleanor laughed. Sam dipped the sponge in his pail of soapy water, then threw it at her, hitting her in the chest. She looked down at the soap circle on her T-shirt.

"Hey, Eleanor's not wet yet," I said.

"Yeah, Mom. No fair."

Eleanor looked at the hose, which she held like a torch, its water spouting upward before spilling down on her hand and arm. She held the hose over her own head. Sam rolled on the hood of the car, laughing and holding his sides, until Eleanor aimed the hose at him again. Then it was war.

I dashed around, throwing sponges. Eleanor sprayed me with the hose as Sam hid behind the car and fired sponges back. I wrestled the hose away from Eleanor, then turned it on her and Sam. Eleanor hit me in the back with two sponges at the same time. With a war cry, Sam ran around the car and poured the bucket of water over me.

Eleanor grabbed the hose again and sprayed all of us. The sun made rainbows in the water. The soap made iridescent bubbles. The cat ran and hid under the bushes. The three of us laughed and laughed and laughed.

I didn't laugh after Eleanor died. I got sick. I was exhausted from the funeral, from the questioning by the police, and from the longer hours at the bookstore, but there was something else wrong, too. While the doctor at the clinic was running tests, I lay on the exam table, staring at the ceiling, wishing my stomach would calm down. I fell asleep for a while. Then the doctor came back in with the test results.

I'd called Sam at Roger's house before I left the clinic, so he was waiting for me on the porch when I got home. We went into the house together, to the kitchen. The empty prescription bottles and the plastic bag with its white residue were still there, where I'd left them three nights ago, lined up in a row on the table. Sam glanced at the bag and the bottles, but he was quiet. I looked at them one last time, then said the only thing that could make him understand.

"I'm pregnant."

Now you know why you kept having miscarriages before, says Dr. Daniels. No, I don't. What are you talking about? *Everything in the universe is connected, Claudia.* I don't understand. *You had miscarriages all those years because you already had a child who needed all of your attention and love.* I shake my head, not understanding. *Eleanor,* she says. *Wasn't she your child?* But she was supposed to be a mother. *You were looking for a mother, and you found one,* she says. *Her name was Claudia.* When she says that, something in me shifts. It's as if the sun has forced itself through layer after layer of dark clouds, as if I've lifted my face to the sky after years of staring at the ground, as if I'm seeing myself for the very first time.

"What are you looking at?" said Sam when he came into the bedroom.

"My legs," I said.

"What's wrong with your legs?"

"Do they look like they've been broken?"

"She might've made a mistake about your legs, Claudia. She's awfully old."

"Do you see any scars?"

"Remember that time she confused you with somebody named Angie?"

He sat beside me on the bed as I ran my hand down my right leg.

"Here, feel this, Sam. Do any of the bones feel funny?"

"Funny?"

"Like they were broken?"

He ran his hand down the outer side of my leg, then up the inner side, first with his left hand, then with his right. I turned my legs out, heels touching.

"Do you see any scars anywhere?"

Sam bent forward and kissed my knee. His lips were warm. He dragged his open mouth upward, along my inner thigh. I touched the top of his head.

"No scars yet," he said against my skin.

He put his arms around my legs, then underneath my hips. His shoulders pressed my legs further apart. I leaned back on my hands, then on my elbows, as his open mouth warmed me, as his tongue darted against me. When I bent my knees and lay back on the bed, my eyes closed and my thighs brushing his cheeks, he wrapped his arms around me and kissed me harder. So hard I could feel teeth against bone. I forgot about scars and braces and broken legs. I forgot about everything except him — his mouth, his tongue, his thick, strong fingers.

When he rolled over onto his back and pulled me with him, yanking my hips down hard so he was in deep, I put my hands on his shoulders. I rocked against him as slowly as I could, to make it last a long time, but he wrenched my hips down as he thrust upward. Skin against skin, bone against bone. He tightened his arms around me, forcing me down against him, my breasts crushed to his chest. Whenever I slowed my movement, his fingers dug into my hips, forcing me into his rhythm. He held me so tight, I couldn't breathe. Then his mouth was open against mine and lights were exploding behind my eyes and his hips were lifting me as he strained upward.

Afterward, we lay in each other's arms, still and breathless, my cheek against his chest, his heartbeat slowing under my ear. God, I loved him so much. Even after all those years. And I believed in him. More than I believed in anyone else.

I thought we'd be together, like that, forever.

CHAPTER SIX

*D*ON'T YOU BELIEVE ME?" I said.

"I just want to see for myself," said Officer Troy. "If you don't mind."

I picked up the prescription bottle and pressed the heel of my hand down on the lid as I turned it: the lid came off. I set the bottle back on the interrogation room table.

"How about this one?" said Troy, handing me another size. "Okay. And this one?"

"Are you going to ask me to open all of those?"

"That won't be a problem, will it?" said Detective Mitchell.

I pressed down on the cap of the next prescription bottle, twisted it, and removed it. I did the same with every bottle they gave me. Each time I opened another bottle and handed it to them, their faces were absolutely expressionless.

"So, you don't have any problem getting these safety caps off?" said Mitchell.

"I told you I didn't."

"Why didn't any of the prescription bottles at the house have childproof tops?"

"We don't have any children."

"What about Eleanor?"

They were both sitting at the table with me, and when I moved my legs, I bumped into one of them. Both of them shifted their positions as I apologized.

"Why were there so many prescription medication bottles in your mother-in-law's bedroom on the day she died?" said Mitchell.

"Those were the empty ones," I said. "She liked to play with them."

"Did you ever leave the full bottles on her nightstand?"

"Of course not."

"Maybe it was your husband who left the pills on her nightstand."

"Why would he do that?" I said, and Mitchell shrugged.

"Maybe he was hoping that while he was out of town, his mother would get hold of the pills and think they were candy."

"Or maybe he was hoping that she'd think it was time for her pills," said Troy, "and take more than she was supposed to."

"Mrs. Sloane," said Mitchell, lowering his voice and leaning toward me, "did your husband help his mother take her own life?"

"Tell us the truth, Claudia," said Troy. "You can trust us."

"Trust me, Eleanor," I said after I picked her up at the police station. "I'm not the one who was lost."

"Where's Sam?"

"He's not lost either. He's out looking for you. He'll be home when we get there."

"Where's your bracelet?"

"It's not lost, Eleanor. It's right here."

After I held up my wrist so she could see the bracelet, she leaned back against the seat. I buckled her seat belt and pushed down the lock on her car door before I closed it. She watched me as I went around the front of the car to the driver's side, as I closed my door and put the keys in the ignition, as I started the car.

"Seat belt," she said.

"Sorry," I said, buckling it before I pulled out of the police parking lot.

The freeway was relatively deserted, so I sped up a little, to get home sooner. Eleanor was quiet, but I put in a cassette to keep her that way.

> *Oh, where have you been, Billy Boy, Billy Boy?*
> *Oh, where have you been, charming Billy?*
> *I have been to seek a wife.*
> *She's the joy of my life.*
> *She's a young thing,*
> *And she cannot leave her mother.*

"My bracelets," said Eleanor, suddenly sitting up straighter and holding out her arm. "They're gone."

"You're wearing it," I said putting my hand on her wrist. "Here's your bracelet. Right here."

"No, the policeman's bracelets . . . I have to have my bracelets. I'll be lost. . . ."

I hurriedly slipped my watch off and stretched it over Eleanor's hand next to her bracelet.

"Here you go. Now you have two bracelets. Okay? All right now?"

> *Can she bake a cherry pie, Billy Boy, Billy Boy?*
> *Can she bake a cherry pie, charming Billy?*
> *She can bake a cherry pie*
> *In the twinkling of an eye.*
> *But she's a young thing,*
> *And she cannot leave her mother.*

Eleanor leaned back into the seat, keeping her right hand over the bracelet and watch. She was so quiet the rest of the way home, I thought she'd fallen asleep, but in the driveway, when I reached over to unbuckle her seat belt, she was looking at me.

"Thank you," she said.

Sam thought he could save her from the disease — that's what all the supplements were for — but he was wrong: she was too lost in the maze of that illness to ever come back. I don't know how much he spent on the vitamins and herbs and supplements, but one day he came home with a huge grocery bag full of them. As Sam tore the protective plastic off one of the bottles, Eleanor sat down at the kitchen table and picked up the others to look at them: ginkgo biloba, gotu kola, phosphatidyl choline, ginseng, cayenne. Now they have even more, like huperzine A and phosphatidyl serine, but no one had studied those supplements then.

"What's this one?" said Eleanor, showing him one of the bottles.

"DMAE. Di-methyl-amino-ethanol. It's found in some types of fish. It's supposed to increase memory. It'll take a few weeks to start working, but I think you'll notice a difference. You'll need lots of vitamin C, too."

"I already take that. What's this, Sam?"

"It's a list of drugs that aren't available yet in the United States."

"Drugs?"

"Relax, Mom. They're not illegal in Germany."

"We're going to Germany to buy drugs?"

"We buy them through the mail, Mom. And they're not illegal in Germany or Switzerland or wherever we'll be buying them. They're for our own private use. Don't worry, Mom: that's legal."

"'Improves memory and learning,'" said Eleanor as she read from the drug list. "'To combat age-related memory loss.' I guess there are some things here I could use. But you know, Sam, my memory seems to be fine these days. I haven't forgotten anything lately, have I, Claudia?"

Sam began opening the bottles and taking a pill from each one. He put the pills in front of Eleanor, then went to the sink to get her a glass of water.

"Oh, my, Sam, are you sure I should be taking that many pills?"

"Just take them, Mom."

"Well, all right, if you really think I should. But let's not tell your father right now. He has enough to worry about with the layoffs: he doesn't need to worry about me. Oh, my, do you really think I need that many pills?"

"It's not that many."

"Well, all right, but let's just keep this to ourselves. I don't want you and your father to have another fight. Like when you were trying to teach me that healing tree memory-stimulation thing."

She took the pills that day, and every day, for a long time. She would have done anything Sam told her, no matter what it was. And Sam? He would have cut his wrist and signed a contract in blood, if only it kept his mother with him forever.

Silent night, holy night,
All is calm, all is bright
'Round yon virgin mother and child,
Holy infant so tender and mild.

Harold was snoring in his easy chair, one slipper fallen off and lying on the floor, the firelight casting flickering shadows on his face. The cats were asleep under the tree. Sam was sitting on the couch, with me on one side and Eleanor on the other. After she leaned against Sam's shoulder, he kissed her on the top of the head. Then he wove his fingers through mine. The grandfather clock ticked soothingly. The wine warmed me, the tree's tinsel glittered at the edges of my vision, and in the dark room, the star on top of the tree was a brilliant point of white light.

Sleep in heavenly peace.
Sleep in heavenly peace.

For all you know, Sam loved you even more than he loved Eleanor at the end, says Dr. Daniels. I don't think it was me he loved. *You were the one he chose. You and your marriage.* There was never anything wrong with our marriage. *Then why did you want a divorce? I didn't. You asked for one.* I didn't mean it. *Did Sam know that? Or was he listening to what you were saying?*

"You're not listening, Sam."

"No, I would not kill myself."

"You see? You never listen. That isn't what I asked you. What I said was would you help someone —"

"Jesus, Claudia, do you realize that's all you ever talk about these days? What the hell are we paying Dr. Daniels for anyway?"

When he closed the book he'd been reading, I saw part of the title: *Final Exit.*

"What are you doing with Lois' book?" I said.

"It was in Mom's room."

"It's Lois' book."

"Well, since Lois isn't here anymore, I guess she won't mind if I have it," he said, shoving the book under the paperwork on his desk. "Listen, Claudia, can we have this extremely exciting and stimulating conversation some other time? I'm trying to itemize all our medical expenses for the taxes. Do you know how much we spent on doctors last year? Do you realize how much Dr. Daniels alone costs? It's incredible what these people charge. If she's not doing you any good, you should stop seeing her. God knows we could use the money."

He buried the book deeper under the papers, cleared the adding machine, and repositioned the stack of checks. He turned the checks over one at a time, entering their totals on the machine before he yanked the tape from the adding machine, crumpled it, and dropped it into the trash can beside the desk.

"Jesus, Claudia, could you please not hover over me like that? You're as bad as Mom: following people around, standing behind them without saying anything. Like a vulture or something."

He punched a few more numbers into the machine before he turned around and frowned at me.

"I'm leaving," I said.

But I didn't mean it. *How was Sam supposed to know that?* By that time we'd been married almost twenty years. *Was he supposed to read your mind?* He should have known me well enough to . . . *He knows you as well as I do, Claudia, and both of us know you don't say things you don't mean.* I didn't want to lose my marriage. *You told him you wanted a divorce.* I didn't mean it like that. I never really wanted a divorce. *But you wanted Sam to save you.* You've got to be kidding, I say, but Dr. Daniels isn't laughing. To save me? To save me from what? *From Eleanor's illness,* she says.

"I'm waiting for you to say something," said the priest from behind his black screen.

I wanted to tell him everything. I wanted to tell him how Eleanor's illness had changed everything. I wanted to tell him how every night before I went to sleep, every morning before I opened Eleanor's bedroom door, every time Sam was alone with her, I prayed for her to be dead. I stared at the priest's outline through the black grate and folded my hands so tightly they ached, but no words came out. I shifted my weight from one knee to the other on the padded wood. When I bent my head over my folded hands, the beads of my rosary were cool and hard against my forehead. The doors of the other confessionals creaked each time they opened and closed, while from behind his iron grate, the priest coughed. But still, no words came. When I was a little girl, I believed in a compassionate and loving God, a God who wouldn't give us more than we could bear. But God gave Eleanor too great a burden. He gave me too great a burden, too.

"Didn't you realize that your husband was being crushed by his mother's illness?" said Detective Mitchell.

"Do you have any idea how much money you were spending on visiting nurses?" said Officer Troy.

"What if we told you that your husband took this amount of money out of the business the last three years?" said Mitchell, sliding a sheet of paper across the table. "What's the matter, Mrs. Sloane? You didn't know it was that much?"

"How much did you think he'd taken out, Claudia?"

I stared at the sheet until the row of numbers blurred and danced on the page. So much money. In so short a time.

"He didn't tell you, did he?"

"You couldn't afford a nursing home for your mother-in-law, could you?"

"Not without selling the business," I said.

"Not even if you sold both of them. Show her the papers, Mitch."

"We audited the company books," he said, taking the first sheet and replacing it with another. "This is how much money your husband borrowed from the bank, using his business and half of yours as collateral."

I stood up, then sat back down again. Both the policemen looked at me.

"You didn't know about this loan either, did you, Claudia?"

"Her illness was draining both companies dry," said Mitchell. "If she'd lived much longer, you and your husband would've had to declare bankruptcy."

I brushed my hair out of my eyes. Troy put the figures back into a folder as Mitchell stared at me.

"Didn't you ever ask your husband where he was getting the money for the visiting nurses?"

"I was too busy taking care of Eleanor," I said.

So Sam could have done other things that you weren't aware of. But he didn't do that. *Not even out of love for you?* He knows how I feel about it. Everybody knows. And he knows I'd leave him if I thought that he had anything to do with it. *That would only mean that he wouldn't tell you,* says Dr. Daniels, *not that he wouldn't do it.* Why are you doing this to me? *Doing what?* Trying to make me doubt my own husband. Trying to destroy my marriage. *I know how hard this is for you to hear,*

Claudia, and I'm not trying to hurt you. I'm telling you, Sam wouldn't do that. Not to Eleanor. Not to his own mother, for Christ's sake. *Not even for you? To save you?* Not to his own mother, I say, but Dr. Daniels still doesn't stop. *Not even if she was a stranger at the end?*

"Who are you?" said Eleanor, frowning at me.

"I'm Claudia. Sam's wife, Claudia."

"Where am I?"

"You're home. In your room."

> *By yon bonnie banks and by yon bonnie braes,*
> *Where the sun shines bright on Loch Lomond,*
> *Where me and my true love were ever wont to go,*
> *On the bonnie, bonnie banks of Loch Lomond.*

Eleanor pulled out a picture from Sam's and my wedding. She turned it over and looked at the names on the back as though she could read them. She turned the picture back around and pointed to herself.

"Mother," she said.

"No, that's not Maida," I said. "That's you, Eleanor."

"Mother."

"It's you, Eleanor."

"Grandmother."

"No, that's not Rose either. It's you."

"Grandmother," said Eleanor, tossing the wedding picture back in the box.

> *'Twas there that we parted in yon shady glen,*
> *On the steep, steep side of Ben Lomond,*
> *When in purple hue, the Hieland hills we view,*
> *And the moon coming out in the gloaming.*

She pulled out an old letter from among the photographs, and when she unfolded it, a few dried rose petals fluttered to the table. She dragged the memory book toward her and began turning its pages. Outside, the trees looked like dark skeletons in the densely swirling snow. Eleanor pushed the book toward me, then laid the letter on the Homecoming page, tapping it several times. I peeled the rosebud and ribbon off the page to get the letter on, then rearranged and reglued everything.

> *The wee birdies sing and the wild flowers spring,*
> *And in sunshine the waters lie sleeping;*
> *But the broken heart, it can't know second spring,*
> *Though the woeful may cease from their grieving.*

After I'd finished and put the page back in its cover, Eleanor held the memory book in her lap. It had gotten darker outside, and snow was falling harder. As I was gathering up the glue and scissors to put them away, Eleanor tugged at my sleeve.

"Who are you?" she said.

> *For me and my true love will never meet again,*
> *On the bonnie, bonnie banks of Loch Lomond.*

How did that make you feel? I don't know. *Did you feel abandoned?* No, not that I remember. *Angry?* Why would I be angry? *Eleanor left you, just like your mother,* says Dr. Daniels, *and you didn't feel anything?* I look at her diplomas, framed on the wall behind her desk, at the figurines on the windowsill and on top of her filing cabinets, at the prisms and stained-glass hummingbirds hanging in the windows. Dr. Daniels looks at me. You're always telling me I should forgive Eleanor, I say. Maybe I have. *And maybe you're still in denial,* she says.

Sam was the one in denial about Eleanor's illness. That was obvious the day I went into the bathroom to get her pills and found him there. When he saw me, he turned his back, and I heard a noise, like a rattling of seeds. Then something hit the water. I got to Sam's side just as he emptied the second bottle of pills into the toilet.

When I grabbed his arm, he jerked away, knocking me off balance, and I fell. After I got up, Sam pushed me back, dropping his elbow so fast it hit me in the face. I yanked on his sweater, pulled at his belt, put my arms around his waist to drag him away, but he was too strong for me. He forced my head back so hard that I slipped on the tile floor and went down on one knee. He opened the next prescription bottle.

After I lunged against him, he leaned forward, away from me, so I had to jump up on his back. Before I could get the pills, though, he rammed me backward, and I skidded across the countertop and sink, scattering hair dryer, toothpaste, razor, brushes, and combs. He poured the next bottle of pills into the toilet. I threw myself at him, hooking my fingers into his mouth and pulling as hard as I could. After I slipped off his back, I smashed the toilet lid down on his hand. He roared and slammed me into the shower doors. The breath exploded out of me, the shower door crashed out of its track and against the wall, and the next bottle of pills fell into the water.

Sam pushed the handle down. The water swirled, rose, and washed away its cargo. When he turned around, holding his left hand up against his chest, I kicked out at him with both feet, so hard and fast that he hit the opposite wall trying to get away from me. Each time I took a breath, pain tore through my side. Sam slid down to the floor, his back and shoulders against the wall. I kicked at the air between us, but all the pills were still lost.

"You bastard," I said. "You stupid, selfish bastard."

I wasn't losing any business by closing the bookstore a few hours early before a holiday, so I locked the door and pulled the blinds. I went to the bookstore kitchen to get the bottle of wine and a glass, then ran up the stairs to the second floor, to the room next to the office, the spare living room. I changed into a pair of sweatpants and a T-shirt before I opened the wine and poured myself a glass. The new books I wanted to read were on the table beside the sofa, its bed already pulled out and made. I put the bottle and the glass beside the books, then crawled between the sheets.

I had all that Saturday night, all day Sunday, and all day Monday, which was a holiday. The bookstore wouldn't open till Tuesday morning, and I wasn't going home till after work on Tuesday. I had a change of clothes, lots of bubble bath in the bathroom, and a huge basket of food in the refrigerator downstairs. I drank some wine, then snuggled down with the blankets and pillows. I took another sip of wine, gazed around the empty room, and opened the first book. Whenever I got hungry, I went downstairs and ate. I thought I'd fall asleep early, but I read most of the night. Not even the wine made me sleepy. All that weekend, I read and ate, read and napped, then read some more. Sam was taking care of Eleanor, the bookstore was closed for the holiday, the phone was turned off, and I was on vacation. I was alone. Completely alone. For the first time in my life, I was happy that way.

"I don't think we're alone," said Eve, turning her head toward the bedroom door. "I'll bet Roger's out there. Listening to us."

"He's in the garage," I said, "working on his car."

Eve got up, tiptoed over to the door, and pressed her ear against it. I turned off the radio. Eve shrugged her shoulders and came back to the bed.

"I told you there was nobody out there," I said. "So, who would you really do it with?"

"Who would *you* do it with?"

"Sam."

"Roger's Sam? Oh, you would not," said Eve.

"He's kinda cute."

"He's losing his hair already. He's gonna end up looking like Harold."

"Yul Brynner doesn't have any hair, and he's dreamy."

"Sam's not Yul Brynner," said Eve, falling back on the bed, hugging the pillow. "Give me Gregory Peck any day."

"They why'd you say you'd do it with Roger? He's not anything like Gregory Peck."

"He's still cute."

"Roger? He's boring."

"No, he's not."

"He's in the Criminal Justice Club, Eve."

"So?"

"Boring. And gross. No way I'd do it with him."

"You just think that 'cause he's your brother," said Eve. "Hey, there it was again. Didn't you hear that?"

"Are you telling me you'd really do it with Roger?"

"Not with anybody else. But with him, I would."

"What about in your mouth?"

"Yeah. But only with Roger."

"That is so disgustingly gross," I said. "Where are you going?"

Eve put her forefinger to her lips as she slipped off the bed and crept to the door again. She turned the knob so slowly, it didn't creak. Then she flung the door wide open.

"I knew it," she said. "What are you doing out here?"

"Nothing," said Sam as I came to the door and stood beside Eve.

"You're spying again."

"I'm looking for Roger."

"Like he's gonna be in here."

"Yeah, you were spying."

"Like I'm gonna spy on you two," he said, making a face as he moved away down the hall. "Like you two are gonna say anything that I'd wanna hear."

"Stop eavesdropping," said Eve. "If you know what's good for you."

"And don't come back," I said just before we slammed the door.

"I heard you didn't cry," said Detective Mitchell, sitting across the table from me, "the day you found the body."

"I cried afterward."

"You mean, when no one else was there?" he said, and I nodded. "So nobody actually saw you cry?"

"Sam did."

"I thought he was out of town."

"When he got home that night. The next morning, really. Early the next morning."

"You know, those pills keep bothering me," said Mitchell, leaning his elbow on the table, rubbing his chin with his thumb and forefinger. "How did you know you weren't giving your mother-in-law too many pills?"

"I gave them to her exactly like Dr. Barnett told me," I said.

"Did you ever give her anything alcoholic with the pills?"

"No, of course not. Why do we have to keep going over the same things?"

"Mitch and I want to make sure we have everything right, Claudia."

"You must have it right by now, Troy."

"Just a few more questions."

The tape recorder clicked off. As Mitchell changed the tape, Troy stood up and stretched, his arms above his head, fingers interlocked, arching his back. When Mitchell turned the recorder on again, Troy sat back down.

"Tell us what you did with the ashes," said Mitchell.

"You know what I did with the ashes."

"Tell us again."

"I put them in the garden."

"You just dumped the whole container, right?"

"I thought you sent some people over to sift the garden soil," I said.

"You don't have to get angry, Mrs. Sloane."

"I'm not angry."

"You're raising your voice."

"You sifted the soil and found the ashes, didn't you?" I said.

"We found pieces of bone," said Mitchell, turning his pen between his fingers like a baton. "And teeth."

"So, why don't you just run some tests on them?"

"Why would we do that?"

"To test for drugs."

"Would we find any drugs in the bone?" said Troy.

"Not an overdose."

"Then what good would it do us to test for drugs in the cremains?"

"You'd know I'm telling the truth about not giving her an overdose."

"We can't test cremains for drug residue, Claudia," said Troy.

"Why not?"

"Nothing organic can survive the fire."

"But you found the cremains in the garden, didn't you, just like I told you?"

"So?"

"Doesn't that prove I'm telling the truth?"

Mitchell took a cigarette out, but when Troy nodded toward me, he slipped the cigarette into his shirt pocket. Troy offered him a piece of gum. He unwrapped it slowly and put it in his mouth, looking at me the whole time. The tape recorder hissed softly.

"You know, I think I understand what you went through," said Mitchell. "Because of my father-in-law. I know how hard these situations can be."

"This isn't the same as cancer," I said.

"Yeah, but I know how hard it is for me and my wife, so it must have been worse for you. Day in. Day out. No hope of improvement. No hope of remission. You start to feel hopeless. You start to feel a little angry, maybe a little resentful."

"What Mitch is saying, Claudia, is that we understand the position you were in."

"God knows, my father-in-law takes me for granted, and I'm the one paying all the medical bills," said Mitchell, leaning back, his hands behind his head, the underarms of his shirt wet with perspiration. "So, the way Troy and I got it figured, one day you woke up and decided you'd had enough."

"Is that what happened, Claudia?" said Troy, touching me on the hand. "Did you wake up one day and say, 'I can't do this anymore'?"

"It's not a coincidence that your husband was out of town when it happened, is it, Mrs. Sloane?"

"You can tell us the truth, Claudia. No matter how awful you think it sounds."

"We'll respect you for telling us the truth."

"And it'll go easier on everybody else if you tell us the truth."

"Then we wouldn't have to implicate your husband."

"Or anybody else who was innocent."

I looked back and forth at the two of them, and though I was sitting down, I felt dizzy.

"You want to change your story now, don't you, Mrs. Sloane?" said Mitchell.

"You want to tell us what really happened, don't you, Claudia?"

"I think I need a lawyer," I said.

CHAPTER SEVEN

*Y*OU'RE SUPPOSED TO HAVE AN ATTORNEY PRESENT when you're questioned."

"They were just asking me a few questions, Ms. Garner."

"Call me Tracey."

"I told them it was all right."

"It's not all right, Claudia. You don't mind if I call you Claudia, do you?" she said, smiling briefly. "And you should never have taken that polygraph test."

"Why not?"

"You didn't pass."

"I didn't fail."

"You didn't pass," she said, uncapping her fountain pen. "That's what's important to them."

"They told me the results were inconclusive."

"Which means they'll interpret the results in their favor, Claudia, not in yours."

Her office was downtown, above one of the restaurants, and the wall that faced the street was covered with windows. Baskets of philodendron and impatiens hung from the ceiling; fig trees, elephant-ear philodendron, and rubber plants in brass or wicker containers stood in the corners near the windows. An old Oriental rug covered most of the wood floor. When Tracey reached across her desk and pressed the intercom button on the phone, her bracelets glinted in the sun.

"Marilyn, clear my calendar for the rest of this afternoon and tomorrow," said Tracey. "Reschedule everyone for sometime next week. Then bring us some coffee, could you? And send down to the deli for sandwiches. Is chicken salad okay with you, Claudia? Two chicken salad sandwiches, Marilyn. And lots of coffee. We've got a long night ahead of us."

"Does that mean you'll help me?"

"It means I'll take the case, Claudia, and I'll try to undo any damage that's already been done."

"Damage?"

"You let them into your home, Claudia, and the circumstantial evidence alone is enough to convict."

"But I didn't do anything."

"Innocent people go to jail, and the guilty go free," she said, writing something down on the legal pad. "It happens all the time. Don't you ever watch television?"

"Roger told me you're one of the best. That's why I came to you, Tracey," I said, scooting my chair closer to her desk. "The police won't listen to me. I thought if you could talk to them for me . . ."

"This has gone way beyond talking," she said, shaking her head. "Now we're into damage control. If they come to you and want any other kind of testing or have any further questions, you call me. I want to be there so I can do the talking."

"They can't really think I killed her, can they?"

"Apparently," she said, "that's exactly what they think."

And you did think about Eleanor's getting hold of all those pills and taking them, says Dr. Daniels. But I never gave them to her. My God, what kind of person do you think I am? *The kind of person who was carrying too great a burden.* When I lean back on the couch, I feel the air-conditioning on my face and throat. On her desk, a crystal vase shaped like a praying angel holds lilies. There's only one thing I was ever guilty of, I say. Wanting to end the suffering. *Whose suffering?* she says. *Hers? Or yours?*

"Everyone here has a loved one who's suffering with the same symptoms, even if they don't have the same disease," said Sharon, the group leader. "The only guidelines for these meetings is that everything you say in this room stays here: we don't share it with anyone outside, not even family members. No one will pass judgment on anything said in this group. That way everyone feels safe here. All right, who'd like to start? Dan? It's Dan, isn't it? Go ahead."

"Yeah, hi, I'm Dan. My wife is the one who's ill. Actually, she's my second wife. My first wife died of lung cancer. Then about five years ago, I remarried . . ."

His hair was silvery white, his face lined and tired. He fidgeted with his wedding band as he talked.

". . . but, you know, everything's fine. We're handling everything. She knows all about the disease, and she's doing pretty good. The only thing she's mad about is that she can't come to these meetings with me. But we're doing good. Of course, she can't drive anymore, and she can't cook anymore, but everything's fine. She's fine. I'm fine. We're handling things good. . . ."

There were thirty-five of us there that night, but only three were men. Almost no one in the room was my age — everyone was older — and everyone looked as tired and worn out as I felt. Half the room looked like a sort of living room, with stuffed chairs and love seats. The other half looked like a dining room, only there were about twenty small round tables, each with four or five cushioned chairs around it. There was a stereo system, a television, and a video recorder on one wall, but they weren't on during the meeting. A couple of the people had dragged over some of the more comfortable chairs and were sitting at the edges of the grouping of tables. The room was decorated for Halloween. Witches and ghosts and jack-o'-lanterns were hanging from the ceiling, and huge dried cornstalks stood in the corner, surrounded by pumpkins. But no matter how comfortable the chairs were, no matter how nicely decorated the room was, nothing could relieve the weight that was crushing everyone there that night.

". . . This is my second marriage. My first husband died fifteen years ago, of a heart attack. When I married Bill, about thirteen years ago, I thought he was old-fashioned and a little stubborn, and sometimes unreasonable, but I didn't want to spend the rest of my life alone. Now I think he must've already had the disease before we got married, but I didn't know anything about it. . . ."

She clenched her handkerchief. One of the women at the table with her patted her hand.

". . . All Bill's children live in Kentucky, so they don't help take care of him, but that doesn't bother me. I'm managing. Except for his temper. If he were one of my grandchildren, I'd say he has temper tantrums. But that's okay. I can handle them. I'm all right. . . ."

". . . My dad has the disease pretty bad. He was living with my sister for five years out in Nebraska, so I didn't really get to see him too much. But I called almost every weekend. Then one day my sister called and said it was my turn to take care of him. She put him on a bus. Can you believe that? I mean, she knows he's sick, but she put him on a bus with his name and my phone number pinned to his shirt. Like he was a kid going to kindergarten. Only she was sending him across the country. She's lucky nothing happened to him: I never would've forgiven her. So, anyway, Dad lives with me now, and I haven't talked to my sister since. And do you know what? He's not as bad as she said he was. . . ."

". . . My mom and me, we've gotten lots closer since she got ill. We used to fight all the time, even after I was married and on my own. But that's gotten better over the years. I'm divorced now, and all my kids are grown, so there's no one in the house but me and Mom. I was worried about her living with me, on account of how we used to fight, but these days I just ignore it when she's in a bad mood. You know, this might seem funny, but sometimes she doesn't seem sick at all. . . ."

My chest tightened with every breath I took. Despite the size of the room, it felt like everyone was crowding in on me. How haggard all these people looked. The man beside me didn't even wipe away the tears running down his face. Then, suddenly, the room was completely quiet, and everyone was looking at me. It was my turn. Time to say how much I loved Eleanor, time to say how the disease hadn't really changed her at all, time to say how I wouldn't do anything different if I were given the chance to live my life over. Everyone sat there, looking at me, waiting.

"She's not even my mother," I said. "Why should I be the one who has to take care of her?"

"Sam, you don't understand."

"You asked me to help take care of her, and I'm trying."

"God, you never listen."

"Claudia, if you'd stop telling me every single thing I'm doing wrong . . ."

"Oh, just let me do this by myself."

"You said you wanted my help."

"If we don't do things exactly the same way every time . . ."

"You're the reason she overreacts in the first place. You make things so goddamned predictable that she goes crazy if we change the routine. What she needs is some variety."

"That's the very thing she doesn't need, Sam. You need to take her hands, like this, and then tell her what to do, like this: Get in the car, Eleanor."

"No," she said.

"Oh, yeah, that's working so much better than what I was doing."

He waved me aside and tried to guide Eleanor into the backseat himself, but she kept holding the doorframe. Every time he got one of her hands free, she grabbed the doorframe with the other. Then he got hold of both her hands at the same time, for about two seconds, before she wrenched one of her hands loose and clutched the frame again. The fallen leaves on the driveway rustled and cracked as Sam and Eleanor struggled.

"We're only going to the doctor's, Mom."

"God damn it, Sam. Now we'll never get her in the car."

"Oh, I'll get her in the car. You don't have to worry about that."

"Don't pick her up like that. She'll . . . fine. Do it your way."

"Mom, stop it. Cut it out. Let go, Mom. Claudia, are you going to just stand there? Ow. Mom, stop it. Damn it, Claudia, give me some help here. Get her other arm. Watch it. Ow. God damn it. Will you help me?"

"Don't hold her arms like that. Ow. Shit. Eleanor, will you stop screaming?"

"Here, get her legs. Get her legs, damn it. Okay, I've got her. Move your head. Claudia, get out of the way. Push. Push, God damn it."

We shoved Eleanor into the backseat and slammed the car door. Eleanor slapped her hands against the windows, shrieking as loud as she could. Most of the trees were bare, so the sunlight blinded me every time I turned around. The dried leaves skittered across the driveway, making a scratching sound.

"God damn it. There's blood on my shirt," said Sam, looking down. "What's bleeding? My nose?"

"And your lip."

"Shit."

"I told you not to say 'doctor' around the car."

Sam wiped his lip and nose while, in the backseat of the car, Eleanor rocked back and forth, holding onto the front seat, wailing, pausing only to catch her breath. Sam started to kick the leaves, sending them flying into the air before they settled, only to have him thrash them away again.

"Where are the goddamned keys? Where are the keys, God damn it?"

"It makes her worse when you yell."

"You're the one who's yelling."

"Nobody's having problems hearing your voice either."

"What'd she do with the goddamned keys? Shut up, Mom. Shut up, I said."

"Oh, that's good, Sam. Hit the car roof again, only hit it harder this time. Let's see if we can make her a little more hysterical."

Sam pounded his fists viciously on the car roof, the blood from his nose and lip flowing again as the wind scattered the leaves. He pounded the roof so hard he dented it. He pounded it so hard, we couldn't hear Eleanor's screams. He pounded and pounded, then laid his head down, his forehead against the car's roof, his feet surrounded by brown leaves.

"Why don't you just die?" he said. "Why don't you just die and leave us in peace?"

So Sam admitted that he wanted her to die? He didn't mean it. Dr. Daniels sighs, shaking her head before she uncrosses her legs and leans forward. *I thought you told me you wanted to face the truth.* I do. *Then stop making excuses,* she says. Excuses? *Be completely honest with yourself, Claudia. Just once. Even if it's only in here with me.* What is it you want me to do? *Admit the truth, for heaven's sake.* About what? *About wanting Eleanor to die. Say it. Just once. Out loud,* says Dr. Daniels. *And I'll never ask you to do it again.* When I reach for something on the table next to the couch, my hand knocks over the pictures of her children. While I'm setting them right again, one of the frames jars the small fountain, spilling its smooth, rounded stones and water. I sop it up with the tissues. When the box is empty and I turn to Dr. Daniels, she still doesn't come over to help me. *Admit that you wanted her to die,* she says. *It's the only way you'll ever be free.*

I didn't want her to die. All I wanted was for her to take a nap. I spooned the chocolate pudding into a bowl, then got her medicines. Over my head, I could hear Eleanor in her room, screaming and stomping her feet. I opened the bottle of tranquilizers and put two of them on the cutting board. As I was crushing them with the rolling pin, I heard a crash from upstairs. Something fell past the kitchen window outside: the screen from Eleanor's room. Then her pillow flew by and hit the ground. I picked up another bottle and took out two sleeping pills as Eleanor started tossing clothes out the upstairs window. Bright colors flashed by, one after the other, as I blended the sleeping pills and the tranquilizers into the pudding. When I heard glass breaking, I didn't know if it was the window or the mirror. I picked up the bottles, took the lids off, and poured out more pills. Upstairs, Eleanor screamed and threw more things out the window. The pills, shiny and bright, lay still as death in my hand.

"So no illicit cause of death was actually established?" said Tracey.

"She was terminally ill," I said. "She had pneumonia for the second time that winter."

"It's my understanding that these patients usually lapse into a coma before they die."

"It was like she was in a coma, that last day."

"What do you mean?"

"When I came in to check on her, I couldn't get her to wake up."

"What did you do to try to wake her?"

"I called her name. I shook her. It didn't do any good. And she was breathing funny: loud and raspy."

"So that's when you called the paramedics?"

"Not then," I said.

She stopped writing to look at me.

"I went downstairs," I said.

"To the phone?"

"To the bottom of the stairs, at the entry hall."

"And what did you do?"

"I . . . sat there."

"You sat there? On the steps?" she said, and I nodded. "Then you called the paramedics?"

"No. I went back up to her room. It was over when I got there."

"What did you do then?" said Tracey, writing again. "Did you touch her? Did you say anything? Did you try to give her mouth-to-mouth?"

"I called for help."

"You went back downstairs to the phone?"

"There's a phone upstairs."

"Upstairs?" she said, her pen stopping once more.

"In the hall. Outside her bedroom."

"Is that the phone you used?"

"Yes."

Tracey took a sip of her coffee and turned the page of her notebook before she wrote something down.

"How long would you say it was, between the time she was in that comalike state and breathing funny, to the time you called the paramedics?"

"I didn't look at a clock."

"Make an estimate, Claudia," she said. "One minute? Five minutes? Half an hour? Two hours?"

"I'm sorry, Tracey. I just don't know."

"All right. Let me make sure I've got this right. You came in to check on her, she was breathing funny, and you couldn't wake her up. Then you left her to go sit on the stairs for — you don't know how long — and when you got back to the bedroom . . ."

"It was over."

Just like you wanted it to be over, all those years, says Dr. Daniels. *Just like Sam wanted it to be over.* She crosses the room and hands me another box of tissues, but I don't wipe up the rest of the water spilled from the fountain on the table beside the couch. *I know this is painful for you, Claudia, and I'm sorry,* she says as she sits back down in her rocking chair, pulling it closer to the couch, closer to me. *But you'll never be free of the past if you don't admit the truth.* I loved Eleanor. *I know you did.* I didn't kill her. *I know that, too.* Sam loved her, too. *I'm not talking about Sam right now,* she says. *I'm talking about you.* I didn't do it, and I didn't help her either. *But you wanted to be free of the disease.*

112

And you believed that the only way you'd be free was if Eleanor died. Dr. Daniels' voice is so soft I can barely hear it over my sobs. *After you found Eleanor, you waited a long time before you called the paramedics, didn't you, Claudia?* She waits, without saying anything, till I finally quiet down a little. If only I could have said good-bye, I tell her. I never got the chance to say good-bye. *When you sat on those steps instead of calling the paramedics,* she finally says, *that's what you were doing* — saying good-bye.

> *Good-bye, Love,*
> *There's no one leaving.*

I closed the bedroom door, even though we were alone in the house. I opened the curtains so the room was bright with light. Outside the window, birds were singing at the feeders. Eleanor was in bed, the blankets drawn all the way up to her chin, her eyes closed. I knelt beside the bed, brushed her thin hair from her eyes, and kissed her on the forehead.

> *I don't know how much you can hear me,*
> *But you seem quite content on your own.*
> *Are you drifting away like the summer*
> *To the days of your childhood at home?*

When she opened her eyes, I held her right hand tightly in mine. She reached over with her left hand, slowly, so slowly, and brushed my cheek with the back of her fingers. Suddenly I didn't care what the disease did to her, I didn't care what it did to me or Sam — as long as she didn't leave me. After I pressed my face against her body, she rested her hand heavily on my head. She took several harsh, short breaths as her music played.

> *Here is the moment of parting,*
> *I can feel all the fear in your hand,*

Leaving a home full of memories
On the verge of a strange new land.

I leaned more over the bed, putting one arm around her head and the other over her chest, to hold her closer. My tears wet her cheek, temple, and forehead as I kissed her. The birds outside the window chirped, the music played in the background, and she held onto me hard, with both hands.

And the stories I tell to my children
Are the ones that you told me before,
But the story now slowly unfolding
Is the saddest story of all.

Gradually, her grip loosened. Finally, her eyelids lowered. And this time, she didn't struggle to keep them open. I held her tighter. God, I loved her. I loved her so much. I would have done anything for her. I would have traded my own life for hers.

"So after she died, you took the silver box, the one with the cremains, and you put the ashes in the garden," said Tracey.

"Yes."

"Did you just dump the cremains in one spot, Claudia, or did you spread them out?"

"Does that matter?"

"It might."

"I scattered them. All over."

"What'd you do with the box after it was empty?"

"I took it back into the house."

"Where in the house?"

"I don't remember."

"How could you forget something like that?"

"I don't know. I just don't remember. Jesus, I'm so sick of going over it all the time."

"I wouldn't want a jury to hear that tone of voice, Claudia."

"A jury? My God, Tracey, I didn't do anything."

"I'm not the one you have to convince."

I didn't do anything, and I was only gone a little while. When I came back from the yard and looked in on Eleanor, she was asleep. She slept almost all the time toward the end. Her breathing was louder than usual, and it sounded a bit strange, but I thought it was the pneumonia. I went over to the bed, touched her, and said her name, but she didn't move, so I left her alone. I know I should have stayed there with her. I know I never should have left her. Not even for a moment. But I couldn't stay in that room. I just couldn't. I only went to the bottom of the stairs — it's not like I left the house. I just went to the bottom of the stairs. I didn't do anything but sit at the bottom of the stairs. I had to get away from all that sickness and dying and death.

You had to get away from Eleanor. Just for a little while. *Just long enough for it to be over,* says Dr. Daniels. *And when you got back, it was all over, wasn't it?* I'll never forgive myself. Never. No matter how long I live. The one time she needed me most, the one thing she ever asked of me, and I couldn't even stay in the same room with her. *It's a grievous burden, Claudia,* she says. *It's a heavier weight than steel leg braces.*

"The hearing and vision tests are all normal," said the neurologist. "The blood count, blood chemistry, and EEG are within normal ranges."

His words fell like heavy boulders all around us, as we sat in the overstuffed, flowered chairs in his brightly lit, pastel-colored office, and the weight of his words crushed all the hope out of us.

"The CAT scan didn't indicate any brain tumors or strokes, and there's been no head injury," he said. "Of course, we can't be absolutely, one hundred percent certain until after death, at the autopsy."

"So you might be missing something," said Harold.

"This is the third doctor, Dad."

"He might be wrong. He's not God, you know."

"They can't all be wrong, Dad. Jesus, why can't you just face the truth?"

"If you know so much, why don't you help your mother?"

"Harold, please don't."

"My son. Mr. Big Shot. He was the first one to notice something was wrong with Eleanor, did I tell you that? He thinks he's so smart. Always reading. Never has his head out of a book. Thinks he knows more than anybody else on the planet."

"I know how hard this must be for you to hear, Mr. Sloane," said the neurologist.

"If he didn't put these ideas in the doctors' heads, maybe one of you could find out what's really wrong with her."

"And if you weren't so damned bullheaded, maybe we could've gotten Mom in earlier. Maybe we could've done something for her when she first started to get sick."

"Stop it, stop it, both of you. Will you listen to yourselves? You act like you're the ones who're suffering."

"Mr. Sloane, Mrs. Sloane, I think it would behoove us all to sit down, take a few deep breaths, and —"

Harold muttered something as he stomped over to the bookcase, breathing heavily as he leaned against it. Sam paced the office, his hands jammed into his pants pockets. The neurologist looked sadly at me.

"I'd advise you to bring Mrs. Sloane in for a reevaluation in a year," he said, "so we can determine if her condition has changed in any way. But I'm afraid I do agree with Dr. Barnett's original diagnosis."

For a few minutes, no one said anything.

"This is going to kill her when she finds out."

"I'd advise you not to tell her," said the neurologist.

"Why not?" said Harold, turning around from the bookcase.

"It'd be unnecessarily distressing for her."

"But she already knows something's wrong," said Sam.

"She'll lose that insight pretty quickly. Trust me: soon she won't know there's anything wrong with her."

"How can you be so sure?"

"That's one of the things that makes patients with this disease so dangerous to themselves and to others," said the neurologist. "They don't know anything's wrong with them, so they try to continue living their lives as they always have."

"She's going to ask us what the tests showed," said Sam. "What'll we tell her?"

"We can tell her that she's having problems with her memory. We can tell her that we're concerned, and that we're doing our best to find out what's wrong. That's usually sufficient to calm patients down."

"What if Eleanor asks us, point-blank, what's wrong with her?"

"Tell her she has memory problems."

"Hell, why don't we just tell her she's fine?" said Harold.

"Don't lie to her, Mr. Sloane."

"Why the hell not?"

"She needs to trust you."

"And I need you to run some of these tests again."

"Dad, will you just stop it?"

Harold grabbed one of the medical texts off the shelf and flipped it open.

"Maybe she had a stroke."

"She didn't have a stroke, Mr. Sloane."

"Well, maybe she's got some other disease. Like Parkinson's or depression or . . ."

"Will you listen to yourself, Dad? When are you going to face the facts?"

"You go to hell."

Harold swung at Sam when he tried to take the book, but he missed. Then Sam shoved Harold down into one of the chairs. I started to get up, to keep everything from getting worse, but Harold covered his face, sobbing. Sam put the medical book away, resting his forehead against the shelf.

"Unfortunately, this disease follows a fairly predictable pattern of deterioration," said the neurologist. "In the later stages, Mrs. Sloane may have to be institutionalized . . ."

"Never," said Harold.

". . . but you don't have to think about that right now. Until then, this is a list of resources, as well as the number of the local chapter. They have support groups that can help you get through this. All the families have been through exactly the same thing."

I took the list from the desk. When Sam touched Harold's shoulder, Harold held onto Sam's hand with both of his. Then, once again, a doctor wrote our family's death sentence on Eleanor's chart. Dementia. Of the Alzheimer's type.

We didn't lose Harold right away, and we spent several nights outside his room in the Cardiac Intensive Care Unit. The last night at the hospital, when Sam took Eleanor downstairs to get coffee, I went back to Harold. He looked so helpless, attached to all those monitors and tubes and wires. The only sound in the room was the beeping and humming and *whoosh*ing of the machines. While I was sitting beside the bed, holding his hand, Harold's eyes fluttered open, and he mumbled something. I thought it meant he had a chance. I thought it meant everything would go back to normal, the way it was supposed to be. But before morning, Harold was dead. And Eleanor had no one else in the world. No one but me and Sam.

I thought it would make me so happy, her needing me like that. *And you were happy, Claudia, a great deal of the time.* I'm not happy anymore. I haven't been for a long time. *I know.* I loved Eleanor. I didn't want her to be sick and helpless and dying, the way she was at the end. *I know that.* I didn't want her to suffer or be in pain. *And that doesn't make you a bad person, Claudia. It makes you human.* But I didn't kill her. I never would have done that. *I never said you did. I only said I want you to admit the truth.* Yes, yes, all right, I wanted her to die. Are you happy now? Is that what you wanted me to say? Yes, I wanted her dead. Those last few years, every hour of every single day, I wanted her to be dead. Every minute of every hour, I wanted her to die. Oh, God forgive me, but I never wanted anything in my life as much as I wanted Eleanor to die.

Every single day, I thanked God for bringing Eleanor into my life, and I thanked Him again that night, as we sat out in the backyard, holding hands, watching the sunset: rose, cream, blue, and violet, all swirled together. The crickets sang, the air smelled clean, and even though Eleanor didn't talk much anymore, I felt closer to her than ever. When Sam came out, he stood behind us, one hand on my shoulder, one on Eleanor's. The fireflies were winking all around us by the time Eleanor and I stood up. After we went in, I made some herb tea while Eleanor and Sam sat at the kitchen table. I brought the teapot over, sat down, and poured us each a cup. Sam lifted Eleanor's hand and kissed her fingers, then pressed them to his cheek. When I touched his arm, he held my hand. God, I was so happy. I was so unbelievably happy.

You can find that happiness again, Claudia, says Dr. Daniels. *You can start by being grateful.* Grateful? *For all the happiness and love you did have with Eleanor. And for the gift she gave you the night she died.* My freedom? I say, but she doesn't laugh. *I meant the other gift.* Oh, that. *You are grateful for that, aren't you, Claudia?* You know I am. *Then thank Eleanor, and send her a blessing.* After I do, I look back up at Dr. Daniels. And if I'm grateful, I say, then one day I'll be happy? *You'll have a chance. But even if you're never as happy as you think you should be, at least you'll be free.* So, I don't have to think that Sam had anything to do with her death. *I do want you to consider that possibility.* Why? If he helped her die, I can't be happy with him. *You need to face the truth, Claudia. All of it. And that includes the possibility that Sam might have helped Eleanor kill herself.* But I couldn't stay with him if he did that. I'd leave him. You know I would. *No, I don't know that,* she says. *I don't know that at all.*

"You don't know what you're talking about," said Sam. "She's innocent, and everybody knows it."

"Mrs. Sloane, you have the right to remain silent," said Detective Mitchell, taking my wrist and putting it behind my back. "If you give up this right, anything you say may be used as evidence against you."

"What kind of friend are you, Troy? And where's Roger? Why isn't Roger here?"

"Don't grab him like that, Sam," said Troy. "Come on, buddy. Don't make us take you in."

"You're using handcuffs? Are you crazy? She didn't do anything, you stupid —"

"Stop it, Sam. Let go. Don't make us arrest you, too."

"How can you do this to us, Troy? After all the years we've known each other?"

"You have the right to have an attorney present during questioning," said Mitchell, taking my other wrist. "If you cannot afford an attorney, one will be appointed for you. Do you understand these rights as I've explained them to you, Mrs. Sloane? Mrs. Sloane?"

"Where's Tracey's number? She'll straighten everything out," said Sam. "This is a witch-hunt, that's what it is."

"You're under arrest," said Mitchell, clamping the metal cold and tight on my wrists. "For the murder of Eleanor Sloane."

Eleanor

It requires more courage
to suffer than to die.

Napoleon

CHAPTER ONE

*D*OOR CLOSES. Eyes open. Sit up. Reach out. Chew. Swallow. Empty. Chew. Swallow. Empty. Noise. Stop. Listen. No one. Chew. Swallow. Cough. Cough. Cough. Chew. Swallow. Empty. Empty. Empty. Lie down. Close eyes. Done.

I open my eyes. It's dark. The voices are loud. The voices are everywhere.

"We're not putting her in that place," she says. "They're just waiting for her to die."

"They won't artificially prolong her life, Claudia, if that's what you mean," he says.

"Why don't we just skip the middleman, Roger, and take Mom right to the cemetery?"

"She has less than six months to —"

"You don't know that, Eve."

"Based on their evaluation . . . Don't look at us like that. They're professionals, Sam. They've dealt with thousands like her. They developed the criteria. . . ."

"If she has less than six months, then she might as well stay here."

"Why are you doing this? Why are you making everything so much harder?"

"I'm helping as much as I can, Eve. Claudia doesn't want her to leave either."

"Yes, she does, Sam. She's afraid to tell you how she really feels."

"Did those tarot books give you the power to read minds, Eve?"

The blanket goes over my head. It's more dark. But the voices are there.

"It's killing you, too, Sam. How much weight have you lost, buddy? You look like a damned skeleton."

"We're not putting her in a home."

"Not a home. A hospice. They'll take good care of her."

"Eve, they won't give her antibiotics if she gets pneumonia again. How is that taking good care of her?"

"The pneumonia's her body's way of saying it's had enough."

"If you had pneumonia, Roger, you'd want them to give you antibiotics."

"I'm not terminally ill."

"She's staying here. With us. I won't starve her to death."

"Jesus, Sam, it's a hospice, not a concentration camp."

"They don't have feeding tubes. How is she supposed to eat after she can't swallow?"

"Do you want them to force a feeding tube down the throat of a dying woman?"

"You'd want one if you were in her place. You'd want everything they could do to keep you alive."

"Not machines."

"They won't accept her anyway. We're not signing their 'Do Not Resuscitate' order."

The voices go more loud. Someone cries and cries. My hands go over my ears. Someone still cries.

"Come on, Mom. Put your hand down. Open your mouth," he says. "You like chocolate pudding. It's your favorite. Mom . . ."

I keep my mouth closed.

"Just a little, Mom. Come on," he says, and the spoon touches my lips. "You like chocolate pudding. Really, you do. And I put in extra cocoa. You like it that way. Just one bite, Mom. For me, please? Look, oh, yummy. Isn't that good? Mmm. It's delicious. Here, now you try some. Okay. Watch this. Mmm-mmm. This is so delicious. If you don't eat some of it pretty soon, I'm going to eat it all myself."

The spoon goes to the bowl. To his mouth. To the bowl. To my mouth. I shake my head. God tells me not to. I listen to God. My mouth stays closed.

"God forgive me for saying this, Dr. Daniels, but I think she wants to . . ."

She looks at me. She looks away. The other one leans forward. Her chair stops rocking.

"You think she wants to do what, Claudia? You can tell me."

"Do you think it was an accident — that time Sam and Harold found her?"

"Yes, I think that was an accident."

"You don't think she wanted to . . . that she wants to . . ."

"No, I don't think that's what she means. She's tired of the illness and she wants it to end."

"I suppose."

She pulls at the cushion. The other one frowns.

"Just to be on the safe side, Claudia," she says, "you probably shouldn't keep any cleaning fluids or things like that in places where she'll have access to them. There's no harm in being cautious. And keep reassuring her that you understand she's suffering. Reassure her that —"

I get up. My feet go around and around.

"What is it, Eleanor?"

"What's wrong with her, Dr. Daniels?"

"I know this must be very scary for you, Eleanor."

"Why is she pacing like that?"

"I know you're suffering, Eleanor."

I look and look at her. She just sits there. Her face looks at me. Her eyes don't. My hands pull my hair. My words go around and around my head. No one hears me.

His hand goes on my head. I'm in bed. My baby's next to me. He's sitting with us. He says, Love-you-always. He turns to a different page. I pull his arm. He shows the picture. He touches my face with his hand. Love-you-love-you-always, Mom, he says. He holds my hand. Love-you-love-you-always, Mom. My eyes go asleep.

I don't see her get in. But she's here. In my room. I put my hand over the clock on my arm. Oh, no, my ring. My heart beats hard. My heart beats fast. I turn my ring around. I cover my clock. Oh, no, my purse. My heart beats harder. The floor in front of me moves around. I grab the bed. The floor stops moving. I keep holding the bed. I hold tight. She sits down at the table-thing. From the bed, I can see what she has: something in a bowl, something on a plate, something white in a glass. I run real fast to the table-thing. I push all the food on the floor. She cries out as she stands up. I go back to the bed. I make my legs and feet go on the bed, too. I hold onto the bedpost with both arms. I don't let go.

She holds my hand. I sit on the table-bed-thing. The woman-in-white holds my arm still. The man-in-white makes the sharp-pointy-thing go in my arm. I cry. She's next to the table-bed-thing. She holds my hand hard. The sharp-pointy-thing makes black on my arm. The black goes back and forth across the red.

"You know, you really shouldn't keep knives in places where she can gain access to them," says the man-in-white. "Alzheimer's patients don't realize that their skills aren't the same as always. In fact, if I were you, I wouldn't let her use a knife at all, unless it was a butter knife. I know you're trying to make her feel useful and helpful, Mrs. Sloane, but don't do it with dangerous implements.

And tell the sitters to keep a better eye on her. Get sitters who are used to dealing with Alzheimer's patients. Once I'm done here, Nurse will bandage it. Keep the stitches dry, Mrs. Sloane. And don't let her pick at them. And please, keep her away from the knives."

The sharp-pointy-thing goes in and out, in and out. She puts her head next to mine. She says something quiet. The sharp-pointy-thing pulls the black in and out, in and out. Water gets in my eyes. He comes running around the curtain. He looks at her. He looks at my arm. His face goes all white.

White pills. Blue pills. Pink pills. I put them in my money-thing. Lots and lots of pills. I close the shiny-thing on the wall. I flush. I go downstairs. She sits on the couch. A thing with towels is there. I sit next to her. She folds the towels. I hold my money-thing in my lap. She folds and folds. I wait and wait.

"Damn it, Sam, you waited too long," she says.

"I just took her a few minutes ago," he says. "She didn't have to go."

She comes over to me. Her hands go on her hips. She looks at him.

"She wouldn't stay there," he says. "I thought it meant she didn't have to go."

She pulls on my arm. I get up. She makes a bad face.

"Jesus, it's all over the cushion. Don't let her sit there. Sam, get her."

"What do you want me to do, Claudia?"

"Take her upstairs and get her changed."

"Me?"

"I've already done it three times today."

"But she's my mother."

"Do you mean you're only going to help out when it's not messy?"

He comes over. He takes my arm. He makes a more bad face.

"Christ," he says.

Domine Jesu Christe, rex gloriæ,
libera animas omnium fidelium
defunctorum de poenis inferni,
et de profundo lacu.

(O Lord, Jesus Christ, King of glory,
save the souls of all Your faithful
from the pains of hell,
and from the deep pit.)

The lights are pretty. The windows have lights in them, too. Red, blue, purple, green, gold. Like a Christmas tree. She's here next to me. When I touch her arm, she smiles.

Libera eas de ore leonis,
ne absorbeat eas tartarus,
ne cadant in obscurum.

(Save them from the lion's mouth,
and from the fiery lake
and from endless darkness.)

She stands. She kneels. She puts her face in her hands. I don't kneel or stand. She says I can sit. I look at the pretty lights. I like it when we talk to God.

Fac eas, Domine, de morte
transire ad vitam.

(Lead them, Lord, from death
into life.)

I look at the Holy Family. Mary's pretty. Jesus is pretty, too. I sit there. She sits next to me. I hold her hand. They talk to God. I listen for what God says.

ELEANOR

Gloria tibi, Domine.
Gloria tibi, Domine.

(Glory to You, O Lord.
Glory to You.)

CHAPTER TWO

GOD DOESN'T ANSWER. The knife's in my hand. It's the most big knife. It has little teeth. Like Harold's wood-thing. I go into the bathroom. I close the door. I sit down. I hold up my arm. God says nothing. The knife moves on my arm. Blood goes on the floor. My arm burns. I hold the knife in my other hand. The knife falls. More blood goes on the towel. My hand drops and drops the knife. The door opens. She sees me. She screams.

"Is she still screaming, Claudia?"

"No. Now she's like a ghost, Dr. Daniels, the way she follows me around everywhere. Sometimes it feels like she's my shadow. She's always right behind me."

"You're the primary caregiver, Claudia. She probably only feels safe with you."

I sit next to her on the couch. I put my hand on her leg. She doesn't look at me. She wipes her face.

"She still keeps saying 'sleep' all the time."

"And what do you say back to her?"

"The things you told me: 'I know you're tired of being sick,' 'I know you're tired of being dependent on somebody else,' but she just won't stop saying it."

"How does Sam respond when Eleanor says 'sleep' to him?"

"She doesn't say it to him."

The other one looks at me. She smiles. She touches my hand.

"We know you want to tell us something, Eleanor," she says. "Can you help us understand?"

"Sleep," I say.

"You see? That's all she ever says. It's making me crazy."

"Eleanor's cognitive impairment makes her more sensitive to the emotional connection between you. When she feels your frustration, she gets scared."

"Scared of what?"

"You're thinking logically, Claudia. Eleanor's reacting emotionally. Your frustration is a signal to her that the environment isn't safe, so she responds in the only way she knows how."

"By saying 'sleep' about a hundred thousand more times."

"She can't process your irritability, Claudia. All she senses is that you're pulling away, so she desperately tries to connect."

"So what should I do, Dr. Daniels?"

"Instead of communicating logically, relate to Eleanor's feelings. When she feels safe and understood and accepted, she may be able to communicate better."

I stand up. I hug her. She says the words that can't get out of my mouth. I hug her again and again.

I hug myself. I stand in the middle of the kitchen. I rock on my feet. They can't hide them forever. I leave all the spoons and forks on the counter. I leave all the boxes and cans on the floor. I leave all the little doors open. Where are they? I look around and around. Then I remember the cookie-pie-cake-thing. I go over and open the door. I bend down to look inside. There's a box. I pull it out. The box is heavy. It makes a noise. My hearts beats fast. I put the box on top where the pans and skillets go. I open the box. Yes, it's the knives.

"Let's just cut to the quick. This isn't working."

"I've been saying that for months. No, longer than that."

"It's not worth the effort anymore."

I go down the stairs. Not all the way. There they are. In the room. I sit down. I hold on to the wood. I hear them.

"I'm leaving."

"You're leaving?"

"That's what I said. I'm already packed."

"That's funny. That you're the one who's leaving. After all I've done to hold this family together."

"Family? Is that what you call it? Being trapped with a sick woman who doesn't even —"

"You think you're trapped? What about everything I've sacrificed? Just to take care of both of you."

"If you cut off both your arms and pulled out both your eyes, you still wouldn't have sacrificed as much as I have. I've sacrificed ten times as much as you. And for what?"

"I've been telling you that for years. You weren't listening."

"I wasn't listening? If there's anybody in this house who doesn't listen . . ."

"Can't we get past the blame? Can't we end this . . . amicably?"

"You can stay here. I'll go. Is that amicable enough for you?"

"You don't have to sound so bitter. It's not my fault, you know."

"Whose fault is it then? Hers?"

"Circumstances."

"You never take responsibility for anything, do you?"

"I don't want to go over this again. It's old territory. Going over it won't change anything."

"No, you're right. It won't."

They go back and forth. I stay on the steps. I hold the wood tight. They don't see me.

"Are you really packed?"

"Yes."

"So am I."

"If it didn't hurt so much, I'd laugh."

"If it didn't hurt so much, we wouldn't be here right now."

"Don't, please. It's too late for that."

"It just suddenly seemed like there was nothing ahead of us but . . ."

"But what?"

"Death."

"You see? That's the difference between us. You've just figured it out, but we've been dead for years."

"Have we? Well, I guess it was harder for me to let go."

The candy's hard. I spit it out. I put another candy in my mouth. A red candy. I try to chew it, but it's hard, too. I spit it out. It falls on the table. It's not good candy. Where did they put the good candy? I look for another piece. Black, black, black. I don't like black candy. White. I don't know what white candy tastes like. I put it in my mouth. It doesn't taste like anything. I spit it out. I pick up a green candy. It's a funny green. It's shiny but not wet. I put it in my mouth.

"Shit," he says.

He runs up to me from behind and hits me on the back. I push him away, but he hits me again. The green candy falls out of my mouth. He leans down in front of me. He pushes my mouth open. He puts his fingers in my mouth.

"You got any more in there?" he says. "Spit them out."

He doesn't take his fingers out of my mouth. I have to bite him. I bite down hard.

"Ow. God damn it, Mom," he says.

"What's the matter?" she says. "What's wrong?"

"She's eating buttons," he says, rubbing his fingers.

She comes over. She scoops up all the candy and puts it back into the clear box. The candy looks pretty in the box. They can't see the piece of candy in my hand. It's a blue candy. They can't take it away from me. He holds his fingers out to her. She looks at them. The blue candy is in my hand. I won't let them take it.

"Christ. Eating buttons," he says. "What next?"

She hits my hand. I touch her again. Her voice goes more loud. "Leave me alone, Eleanor," she says. "I'm taking a nap."

She's on the bed, but it's daytime. She turns over on her side, so she can't see me. He's outside. I hear the grass-cutting-thing. She won't turn around. She won't look at me. I put my hand on her shoulder.

"Sleep," I say.

"Not again," she says. "I can't take any more."

I let go of her hand. I go to the bathroom. I open the shiny-thing on the wall. My hands shake. I take out the bottle. I go to the bed. She looks at the bottle. She looks at me. I kneel down. I empty the bottle on the bed. She shakes her head. I put my arms around the pills. I lay my head down on them. I close my eyes.

I close the drawer. I open the other. Big spoons, little spoons, spoons with holes, big forks, little forks. But not them. Where are they? Where did they put them? I push the spoons and forks away. They keep falling back, so I take the spoons out of the drawer. I take the forks out, too. I put them all on the counter. What did they do with them all? They're supposed to be in the drawer, but they're not. I leave that drawer open. I do another drawer. I leave that one open, too, so I can remember. I keep opening drawers. Where did they put all the knives? I close the door to the cold-white-thing. No knives there. No knives anywhere. Not in the cold-white-thing. Not in the drawers. Not behind the little doors. I know they have them. He sharpens them on that long steel-thing. It makes a funny noise when the knife hits it. I open the door where the food is. Pudding, corn, pancake stuff. No knives. I push all the cans out of the way. I push all the boxes out of the way. Nothing can stop me. Nothing is as hard as this.

"It's so hard to figure out what she wants," she says. "Something's wrong with her, Dr. Daniels. Something besides the disease, I mean, but I can't figure out what it is."

"Eleanor, is there something bothering you that you want to talk to Claudia and me about?"

Yes, it's all in my head. Everything I want to tell her. I just have to say it. It goes like this: I don't want to break things. I don't want to lose things. I want my husband. I want my house. I want my car. I want my keys and my money. I don't want to be scared. I don't want to be lost. There it is, all of it. Now I just have to say it.

"Sleep," I say.

"She follows me all over the house saying that. No matter what time of the day it is, Dr. Daniels, that's all she says. I don't understand what she wants."

"Sleep," I say.

"First of all, Claudia, we have to relate to Eleanor on an emotional level, rather than on a physical one. Eleanor's probably not saying that she wants physical sleep. She's telling us that she's tired on an emotional level, Claudia. She's tired of being sick. She's tired of the toll the illness is taking on her."

"Is that what she means, Dr. Daniels?"

"Yes, I think that's a reasonable interpretation."

"You wouldn't believe what I thought she meant."

"Well, we don't want to look for things that aren't there, do we, Claudia?"

"Goodness, I didn't see you, Eleanor," she says. "You scared me. I thought you were in the living room."

She closes the cold-white-thing. She wipes the counter. I touch her back. She turns to look at me.

"Eleanor, you've been following me around all evening," she says. "Why don't you just tell me what you want?"

She sits down at the table. I sit down. She takes my hand. I have to take the words from the darkness. I'm strong today. I push the darkness into the corners. Yes, I can tell her now. This is what I want: I want to be myself. I want things to be the way they're supposed to be. I want my husband. I want my furniture and my dishes. I want my wildflowers and my garden. When I look in the mirror, I don't want to see that old woman. I don't want to be sick. I don't want to be afraid. I want me. Yes, that's what I want most of all: me. And today, I can say it to her. I hold her hands as tight as I can. The darkness is coming back. It wants to take me away from her. It wants to lock me up so no one can find me. The darkness makes my words so they don't come out right. I have to say it now. Before the darkness covers me. Before there's none of me left. I kiss her fingers. I kiss the back of her hands. I hold her hands and fingers to my heart. I lean closer to her. I whisper, so only she will hear.

"Sleep," I say.

CHAPTER THREE

*L*ISTEN TO THIS, CLAUDIA," he says.

He puts the paper down so he can look at her. The clock says, *Tick-tick-tick*. I pet the ball of yarn in my lap. The yarn is soft. Like a kitten. He's talking. He's saying it. I want it so bad. She says no. He says not now, Mom, not now. The yarn is pink with silver sparkles. But it's not a kitten. He reads to her.

> *Physician John Smith, nicknamed the "death doctor" by the media because of his controversial involvement in physician-assisted suicides, has once again been present at an assisted suicide in Kansas.*

I stop petting the yarn. The clock goes, *Tick-tick-tick*. I lean closer to him. He holds up the newspaper. He reads from it.

> *Fifty-eight-year-old Lotta Jones, suffering from the late stages of ovarian cancer, took her own life at her home Saturday night by ingesting a combination of barbiturates and narcotics. Mrs. Jones' husband and three grown children were in attendance.*

She drinks her coffee. She puts her feet on the couch. Against his leg. The yarn is in my hands. He reads. I look at her.

"We don't think of it as an ending, but as a beginning," said Martha Thompson, Lotta Jones' oldest daughter. Her brother and sister nodded their agreement. "After all, Mom's been suffering so much lately," said Jeff, the youngest sibling. "Where she's going has to be better than what she's going through here."

My heart beats fast. My heart beats hard. There is no darkness around me now. I'm in the living room. I'm with them. I'm not lost. I look at her. I push the ball of yarn out of my lap. It falls on the floor. I kick the yarn. It rolls over to her. He reads out loud.

Friends of the Joneses gathered in their home the night before the suicide to share in a farewell dinner and in communal prayer. Lotta Jones was reported to have wept, expressing her gratitude for the love of her friends and family in supporting her.

She bends over. She picks up the yarn. She winds the loose string. The clock says, *Tick-tick-tick*. She comes over to me. She holds out the ball of yarn. I put both my hands around hers. I don't let go.

An attorney for Dr. Smith, who himself was unavailable for comment, stated that the physician stood by his oft-repeated claim that "the terminally ill have a right to die with dignity, with a physician's assistance, without additional pain and suffering." Through his attorney, the doctor insisted that he was not taking a life, but ending suffering. State attorneys say they intend to prosecute the doctor for murder.

I hold her hand. I hold it and hold it. She looks at me. Her mouth makes a funny smile. She tries to pull her hand away. I don't let go. I look at her and look at her. She stops smiling. He puts down the paper. She pulls her hand away hard. She goes and sits on the couch next to him. Her hands go fast. Back and forth, back and forth. Around her hair, around her throat. The clock goes, *Bong-bong-bong*. She looks up. He drinks his coffee. Her hands go back and forth.

Around the coffeepot, around the sugar, around the milk. I look and look at her. He lifts the paper to turn the page. She looks back at me. Yes, I say with my head, Yes. She doesn't move.

He leaves. I move fast. She's outside. In the flowers. I close my door. I go to the bed. I reach under it. I pull out the gun. I open the black-thing at the back. Put the bullet in. Close it. Turn the gun around. Put it on my heart. I close my eyes. Love-you-always-good-bye-goodbye. I pull the trigger. Nothing happens. I put my thumbs on it. I push and push. Nothing happens. I turn the gun around. Open the back. Yes, the bullet's there. I close it. Turn the gun around. Put it on my heart. Love-you-love-you-always. I push the trigger as hard as I can. It doesn't move at all.

I stay still when he comes into the kitchen. I don't make any noise. He opens the cold-white-thing. He takes a box out. He drinks out of the box. She says that's bad. I'm bad, too. I don't know how it happens. I try not to do it. But my panties are wet. My dress is wet, too. The chair's wet. He says I have to wear a diaper. But I'm not a baby. Why am I wetting myself? What's wrong with me? He opens the cold-white-thing and puts the box back.

"Mom, there you are," he says. "What are you doing out here all by yourself? Why don't you come in the living room with me?"

Not him. No diapers. He pulls on my arm. I stand up. Some of the wet runs down my leg.

"Christ," he says.

"God, if this didn't hurt so much, it would be easy."

"It could never be easy."

"If we didn't love each other . . ."

"Well, if we both hated each other, it might be easier. But I don't think so."

The door is closed. They're in the room. My face is against the door. I hear them.

"We do still love each other, don't we?"

"I know I love you."

"And I still love you. It's just that . . ."

"I know. But she's not going to get any better."

"So the real question is, considering the fact that she's only going to get worse . . ."

"Do we want to stay together?"

"Yes. Or do we want to . . . throw in the towel?"

"Don't say it like that. It makes it sound so . . . trivial."

"I didn't mean it that way. It's just that I don't know how to talk about it without getting . . ."

"Emotional?"

"Yes. Emotional."

"They say once you've let the word itself in, it's sometimes hard to go back. You know, to what you were before you said it."

"It's just a word."

"Can you say it?"

"Can I? Of course I can."

"Well, then, say it."

"You say it."

"I have said it."

"Not to me, you haven't."

"No, not to you. It is hard, isn't it."

"It's hard because we still love each other."

"Yes, I do still love you. I know sometimes I may not act like I do."

"I'm guilty of that, too."

"So, what does this mean? Are we not talking about it anymore?"

"About a divorce?"

"Yes. About a divorce. There, now we've both said it. Are we . . ."

"I don't think we need to do that. Do you?"

"Not anymore. Talking about it helped."

"It helped me, too. It made me realize that I don't want to lose you."

"I've always known that. I just felt so . . . frustrated."

"It's time we started looking into some options for her. So her illness won't destroy us."

"So it won't destroy our marriage. I'm sorry. You weren't ready to hear that."

"I'd never choose her over you. Don't you believe me?"

"It doesn't matter now. Let's not talk anymore."

"No, let's not talk. Let's not say anything at all."

"Let's just listen to our hearts."

"Can you hear what my heart's saying?"

"Yes, oh, yes."

"Eleanor, are you listening to me? What is that mess? What'd you do? Oh, never mind. I'll clean it up in the morning. Just get into bed. What's this under your pillow? *Final Exit.* Jesus, Eleanor, you don't have to tear it out of my hand like that. Isn't that Lois' book? I thought you told me once it was Lois' book. Well, don't you want to give it to Frank? How about giving it to one of their sons? Not to them either? Come on, Eleanor. Quit kicking the covers off. Don't . . . All right. Fine. Keep Lois' book. It won't be very comfortable sleeping with it under your pillow, but that's your business. There, are you happy now? Okay. Here, take your medicine. There you go. Now sleep tight. All right, here's another kiss, and a really big hug. There you go. Yes, I love you, too. Love-you-love-you-always, Eleanor. Now close your eyes and go to sleep."

I open the dresser drawer. I move the clothes all around. No, it's not there. I close the drawer. I get down and look under the bed. No, not there. I open the closet. I put my hands on the shelf. I push the clothes so I can see behind them. No, not there either. But it's here. Somewhere. I see him with it when she's not here. I get on my hands and knees. I look in the shoes. Not in her shoes. Not in his shoes. I pick up one of his boots. It's heavy. My heart beats fast. My heart beats hard. I turn the boot over. The gun falls out.

My heart beats hard and fast. He comes in. The door slams. He doesn't look at me. He goes to the dining room. I follow him. He's wet. Water goes into his eyes and down his face. Water goes on the floor.

"Leave it, Mom," he says. "If I want to throw my coat on the rug, I will."

He opens a bottle of brown stuff. He pours it in a glass. He drinks it fast. He pours more. He looks at me.

"She lost it," he says. "And the doctor says she's got to stop trying for a while. He says it's killing her."

He drinks more. He holds the glass hard. It breaks. Red goes in the brown. He holds up the glass. He makes his finger go on it. More red goes in the brown in the glass.

"It's all your fault," he says. "If she didn't have to take care of you, she wouldn't have lost this one."

He throws the glass. It makes a bad noise. He throws another one. I cover my ears. He throws and throws. The glasses break. He sits at the table. His head is down. His shoulders shake. I don't move.

"Don't, Mom. Don't," he says. "Don't do that."

"Try not to let it bother you, Sam."

"She doesn't have to do it, Claudia. She can stop it if she wants to."

"She's not doing it on purpose. It's the disease."

"Mom, not with your fingers."

I put some potatoes in my mouth. I like potatoes. I like gravy. I'm hungry. He's holding my hand away from the plate. I want to eat. I use my other hand.

"Mom, will you at least . . . Use a spoon, for Christ's sake. Jesus, she's getting gravy all over everything."

"That's why there's a plastic mat on the floor, Sam. That's why she's wearing the smock."

"Mom, stop it."

"Sam, when she makes that noise, she's about to —"

"Let me handle it."

"I spend more time with her, Sam. I know her better. When she makes that noise, she's about to —"

"Will you let me handle this, Claudia?"

"I'm just trying to keep this from turning into —"

"She's my mother, okay? Not yours. Mine. And you don't have any idea what it's like to see your mom at dinner wearing a bib."

"It's a smock."

"A bib is a bib is a bib. Let's call things what they are."

"We shouldn't talk about this now. Not in front of —"

"Why not? You think she doesn't know she's wearing a bib? You think she doesn't know she's playing with her food? What's next, Claudia? Diapers? And why is her damn purse on the table? Why does she have to carry it around everywhere? She lives here, for Christ's sake. Nobody's going to steal her purse."

He picks up my purse. I stop eating. He puts it on the shelf. When he sits down, I can't see it.

"The purse, Sam. That's what that noise means."

"God damn it."

He stands up. He gets my purse. He puts it back on the table. He looks away from me. She reaches over and pats my hand. She smiles. I eat my potatoes and gravy. He gets up from the table. He stands in the doorway. He shakes his head. I open my mouth. Potatoes are good. Gravy's good.

"She's a damned zombie," he says.

"As long as she's eating," she says.

Someone's mouth is open on mine. I try to push him away. But my hands won't work. He's too big. He's too strong. He keeps his mouth on mine. I'm on the floor. It's cold. It hurts my head. He pushes hard on my chest. His breath goes in my mouth. Then his hands go hard on my chest again. I open my eyes. I push him away. Smoke is everywhere. I'm in the garage. He makes his breath go into me again. He starts to cry. I wipe his breath off my mouth. I make a fist. I hit him as hard as I can.

CHAPTER FOUR

$\mathcal{D}$R. JUDITH'S HAND COVERS MINE. Claudia shakes her head.

"I feel so stupid," she says. "I didn't understand what Eleanor was saying."

"How could you? Have you ever dealt with Alzheimer's before? Have you ever dealt with any neurological or mental illnesses before? You couldn't possibly decipher what Eleanor was trying to tell you."

"But I thought . . . you won't believe what I thought, Dr. Daniels."

"Don't interpret what she's saying from your perception of reality, Claudia. We have to interpret what she says from her own reality. We don't know what Eleanor wants unless she communicates it to us herself."

"Sleep," I say.

"Yes, we know you're tired of being sick, Eleanor," says Dr. Judith. "I know how scary this is for you. And for you, too, Claudia. But you're not alone anymore. You don't have to deal with this illness alone. That's what I'm here for."

Claudia tells Dr. Judith about my room and about Sam. They talk and talk. I hold Claudia's hand. Sometimes Dr. Judith holds my other hand. Then she looks at her clock. She says good-bye. She gives me a card. Eleanor, it says: Tuesday 1:00. I hold the card. I take it with me wherever I go.

We go in my room. I get into bed. He pulls the covers up to my shoulders. He tucks the blanket around me. He turns on the little light next to the bed. He kisses me on the cheek. He kisses my baby on the top of her head. He gets our book. He opens it. He sits next to me. He holds the book so I can see the pictures. He reads. I make my head go sideways. My cheek touches him. He puts his hand on my hair. My heart beats slow. He says love-you-always. His hand goes on my face over and over. My eyes go closed. His voice goes away slow. Love-you-love-you-always.

He goes away. I look all around. No one is in the living room. I go to the kitchen. No one is there. I look out the windows. Yes, there he is. By the tomatoes and flowers. He can't see me. I go fast to the garage. I put my hand on the knob. I close the door behind me. I go down the steps into the garage. The truck is gone. The car is there. I look in the car. Yes, the keys are there. The big garage door is closed. The little garage doors are closed. I get into the car. My hand is on the key. My foot is on the gas. No one sees me. I hold on to the steering wheel. My hands are cold. My throat makes me cough. I push the mirror up. I can't see my eyes. The doors are closed. I turn the car on. I push my foot on the gas. I push down hard. The car doesn't move. Smoke comes out of the back of the car. Smoke fills the garage. Smoke fills the car. I take a deep breath. I push my foot down harder. I take another deep breath. The smoke covers me.

I cover myself. She can't see me. It's not dark. She's not my husband. She has to get out of the bathroom before I take my clothes off. I don't even undress in front of Harold.

"Unbutton your shirt," says Claudia.

"I don't want to take a bath," I say.

"Undo this button," says Claudia.

I try to make my fingers stop what they're doing, but my fingers are listening to Claudia. My head says, No, but my fingers do what she tells them to do. Stop that, you bad fingers. Every time Claudia touches a button, my fingers obey her. Then Claudia touches my arms, and my hands move so she can take my blouse off. Bad fingers.

Bad hands. I wrap my arms around myself. Claudia puts my blouse by the sink. When she comes back, she touches the side of my skirt.

"I don't want to take a bath."

She can't see me in my underwear. She's not my husband. It's not dark in here. Stop that, fingers. Stop that, hands. They don't listen to me. Claudia's the boss of my fingers and hands. After the skirt falls down, Claudia touches my ankle. My foot lifts up. She touches the other ankle. My other foot obeys her, too. She's the boss of everything. She picks up the skirt and puts it with my blouse. I turn around so she can't see me.

"I don't want to take a bath."

She taps me on the shoulder. My arms move. The slip goes up over my head. Claudia puts the slip on top of the skirt and blouse. All I have on is my bra and panties. Claudia puts her hands on my shoulders and turns me around. She unhooks my bra. Children shouldn't see their parents naked. I look for my bathrobe. There it is, on the back of the door. When I pull it down, Claudia takes it out of my hand. I hold a towel up in front of me. Claudia takes it away. She leads me over to the tub.

"I don't want to take a bath."

It's filled with water, but there's no bubbles. I never take a bath without bubbles. I look all around for the bubbles, but I can't see them. Claudia pours water all over me. I make my legs go out in front of me, under the water. I put my hands over my legs. This is bad. She's my daughter. There's no bubbles. Claudia takes my hand and puts something in it.

"Here's your washcloth, Eleanor. There you go. Nice and soapy."

"I don't want to take a bath."

"Okay, Eleanor, let's do this arm now. There you go. That's good. Now, let's do your face. That's a girl. Here comes the warm water to rinse all the soap off. Close your eyes. Okay, all done. Stand up."

My legs get up. Claudia gets the big towel and puts it around me. The towel is warm. She rubs the towel all over me. I try to keep the towel, but Claudia takes it away and hangs it up. She sprinkles powder on me. She rubs it all over. She puts my nightgown on. She holds up my bathrobe. My arms go in. Claudia ties the belt. She rubs the towel on my head. She combs my hair. She kisses me on the face.

"There, doesn't that feel good?" she says. "Now you're all nice and clean."

"I don't want to take a bath," I say, and she kisses my face again.

The pillow keeps getting off my face. I hold it harder. It works in movies. But that noise comes in my ears. It goes, *Pound-pound-pound*. When I let go of the pillow to cover my ears, my body takes a big breath. Bad Eleanor. I take my hands away from my ears. I push the pillow harder on my face. I don't take any breaths. I don't even open my mouth. I don't fight. I don't punch or kick. My chest hurts. I don't let go. I hold the pillow harder. My chest hurts more. My ears go, *Pound-pound-pound*. That noise gets loud in my ears. My hands let go of the pillow. My mouth takes a big breath. Stupid body. Stupid pillow. Bad, stupid Eleanor.

"You're so stupid sometimes. How can you be so stupid?"

"That's it. This conversation is over."

"It's over when I say it's over."

"Like hell."

The door slams. The door slams again. I go to the window. They're in the yard. Snow is up to their knees. Snow falls all around them. Her mouth moves. White comes out. He shakes his head. Her hands and arms go back and forth. She grabs his sleeve. He pushes her away. She points to the house. To my window. I go behind the curtain. No one comes. I look out the window again. She has her hands over her ears. He picks up something in the snow. He throws it hard at the tree. His mouth moves fast. Her mouth moves fast. He puts his hands over his ears. The air is white between them. So much white. The window is cold on my face and hands.

I close the window. I lock it. I pull the curtains. I go across the room. I can't move the dresser. I push and push, but it's too heavy.

The chair's not too heavy. I push it over to the window, against the curtains. I pile all my things in the chair. I go to the bed. There's a little light next to the bed. I make the light go off. Now it's almost dark. I pick up the pillow. I lie down. I close my eyes. I can't see anything. I hold my breath. I hold the pillow over my face.

He doesn't see me. He goes past my room with it. I go after him. He goes up the stairs. To the top of the house. No one else is with him. He takes it to the corner. The sun shines on it. He makes his fingers go along the wood. When he touches it, it rocks. He wipes his face with his hand. He makes the blanket go all around it. But he doesn't get up. He stays next to it. On the floor. He puts his hands over his face. His shoulders shake. He makes a funny noise. I go down the stairs. I sit on the steps. I put my arms around myself. He stays up there a long time. I hold myself harder. He makes that noise over and over. No one hears him. No one but me.

"Did you hear me, Sam? Where are you?"

"Here she is, Claudia. I found her."

"Where?"

"In the bathroom. In the tub."

"What's she doing in the tub?"

I don't move. A little bit of breath goes out. There's bubbles. Not real bubbles. Mouth-bubbles.

"She's pretending it's a swimming pool," he says.

"A swimming pool? What do you mean? Sam, don't let her put her head under the water."

She reaches in and grabs my arm. I try to push her away, but then he gets my other arm. My eyes open. My body takes a breath. The water chokes me. It makes me cough. They pull me out of the tub.

"Maybe we should buy her a kiddie pool."

"Here, put this towel around her, Sam. Careful: she's getting water on the —"

"Has she got a bathing suit?"

"I don't think she's pretending it's a pool."

"Why else would she have her clothes on in the tub? I thought you said she didn't like baths."

"Eleanor, stop it. Help me, Sam. Don't let her put her head back under the water."

"Come on, Mom. That's enough. Get out of the tub. Let's get you some dry clothes."

Sam pulls me. My feet go on the floor. He makes me get out of the bathroom. I try to turn around, but he holds my arm tight. He takes me into the hall. Claudia stands next to the tub, looking down at the water. Sam makes me go with him. There's nothing I can do.

CHAPTER FIVE

*B*UT THEY HAVE TO DO IT, EVE."

"No, they don't, Claudia."

"Sam and I need them."

"You'll have to find someone else to sit for Eleanor," says Eve. "The twins aren't going to do it anymore."

"What if we gave them a raise?"

"Claudia, the twins are afraid of her. She hit Sarah."

"What about Matthew? She wouldn't hit him. He's bigger than she is."

"He has a job at the mall now. Besides, even if he wanted to baby-sit, I wouldn't let him. She's getting violent. I'm not going to put my children in that situation."

"I don't understand you, Eve. You've been complaining for months that I don't help out enough at the bookstore, but when I ask the twins to sit for Eleanor so I can go to work, you won't let them."

"Why don't you get another professional sitter like Marie?"

"I thought you wanted the kids to have a grandmother figure, now that your parents are in Tucson."

"Jesus, Claudia, haven't you heard anything I've said?"

"Shhh. Not so loud. She'll hear us."

"I don't want the twins to sit for Eleanor anymore, and they don't want to do it either. End of story."

"What if we went ahead and put her name on the home's waiting list. Could the twins sit for her till she goes in the home?"

"The waiting list is a year and a half long."

"Could they sit for her till then?"

"Put her in the assisted living unit, Claudia. You can go visit her whenever you want."

"We don't want Eleanor to be with strangers."

"This isn't like what happened to you, Claudia. She's not an orphan."

"If you won't let Matthew or the twins sit for her, I'll have to stay home and do it myself."

"She's not even your mother, for Christ's sake. Why should you take care of her?"

He shows me the picture of the mother. I look and look at it. He lets go of my hand to turn the page. He holds my hand again. I look at the man and the baby in the picture. The man sings to the baby. Love-you-love-you-always. He closes the book.

"The end," he says.

He puts the book next to the bed. He stands up. He makes his face go next to mine. I make my arms go around him. He kisses me. He kisses my baby. He stands up. He makes the light go off. He goes to the door. He smiles at me. He makes a kiss.

"Love-you-always, Mom," he says, and he closes the door.

I hear the door. I go to the window. Claudia's in the yard. So is Sam. It's snowing and snowing. Claudia holds her arms out. She falls backward into the snow. She moves her arms and legs. The snow goes flat like a long skirt, like wings. Sam falls down next to her. He does it, too. Claudia opens her mouth. Snow falls in it. Sam sticks out his tongue. He eats snow. They stand up. The snow-people-with-wings stay down in the snow. Sam and Claudia throw snowballs. Some snowballs hit the tree. Some hit the snow. Some hit Sam and Claudia.

She runs. He catches her. He picks her up. She laughs and kicks. Sam falls in the snow. She falls on top of him. They laugh and laugh. Snow falls on their cheeks. It melts. Like tears.

Someone's crying. When I wake up, I hear it. I get out of bed. No lights are on. I go down the hall slow, my hand on the wall. The floor stays still. I don't fall. The crying is louder. The door with the sign "Sam's and Claudia's Room" is closed. The "Bike Room" is closed. The "Bathroom" door is open a little bit. I push it open more. The streetlights shine in the window. I see Claudia, sitting there. She's crying. When I go over to her, she looks up at me.

"The baby . . ."

I put my arms around her. Her face is against my body. She's shaking. I rub my hands on her shoulders and back. I hold her. The door opens wider. It's Sam. I move so he can hug her to him. I stand there, next to the wall. Sam goes to the sink. He takes a washcloth and turns on the water. He wipes the wet washcloth on Claudia's face. Then he holds her again. He kisses her over and over. He rocks her in his arms. I stay with them, there in the dark. But I don't say anything. Sam holds Claudia for a long, long time.

"Here, let me hold your hand," says Claudia. "Watch the step. There you go."

She puts her arm through mine. We walk across the yard.

"Isn't this a beautiful day?" she says. "Look at the leaves. Aren't they lovely?"

The ground is covered with leaves: orange, yellow, red, brown. Our feet make noise when we walk. She holds my arm so the ground won't make me fall. We walk slow. We go all the way to the fence. We turn around.

"I love this time of year," she says.

She's so pretty. When the sun goes down and comes back up, it's her birthday. I'm making a picture for her birthday. Sam's making a chocolate cake, but I can't tell. It's a secret. I like chocolate cake. I like chocolate pudding. The leaves run around and around. Some of the leaves are the color of her hair. I like those leaves best. When I touch her hair, she smiles at me. Then she holds my hand.

"Oh, your hand's chilly. Are you cold, Eleanor? Do you want to go back?"

We walk again. The wind blows. The leaves run back and forth in front of me. I try to step on them. Some of them jump up in the air. I look up at the sun. It's bright. I close my eyes, but I still see it. The wind blows hard. The leaves dance. I hold out my hands to catch them. They run out of my hands. They fall back on the ground. She laughs. I stop walking to put my arms around her. I hug her and hug her. All around us, the wind blows. The sun shines. The leaves dance and sing.

"Yes, that's her. She's singing a song for me," says the Uniform Man into the phone. "At first, when she kept hitting him, he thought she was drunk. But then he saw the bracelet and called us. So she's safe and sound."

The Uniform Man is sitting on the end of his table. I'm sitting in the chair. This table has lots and lots of drawers. I like drawers: I like to fold. I'm a good folder. I open the drawer. There's no clothes to fold. There's paper. I pull it out. The Uniform Man reaches over. He takes it out of my hand. He hides the paper. He puts new paper in front of me. I fold it.

"Oh, she knew we were the police, all right," says the Uniform Man. "As soon as we pulled up, she ran right over to us. She was more than happy to get into the cruiser. She wanted us to arrest the guy who found her."

The paper is folded. Now I want to make something on it. I look in the drawer. There's no pencil in the drawer. There's some stretchy brown circles. There's some sharp silver things. There's two bracelets hooked together. I like bracelets. I take them out. The Uniform Man leans over. He touches the bracelets: they open. I put one bracelet on. I put the other bracelet on. When I move my arm, the bracelets fall off. The Uniform Man picks the bracelets up. He puts them both on one arm. He pinches them. They don't fall off. Now I have lots of bracelets. They're pretty. I look for the pencil. I move all the little cards. I move the little white bottles. I move the flat stick with marks on it. No pencils. I look at the Uniform Man. He opens a different drawer. He takes out a yellow and green box. He empties it next to the paper. Crayons. I like crayons. I pick up red. I like red best. I make red on the paper. I make yellow. I put the yellow and the red down. I pick up the one that's like green, but not green. I make a flower. The bracelets make pretty noise. I show the Uniform Man the flower. He smiles. He pats me on the head.

"Just ask for Officer Jenkins. No, no problem at all. She hasn't caused us a bit of trouble," he says. "She's as good as gold. Just like an angel."

She wears a sparkly gold heart pin. That's good. That helps me remember she's Marie. I like Marie. She talks slow. She talks words I know. Claudia kisses me on the cheek. Sam kisses me on the cheek. Claudia and Sam go away. Me and Marie stay. She has a big purse with lots of surprises: candy, popcorn, movies in a black box. Marie sits next to me on the couch. We turn off all the lights. We take our shoes off. We make our feet go on the couch. We cover up with blankets. Marie makes the movie in the black box go on. We watch the movie. We eat popcorn. We eat candy. Sometimes Marie holds my hand. I like that. Sometimes she hugs me. I like that, too. I sit close to Marie. When something bad happens in the movie, she cries. When something good happens, she laughs. When Marie cries, I hug her and hug her. When she laughs, I laugh, too. I sit so close that my leg touches hers. Marie likes that. She puts her arm around my shoulders. I hold her hand. She kisses me on the cheek: I like that most of all.

He holds out his hand in front of her. His hand is closed.

"Hit this," he says.

She makes her hand go closed. She hits his hand. His arm goes all the way around without stopping. His closed hand hits her on the top of her head. She makes her hands go up and down her face real fast. Her feet and legs dance around. But she doesn't go anywhere.

"Whoop-whoop-whoop-whoop-whoop," she says.

He makes his two fingers stick out. They go near her face. She puts her hand up fast. His fingers hit her hand.

"N'yuk-n'yuk-n'yuk," she says.

"Why, you . . ." he says, and her legs dance fast without going anywhere.

"Whoop-whoop-whoop-whoop-whoop," she says.

He hits her on the top of her head again.

"Boink," he says.

She doesn't cry. She makes her hand go flat on her hair. She moves it up and down. Like she's waving. Only on top of her head.

"N'yaah-aah-aah," she says.

"We're getting nowhere fast," he says.

There's only two of them. Not three. They're not pudgy and fat. But they do it good. They do it real good. They do it over and over. They never get hurt. They never cry. It's just like the movies. I laugh and laugh and laugh.

She's crying. She's sitting on the bed. He sits next to her. He puts his arms around her. I'm in the hall. Near the doorway.

"It's not too late," he says. "We'll just have to keep trying."

Her hands cover her face.

"The other day I read about a woman who had a baby at age forty-eight," he says. "That gives us plenty of time."

His hand goes back and forth on her hair.

"You know, I've been thinking about what you said, about what Roger and Eve said. Maybe we should start looking into a home for Mom. I'm not saying that just to make you stop crying. I mean it. With Mom in a home, you'll have enough time and energy to run the bookstore again and to take care of a baby. In fact, I'll bet once Mom's in a home, you'll be pregnant in no time. Please don't cry, honey. This is no way to spend your birthday."

She doesn't stop crying. She doesn't uncover her face. His hand goes on her hair.

"We could always adopt," he says, and she cries even harder.

Martha cries when I hit her, and Angie comes. She takes the box from Martha. She gives me the box.

"Eleanor's the boss of the ornaments, okay?" says Angie. "And Eleanor, no more hitting."

"No snowflakes on the tree," I say.

"Martha can put snowflakes on the tree if she wants to," says Angie. "Now, no more hitting, Eleanor, or you can't be the boss of the ornaments."

Angie goes back to the snowflakes. Claudia comes. She stands by Gaby and Deedee at the desk. Gaby points to the tree. Claudia looks around and smiles at me. She waves her hand for me to come over. I take the box with me.

"We have an appointment with Dr. Judith," she says. "What's in the box?"

"Eleanor's in charge of the ornaments," says Deedee. "Without her, we can't do the tree right."

"How much is left?" says Claudia.

I show her the box. She shows me the clock on her arm. She points to it.

"When the hand gets to here, we have to leave," she says.

I go back to the tree. Martha holds out her hand. I give her the red one with white glitter. She puts it on the tree. Angie is hanging snowflakes. Only Angie or Deedee or Gaby can hang snowflakes. Angie stands on a chair. Dick holds the chair for her. John holds the snowflakes. There are some snowflakes on the tree, too. Martha put them there. Snowflakes don't go on the tree. Martha holds out her hand again. I give her the white one. Martha goes to the other side. I take the snowflakes off the tree. I drop them on the floor, under the tree. Bill comes over to me. He looks in the box. He points to the shiny green one. I give it to him.

God rest ye merry gentlemen;
Let nothing you dismay.
Remember Christ our Savior
Was born on Christmas day
To save us all from Satan's power
When we were gone astray.

Claudia moves her hand again. She points to her clock. I go over. Martha goes with me. Claudia looks in the box: it's empty. I give the box to Deedee. Martha stands real close to Deedee. Martha sings. Claudia gets my coat.

From God our heavenly Father
A blessèd angel came
And unto certain shepherds
Brought tidings of the same
How that in Bethlehem was born
The Son of God by name.

Martha sings. I sing. I love singing. I love the tree. I love snowflakes, too. But not on the tree. Claudia has my coat. She does the buttons. Angie gets down off the chair. She comes over to the desk. Dick keeps on holding the chair. Dick holds chairs good. Deedee gives Angie more string. Before Angie gets on the chair again, the record stops. Angie goes over to the record. She makes it sing again. Angie goes back to the chair. Dick holds her hand when she gets up on it. Angie hangs up more snowflakes.

The shepherds at those tidings
Rejoicèd much in mind
And left their flocks a-feeding
In tempest, storm, and wind,
And went to Bethlehem's great way
The Son of God to find.

"Mittens," says Claudia.

I hold out my hands. Claudia makes my hands go in. She puts my hat on. She makes the blanket-thing go around and around my neck. We say good-bye to Angie and Gaby and Deedee. We say good-bye to Martha and John and Bill and Dick. I go with Claudia to the car. I sing.

> Oh, tidings of comfort and joy,
> Comfort and joy,
> Oh, tidings of comfort and joy.

"You did a good job with the tree," says Claudia. "I'm so proud of you."

"I love singing with Mitch," I say.

"Which one's Mitch?" says Claudia.

Which one's mine? Where is it? I don't see it anywhere. Someone moved it. I walk up and down the sidewalk. It's dark out here. It's cold. I don't have a coat. I don't have a sweater. I rub my hands on my arms. I cross the street. No, my house isn't there either. I cross the street again. Why did Harold let them take our house away? I look for that church-thing, but I can't see it anywhere. It's too dark. I walk back and forth, back and forth.

"Hey, lady, you lost?"

I turn around. Who is this man? I don't know him. He's not Harold. He's not Sam. My heart goes fast.

"Hey, what're you doing?" he says. "Don't run away."

He catches me. He holds on to my arm. He won't let go. He pulls me toward a house. It's not my house. My heart goes faster. He pulls on my arm.

"Just come up on the porch under the light for a second," he says.

He touches my bracelet. He turns it around. I have to stop him. Without my bracelet, I can't get home.

"Just lemme see what this says. Ow. What'd you go and do that for?

Hey, watch it," he says. "I ain't gonna hurt you. I just wanna read it. Hey, cut it out."

He's not Harold. This isn't my house. I have to get away from him. My heart hurts. My arm hurts. I push at the man. I can't take my bracelet off: Claudia says so. The man bends closer to my bracelet. He turns it around.

"Yeah, this is just like Dad's," he says. "'Memory-impaired. To help Eleanor, call 1-800 . . .' Hey, don't do that. Come on, now, Eleanor."

How does he know my name? Why is he saying bad things about me? My head goes around and around without moving. There's a funny noise in my ears. I can't breathe. He pulls on my arm as he goes toward his front door. This isn't my house.

"Hey, come on," he says. "Quit hitting, willya? I just wanna go inside and call somebody to take you home. You wanna go home, don't ya, Eleanor? Hey, cut it out. Eleanor, quit hitting. Don't you wanna go home?"

I scream until someone comes to help me.

CHAPTER SIX

It's nice when Claudia helps me. Sam puts on too much powder. And he doesn't do the right lipstick. But Claudia does it good. She's sitting next to me. I can see both of us in the mirror. Claudia smiles at me and pats my cheek.

"Do this side now," she says. "Put some powder over here."

I do what she tells me. Claudia's good. She makes mashed potatoes with gravy. She walks with me outside. She tells me stories about lots of mothers. Claudia takes the powder brush out of my hand. She puts it on the table. She opens the lipstick. Yes. It's the right one. Sam doesn't do the right one, but Claudia does. I hold out my hand. She puts the lipstick in it. She closes the powder. Something's wrong with the lipstick. I hold it as hard as I can, but it keeps on shaking. It shakes so much, I call Claudia, and she puts her hand on mine.

"Here, I'll do it for you."

She turns my face toward hers. She touches my mouth with her fingers.

"Open," she says.

I make my mouth like hers. She puts the lipstick on for me. Then she turns me back around to the mirror.

"There you go," she says. "You look beautiful."

The lipstick is good. It's my best color. Harold likes it, too, but I don't know where Harold is. I can't find him. I go closer to the mirror. There's not enough black on my eyes. And somebody spilled baby powder on my hair. I move my hand over my hair, to get the powder off. Claudia picks up the brush. She brushes my hair. The powder doesn't come off, but it feels good when Claudia brushes it. She does it just like Harold. Where is Harold? Will he like my hair? I close my eyes. Claudia brushes and brushes. Then she stops and puts the brush down on the table, next to the powder and lipstick.

"There," she says. "How's that?"

She puts her face next to mine. Now both our faces are in the mirror. I look at the two of us. She doesn't look like me, but she's my daughter. My Claudia. She makes me so happy, I put my arms around her and kiss her.

I follow my Claudia all around. She's taping cards on the doors of all the rooms. The cards have words written on them. I go over to see what they say. "Bathroom," says the first card. I open the door: yes, it's the bathroom. "Sam's and Claudia's Room," says the next one, and it's right, too. "Exercise Room," says the next. Yes, the bike with no wheels and the walking-thing are there. 🛑 says the sign on the next door, so I don't open it, but I look out the window. I can see the backyard. The very last sign says, "Eleanor's Room." I open the door. Yes, it is my room. My bedspread is on the bed, and my curtains are at the window. Claudia smiles at me.

"Now you won't get lost," she says.

My house is lost. I have to find it. The door is open, so I go out. It's cold out here, but it's not dark yet. I go down the steps, through the yard, to the sidewalk. I look up and down the street. I look all around, at all the houses. Which way is my house? Far away, over the roof of one house, I see a church-thing that sticks up in the air. My house is near a church. I can walk to the church from my house. If I can get to that church-thing, I can get back to my house. It's cold on my arms, but I don't care. I want to go home. I walk toward that big church-thing in the air. I walk and walk. I'm going home.

"I want to go home," I say.

"You are home, Eleanor," she says. "You live with us now. Remember?"

No, my kitchen has a round table, with chair cushions that match the curtains, and flowers on the table. This is not my house. She cuts the white thing in her hand and drops the pieces into the pot in front of her. There's water in the pot, and sometimes it splashes when she drops the white things in. I go to the cupboard and open it. These dishes have strawberries on them. My dishes have silver on the edges and tiny white flowers. My wedding dishes have gold on them. This is not my house.

"Take me home," I say.

"Oh, Eleanor. Please don't start this today," she says. "I'm really not in the mood for it."

She stands up, picks up the pot, and takes it to the thing that has fire. I follow her. She turns a black circle on the front, and fire jumps up around the pot. I'm not allowed to do fire. Fire is hot. She opens the white door and cold air comes out. The cold air hits my arms and legs. I shiver. She pulls something out and closes the white door. She goes to the sink and turns on the water. I follow her over to the sink. She opens one of the doors by her head and takes out a bowl. I look at it. No little white flowers, no silver edge, no gold edge: just more strawberries. No, this isn't my house. She puts something in the bowl. She turns off the water. I'm behind her. When she's not looking at me, she can't hear me. I touch her arm so she turns around.

"Take me home," I say.

"You are home, Eleanor. God, how many times I have to say it?"

"Take me home."

"You're going to drive me crazy, you know that, Eleanor?"

"Take me home."

"I'll tell you what, Eleanor: as soon as Sam gets here, he'll take you home, okay? Would you like that? Now why don't you be good and go sit in the living room while I finish dinner?"

Who's Sam? Does he know where I live? I look around the room for Sam. I don't see any Sam. There's no one but her and me. She's not Sam, is she? Am I Sam? She takes my arm and makes me go to the other room. She sits me down in a chair by the window. I put my purse on the floor by the chair. This isn't my chair. That's not my couch either. I look at the floor. There's no carpet here. There's wood on the floor. There's a rug in front of the blue couch, but it's not my rug. Whose house is this? She turns my head so I look out the window. There's a tree in the front yard. I don't see any Sam. Is he hiding behind the tree? I move my head, to see Sam behind the tree, but I don't see anyone at all. Nobody's there. No Sam, no Harold, nobody. I look down at my purse. Yes, it's still there. Outside there's nobody. Just the tree and the street. I turn around.

"Take me home," I say, but I'm all alone.

I can do it by myself. No one has to help me. I open the dresser drawer. The clothes are just thrown in. That's not good. I take all the clothes out of the drawer and pile them on top of the dresser. Then I pick up one thing at a time and fold it. I fold very careful, so it's done right. I fold a pair of panties as small as I can. Then I put the panties back into the drawer. I press them against the front and side of the drawer so they'll stay neat. Then I pick up the next panties to fold. While I'm folding, Claudia comes into the room. She has her bathrobe on, and her hair is all wet. I never go around with wet hair, but sometimes Claudia does. She doesn't say anything. She just rubs the towel on her head and watches me fold. After I finish all the panties, I fold the bras. They're hard to fold. Those straps and hook-things don't want to stay folded with the rest of the bra. They want to fall all over the drawer. It's hard work, but I finally get all the bras folded. When I pick up a nightgown, Claudia comes over to me. She holds out the towel to me.

"Eleanor, could you fold this for me?" she says.

She knows I'm a good folder. I take the towel from her. She reaches around me, into the open drawer. I have to be careful with the towel. If I don't pay attention, the towel will unfold itself. I do the towel real slow. When Claudia kisses me on the cheek, I look at her. She's not wearing the bathrobe now. She's wearing her bra and panties. But her hair is still wet. She smiles at me before she pulls her T-shirt over her head. I like Claudia. She tells funny stories about mothers. I put the folded towel on top of the dresser. I fold the nightgown and put it in the top drawer. There, now everything is the way it's supposed to be. I close the top drawer and open the next one.

When the door opens, the Uniform Man comes in the room. I don't know who he is, or how he got in my house. My heart starts to hurt, it's pounding so hard. I look out the window. I see flashing red and blue lights. I scoot closer to the good man, sitting next to me on the bed. I hold him as tight as I can.

"I'm sorry, Roger. She doesn't know what's she's doing."

"I know," says the Uniform Man, coming closer to the bed. "Don't you remember me, Eleanor? I'm Roger. Sam's friend. Claudia's brother. Remember? I broke my arm falling out of the tree house when Sam and I were kids."

I look and look at him. I know Roger, and he's not Roger. He's too old. And his arm's not broken. I hold on to the good man with both hands. He doesn't leave me alone with the Uniform Man. My heart starts to slow down. My stomach is less sick. I look at the good man. His eyes are brown, like Harold's.

"I'm sorry the neighbors called you," he says. "She's never screamed like that before. And she's never broken a window. I just don't know what's gotten into her today."

"No problem. I just wanted to make sure everything was all right, you know?"

"Where's Harold?" I say, and they both look at me.

"Roger's going to go look for Harold, aren't you, Roger?"

"Yes . . . yes, that's what I'm going to do. I'm going to go out and look for . . . Harold. Right now."

I smile at him. I let go of the good man. I lie back on the pillows. The good man pulls the quilt up to my chin. He brushes my hair out of my face. I miss Harold. I wish he'd come home. The good man stands up. He goes with the Uniform Man out of the bedroom. They shut the door. Even though my eyes are closed, I can see the flashing lights outside. I hear them talking to each other in the hallway, but I don't know what they're saying. The Uniform Man will look for Harold. The good man will protect me until then. When Harold comes home, everything will be all right.

Everything's happening just the way it's supposed to. I did it. Now I wait. My arms and legs are cold. I move them, then stop. Maybe I'm supposed to be cold. I stay still, and it gets colder. So this is what it feels like: cold. And there's a noise in my ears. Like the ocean. Like thunder that won't stop. So this is what it sounds like: thunder. And darkness is wrapped around me. I want to see if the darkness is really there in the room with me or just in my head, but I don't open my eyes. If I open my eyes, God will think I changed my mind and call the darkness back. It gets darker and darker. My head feels funny. My stomach doesn't feel good. I keep my eyes closed, but it doesn't help. I sit up and get sick over the side of the bed. My hands slip on the picture frame. Now the darkness is lighter, and the thunder is fainter. Oh, no, is it ruined? Do I have to start again? But when I close my eyes, the darkness and the thunder are still there. I hold the picture of Harold and Sam as I lie back down. Then someone touches me. No. No. Don't. I can't go back. Hands lift me up and pull me. Hands drag me off the bed. My feet touch the ground. No. No. Stop. No one's supposed to be here. Harold's at work. Sam's with Claudia. Go away. Go away. The thunder is too loud. I have to shout, so they'll hear me.

"What'd she say?"

"I don't know. Eleanor, can you hear me?"

"Mom? Can you hear us, Mom?"

One shoves me, and the other one drags me. When they make my feet go across the floor, my eyes open by themselves. It's Harold. Sam's with him. They pull me away from the darkness. They carry me to the car. They put me in the backseat. I punch, I kick, I scream.

Harold gets into the backseat with me. Sam gets in front. He starts the car. Every time the car moves, I get sicker. The darkness changes. The thunder changes. Harold's face is wet on my cheek and neck. I push him away. Now everything will be hard. And it's all his fault.

"Is it hard to do this guided imagery, Sam?" I say.

"Not hard at all, Mom. And this memory-stimulation imagery will keep your memory strong."

"Actually, my memory seems to be all right these days. I haven't forgotten anything lately, have I?"

"Are you sure this'll work?" says Harold. "She never went to college like some people in this family."

"One year of college, and he's never going to forgive me for it. You'd think I was a criminal."

"Don't mind him, Sam," I say, and he sighs.

"Close your eyes, Mom. Now think of a tree with bare branches. Think of those bare branches reaching out to the branches of another tree, right beside it —"

"How are bare tree branches going to help your mother?"

"That's what the nerve endings in the brain look like, Dad. Like bare tree branches. And messages get sent along those branches. They're called dendrites."

"I know what they're called."

"Since when?"

"Don't start with him, Sam," I say. "He's just trying to pick a fight."

"How does this help her memory?" says Harold. "That's all I asked."

"If you don't have lots of branches — dendrites — the information can't go from tree to tree so there isn't a memory. Stroke victims' brains relearn things. . . ."

"Your mother didn't have a stroke."

"This imagery is based on that same concept, Dad."

"I do imagery for my headaches, Harold," says Claudia.

"And you still get headaches."

"Just don't pay any attention to him, Sam," I say. "You know your father's behind the times."

"Close your eyes, Mom," says Sam. "Okay, now image the dendrites in your brain. Picture their branches stretching out toward each other. Image new branches sending your brain's messages around the old, broken, and tangled branches. Picture lots of branches, complex branches, with lots of twigs. Okay? Now image the neuropeptides as raindrops —"

"Raindrops? In her head?" says Harold, and he makes a noise. "Where'd you get this shit anyway?"

"Eve told us about it," says Claudia.

"Eve? Jesus H. Christ. Fairies, moon goddesses, crystals, reincarnation . . . Eve's a hippie, for Christ's sake. No wonder this shit's weird."

"Alternative medicine is not weird, Dad."

"But only people from alternative planets use it, right?"

"Neanderthals don't use it, Dad, if that's what you mean."

"Why, you smart-ass little runt. You think you're the only one who knows anything? Let go of my arm, Eleanor. He does this all the time: reads something in a goddamned book, then thinks he's the only person in the world who knows anything."

"I know a hell of a lot more than you do, Dad."

"You don't know anything. Your mother's not doing any more of this tree crap."

"It's called guided imagery, Dad."

"I don't care what it's called. Your mother's not doing it. Let him go, Eleanor. Claudia can stay if she wants. Fine. Go with him. When he gets down from that mountain he's on and wants to mingle with the rest of us regular folk, you let us know," says Harold as they get into their car, and I grab his arm. "Damn it, Eleanor. Don't you start with me. Hey, watch it. Ow. Jesus, Eleanor, you hit me. I can't believe you hit me. What the hell's gotten into you?"

"Hey, watch what you're doing," he says. "Careful: you're gonna hit the curb."

Stupid man. He's trying to make me have an accident when I'm trying to park. I hold the wheel tight and step on the gas. The car bumps up over something. The man curses and jumps out of the way.

"You almost hit me," he says. "Whatsa matter with you? Didn't you hear me tell you to watch out?"

I turn the wheel and take my foot off the brake. I put my foot on the gas. The car goes back down on that side. I turn the steering wheel. I step on the gas. There's a funny noise. The car stops.

"Jesus, look what you did. Somebody oughta call the cops. You did that on purpose."

I put the car in reverse. I turn the wheel the other way. The car goes up in the back.

"What're you doing?" he says. "You trying to kill somebody now, or you just wanna hit some cars? Ain't it enough hitting a . . . Jesus, stop that, you stupid old broad."

He comes around the car. He comes over to my window. He's an ugly man. He has hair all over his face. He has a baseball cap on backwards. Stupid man. He puts his head and arm in through the open window. Oh, no, he's one of those carjacker men. I hear about them on the news. I'm not going to let him carjack me.

"Hey, cut it out. Stop that, you crazy old dame."

"Hey, man, you need some help?" says a boy who runs up to him.

The carjacker-man grabs the keys and pulls them out. He goes back to the sidewalk and stands there, holding my keys, next to the boy. The front of my car is in the street. The back is up on the sidewalk. He won't let me fix it. The ugly man and the boy both stare at me.

"So, is she, like, drunk or something?" says the boy.

"Crazy, more like it," says the man. "You know what beats it all? I told her, 'Be careful.' I didn't have to say nothing to her, but I said, 'Watch out. You're gonna hit the curb.' So what does she do? Goes right up over the curb and plows into the mailbox anyway."

"So, like, whatdya think happens when you smash a mailbox like that?"

"If I was the post office, I'd make her buy the city a new one, you know? They ain't gonna be able to fix that one."

"Man, if she did that to my car, like, I'd be looking for a baseball bat or something."

"Stupid old cow," says the man, and he kicks my tire. "That's what you get for trying to be nice to people."

"Yeah, man, like, old people shouldn't drive, you know? Half of 'em are blind, and the other half, like, never take their damn foot off the brake, you know?"

"Post office sure ain't gonna like what she done to that box."

"Think she's got insurance?"

"She probably ain't even got a license."

He's a bad, ugly carjacker-man. He's a stupid, dirty boy. I put my hand on the horn, to make the police come. The man and the boy both jump.

"Shit," says the boy.

"Crazy old bat. They oughta lock her up."

"Yeah, and like, throw away the key."

I put the key in the box. I open it. Yes, they're still there. I unfold the first one.

> *To my Family, my Physician, my Lawyer, my Clergy; To any Medical Facility in whose care I happen to be; To any individual who may become responsible for my health, welfare, or affairs . . .*

I close the box. I put it under the bed. I keep the key in my hand. I don't let go.

Lois' hand is in mine. Her eyes are closed. The house is quiet: Fred's fishing with Harold. I'm alone with Lois. Her breathing is noisy and loud, but I don't let go of her hand. I hold it as hard as I can. No one loves Lois as much as I do. All afternoon, I wait, holding her hand. Until it's finished. When the sun is starting to go behind the trees, Fred and Harold come home. I hear the car when it pulls into the driveway. I hear them laughing when they come into the house. Lois doesn't move or open her eyes. The room is quiet. There's no sound at all. It's all over. I let go of her hand. God understands.

CHAPTER SEVEN

Non nobis, Domine, non nobis:
sed nomini tuo da gloriam.

(Not unto us, O Lord, not unto us:
but unto Your name give the glory.)

THE PRIEST'S SAYING IT WRONG. He doesn't do Mass very good. Everyone else is saying it like the priest. What's wrong with them? Don't all churches use the same words? Lucky for them I'm here today. I pray louder, so they'll say it right.

Os habant, et non loquentur:
oculos habent, et non videbunt.

(They have mouths, and speak not:
They have eyes, and see not.)

The man near me gives me a funny look before he moves away, all the way down to the other end of the pew. When the two old women in front of me turn around to look at me, I smile at them. They don't smile back. I pray louder.

Benedictus Deus,
et Pater Domini nostri Jesu Christi,
Pater misericordiarum,
et Deus totius consolationis,
qui consolatur nos
in omni tribulatione nostra.

(Blessèd be God,
the Father of our Lord Jesus Christ,
the Father of mercies,
and God of all consolations,
who comforts us
in all our tribulations.)

After the two women in front of me turn around again and give me a mean look, they pick up their purses and go to a pew across the aisle. The priest prays louder, but he's still not saying it right. Those two women keep giving me looks.

Non mortui laudabunt te, Domine:
neque omnes, qui descendunt in infernum.
Sed nos qui vivimus, benedicimus Domino:
ex hoc nunc, et usque in sæculum.
Gloria Patri, et Filio, et Spiritui Sancto.

(The dead shall not praise You, O Lord:
neither shall they that go down into hell.
But we who live bless the Lord:
from this time forth and for evermore.
Glory be to the Father, to the Son, and to the Holy Spirit.)

Someone behind me laughs. I turn around. When the mother pushes on the little boy's shoulder, he puts his hand over his mouth. I turn back around. The prayer book is shaking in my hands. I sit down. My prayer book slides off my lap. I feel cold and sweaty at the same time. The little boy behind me laughs and laughs. My God, what's happening to me?

"What's going on, Eleanor?" says Claudia, over the phone. "Is everything all right?

"Of course, dear," I say. "Why do you ask?"

"We were supposed to have lunch today, and when you didn't show up . . ."

"Lunch?"

"Wednesday? At D'Amico's?" she says. "This is Wednesday, isn't it?"

My heart starts to beat fast. I look at the calendar hanging by the phone. What day is it today? Is it Wednesday? Which square is Wednesday? I stare at the calendar hard, but I still don't know what day it is.

"Oh, dear," I say. "I wrote down that . . . that we were having lunch on . . . Thursday."

"Thursday?"

"Yes, here it is, in black and white: lunch with Claudia. At D'Amico's."

"I thought we were having lunch today," she says.

"I'm sure you're right, dear. I must've written it down on the wrong day. I'm so sorry. Do you want me to come down now?"

In the background I can hear the clatter of dishes and the faint noise of traffic. Why doesn't she say anything? Doesn't she believe me?

"I have to get back to the bookstore," she says.

"I'm sorry, Claudia."

I listen to the sound of the dishes and the traffic until she says good-bye. Then we hang up. I hit myself in the head with my hand: I'm so stupid. There's nothing written on the calendar. Not on any of the Wednesdays, or any of the Thursdays, or any of the other days. But I do remember: we said we'd have lunch at D'Amico's. No, that's not right. I was the one who invited Claudia to lunch. I was the one who said, "Let's have lunch at D'Amico's this Wednesday." How did I forget something like that? Why didn't I write it down? Poor

Claudia went all the way over to D'Amico's, and I forgot the whole thing. Stupid, Eleanor, stupid. And it's my fault for not writing it down. Harold keeps reminding me that we're both getting older. He keeps telling me to write things down so I won't forget that I'm supposed to have lunch with Claudia, or that I invited Lois and Fred over for dinner, or that the phone rang for Harold when he was in the yard. Yes, I'll write everything down, and then I won't forget. That's all I need to do. Then everything will be fine.

"Everything will be fine, Lois. I'm here now. Don't worry. What? No, Fred's not here. Harold took him down to the cafeteria. Shhh, it's all right, dear. No, I didn't forget. Here, let me close the door. All right. I promised you that if you had another stroke . . . I remember. Now, Lois, I just want to be sure. Blink if you want me to keep my promise. All right, dear. Calm down. But I can't do it here. You know that. I have to wait till you get home. No, Fred's not going to put you in a home. I won't let him. I love you, Lois. And I'll keep my promise. Just as soon as things calm down. As soon as you're home. Oh, Lois, I don't mean to cry. But you've been my best friend since the second grade, and I can't imagine my life without you. No, don't worry. I couldn't let you spend the rest of your life like this. You know I couldn't. I love you too much. And I'd never forget my promise."

"I haven't forgotten anything since . . . oh, in ages and ages," I say as the nurse sits down across the table from me. "I haven't been sleeping well, but other than that, I'm fine. I really don't know why I need all these tests."

"We just want to make sure that everything's fine, Mrs. Sloane. Is that all right with you?"

"I suppose. Is the test hard?"

"Not hard at all, Mrs. Sloane. Let's see, could you tell me what year you were born?"

"Oh, long before you, dear."

"Can you tell me what year, Mrs. Sloane?"

"Nineteen hundred and . . . twenty. I think it was a little after three in the afternoon."

"Could you count for me, Mrs. Sloane? Backwards, from twenty, by twos."

"Backwards? Let's see: twenty, eighteen, sixteen, fourteen, twelve, ten-nine-eight-seven-six-five-four-three-two-one-zero. I really don't understand why I have to take all these tests. I'm just a little tired these days."

"Can you do these problems for me?" says the nurse.

"I was never very good at math."

"Just try."

$$24 + 37 + 12 = 73$$
$$(6 \times 5) - 2 = 38$$
$$(3 \times 15) + 5 = 40$$
$$(5 \times 2) + (3 \times 3) = 16$$
$$13 + 12 + 9 = 34$$

"Do you know what year this is?" says the nurse.

"Doesn't everybody?"

"Who's the president?"

"Of the United States?"

"Yes, of the United States."

"Nobody I voted for, I can tell you that. I'm so sorry we're wasting your time, dear."

"You're not wasting my time at all, Mrs. Sloane," she says as she holds up a pencil. "Do you know what this is?"

"Pencil."

"And this?"

"Bracelet. Oh, no, I'm sorry. It's a clock. Your sleeve was over it: I didn't see it right."

"I'm going to draw something," says the nurse. "There. Can you draw one just like it for me? Okay. Now, I'll turn the paper over. Can you draw that from memory? Thank you. Now, look at this picture, Mrs. Sloane."

In the picture, a young girl is rocking her doll in a cradle. Beside the girl, a puppy and a kitten are asleep on the floor, curled together in a pile. Outside the window, a boy in a red snowsuit throws snowballs at a crooked snowman.

"Can you tell me a story about what's happening in this picture, Mrs. Sloane?"

"Oh, yes. I mean, it won't be a very good story. I've never been very good at telling stories. My son's wife, Claudia, now she tells the most wonderful stories. But I'll try. Let's see: Once upon a time . . . is it all right if I start like that? Okay, once upon a time, there was a beautiful young princess who lived in a castle with her baby, her cat, and her dog. The little princess was so upset. You see, the wicked old witch wanted to take her baby away, and the princess didn't know what to do. Of course, the princess really needs a husband if she has a baby. When I was young, there was this girl who was going to have a baby, and everybody knew she didn't have a fiancé or even a proper boyfriend. It was so sad. One day she went away pregnant and the next day she came back not pregnant but without any baby. Everybody knew she'd had an abortion. She was lucky she didn't die. Lots of girls died from those operations back then, you know. I'd never do anything like that. Not with all the couples in the world who want babies. My son and his wife are trying to have a baby. Poor Claudia, she keeps getting pregnant, but she keeps losing them. It's so sad, but the doctors say there's nothing they can do. Can you believe that? With all the technology and medicine we have today, they can't do a thing."

"Can't . . . no," says Lois. "No . . ."

"You got better after the other strokes," I say. "You'll get better after this one, too."

"Not . . . not . . ."

"This stroke is just a little bigger than the others, that's all. Fred and I will both help, you'll see. You'll be back to your old self in no time."

Lois opens and closes her right eye. She moves her mouth, but only on the right side. Her nails dig into my hand.

"Try to rest now, Lois. You can tell me later. When you're stronger."

"No . . . home . . . no . . ."

I sit down by the bed. No one is in the room with me and Lois. Fred is with Harold. I wipe away the drool that comes out of the corner of Lois' mouth.

"Shhh. Don't worry, Lois. Fred won't put you in a home. The doctor says it's just another stroke. And not a very big one. After some physical therapy and some medicine, why, you'll be good as new, you'll see. Shhh. Hush now. You need to rest, dear. Otherwise, you won't get better. Shhh. Don't worry: you won't end up like your father. I swear, I won't let you."

"I swear, Harold. I paid the phone bill."

"Then what's this disconnect notice for?"

"I distinctly remember writing out the check for . . ."

Harold crosses the room, picks up my purse, and opens the checkbook.

"Here's an entry for check 5306, Eleanor," he says. "And here's one for 5315, but there's nothing in between."

"I must have written them down somewhere else."

"Damn it, Eleanor, I don't ask much of you. Put that damn magazine down and find these checks for me."

"I know I wrote them down, Harold, and I know I paid the phone bill. Give me the purse. What are you doing home in the middle of the day anyway? Did something happen on the site, or did you just decide to come home and start an argument? Look: here they are, Harold. Just like I told you. Checks 5307, 5308, and 5309. Are you happy now?"

"You wrote them on a napkin? Why did you write them on a nap-

177

kin? Where are you going? We still need the record of checks 5310 to 5314."

"My other purse is upstairs."

"Go get it."

"You go get it, Harold."

"God damn it, Eleanor. That's it. I've had it. I'm taking the checkbook away from you. And I'm taking your car keys."

"What do the car keys have to do with the checkbook?"

"If you can't handle the checkbook, you can't drive."

"I do everything in this house, Harold: all the shopping and the cleaning and the cooking. And I know I paid the phone bill. So don't you dare talk to me like I'm a child."

All of the sudden, a picture comes into my head. A terrible picture. A picture of an envelope addressed to the phone company, with a stamp on it, all ready to go in the mail, but still sitting in my red purse upstairs. No, it can't be. I put that envelope in the mail ages ago. I'm remembering wrong. But if Harold opens my purse and the envelope is there . . . I get up and go to the stairs. Something must have interrupted me when I was going to the mailbox. Something about Sam's and Claudia's wedding, or Claudia's engagement party. Harold will be furious if he finds that phone bill. I'll write myself a note and put it in the checkbook. And when I do the bills, I'll mail them right away. First, though, I have to get to that envelope in my purse. So Harold won't see it.

I get to look at him whenever I want. I go over to the bassinet to see him. He's so beautiful. I cover him with the blanket and tuck it all around him. I stand there, listening to the sound of his breathing. I pull the rocker close so I can sit there and watch him. He makes a noise in his sleep. I put my hand on his back. I sing to him, softly, my mother's song.

Sleep, my love, and peace attend thee,
All through the night.

Guardian angels God will lend thee,
All through the night.

It's like a dream, having him here. I lean over my baby, so I can breathe the very same air he breathes. My lips brush his tiny hand.

Angels watching ever 'round thee,
All through the night.
In the slumbers close surround thee,
All through the night.

I stay beside him for hours. I put my fingers by his nose and mouth, to feel his breath. I press my ear to his back, to hear his heart. I sit back down. My fingers touch the top of his head softly, so softly. He sighs in his sleep. Then he smiles. Yes, my darling, have sweet dreams. Sweet, beautiful dreams for Sam. My sweet, belovèd gift from God.

They should of all fears disarm thee,
No foreboding should alarm thee,
They will let no peril harm thee,
All through the night.

Sam

Give me where to stand,
and I will move the earth.

Archimedes

CHAPTER ONE

𝓜Y WIFE DIDN'T KILL MY MOTHER. Jesus, what does it take for people to get the picture in focus? Every time Harlan Graham gets on his soapbox, every newspaper in the area starts running articles about Claudia's trial. That's why we moved here in the first place — to get away from it all — but it keeps following us. It's over. It's in the past. We've paid for what happened, and we shouldn't have to keep going through this for the rest of our lives. If the reporters had watched the tapes of the trial and read the transcripts, they wouldn't be writing the type of articles they've been printing about Claudia. For Christ's sake — why don't they just let it go? My wife is innocent. She did not kill my mother. It's Harlan Graham's fault that it keeps coming back up. If he weren't in politics, no one would remember us. God, I hate that man. He's had a God complex ever since he was the district attorney at Claudia's trial.

The way he pranced around in the courtroom, wearing those shiny suits and wing tips. I never saw a man with as many clothes as Graham had. And matching handkerchiefs and ties — Christ. What was he, a lawyer or a fancy-boy, that's what I used to wonder. Every time he opened his mouth in court, I wanted to twist those matching ties and hankies around his bony little neck.

"Claudia Sloane doesn't look like a murderer," said Graham in his opening statement. "She doesn't look cold-blooded or evil. In fact, the defense is going to tell you how the defendant sacrificed her own life to take care of her terminally ill mother-in-law. But the state will prove that the defendant planned this murder with great deliberation. The testimony will establish that on the day of the murder, the defendant's husband went out of town on business and wouldn't be back for several days. The evidence will prove that the defendant took a gallon-sized plastic bag and crushed all the deceased's medications — toxic levels of prescription medication — and force-fed them to a helpless woman, giving her an overdose that resulted in Eleanor Sloane's death. Then the defendant had the body cremated, despite the fact that a burial plot had already been bought and paid for. Testimony from the police will show that she scattered the ashes so they couldn't be recovered. All of this, ladies and gentlemen, Claudia Sloane did to cover up her heinous crime.

"But the defendant made mistakes, ladies and gentlemen," he said as he leaned on the podium to look at the jury. "The police discovered the empty medication bottles and the plastic bag that Claudia Sloane used to crush the pills. Testimony from investigators and police will establish that the defendant's business, BookLovers, and the family business, Sloane and Son Construction, were both being bankrupted by Eleanor Sloane's illness. All the life insurance policies had already been cashed to pay for visiting nurses. The evidence will show that the money was running out, so the defendant determined to put an end to it. The evidence will show that the defendant, Claudia Sloane, murdered her mother-in-law.

"She waited to commit her crime until her husband was going out of town on business," said Graham. "Then she crushed all the bottles of prescription medication, mixed them with some chocolate pudding, and fed that toxic pudding to her mother-in-law. We'll present witnesses whose testimony will show you Claudia Sloane's state of mind in the months preceding the death. The police will testify that the defendant told them that Eleanor Sloane had a difficult time breathing before her death. Police Detective Mitchell will tell you that Claudia Sloane, by her own admission, did not call for help while her mother-in-law was struggling for breath. Police and paramedics who responded to the 9-1-1 call will testify that Claudia Sloane showed no emotion whatsoever when they were unable to revive the victim. You'll hear the 9-1-1 call that the defendant made. You'll hear her tell the police dispatcher that her mother-in-law has died — not that there's something wrong with her breathing or that she needs help — but that she's dead. We'll show you that Claudia Sloane had the motive, the means, and the opportunity. We'll prove her guilty beyond a reasonable doubt, ladies and gentlemen, then we'll ask you to dispense justice."

Graham didn't care who was on that stand, as long as somebody got punished for my mom's death. Hell, he would've put me on trial if I hadn't been out of town on a job. I was supposed to stay at the job site for another week, but I left as soon as I got the news. I didn't even go back to my motel room. I just grabbed my keys and headed for the truck. The sun was already starting to come up the next morning by the time I made it home. The house was dark, but Claudia wasn't in bed. She wasn't in the bathroom or the living room or the kitchen. My chest started to feel like a safe got dropped on it. But then I found her. In Mom's room, on the bed. She had all the pillows hugged to her chest, and her back toward the door. She didn't move when I turned on the light. She didn't move when I sat on the bed beside her. When I touched her shoulder, she let out a little sob and covered her face.

"It's all my fault," she said as I lay down behind her.

"No," I said. "I should've been here with you."

Not that it would've made a damned bit of difference. Once Graham got his teeth into us, somebody had to get mauled, even if it didn't bring my mom back to life. What I never understood is why my mom's death had to be somebody's fault. She had an incurable terminal illness, so she was going to die anyway. I'm not saying we didn't make mistakes. Everybody makes mistakes. Everybody has regrets, too. Nobody needs glasses to look backwards, right? But the first time I thought there was something wrong with Mom, I never thought of that disease. I thought she was just getting old. I thought all old people lost their common sense. Jesus, what did I know?

"What did you lose, Mom?" I said, setting the bags of groceries on the kitchen table.

"You know. That thing I keep my money in."

"Your billfold?"

"No, not that."

"Your purse?"

"That's it. My purse. Could you help me find it, Sam? It'll only take a couple of minutes."

I went into the dining room, looking for her purse, and I heard a strange humming that sounded like it was coming from the walls. As I went up the stairs, that noise got louder.

"What's that noise, Mom?"

"What noise?" she said.

When I pushed open the bathroom door, I found out what it was. She'd left the water running in the tub, and it was pouring over the sides onto the floor. By the time I ran over there and turned it off, there was at least an inch of water on the floor. Then Mom made this little squeal. There was her purse, bobbing around the tub like a damned boat. She grabbed it and shoved her hand around in it, looking for something, with water sloshing all over our feet, and I thought it was a normal part of getting old. But the disease already had her by then. It had her good.

"Eleanor Sloane was terminally ill and in the final stages of her disease," said our lawyer, Tracey, when she addressed the jury for the first time. "She died of pneumonia, brought on by the final stages of

Alzheimer's, and not because of any wrongdoing on the part of my client. In fact, up until a few weeks ago, the cause of death listed on Eleanor Sloane's death certificate was pneumonia. We'll submit a copy of that original death certificate as evidence. The Prosecutor's office altered that death certificate, without a medical inquest, so that it listed drug poisoning as the cause of death, and they did that only to make their case look better. But our testimony will show that the medications in the bottles found by the police were all prescribed by the attending physician, Dr. Barnett, and he'll testify that they were safe when taken as directed. Claudia Sloane used the plastic bag to crush the medications, to make it easier for Eleanor to swallow them, just as she pureed her mother-in-law's food so Eleanor wouldn't choke. Claudia Sloane didn't do anything wrong. In fact, no one besides the police and the prosecutor has ever thought that any crime was committed.

"In the months following Eleanor Sloane's death," said Tracey, "the police and their investigators relentlessly pursued Claudia, but our evidence will show that my client's care of her mother-in-law extended the sick woman's life. My client sacrificed her own career at her bookstore so that she could nurse Eleanor Sloane. The evidence will show that Claudia took on a partner, selling half of BookLovers, so that she could stay home and care for her terminally ill mother-in-law. She and her husband could have put Eleanor Sloane in a nursing home, but they wanted to keep her at home with them, with the family who loved her. Our evidence will show that it is only the circumstances that made the police investigate Claudia Sloane for murder. Our testimony will show that the police misinterpreted innocent events and remarks. They wanted to see murder, so they saw murder. But our evidence, ladies and gentlemen, will prove that Claudia Sloane is innocent."

"Maybe Gina didn't do anything," I said. "Maybe she's an innocent victim."

"You think Roger lied?" said Claudia, closing the apartment door behind her.

"Maybe he just thought he saw her with somebody else."

"Sam, he caught her in bed with the guy. When they raided the party for drugs."

"But she might not have been doing anything. She might've been just taking a nap. Or something."

Claudia put her purse on the counter before she started collecting the empty beer cans.

"Put something on," she said. "You're not decent."

"My bathing suit covers less than this," I said, looking down at my-self.

"How much have you had to drink?"

I got back into the sofa bed and hugged one of the pillows to my chest, watching her. She dumped all the beer cans into the trash, then emptied the trash can into a plastic garbage bag. The empty cans rattled as she knotted the bag and shoved it into the corner by the apartment door.

"You don't think Roger could've made a mistake about Gina? He's been wrong before, you know."

"Get under the covers if you're not going to put any more clothes on."

I pulled the blankets up over me as she went to the sink. She made a face before she forced the half-eaten hamburger and soggy fries into the garbage disposal and turned on the water. She picked up the pizza box.

"Not that," I said. "That's leftovers."

"It's moldy," she said and dumped it into the running disposal.

She threw all the paper plates away, too, then scrubbed the counter and sink. When she finished, she turned around and looked at me, drying her hands on a dishtowel.

"You'd never cheat on me, would you, Claude?"

"I'm not your girlfriend," she said.

"But if you were, you wouldn't screw around on me, would you?"

She came over to the sofa bed, brushing my hair back with her fingers.

"You're going to have a hell of a hangover tomorrow," she said.

I fell back against the pillows, groaning.

"I wish Roger hadn't told me," I said.

"You wouldn't have wanted him to keep something like that from you."

I put the pillow over my head, but it smelled like Gina. I pushed it onto the floor. Claudia picked it up.

"Hey, you wanna sleep over?" I said.

She laughed as she lifted my head and stuffed the pillow under it.

"*Plan 9 from Outer Space* is on. Come on, Claude: let's do a sleep-over, like we used to."

"We're not kids anymore."

"We can put the blankets and pillows on the floor in front of the TV," I said. "We can make popcorn and you can make jokes, just like you always do, and we can . . . we can . . ."

"Oh, Sam," she said, putting her arms around me. "Don't cry."

"I really love her, Claude."

"I know."

"What did I do wrong?"

"You didn't do anything wrong."

"She cheated on me."

"That's just the way some people are. You don't do anything to make them cheat, and you can't do anything to change them."

She lay down on the bed beside me, but on top of the covers, and put her arms around me.

"You love me, don't you, Claude?"

"You know I do."

She held me for a long time. After I was quiet again, she kissed me on the top of the head.

"What would I do without you, Claude?"

"You'll never have to find out," she said.

"But, Marie, what are we going to do without you?" said Claudia. "Who'll sit for Eleanor?"

The sitter took off her hat and handed it to me. I put her coat and hat on the coat tree in the entry hall.

"I'm sorry, Mrs. Sloane. Really, I am," said Marie. "But my son's been transferred to New Mexico. You know I live with him and his family."

"Couldn't you go live with your daughter instead?"

I called upstairs to Mom. Still holding the damp dishtowel, Claudia slumped against the banister. The sitter picked up her needlepoint tote, pulled out the sparkling gold heart, and pinned it on her dress.

"I won't be leaving for six more weeks," said Marie. "That'll give you time to get Eleanor used to someone else from the agency. Here, I wrote down some people I think she'd get along with."

Claudia didn't take the card, so Marie handed it to me. There were three names on the back, but I didn't recognize them. I slipped the card into my pants pocket before I called Mom again.

"I wish you'd waited till we got back from dinner to tell us," said Claudia. "This is our anniversary."

"Marie," said Mom, bouncing down the stairs and slamming into the sitter with a bear hug.

"There's my Eleanor," said Marie, kissing Mom on the cheek as Mom stroked the heart pin. "Wait'll you see what I've got for you tonight. Something special from my garden."

"Oh, Marie," said Mom, a huge grin on her face when she saw the red tulips. "Look, Sam. Look, Claudia."

"Nice flowers," I said. "Say 'thanks, Marie.'"

"Thanks, Marie," said Mom.

"You're welcome, Eleanor. I know how much you like flowers. Let's go into the living room so your son and his wife can get ready. Guess what movie I brought. It's one of your favorites."

They went into the other room, their arms around each other, chattering away like Roger's twins always did. Claudia snapped the wet dishtowel out into the air behind them. She didn't look happy anymore.

"I knew it was too good to be true," she said. "What are we going to do now?"

"We're going out to dinner to celebrate," I said, putting my arm around her shoulders and guiding her back upstairs so we could get dressed. "It's our anniversary, remember?"

What else could we have done? Staying home wouldn't have stopped Marie's son's transfer. Crying and moaning wouldn't have slowed down Mom's disease. We had to live the best we could, didn't we? Still, you'd think we would've been used to loss by then. I mean, we'd already lost Mom to the disease and Dad to the heart attack. What difference did it make if we lost a few more people? Claudia and me, we didn't have anybody but each other. It was me and her against the disease. At least, that's how it felt. And nobody else understood what we'd been through. Even our lawyer didn't at first. I hated Tracey when I first met her. Especially when she asked me about Claudia. But maybe that's what lawyers are supposed to do. Maybe that's why nobody likes them.

"This isn't about bail?" I said.

"No, that's not why I asked you here, Sam," said Tracey. "I have to talk to you about something. Alone."

"You're not saying we can't get the bail lowered, are you? She won't have to stay in jail, will she?"

I sat down. Tracey's office held as many plants as books, so it was like a rain forest or something. Little trees, hanging plants, flowers — all crowded in front of the windows. And the sunlight pouring down through the skylights. I had to take my jacket off and roll up my shirtsleeves, it was so muggy in there. Tracey's bracelets jingled and jangled every time she moved her arms. She folded her hands over her notebook and looked me right in the face.

"I need to be extremely blunt with you, Sam," she said, "and I need you to tell me the truth. No matter what you tell me, it'll never go further than this office, and I'll still give Claudia the best defense I can. But I need to ask you a really tough question, okay?"

I shrugged and nodded.

"Do you think your wife killed your mother?"

CHAPTER TWO

*T*HE PROSECUTION IS GOING TO TELL YOU that Claudia Sloane committed murder," said Tracey as she continued her opening statement, "but we're here to tell you the truth about the facts in this case. Claudia Sloane lives in a small village, where people trust the police. You'll hear how she cooperated with the investigation, allowing detectives to enter her home without a search warrant. She answered their questions fully and honestly. That isn't the behavior of a woman with something to hide. That's the behavior of an innocent person. And what did the police do?"

Tracey moved her arm toward Graham and the detectives sitting behind him. At the table next to Graham, his assistant leaned so far back in his chair, it looked like it'd fall out from under him.

"The police lied to Claudia Sloane," said Tracey. "They purposely misled her, lying about what other people had said during interviews. You'll hear how they tried to coerce Claudia Sloane into a confession of murder, but they didn't get one. You'll hear from Dr. Barnett, the primary physician, who'll describe the progress of Eleanor Sloane's disease and the cause of her death.

"Like a lot of families, the Sloanes suffered under the stress of this devastating terminal illness. At times, they disagreed about courses of action and treatment, as any family might. Yet they always remembered the love and the affection they felt for each other. But their love wasn't as strong as the disease. No one's love could be. Our evidence is the same as the prosecution's, yet you'll see that Claudia Sloane couldn't have committed any crime. You'll see that the police have interpreted the circumstances surrounding Eleanor Sloane's death in the darkest light possible. You can rectify that, though, by finding my client innocent of the crime of which she's accused. You can right the wrong, ladies and gentlemen."

Our lives depended on those words, but by the time the trial was over, words didn't mean a damn thing. You can't live through that disease and think in terms of "right" or "wrong." You only think of one thing when that disease has you by the short hairs — how to survive.

"Hey, what's wrong with you?" said Ace when we got there. "Didn't you hear what we said? We're playing three-on-three, half-court."

"We've got three," I said.

"No, you don't."

"What's Claude — chopped liver?"

"She's a girl."

"She can kick your butt any day of the week," said Roger, bouncing the ball back and forth, back and forth.

"Oooh, I think I just wet my pants, I'm sooo scared," said Ace, snatching the ball away and dribbling it as he talked. "I ain't guarding no girl."

"Watch who you're calling a girl," said Claudia.

He faked a pass, then turned and shot, sending the ball neatly through the net. Roger grabbed the ball and passed it to me while Gun covered Claudia. Ace dropped down in front of me, waving his arms, trying to trap me at the fence.

"Come on, mama's boy," he said, poking and slapping at the ball.

I shoved him with my shoulder and spun to my right, passing the ball to Claudia. She raised up and nailed a jumper — *swish*.

"Who's a girl now?" she said as she moved outside, but Ace ignored her.

Roger knocked the ball out of Hondo's hands, but Gun intercepted his bounce pass. Gun pivoted, but Claudia was right there. He ducked and twisted, faking left and right, but she played him tight. She stole the ball and tipped it to Roger, who scored. We could always depend on Claudia. She never let us down.

"Sit down, Mr. Whitman," said Prosecutor Graham to the first witness, a neighbor from my parents' old neighborhood. "How long did you live next door to the Sloanes?"

"More than twenty years."

"In all that time, did you ever hear Claudia Sloane refer to the deceased, Eleanor Sloane, as 'Mother'?"

"No," said Mr. Whitman.

"When the defendant addressed the deceased, did she call her 'Mom'?"

"No."

"How about 'Mother Sloane' or 'Mom Sloane'?"

"No, I don't remember her ever calling her anything like that."

"Are you telling me, Mr. Whitman, that in all the years the defendant was in the family, she never called Eleanor Sloane 'Mom'?"

"No, sir, to the best of my recollection, she never did."

Graham's story of what happened made everything sound dirty and ugly. He could've made Christ seem guilty. Whenever I turn on the news and see one of Graham's commercials, I want to grab him by the throat and teach him some manners. God, I hope he doesn't get elected. It wouldn't give us back what we lost, but it would sure as hell make me feel he got what he deserved after what he did to us.

"Killing yourself won't make her any better," said Eve.

"It's time to put Eleanor in a home," said Roger.

In the flickering light of the citronella candles, I could see Claudia beside me, but I could hardly see Roger and Eve, sitting across the picnic table from us. Though the windows of their family room were closed, I could hear the video their twins were watching. From Eve's garden, the smell of lavender and geranium, mixed with the citronella, was too strong. Claudia slapped at a mosquito on her bare arm, then pulled her sweater around her shoulders.

"Even if we ignored our promise to Dad and wanted to put Mom in a home — which we don't," I said, "we couldn't afford it."

"You could sell the business," said Roger.

"Dad's business? You can't be serious."

"You could take on a partner, then, so Claudia can go back to work full-time."

"She doesn't want to work full-time, Eve."

"Yes, she does."

"She's never said anything to me about it."

The back door to the house swung open and Eve turned around. One of the twins, holding the phone to her chest, leaned out the door.

"Mom, Matthew wants to know if he can stay with the guys for one more hour."

"Tell him to be home by eleven. No later," said Eve.

The twin repeated Eve's answer into the phone, listened a second, then went back into the house, closing the door behind her. Claudia tore at the edge of her paper plate. Eve relit one of the candles after a breeze blew it out.

"Listen, Sam, money will be a little tight," said Roger, "but Claudia's freedom will be worth it."

"Claudia and I have already discussed this," I said. "I'll be staying home more to help take care of Mom."

"Harold's dead, Sam. You don't have to prove anything anymore."

"Jesus, Roger, she's my mother. You didn't put Grace in a home."

"She didn't have a terminal disease that was killing everyone else in the family."

Claudia began to shred her napkin, dropping pieces onto her cold baked beans. After the back door opened again, Eve cursed under her breath. When the twins saw the look on her face, they closed the door fast. Claudia mixed the napkin shreds into her leftover beans with a fork.

"It's time to put Eleanor in a home," said Roger.

"We love her," I said.

"This isn't about love," said Eve.

If it wasn't about love, then I sure as hell don't know what it was about. Claudia doesn't tell me what she thinks it all meant. She's a very private person, even with me, especially about things like that. Who could blame her, after what happened at the trial? Jesus, the things we got accused of. The names we got called. Claudia says none of that matters now — "a rose by any other name" and all that. But I don't know. If you call somebody a name long enough, does he think of himself like that? Does he ever call himself that name, accidentally, when he's all by himself? Do we become the names other people call us?

"Come on, Stupid-heads," said Claudia. "Open up."

"Not till you say the password."

"I've got popcorn," she said. "Mmmm, it smells so good. Extra butter, extra salt . . ."

Roger opened the bedroom door.

"Hey, Sam," she said, nodding to me after he let her in. "What's on?"

"The Curse of Frankenstein."

"With Peter Cushing and Christopher Lee?"

"That's the one."

"Cool."

"Hand over the popcorn," I said, reaching for the bowl.

"Hand over the Milk Duds."

"Come on, Claude."

"Candy first," she said.

She held onto the bowl of popcorn until I'd tossed her the candy. Roger closed the bedroom door and got back into the sleeping bags,

197

spread out on the floor by the bed. I stuffed a handful of popcorn into my mouth as Claudia kicked off her slippers. Her feet were bare.

"Put socks on," I said.

"The movie's already started."

"Get away, Iceberg-feet."

"Get a pair of my socks," said Roger, grabbing some popcorn.

"I hate tube socks. They go all the way up to my knees."

"That'll protect me from freezer burn."

"Come on, Sam . . ."

"Just get the socks, Claude, and hurry up," said Roger.

She stumbled over the sleeping bags to the dresser, grumbling the whole time. She dragged the socks up her legs, then stepped over Roger to crawl between him and me. The television flickered black-and-white images out at us as we leaned back against the bed, our shoulders touching, the bowl of popcorn in Claudia's lap so we all could reach it. On the screen, Peter Cushing, as Dr. Frankenstein, walked an older man up the stairs of his house.

"The old man's some kind of genius professor," said Roger, digging into the popcorn, talking with his mouth full. "Frankenstein wants him for his brain."

"Yeah, that's what all the boys say," said Claudia as she opened the Milk Duds.

In the film, just as the two characters reached the top of the stairs, Dr. Frankenstein told the professor to look at an old portrait hanging on the wall, then told him to step back to get a better view of it.

"Watch out," said Frankenstein, and he shoved the professor backwards.

"Oh, that was subtle," said Claudia.

The banister broke apart, and the old professor fell like a sandbag, slamming into the entry hall's marble floor.

"What a cheap banister," said Claudia. "It looks like it was made out of Styrofoam."

Dr. Frankenstein stared down at the dead professor with no emotion on his face.

"Hey, man, watch that first step: it's a killer," said Claudia, while Roger and me laughed. "Man, he sure died easy. That's what happens when your studio contract runs out. He should fire his agent, pronto."

Later in the movie, after Dr. Frankenstein's friend found out what really happened to the professor, he got into a fight with Frankenstein in the laboratory. The friend tried to snatch the black bag holding the dead professor's brain. Frankenstein fought him.

"I got dibs: it's my brain. Give it back," said Claudia, doing two different voices as the men wrestled on-screen. "You give it back: I'm better looking than you. No, you give it back: I get paid more than you do. And I get the girl, too. Hey, man, no fair. I'm talking to my agent."

Our fingers bumped into each other in the bowl of popcorn. Our feet tangled up together in the sleeping bags. The black-and-white images flickered across our faces all night long. Roger and me laughed at all her jokes. It was just the three of us. Like always. Porthos, Aramis, and D'Artagnan. Larry, Curly, and Moe.

No one was laughing at the trial, though sometimes it felt like we were stuck in some real bad movie. I wanted to change the channel. Anything to get us out of there and back into our real lives.

"Mr. Whitman, you testified that you never heard the defendant call Eleanor Sloane 'Mother' or 'Mom,'" said Tracey when she cross-examined the neighbor. "Yet you lived next door to the Sloanes for twenty years?"

"That's right, ma'am."

"Twenty years is a long time. So you must have known the Sloanes pretty well, Mr. Whitman."

"I guess you could say that."

"During those twenty years that you lived next door to the Sloanes and you were so close to them, how many times did you celebrate Christmas with them?"

"Christmas?" he said, looking surprised. "Why, I never celebrated Christmas with them."

"Never? Not even once?"

"I spent Christmases with my own family," he said.

He straightened his tie, smoothing it over his belly, and adjusted his too-tight jacket. The television reporter, sitting behind the prosecution's table, turned the tape in his recorder over. Next to him, the artist glanced up at the witness occasionally while she drew him.

"Mr. Whitman, did you ever celebrate any holidays with the Sloanes?" said Tracey.

"No, ma'am, I can't say that I did."

"During the twenty years you were so intimate with the Sloanes, how many meals did you eat with them?"

"None."

"Did you ever go inside the Sloanes' house?" said Tracey.

"Oh, sure."

"How many times?"

"A couple of times."

"How many is a 'couple,' Mr. Whitman? Two times?"

"More than that. When I was collecting for the Heart Association. Or the American Cancer Society," he said. "Oh, and when one of my granddaughters was selling cookies. Mrs. Sloane always bought some of the cookies, and when I helped my granddaughter deliver them, I went in."

"So you never celebrated any holidays with the Sloanes, and you never had any meals with them, but you did step in once or twice for a few minutes when you delivered cookies that Eleanor Sloane bought from your granddaughter. Is that correct?"

"Yes, ma'am. But me and Mrs. Sloane — Eleanor — we used to talk all the time across the fence, especially during the summer when we had our gardens."

Mr. Whitman looked over at the jury as he waited for Tracey's next question. The artist turned the page in her sketchpad, changed her position so she was facing Claudia, and started drawing again. Mr. Whitman cleared his throat several times, then took a drink of water.

"Were you acquainted with Harold Sloane, the deceased's husband?" said Tracey.

"Yes, ma'am," said Mr. Whitman.

"Do you remember when he died?"

"Yes, ma'am, I went to the funeral."

"Do you remember what year it was?"

"He died quite a while back," said Mr. Whitman, frowning. "Let me see now. I think it was around 1989 or 1990 when he died. No, wait a minute. 1988. Or 1989. No, it was 1990. Yeah, I'm pretty sure it was 1990."

"Did Eleanor Sloane continue living next door to you after her husband died?"

"No, she moved in with her son and his wife."

"Did you see Eleanor Sloane after she moved in with her son?"

"No, ma'am."

"So if Claudia Sloane started calling Eleanor Sloane 'Mother' or 'Mom' during those years they lived together, you wouldn't have known that, would you?"

"No, I guess not."

"Are you married, Mr. Whitman?"

"Yes, ma'am," he said, turning again to the jury and smiling. "Thirty-seven years now."

"Is your wife's mother still alive?" said Tracey.

"Yes, ma'am."

"Do you call your mother-in-law 'Mom' or 'Mother'?"

"No, ma'am."

"What do you call her, Mr. Whitman?"

"Old bat," he said, and there was tittering in the courtroom. "But only because that's what she is."

CHAPTER THREE

COULD YOU STATE YOUR NAME and profession for the court?"
said Graham to the witness.

"Carl Thompson. I'm a pharmacist."

"Could you tell the court what this is?"

"It's a prescription ledger for the Sloanes."

Graham had the ledger entered into evidence. Tracey's assistants
looked through the stacks of paper on the table in front of them until they found one and passed it to Tracey. She tapped her eraser
against her notepad, then put her pencil down. She didn't wear any
of her bracelets in court, but that day she was wearing that pink suit.
After Graham's assistant set up the poster-sized reproduction of the
prescription ledger on an easel facing the jury, Graham pointed out
some of the lines on the poster.

"Mr. Thompson, your ledger indicates that Eleanor Sloane had a
prescription for sleeping pills, and Claudia Sloane had a separate prescription for sleeping pills, is that correct?"

"Claudia had three prescriptions for herself."

"When you say 'three prescriptions,' do you mean that she had a
prescription with two refills?"

"No, she had three different prescriptions for sleeping pills."

"Are these the three sleeping pill prescriptions?" said Graham,
pointing to another line.

"Yes."

"Each prescription is for a different sleeping pill," said Graham, "and it looks like a different doctor wrote each prescription, as indicated by the physicians' names here on these lines. Is that correct?"

"Yes, sir. Three different prescriptions, by three different doctors."

Graham put the pointer down in front of the poster. Mr. Thompson took his glasses off and cleaned them with his handkerchief.

"So you filled three different sleeping pill prescriptions for Claudia Sloane, in addition to all the prescriptions you filled for Eleanor Sloane?"

"Yes, sir. That's correct."

"And you put childproof tops on all the prescriptions, correct?"

"No, sir."

"Why not?"

"Claudia asked me not to."

"Claudia Sloane specifically requested that you not put on childproof safety caps?" said Graham.

"That's correct, she did."

We didn't need childproof tops: we didn't have any kids in the house. During the trial, I was glad we didn't have any kids. Can you imagine kids suffering through something like that? One of the clerks in the grocery last month said it sure is lucky how some things turn out. The guy at the auto store where I bought spark plugs said it sure is lucky we don't have capital punishment in this state. Lucky? They think we've been lucky? Yeah, it sure was lucky for us that the police misinterpreted the circumstantial evidence and arrested Claudia. And we sure were lucky that Graham wanted to be a judge and needed a sensational case to get him some national media attention. And, hey, weren't we lucky that we had to sell our house to pay the legal fees of the defense team and the investigators who worked for Tracey? Yeah, we were so damned lucky that Claudia had all those miscarriages, and that Dad died of a massive coronary without ever letting us know what it was really like taking care of Mom, and that

I lost Dad's business paying for all the goddamned visiting nurses and sitters and psychiatrists and psychologists. Oh, man, were we lucky or what? And, hey, let's not forget Mom — if the rest of us were lucky, then she hit the damn jackpot.

"It's just our luck," said Claudia after I got to Mom's bedroom. "Now that company's here . . ."

"She's been in a good mood all day. What did you do to her?"

"I didn't do anything, Sam."

"Mom, stop screaming. Stop it," I said, taking her by the arm. "You remember what we said about screaming, don't you? You must have done something, Claudia. She wouldn't hit you for no reason."

"She does it all the time, Sam. Do you have to see bruises before you believe me?"

"Jesus, don't you start yelling, too. Not with Roger and Eve and the kids downstairs."

Claudia gave me a look and crossed her arms over her chest.

"I got her dressed," she said. "You get her downstairs."

"Mom. Hey, Mom, look at me. We're going to have Thanksgiving dinner, Mom, remember? Everybody's here: Roger, Eve, their son Matthew, their twins Sarah and Laura, Tommy. Hey, stop it. Jesus, Mom. What's the matter with you?"

"My dress."

"What about your dress?"

"My dress."

"Claudia, what's she talking about?"

"She thinks I'm wearing her dress."

"Take it off."

"It's not her dress, Sam."

"Take it off anyway, Claudia; it's not worth the . . . Damn it, Mom, don't do that."

"Why should I have to change just because she's got it in her head that —"

"God damn it, Mom, stop it. What the hell's the matter with you?"
Mom grabbed Claudia's forearm so hard she cried out.

"You little thief," said Mom. "I'm telling."

There was only one thief in our lives, and that was Mom's disease. It stole Mom, it stole our kids, it stole the business. It blasted us just like a bomb, and after Mom was dead, Claudia and I were still there, picking through the rubble, trying to rebuild our lives. You can't believe how much damage that disease does to your life. The kind of damage no doctor on earth can repair.

"Each doctor at the Glenview Clinic works there only a couple days a week," said Tracey after she approached the pharmacist on the witness stand. "Were you aware of that, Mr. Thompson?"

"Yes," he said.

"So if a patient calls in for a prescription refill on a day when her usual physician isn't present, whichever physician is on duty authorizes the refill, correct?"

"That's correct."

"That means a patient could have the same prescription with three different doctors' names on it," said Tracey, "depending on who was working in the clinic on the day she called for a refill, doesn't it?"

"Yes, there could be a different physician's name on each refill."

Tracey stood beside the poster-sized reproduction of the prescription ledger and pointed to the three lines the prosecutor had indicated earlier.

"Are these the names of the physicians who authorized the prescriptions?"

"Yes."

"All three of these doctors work at the Glenview Clinic, don't they?"

"Yes, they do."

"And if Claudia Sloane hadn't liked the side effects of the sleeping pill that Dr. Barnett had originally prescribed for her, let's say, and she called the clinic for a refill when he wasn't on duty, the clinic would have called in a change in prescription with another physician's name on it. Isn't that correct, Mr. Thompson?"

"Yes, that's possible, of course, but . . ."

"So Claudia Sloane could have had three different sleeping pill prescriptions, authorized by three different physicians, all of whom worked at the Glenview Clinic, and she could have had those prescriptions legitimately and without any criminal intent, couldn't she?"

"Objection."

"Overruled."

"Yes, I guess she could've had those prescriptions legitimately," said Mr. Thompson.

Criminal intent? God, they didn't understand how much Claudia needed those pills. It's hard enough taking care of somebody with a terminal illness, but somebody with a dementia — Jesus, you can't even begin to imagine how tough it is. She needed those pills to sleep. I needed them, too. They let us sleep without dreams.

Our dream of having kids was dead. After the last miscarriage, the doctor told Claudia to give up trying. He told her she was risking her own life with every pregnancy. That's why I put all the baby furniture up in the attic. I wasn't going to risk losing Claudia. The last pieces I took out of the room were the rocking horse and my old cradle. Dad had made the cradle when Mom was pregnant with me, saving it for their grandkids, but he'd died before he finished the rocking horse. I picked up the unassembled pieces and laid them in the cradle. When I picked it up, the pieces made a clacking noise, so I stopped and wrapped the baby blanket around them. Claudia was in bed: I didn't want to wake her. I don't know where Mom was. I went out to the hall with the baby furniture and carried it up to the attic. I set the cradle and rocking horse down under the eaves, next to the bassinet, the changing table, and the dresser. When I stepped back, dust swirled around in the sunlight and made me cough. I picked up some of the old blankets, shook them out, and tucked them around the baby's furniture. Those blankets were so big, and that cradle was so small. And it would never hold a baby. It was small and dead and empty. Like my life.

"Mr. Thompson, you said you didn't put childproof caps on the Sloanes' prescriptions," said Tracey to the pharmacist. "Doesn't the law require you to do so?"

"The Sloanes don't have any children in the house."

"That wasn't the question," said Tracey. "Doesn't the law require you to put childproof caps on all prescriptions?"

"Claudia asked me not to. You don't have to do it under those circumstances."

"Could I see the paper she signed requesting that?"

"I . . . uh . . . well, you see, I don't have it in writing," said Mr. Thompson.

"Doesn't the law require you to get those statements in writing?"

"Well, yes, but . . ."

"So you have — in writing — Claudia Sloane's request that you not put childproof tops on the prescriptions?"

"It's an awful lot of paperwork," said Mr. Thompson, glancing up at the judge. "Nobody does it."

"Did you change the law for everyone or just for yourself?" said Tracey.

"Objection."

"Withdrawn. So you're telling us that you don't have the written requests required by law?"

"I've known Claudia for years. . . ."

"So you don't have to follow the law for someone you've known for years?"

"It's a small town," said Mr. Thompson, turning so he faced the judge. "You get to know people pretty well over the years. Claudia wouldn't have let Eleanor get into the medicines."

"But if Eleanor had gotten the medications, accidentally, she could have gotten those tops off pretty easily, couldn't she?" said Tracey.

"She could've," said the pharmacist, "but Eleanor didn't get into the medications."

"Were you at the Sloanes' house the day Eleanor died?"

"No."

"Then how do you know Eleanor Sloane didn't get into the medications?"

"Objection, Your Honor."

"Sustained."

Tracey went over to the table where Claudia sat and picked up a piece of paper.

"These prescriptions that you filled on January seventh and then again on January twelfth — did Claudia tell you why she needed them refilled so soon, Mr. Thompson?"

"Objection."

"Overruled."

"She told me she lost them."

"Did she say how?"

"She said they fell in the toilet."

"Mr. Thompson, do you take any prescription medications?"

"Blood pressure pills."

"Where do you keep those pills, Mr. Thompson?"

"In the medicine cabinet. In the bathroom."

"Do you have childproof safety caps on your prescriptions?"

"No."

"Did you ever drop any pills, Mr. Thompson?"

"Once or twice."

"When you dropped your blood pressure pills in the bathroom," said Tracey, "where did they go?"

"A couple went down the sink. A couple hit the toilet lid and rolled off onto the floor. A couple . . ."

"Some pills hit the toilet lid? Does that mean that if the lid had been open, those pills you dropped would have gone into the toilet?"

"Yes, I guess they would've. But we keep the lid down so Butch — that's our dog — so Butch won't drink out of it."

Several people in the courtroom laughed. The judge and a couple of the jury members smiled.

"So, Mr. Thompson, if you'd dropped the whole bottle of pills, with its top off, let's say, then all the pills would have gone into the toilet?"

"I suppose," he said. "But we don't keep the lid open, on account of Butch."

"And so you don't lose any pills," said Tracey.

CHAPTER FOUR

*D*ON'T," I said when Claudia reached out for me.

"Don't you want me to?"

"What about Gary and Angela?"

"They deserve each other."

"You don't love me."

"Yes, I do."

"Don't say that."

"I do love you."

"Don't say that. Not tonight."

"What if I mean it?"

"You're hurt, that's all."

"No, that's not it. I've always loved you."

Then, somehow, she was in my arms again, her mouth open on mine, her fingers fumbling with my zipper. When she yanked up her gown and put my hand between her bare thighs, I couldn't help kissing her back. I tried to touch her, but she pushed my hands away, lifting herself with a little hop so she could hook her legs around my hips, using her fingers to bring me closer and guide me into her. Outside in the reception hall, I heard the laughter and talking of the other wedding guests, but in that coatroom, all I could hear was her breath in my ears as she clutched me to her, the dull thud of her back against the door as she tightened her legs against mine, the sweet sound of her voice as she said my name, over and over, like a spell.

"So, you're saying that Eleanor Sloane lost her ability to make competent decisions about her life?" said Prosecutor Graham after the psychologist took the witness stand.

"Alzheimer's patients aren't able to make rational decisions," said Dr. Daniels. "That's the nature of their disease."

"You told us that Eleanor Sloane was a client of yours: did you see her alone or together with her daughter-in-law?"

"At the beginning, I saw them together. Then as Eleanor's disease progressed, I saw Claudia alone."

"How well did you get to know Eleanor Sloane while she was your client?"

"Quite well, I'd say."

"So you feel confident in your assessment of her character?"

"Yes, quite confident," she said.

"Do you think Eleanor Sloane wanted to commit suicide?" said Graham.

"Objection: asks for supposition on the part of the witness."

"Overruled. Answer the question."

"During the time I was seeing her, I don't believe she wanted to commit suicide."

"Even if she'd wanted to, she couldn't have done it herself, could she?"

"Objection."

"Overruled."

"What do you mean, 'she couldn't have done it herself'?" said Dr. Daniels, frowning.

"Eleanor Sloane couldn't have taken all those prescription pills that —"

"Objection," said Tracey, standing up quickly. "It's never been established that death was by anything other than natural causes brought about by the disease process and the pneumonia."

"Sustained."

"Dr. Daniels, if massive numbers of prescription pills were left at the bedside table of an Alzheimer's patient —"

"Objection, Your Honor."

"I'll rephrase the question," said Graham, without even looking at Tracey, who was standing again. "Dr. Daniels, do you advise clients to keep prescription medications by the bedside of patients who are sick with Alzheimer's?"

"I advise them to keep dangerous things as far away from the sick person as possible."

Mom's illness was more dangerous than any pills could've been, even if she'd taken pills by the bucketful. God, sometimes I feel like we're still in the middle of it all. Every day I saw my mom change into some other person, and every day, I saw my wife changing, too. It was almost like they were hanging over the roof of a tall building, and I was trying to keep them from falling. But the weight of the disease was too damn much for us. It stole my wife and mom away from me, then slammed them into the ground, leaving me nothing but broken pieces. It's a terrible memory. Nobody deserves memories like that.

"I can't remember the last time I heard you laugh," I said.

Claudia stared out the bedroom window. From where I was sitting, I could see out into the yard. The trees were so covered with ice, their branches bowed under the weight. Claudia didn't answer me, but there were some things she never talked about, no matter how long we were married and no matter how careful I brought up the subject. Like the miscarriages, or Dad's death. Or even her foster mother Grace's death, for that matter. And Claudia never, ever wanted to talk about putting Mom into a home.

"What if Mom lasts another five or ten years?" I said. "What if she lasts another twenty years?"

Claudia put her finger on the bottom of the window and held it there until the frost dissolved.

"At the very least, we should probably put her name on the home's waiting list," I said. "In a year and a half, you might change your mind."

"They say it's hereditary," she said. "Maybe you should get that genetic testing done."

She pressed her palm to the glass, leaving a bare outline of her hand surrounded by frost.

"What do you want me to do if you get it, Sam? Take care of you? Put you in a home? Or just shoot you?"

Claudia says she doesn't remember saying that. She says I must've dreamed it. Once she even told me that I must've been drunk and imagined the whole thing. But I can't forget it. I'll never forget it.

"What's the matter, Mom?" I said.

"I changed my mind."

"About what?"

"Don't tell me what to do."

"I was just trying to take your coat so I could put it in the closet."

Mom pushed me aside and went over to the couch, plopping down and pushing the throw pillows off onto the floor. When Claudia looked at Dad, he shrugged.

"If she hadn't gone through the change," he said, "I'd think it was that time of the month."

"Why doesn't she want to take her coat off?"

"I don't know. Last week we went out to dinner at that new Mexican restaurant you told us about, and she wouldn't get out of the car. Hey, the place looks nice. It's not as small as I thought it'd be. You did a good job, Claudia."

"Thanks, Harold."

"She made all the curtains and the throw pillows herself."

"Grace and Eve helped me."

"Did you ever think of a career in interior decorating?"

"If I ever get a bookstore, that'll be enough of a career, thanks."

"Didn't Claudia do a great job, Eleanor? Did you see these curtains?"

"I'm hungry," said Mom. "I want to eat."

Dad looked out the front windows, his hands jammed into his pants pockets. Claudia picked up the throw pillows that Mom had pushed off the couch and put them back, but as soon as Claudia turned away, Mom knocked one of them off again. Claudia went to the kitchen. As soon as I joined her there, we heard Dad say something to Mom.

"No," said Mom, and again, even louder, "No."

Claudia arranged the crackers on the board and placed the knife next to the cheese while I took the corkscrew out of the drawer and opened the wine. When we got back to the living room, Mom was sitting on the opposite end of the couch, and Dad was picking up all the throw pillows and putting them in the chair. Mom was trying to get her coat rebuttoned. I set the wineglasses down as Claudia put the cheese and crackers in the center of the coffee table.

"I don't like cheese balls," said Mom.

"Sammy, pour me a glass of that wine," said Dad.

"I hate red wine," said Mom.

"Pour me about twice that much," said Dad.

"I hate cheese balls," said Mom.

Dad took the wine and drank it down fast. Claudia picked up one of the small plates, put it down, slid it next to the cheese knife, moved the napkins, moved the plates, moved the napkins back to their original place. Dad poured himself more wine. Mom bit one of the crackers, made a face, then put the cracker back onto the tray with the rest of them.

"Goddamn it, Eleanor," said Dad as he leaned forward and snatched the cracker from the tray.

"I don't like that kind," said Mom. "You know I don't like them. I told you."

"Maybe we should just eat dinner," said Dad.

"It's not done yet," said Claudia.

"I'm not hungry," said Mom.

"Maybe we better do this some other night," said Dad.

"I didn't want to come."

"Then you should've told Claudia that when she asked you," said Dad. "Now look what you've done. You made Claudia cry."

"You're the one who made me do it. I told you I didn't want to come. I told you I changed my —"

Dad dragged Mom out of the apartment, Claudia sat sobbing on the couch, and I stood there wondering what the hell was happening to our family. One day we were happy, and the next day we were shipwrecked. Thrown into an ocean with no life vests, no compass, no oars. And no lighthouse to guide us to shore. No matter how many families have wrecked in that sea before you, no matter how many stories of survival you hear, when you're out in that dark night, in the raging sea of that disease, it feels like you're all alone. Even if you read all the books — The 36-Hour Day, Understanding Difficult Behaviors, Final Exit — you'll never be prepared for what's going to happen. Nothing can prepare you for how terrifying it'll be.

"Dealing with Alzheimer's must be frightening for the families," said Tracey after Dr. Daniels adjusted the microphone at the witness stand. "Would you consider yourself an expert on Alzheimer's?"

"That's one of my areas of specialty, yes," said Dr. Daniels.

"So you're considered an expert in dealing with Alzheimer's patients?"

"And their families."

"How long have you been practicing?"

"Twenty-three years."

At the prosecution's table, Harlan Graham's assistant refilled his water glass. When he set the pitcher down, he banged it against the light on their table. Tracey and the jury glanced over at the noise. The assistant winced and whispered an apology. Tracey turned back to the witness.

"Dr. Daniels, have you ever had an Alzheimer's patient commit suicide?"

"Yes."

"So Eleanor Sloane could have committed suicide, couldn't she?"

"She was physically capable of it," said Dr. Daniels, "but I don't believe she did."

"Why not?"

"She was in the late stages of the disease when she died."

"Does that make a difference?" said Tracey.

"Earlier in the course of the disease, the patient has more mental competence to make a decision about suicide."

Tracey walked closer to the witness box. The elderly jury member wearing the plaid jacket and polka-dot tie adjusted his hearing aid. Graham leaned back slightly in this chair, stretching his legs out under the table, wing tips shiny as a mirror. Sitting next to me on my right were Roger's twins: they came whenever they could. Sarah and Laura both watched the court artist that day. Roger and Eve were on my left.

"I thought you said that Alzheimer's patients had no mental competence," said Tracey.

"They lose their mental competence due to the disease."

"When do they lose their mental competence?"

"That varies with each patient."

"So when did Eleanor Sloane lose her mental competence?"

"I'm afraid that can't be determined specifically."

"That means she could have been mentally competent enough to take her own life, doesn't it?"

"I don't think she did, though," said Dr. Daniels, shaking her head. "And with Alzheimer's, all of her mental functioning would be suspect."

"But you just told us that earlier in the disease, patients have more mental competence," said Tracey.

"That changes as the disease progresses."

"At what point, what date, would you say that Eleanor Sloane lost her mental competence?"

"I can't determine an exact date."

"Give us a rough estimate, Dr. Daniels. How long after she was diagnosed did Eleanor lose her mental competence?"

"I can't determine that."

"You're an expert in the field, yet you can't determine how long Eleanor Sloane was mentally competent?"

"No."

"You can't even make an educated guess?"

"No. No one would be able to do that."

If at any time a situation should arise when I am in an irreversible or incurable terminal condition from which there is no reasonable expectation of my recovery, and if I am unable to communicate my instructions, or when the use of life-sustaining treatment would only prolong artificially the moment of my death . . .

The paper was in the wooden box I'd made for Mom when I was in high school. I found it under her bed, shoved up against the wall. It wasn't locked. The papers on top were the usual legal stuff: my parents' marriage license, social security cards, deeds to the cemetery plots, automobile titles, my birth certificate. I didn't understand why she'd hidden the box under the bed until I'd opened the last three documents.

. . . I direct that such procedures be withheld or withdrawn, including withdrawal of the administration of nutrition and hydration . . .

The other two documents were the same as the first, and they'd all been done by the same lawyer. Not the family lawyer. After I folded the three papers and buttoned them inside my shirt, I put everything else back in the box. Then I put the box back under the bed, against the wall. Right where I found it. I never told anyone about them. Not even Claudia. Not even after Mom's death. When it was all over.

CHAPTER FIVE

$\mathcal{D}$O YOU BELIEVE THAT TERMINALLY ILL PATIENTS have the right to end their suffering?" said Tracey.

"Yes, I do," said Dr. Daniels on her second day of testimony.

"So Eleanor Sloane had a right to end her suffering?"

"No, Alzheimer's patients don't have that same right to end their lives."

"Why not?"

"Alzheimer's, by its very nature, takes away a patient's mental competence to make a decision like that."

"But you just said it was a terminal disease, and that you believe the terminally ill have a right to end their suffering."

"Yes, but not Alzheimer's patients," said Dr. Daniels.

Tracey paused in front of the jury. Most of them had the same expression on their faces as she did.

"Why are Alzheimer's victims deprived of the rights available to other patients with incurable terminal diseases?" said Tracey.

"Because of their lack of mental competence."

Harlan Graham uncapped his gold fountain pen and held it over his legal pad, but he didn't write anything. Roger and his eldest son, Matthew, were the only ones in court with me that afternoon. Eve was home with their youngest, Tommy, who had the measles, and the twins were working at the bookstore. In his tortoise-shell glasses and wearing one of Roger's ties, Matthew already looked like a lawyer, and that was even before he went to law school.

"You said you saw Claudia alone after Eleanor was no longer able to see you, is that correct?" said Tracey.

"Yes, that's correct," said Dr. Daniels.

"Would you say you got to know Claudia well?"

"Yes, very well."

"Do you consider Claudia honest and trustworthy?"

"Very honest," said Dr. Daniels. "And very trustworthy."

"So if she told you something, you'd believe it?"

"Yes."

"If she told you she did not help Eleanor commit suicide —"

"Objection."

"Withdrawn. What kinds of things did you and Claudia discuss when she saw you alone?"

"Mostly how to handle Eleanor's disease."

"Did Claudia ever tell you she was going to murder Eleanor?"

"No, of course not."

"Why did you laugh?" said Tracey. "Did you find that question funny?"

"Claudia doesn't even kill spiders," said Dr. Daniels. "She catches them and takes them outside."

Claudia's never talked to anyone about what happened. Except for Dr. Daniels, and Claudia started seeing her when Mom was first living with us. I never met Dr. Daniels myself, so before I saw her in court, I thought she'd look like Claudia's best friend, Eve: wearing hippie skirts and peasant blouses. Especially since Dr. Daniels is always coming up with that New-Age-y stuff, like Eve is. But Dr. Daniels wasn't anything like I expected. I mean, to look at her, you'd never know she believed in all that hoodoo rigmarole. How could a woman who looks that good in a tailored suit believe in all that weird stuff? Claudia always wanted me to come to therapy with her, but I didn't think I'd get along too well with Dr. Daniels — once she started on that "pulling down the negative energy of the universe" stuff, I'd be gone. How could I talk to someone if I don't think she's really hearing everything I'm saying?

"Listen, Claude . . ."

"Please, don't call me that. Not now. Not like this. You promised."

When she sat up, the sheet slipping down from over her breasts, I got out of bed and yanked on my sweatpants. I went to the refrigerator and got some juice. All the cups and saucers had candles in them, so I had to drink out of the carton. The juice was sour. I leaned over the sink to spit it out, then emptied the rest. Claudia pushed back the blankets and got out of bed, her legs flashing white as she went over to her dress, lying in a heap on the floor.

"Jesus, Roger's going to kill me," I said.

"What does Roger have to do with this?"

"You're his kid sister, for Christ's sake."

"I wish you'd stop saying that," said Claudia, picking up the maid of honor's dress and holding it against her. "It's not like I'm your sister, Sam."

I tossed the emptied juice carton into the trash can, then leaned against the sink, my eyes closed.

"Have you got something I can wear home?" said Claudia.

I went over to the dresser, pulled out a T-shirt and another pair of sweatpants, and tossed them onto the unmade bed. She shook out the dress and laid it beside my clothes. A gust of wind rattled the windows as icy snow tapped against the glass. My head throbbed when I opened the cupboard above the sink. I pushed aside the box of crackers and cans of soup, but I couldn't find any aspirin. Claudia pulled the T-shirt over her head, flipping her hair out from under its collar, her breasts and nipples pressing against the thin fabric. I began picking up the candles and dropping them into the trash. Some of the candles had melted over the saucers, their wax spreading out on the countertop and stove before cooling. When Claudia came up behind me, I got a knife out of the drawer and scraped up some of the hardened wax on the stove's burner. The knife slipped off the burner and gouged the stove's enamel. I cursed under my breath. When I slammed the bits of candle and melted wax into the sink along with the knife, their clatter made my head hurt more. Claudia put her arms around my waist, her cheek against my back.

"I can feel your heart pounding," she said.

She slipped her hands behind my waistband to touch me. When she led me back to the bed, I went with her. After she flung off the T-shirt, her breasts swayed above me, high and firm. I closed my eyes as she eased my sweatpants down over my hips and legs, her hair brushing down over my chest and stomach. She knelt between my legs. I don't know how long we were together like that, but when I dragged her up on top of me so I could be inside her, when I moved in her, the rest of the world stopped. And when I came in her, I felt like the strongest man in the world.

But I wasn't strong enough. Not when she really needed me to be strong. I promised to love, honor, and protect, but it was too much for me. And the one time Mom asked me to be strong for her — the only thing she ever asked of me — I couldn't keep that promise either.

I'd promised Dad I'd finish the rocking horse. He'd cut out all the pieces and assembled some sections, but he'd died before it was done. After I laid the horse out on the kitchen table, Spike went to each piece, rubbing his face against it to mark it. The knotted-cotton tail and mane that Mom made were lying there, too, slightly yellowed from being in the attic. Spike started to wrestle with them. He was just a kitten then, and he loved wrestling with things. All my tools were on the counter, and the carver's chops was mounted on the carver's bench in the corner of the kitchen. While Claudia was away, it was better to work there than in the basement. I picked up the horse's head, its eye- and earpieces already glued on, and I ran my fingers over the wood. I could feel the horse struggling to get free. I could feel something else, too. I clamped the head and picked up the coping saw to separate the ears. I needed to finish the horse. I needed to start living again.

"Did Claudia ever tell you she was going to help Eleanor kill herself?" said Tracey as she continued the cross-examination.

"No, she didn't," said Dr. Daniels.

"Did Claudia ever tell you she was going to leave all the prescription medications out on the bed-side table so Eleanor could commit suicide with them?"

"Objection," said Graham, without getting up.

"Overruled."

"No, Claudia never told me she was going to leave the medications out so Eleanor could commit suicide with them," said Dr. Daniels.

"If Claudia had ever told you that she was going to do something to hurt Eleanor, you would have had to report that to the proper legal authorities, wouldn't you?"

"Yes, I'd be legally and ethically required to inform the authorities."

"Dr. Daniels, would you say that Eleanor Sloane was an intelligent woman?"

"Yes."

"Would you sat that she was intelligent enough to recognize that she was ill?"

"Oh, yes. In the beginning she would have recognized it."

"Would you say that she was intelligent enough to figure out what her illness was?"

"Early in the disease, while she was still capable of doing that, she may have understood what illness she had," said Dr. Daniels, "though I don't believe the family ever told her the diagnosis."

"But Eleanor may very well have known that she was terminally ill with Alzheimer's," said Tracey.

"She may have, but she would have forgotten."

"Once she realized she had Alzheimer's, though, Eleanor may have decided to take her own life."

"I don't think so."

"The medical literature describes cases of confirmed Alzheimer's patients who commit suicide at later stages in their disease," said Tracey.

"But I don't think Eleanor took her own life," said Dr. Daniels.

"Are you telling us that despite all the medical evidence to the contrary, you don't believe it was possible for Eleanor Sloane to take her own life?"

"Anything's possible," said Dr. Daniels. "But that doesn't mean it's probable."

When we went to the doctor's office to get the results of the tests, Claudia gripped the arms of the chair so hard, her knuckles looked like they were going to tear through her skin. I started to say something once, but after the look she gave me, I just sat there. A small grandfather clock was on the wall behind the doctor's desk, its pendulum moving rhythmically. When the door opened and the doctor came in, Claudia grabbed my hand, like she'd forgotten what we'd said to each other the night before.

"I know you've been very worried about the results of the amniocentesis," said the doctor as he sat down at his desk, "but I want you to know that all the medical tests indicate that you're going to have a normal, healthy baby. There are no indications of any birth defects or abnormalities."

"I told you this time was different," said Claudia, turning toward me. "I knew it'd be all right."

"He'll be a healthy boy, with two very happy parents."

"Boy? Did you say 'boy'?" said Claudia. "I wanted to be surprised."

"I'm sorry. I thought you were more concerned with his health than his sex. Now, we've still got a few months to get through, Mrs.

Sloane," said the doctor. "And given your history of miscarriages and the fact that you're over forty, this is an extremely high-risk pregnancy. You're going to have to take extra care of yourself if you want to carry this baby to term. I may even have to recommend complete bed rest in the later months. In the meantime, we have to watch for warning signs, like . . ."

The doctor's voice faded as I looked at Claudia's belly. Behind that thin, barely rounded wall of skin, my son was growing. My son. Breathing, moving, dreaming. So we weren't cursed, after all. We didn't have to think about ending it. Claudia would forgive me for what I'd said because God was giving us another chance to have a family. He was giving me a son. The love I felt for Claudia was just a spark next to the flame of love I felt for my son. I didn't understand it myself, but as soon as I heard the doctor's words, I loved my son. Then I closed my eyes as the love and the shame rushed over me.

"Many people choose to end their lives rather than to face a terminal illness, isn't that true, Dr. Daniels?" said Tracey.

"Yes, that's true."

"So Eleanor Sloane may have decided to take her own life rather than —"

"Objection."

"Withdrawn. Dr. Daniels, were you aware that Eleanor Sloane was admitted to the Mercy Hospital Emergency Room several years ago?"

"She wasn't my client at that time, but I was aware of it."

"Do you know the reason she was admitted on that date?"

"Objection, Your Honor," said Graham, buttoning his suit-jacket as he stood. "Beyond the scope."

"I plan to show relevance, Your Honor."

"Overruled. Proceed, Ms. Garner."

Graham sat back down, undoing his jacket button. As he picked up his pen, I looked back at Tracey.

"Did you know that Eleanor Sloane was admitted to Mercy Hospital on that date because she took an overdose of sleeping pills?"

"I don't know that her taking those pills was intentional."

"I didn't ask you that, Dr. Daniels," said Tracey. "I asked you if you were aware that Eleanor Sloane was admitted to the hospital because she took an overdose of sleeping pills."

"Yes, I was aware of that."

"In fact, Eleanor Sloane took so many sleeping pills that if her husband hadn't found her and rushed her to the emergency room, she would have died, correct?"

"I'm not able to answer that question. I didn't speak with the attending physician."

Tracey went to the defense table and accepted the paper her assistant held out. She showed it to Graham before she handed it to the judge, who read it before he passed it down to the court reporter. Tracey took the paper back to the witness stand and handed it to Dr. Daniels.

"Dr. Daniels, this is the attending physician's report for the date Eleanor was admitted to the hospital. Could you read his diagnosis at the bottom of the page?"

"'The patient was treated for ingestion of toxic levels of narcotics and sedatives.'"

"'Toxic levels.' Doesn't that mean that Eleanor would have died if she hadn't been taken to the hospital?"

"Yes, it seems to indicate that."

"Dr. Daniels, did you know about the time Eleanor was found in the downstairs bathroom, cutting her wrist with a steak knife?"

"I believe she cut her forearm."

"She cut her wrist so deeply that it required an emergency room visit and stitches, correct?"

"Yes."

"Wasn't Eleanor trying to kill herself?"

"I don't know."

Tracey turned, her hands on her hips, and looked at the jury members.

"What else would a terminally ill woman be doing behind closed doors cutting her wrist with a serrated steak knife," said Tracey, "except trying to kill herself?"

"I don't know," said Dr. Daniels. "I'm afraid there's simply no way for any of us to know."

CHAPTER SIX

$\mathcal{D}$O YOU KNOW WHAT THIS IS?" said Prosecutor Graham, holding up a piece of evidence.

"It's a plastic food storage bag that was retrieved from the defendant's residence, from a trash can in the garage," said the cop on the stand.

"When you first saw this bag, was it empty?"

"Except for the powdery residue that's in it."

"And you examined this bag for fingerprints, didn't you, Sergeant Thornton?"

"Yes."

Graham held the bag up so the jury could see it as he continued asking questions.

"Were you able to lift any fingerprints from this bag, Sergeant?"

"Yes. There were two sets of prints."

"Were you able to determine whose prints those were?"

"The set with the fewest prints belonged to Mr. Sloane, the defendant's husband."

"Would you say that the prints belonging to Mr. Sloane were consistent with his not handling the bag extensively?"

"Objection."

"Withdrawn. You said there were two sets of prints. Were you able to determine to whom the second set belonged?"

"To the defendant, Claudia Sloane."

Graham took the plastic bag back to the table and picked up another evidence bag. Claudia massaged the small of her back with her hand, then leaned further into her chair. Before showing the evidence to the witness, Graham walked past the jury box. The jury member in the plaid jacket moved aside as the other jury members in the row against the wall craned their necks to see the bag.

"Could you identify the contents of this bag for the court, please."

"They're prescription medication bottles discovered in the bedroom of the deceased."

"Were you able to lift any fingerprints from these prescription bottles?"

"Most of them were blurred and therefore unidentifiable. But some of the prints belonged to the defendant, Claudia Sloane."

"Would you say your analysis of the fingerprints is reliable, Sergeant Thornton?"

"Fingerprints don't lie," he said.

"You can tell me the truth, Sam," said Mom one night when we were alone in the house together. "It won't hurt my feelings."

"We're not sorry at all," I said. "Are you?"

"No. I like living with you and Claudia."

"And we like having you here, Mom."

She sat at the kitchen table with me, slowly snapping the ends off green beans from the garden. By the time I'd finished my pile, Mom's was still large, so I took some of hers.

"I miss your father," she said.

"I miss him, too, Mom."

"It doesn't seem like home without him."

When I tried to put my hand on hers, she picked up another bean. After all the beans were done and I'd put them in a colander, she took them to the sink. I scooped all the ends into the garbage bag, then wiped off the table. Mom poured the rinsed beans into a pan.

"Should we put onion in the green beans, Sam?"

"I'll do that, Mom."

"What about bacon?"

"I'll do that, too."

"I can still use a knife, you know. I'm not crippled."

I went to the refrigerator, opened the meat drawer, and got out the bacon. After I put the onion and bacon in with the green beans, I lowered the flame, and put the lid on the pan. Mom was so close behind me that I bumped into her a couple of times. As I opened the oven door, I glanced up at the clock. It was still early: Claudia wouldn't be home from the bookstore for at least another hour. The meatloaf was getting done too quick, so I turned the oven down. As I laid the mitt on the counter, Mom touched my arm.

"Do you think my memory's any better since I moved in with you and Claudia?"

"Does it feel like it's better, Mom?"

"A little. I think."

"Then it must be better. Are you still taking the supplements?"

She nodded, but then she frowned.

"Sam, I need to ask you something, and I need you to tell me the truth," she said, twisting her hands together several times before she looked up at me. "Do I have . . . have I got . . . I've got Alzheimer's, don't I?"

I swear, it was like she'd sucker punched me. After what the doctor had told us about her memory's deterioration, I never expected her to ask me that. The doctor said we needed to tell Mom the truth and that Mom needed to trust us, *blah-blah-blah*. But the doctor didn't see the look on my mom's face when she asked me that question. He didn't have to live with her every day or see her suffering. Sometimes you can't listen to the experts or the professionals. Sometimes, no matter what anybody else tells you, you've got to listen to your own heart.

"No, Mom," I said, holding her tight. "You don't have Alzheimer's."

"Oh, you wouldn't do that, would you?" said Claudia, and I stopped in the hallway in front of her closed bedroom door.

"Cross my heart and hope to die," said Eve.

"In your mouth?"

"Not with anybody else. But with him, I would."

I glanced toward Roger's room. The door was open, but the room was dark. He wasn't there. Grace was outside in the front yard, weeding flowers. I moved closer to Claudia's closed door.

"I can't believe you'd do that," she said. "That is so disgustingly gross."

"You're saying that just 'cause he's your brother."

"I'd say that about anybody."

"What about Sam?" said Eve.

I rested my hand on the door, my cheek against the wood.

"Admit it, Claudia. You would. If it was Sam," said Eve. "What's wrong? Where are you going?"

Suddenly the bedroom door swung open. I jumped back. Claudia glared at me, her fists on her hips.

"I knew it," she said. "What are you doing out here?"

"Looking for Roger."

"You were spying."

"On you two? What are you gonna say that I wanna hear?"

Eve came to the door and stood beside Claudia. Frowning, they crossed their arms over their chests.

"I told you, I'm looking for Roger."

"Like he's gonna be in here," said Claudia.

"He thinks he's 007 or something," said Eve.

"Oh, and you two think you're Pussy Galore," I said.

"Get lost."

"Make me."

"You were spying again. I'm telling. Mom . . ."

"I'm gonna go find Roger," I said as I moved away down the hall.

"And don't come back," said Claudia just before she slammed the door.

"How many times do I have to tell you, Eleanor?" said Dad, loud enough for us to hear it. "Jesus, you're driving me crazy."

Upstairs, something hit the wall. There was a scrambling noise, then another thud. Then Dad started shouting again.

"I thought your parents were out," said Claudia.

"He told me they'd be at the mall," I said.

"God damn it, Eleanor. Stop it," said Dad.

They were in the master bedroom. Dad's back was to us, so he didn't see us come in. Mom was clinging to his arm. She whimpered as Dad pried her fingers free. When he yanked his arm loose, she cried out and held him in a different place. As Claudia and I stepped closer, Dad wrenched himself free. When Mom reached for his arm again, he shoved her. He shoved her so hard she fell backwards. Against the wall.

I don't remember rushing at him. I don't remember grabbing him by the throat, or throwing him down, or hitting his head against the floor. But Claudia says that's what I did, and she wouldn't make it up. Dad and I never talked about it, and if he had any bruises, I never saw them. All I remember is the look on Mom's face, the sound of her body as she hit the wall, and the bitter taste that flooded my mouth. How could he do that to her when he knew she was sick? I swore I'd never forgive him. Ever. God, how I wish I had.

I used to wish that Dad had finished the rocking horse before he died, but then I was glad he hadn't. I'd already separated the horse's ears with the coping saw and shaped them, but I had to carve them so that they angled back. They turned out good. I cut away the corners for the horse's nostrils, pushing the gouge across with wood with my thumb, the slivers peeling away. I tapered the head from the eyebrow to the mouth, then pared the cheekbone with the spoon gouge. It took a while, but I didn't mind. After I finished one side of the horse's head, I turned it over, reclamped it, and began to carve the other side. Spike slept on the corner of the kitchen table, the tip of his tail twitching as I worked, and even though the cat and the horse were the only ones there in the house with me, it felt like I wasn't alone at all.

"What work do you do, Dr. Peters?" said Harlan Graham to one of his expert witnesses.

"I'm a chemist."

"Could you tell the court what these are?"

"Those are prescription medication bottles, taken from the Sloane residence."

"Did you analyze the chemical residue left in these empty prescription bottles?"

"Yes, I did."

"Were you able to determine what medications had been in them?"

"Yes. May I consult my notes?"

"Please, do."

When Dr. Peters lifted his briefcase and set it on the edge of the witness box, it bumped the microphone, so he pushed it aside before he took out a folder. After he put on his reading glasses, he opened the folder and flipped through it. Graham stood there the whole time, holding the evidence bag with the prescription bottles. The witness stopped turning pages and read from one.

"The bottles contained antidepressants; antipsychotics; anxiolytics, which are antianxiety drugs; antirage agents; sleeping pills; and narcotic pain relievers."

"Would a doctor prescribe all these medications for one patient?" said Prosecutor Graham.

"Objection. The witness is a chemist, not a physician."

"Sustained."

"Could one person take all these medications?" said Prosecutor Graham.

"Objection."

"Sustained."

"If a person took all the pills in all these bottles, would it be dangerous?"

"Objection."

"Overruled," said the judge. "Answer the question, please."

"If a patient were to take the pills as instructed by his physician, it wouldn't be harmful."

"But I asked whether it would be harmful to take all the pills in these bottles at one time," said Graham.

"That combination would be toxic."

Graham was obsessed with my mom's death, but she was dead, for Christ's sake. There wasn't anything he could do for her. Why didn't he have some compassion for those of us who were still alive? Why didn't he give a damn whether or not Claudia lost the baby she was carrying? I still get pretty heated up when I think about it all. Claudia says I should just cut it all loose. She says Dr. Daniels taught her how to let go of the past, how to cut the tethers and move on. Forgive and forget, turn the other cheek, cut your losses, and all that other crap. God, I wish I knew how.

I took an ax and went out back to cut up the pile of dead trees in the yard. Spike stretched himself out on top of the woodpile and watched me as I picked up a piece of wood. I set it on the flat tree trunk, raised the ax, and brought it down with all my strength. Spike jumped the first few times, but then he got used to the noise. It was good for me. There was something about the strain of my shoulders and arms, something about the heavy *thunk* of the ax slamming into the wood, something about the ripping and tearing of the wood. With every blow of the ax, I was chopping everything that ruined our lives into smaller and smaller pieces: the prosecutor, the cops, the

Alzheimer's. Some weekends, I chopped wood until my hands blistered, until the blisters broke open and bled, until I dropped the ax in the trampled, bloody snow.

If only we could've really beaten the disease like that.

If only a few blows of an ax could've really cut it out of our lives.

CHAPTER SEVEN

So WHATEVER WAS IN THIS PLASTIC BAG had been cut up before it was put into the bag?" said Prosecutor Graham to the chemist.

"Not cut up," said Dr. Peters. "Crushed."

"And you were able to determine that at least six different kinds of pills had been crushed in this bag, is that correct?"

"That's correct."

Several of the jury members began jotting in their notebooks. At the defense table, two of Tracey's assistants were writing notes on their legal pads and sliding them back and forth to each other.

"Dr. Peters, did the residue in this bag match anything else you examined?"

"Yes, it matched the residue in the emptied prescription bottles."

Graham held the plastic bag up by one of its corners.

"This is a pretty large bag, isn't it?"

"I believe it's a one-gallon size."

"How many pills do you think a bag this size could hold?"

"Objection."

"Withdrawn. If someone took all the pills in a bag this size, she'd sleep for a very long time, wouldn't she?"

"She'd never wake up."

Tracey objected, but the witness answered before the judge could rule. Graham played that game through the whole trial, asking incriminating questions just so the jury would hear them. It didn't matter if he withdrew the questions himself, or if the judge sustained Tracey's objections, or if the questions were stricken from the record. The jury members weren't deaf. They heard every single thing he said, and they understood what he meant, just like he wanted them to. I always thought somebody should've filed a complaint with the disciplinary committee about Graham's behavior. Either that, or put a gun to his head.

I've been around guns all my life. Dad taught me to hunt when I was a kid. But after Mom moved in with us, Claudia didn't want any guns there, so I had to keep them at Roger's house. I wasn't happy about it, but I got tired of arguing with her. I cleaned all the guns before I stored them. When I was on the last gun, Claudia came into the room and watched me as I put another saturated patch on the rod and pushed it through the barrel. I pushed the dry patches through, too, then held the barrel up to the light: it was clean and shiny. I put a drop of oil into the cylinder hand and into the recess at the bottom of the frame. I wiped off the excess oil and dried the barrel with a clean cloth. When I put that gun down into its storage case, Claudia started in on me again.

"We need to protect your mother from the guns," she said, "more than we need them to protect us."

If Mom had taken my pistol and blasted away part of her brain, it wouldn't have done as much damage as the Alzheimer's did. That disease was the only thing she needed to be protected from. And nothing I did could protect her from that. I couldn't protect any of us. No matter how hard I tried.

I was ready for the hardest part. With the rocking horse in the carver's chops, I could start the rough carving. I tapered the horse's neck, carving off bits of the leg muscles that stuck out, tapering the muscles so they flowed smoothly into the legs. I turned the horse upside down and reclamped it. After I shaped the area between the horse's front legs and hollowed the area between its rear legs, I repositioned the horse on its side. I rounded the rump and shaped the area where the saddle would fit. Spike was out in the backyard, enjoying the first warm day. It was still too early to open the kitchen windows: the humidity would've affected the rocking horse before it was finished. I spent a long time on that horse: carving, removing the gouge marks, sanding, sanding, sanding. I had to go over to the sink a few times. To rinse my face and eyes. To get rid of all the residue.

"You analyzed the residue in this bag, correct?" said Tracey to the chemist.

"That's correct," said Dr. Peters, pushing his black-framed glasses up on the bridge of his nose.

"And you say the residue was identical to that found in the empty prescription bottles, correct?"

"Yes."

"Dr. Peters, do you know how the residue from the bottles got into that plastic freezer bag?"

"No, I can only analyze the residue itself."

"So if the defendant had put the open prescription bottles into the plastic bag, to throw them away, let's say, that could have left the residue, couldn't it?"

"I don't think it would have left as much as I found, but it's within the realm of possibility, yes."

"What if something heavy were put on the plastic bag after it was in the trashcan?" said Tracey. "Couldn't that have crushed any pills which might have fallen out of the bottles and were lying in the bag?"

"I concluded that the pills in the bag had been crushed before the bag was thrown into the trash can."

"But they could have been crushed afterward, couldn't they, by a heavy object thrown into the trash can on top of the bag?"

"I think they were crushed first," said Dr. Peters.

"Couldn't the pills have been crushed *after* they were thrown into the trash can by a heavy object thrown on top of them?"

"The particles were so uniformly fine . . ."

"Your Honor, could you please instruct the witness to answer the question with a yes or no?"

The judge stopped rocking in his leather chair and looked down at the witness.

"Dr. Peters, a yes or no will be sufficient," he said. "Please don't add any information that Ms. Garner hasn't questioned you about."

"Isn't that scenario possible?" said Tracey. "Couldn't the drugs have been crushed after they were in the trash by a heavy object thrown in on top of them?"

"Yes," he said. "It's possible."

Possibility, probability, postulation, speculation — all of it was bullshit. Somebody needed to put those expert witnesses into a Dumpster and crush them into residue. I was the only one who ever saw Claudia with that plastic bag, so I was the only one who knew what happened.

"I thought you were done with everything," I said after I found Claudia in the kitchen.

"And I thought you were carrying your stuff out to the car," she said. "Aren't you going to be late?"

"No, I've got time," I said, opening the refrigerator. "Don't we have any juice?"

"Behind the milk."

I drank some juice, then went over to the table where Claudia was.

"I wish you wouldn't drink out of the carton, Sam. Yesterday I caught Eleanor doing it."

Bowls and jars and prescription bottles were spread out everywhere. In front of Claudia was the plastic bag with Mom's medicines.

"What are you doing?" I said.

"Crushing your Mom's pills. What does it look like?"

"I just gave her some. About half an hour ago, when I gave her the pudding."

"This is for later," said Claudia.

"In that big of a bag?"

"We're out of small ones," she said.

After she picked up the bag and shook it, she put it down and ran the rolling pin over it again. Then she opened the bag and poured the crushed pills back into the bottle. She did only one bottle at a time. After she recapped the first bottle, she put it aside before she emptied the next one into the bag. I drank the last of the juice and set the carton down on the table.

"After they're all crushed," I said, "how do you tell how much is one pill?"

"I measure it," she said. "How do you think?"

The measuring spoons were right there on the table, beside the bag, and she was real careful about getting all the crushed pills into the right bottle before she did the next one. I told the cops that, and if Graham had talked to me before the trial started, I would've told him, too. None of them cared about the truth. The cops wanted a bad guy, and Graham wanted to go into politics. Sometimes I think that if Mom had died a year before or after, none of this would've happened.

"So despite the fact that these patients are dying, you'd never prescribe all these pills for an Alzheimer's patient, correct?" said Graham to the witness.

"Alzheimer's patients' bodies are already waging war with the disease," said the physician. "I don't like to stress their systems with drugs and their side effects."

He spoke so slow, I wondered if he thought he was in a kindergarten classroom rather than in a courtroom. Tracey brushed her hair from her forehead as she shifted in her chair.

"So, Dr. Jamison, you don't prescribe sleeping pills for Alzheimer's patients?" said Graham.

"Not ordinarily."

"What about anxiolytics: antianxiety drugs?"

"I prefer not to dispense those."

"What about antirage agents, or antipsychotics?"

"Only if the patient is so violent that he's doing physical harm to himself or others."

"And why are those the only circumstances under which you'd prescribe these kind of drugs?"

"I've found that when this many drugs are prescribed for an Alzheimer's patient," said Dr. Jamison, "the drugs are more for the benefit of the caregiver than for that of the patient."

Had he ever been kept awake by an Alzheimer's patient wandering around all night? Had he ever been slugged by an Alzheimer's patient having a tantrum? The prosecution's witnesses weren't experts. There's only one way to become a real expert on Alzheimer's — to live with one of its victims. Not for a few months, or for a year or two, but for years and years and years. And then, live through a few of their rampages. Like we did. Over and over again.

I rushed into the kitchen as, upstairs in her bedroom, Mom shrieked.

"What set her off this time?"

"Who knows?" said Claudia. "I've given up trying to figure it out."

"She's blocked her door so I can't get in. I'll have to take it off its hinges."

Claudia took some pills out of the bottles and picked up the rolling pin just as something flashed by outside the window.

"Whoa, what was that?" I said.

"It looked like the screen from her window."

"Are you sure you didn't say anything that —"

"Don't even start blaming me today, Sam."

"Hey, that's her pillow. She's throwing things out the window. Give her a couple of sleeping pills, too."

"With the tranquilizers? Are you sure?"

"Maybe we can get her to take a nap."

"We're still going to have to get into her room."

"We'll get into the room: don't worry about that."

I got the chocolate pudding out of the refrigerator and put some of it into a smaller bowl.

"Damn, there go her clothes. What's wrong with her today?"

Claudia emptied the crushed pills from the bag into the pudding. From upstairs, we heard the sound of glass breaking.

"Shit, was that the window or the mirror?"

"They never told us she'd do things like this."

"Goddamned doctors," I said. "Why don't they tell you everything?"

"Would you say you're an expert in the field of Alzheimer's treatment?" said Tracey to the prosecution's medical witness.

"I've treated several Alzheimer's patients," said Dr. Jamison.

"But geriatric medicine isn't your specialty, is it?"

"I'm an internist."

"Which means your training wasn't in geriatrics, correct?"

"I do know something about the treatment of Alzheimer's."

"But your training wasn't in that area, was it?"

"Not specifically, no."

Tracey was wearing a new suit with her new haircut, and she looked very professional. For once, the suit wasn't pastel. She looked pretty good. Like a real lawyer. Claudia was wearing a new maternity dress. She looked nice, too. Tired, but nice.

"Have you conducted any research or published any articles about Alzheimer's?" said Tracey.

"I'm a contributing editor of the journal of the country's leading medical association."

"Yes, I saw your articles on coronary artery disease," said Tracey. "But I couldn't locate your articles on Alzheimer's treatment. In which issue did those articles appear?"

"I believe I've already indicated to you that I haven't authored any studies on Alzheimer's."

"So you're not an expert in the treatment of Alzheimer's, are you, Dr. Jamison?"

"I've treated a few patients with the disease."

"Your Honor," said Tracey, turning to the judge, who looked down at the witness.

"Dr. Jamison, answer Ms. Garner's questions with a yes or no, please."

"You're not an expert on Alzheimer's, are you?" said Tracey.

"No. But I have treated Alzheimer's patients. And my mother had Alzheimer's."

"You didn't treat your own mother, did you?" said Tracey.

Some of the jury members stopped writing in their notebooks to look at the witness.

"I am a physician, Ms. Garner."

"Didn't you have to worry about a conflict of interest, Dr. Jamison?"

"Objection."

"Withdrawn. Dr. Jamison, how long did your mother live with you after she got Alzheimer's?"

"She didn't," he said. "She lived alone."

"With Alzheimer's?"

"She lived alone until she went into the assisted living unit," said the doctor.

"Oh, I see. And how long did your mother reside in the assisted living unit?"

"About five years."

"Until she was transferred to your home?"

"No," said Dr. Jamison. "Until she was moved to a full-care facility."

"A nursing home, isn't that what you mean?" said Tracey.

"I believe that's what I just said, yes."

"So your mother had Alzheimer's, and after she couldn't live alone anymore, she went to an assisted living unit, where she stayed until she was put in a nursing home, correct?"

"That's correct."

"So you were never actually a caregiver, were you, Dr. Jamison?"

"Not in the sense you mean," he said.

What other sense was there? No wonder he didn't think we needed drugs to take care of Mom. Sometimes Claudia and me, we needed those drugs more than Mom did.

Those pills gave us some peace.

Those pills saved us.

CHAPTER EIGHT

*T*HE EMPTY PRESCRIPTION BOTTLES were on the table, in a row, between Claudia and the detective. As I came into the kitchen, he picked up one of the bottles in his latex-gloved hands and showed it to her.

"What was this one for?" he said.

"That was to help her sleep," said Claudia.

"And this one?"

"For her depression."

"What about this one?"

"To keep her from getting violent."

Each time Claudia answered, the detective turned the bottle around to see its name, then wrote it down in his notebook. While he did that, a cop looked through the pantry, and another one opened the cupboards. I could hear the noise of other cops searching out in the garage. In the dining room, one of them was rummaging through the hutch and sideboard. Roger wasn't there. He wouldn't have done that to us. I walked over to the kitchen table as the detective showed Claudia another bottle.

"What's going on?" I said, and they both looked up at me. "Do you have a warrant?"

"Your wife gave us permission."

"You can't search without a warrant. That's the law."

"There's no need to raise your voice, Mr. Sloane. Your wife gave us permission."

The cop at the pantry came over, leaving the canned goods on the floor. He stood at the table, beside the detective.

"Claudia, did you call a lawyer?" I said.

"A lawyer? Do you think we need a lawyer?"

I grabbed the remaining medication bottles from the table. The detective stood up fast.

"Mr. Sloane, give those back."

"This is America, buddy," I said, stuffing the bottles into my jeans pockets. "You can't march into my home and take anything you want."

"Mitch, we've got a situation in here," said a third cop, going to the open garage door.

"Take it easy, Mr. Sloane. Just hand me those bottles," said the detective.

Then somebody's arm swung out at me so fast I didn't even have time to think. I was only trying to protect myself, but they jumped me. I tried to get away from them, but every time I got an arm or leg free, another one of them would get me. Somebody was trying to get the prescription bottles out of my pockets, too. I defended myself as best I could, but there were too many of them for me. I didn't give up, but eventually they dragged me down to the floor with them.

"Don't hurt him. Please. He didn't mean it," said Claudia. "Sam, tell them you didn't mean it."

"You're under arrest, Mr. Sloane. You have the right to remain silent. . . ."

"Don't use handcuffs. Sam, stop fighting them."

"You have the right to have an attorney present during questioning. . . ."

"Sam, please, stop it . . . you're making everything so much worse."

"Listen to your wife, Sloane. Obstructing an investigation, assaulting a police officer . . ."

They yanked me up from the floor and slammed me in a kitchen chair. The detective with the latex gloves wiped the blood off his face. Detective Mitchell picked up one of the other chairs and sat down, breathing heavily. One of the cops offered Claudia his hand-kerchief.

"Hey, look what I found," said Troy, coming in from the garage, and everyone turned toward him. "Whoa, Mitch, what's going on in here?"

"We got it under control," said Mitchell. "What'd you find?"

Troy held up his gloved hand. In it was the plastic bag.

I've never understood what was so earthshaking about finding that stupid plastic bag. If they'd found empty shell casings in the bedroom and gunpowder residue on Claudia's hands, or if they'd discovered a bloodied knife with Claudia's fingerprints and slashes on my mom's throat, then I could've understood their thinking a crime had been committed. But a plastic food storage bag? It's not like they found the damned thing over my mom's head with a rubber band around her neck. I'll never understand why something as ordinary as a plastic bag made anybody think my mom's death was murder.

Claudia was so upset and depressed after Mom's death that she stayed in bed most of the day, every day. When she did get up, she didn't take a shower or do her hair or even get dressed. Not even when Eve came over and tried to talk her into coming down to the bookstore. Not even after she promised Roger that she'd start seeing Dr. Daniels again. Then one day after work I found her sitting on the couch, with that silver box of cremains in her lap. The box with my mother's cremains. Just sitting there. Holding that box. Staring at it. It was too much. I had to do something. When I tried to take it away from her, she wouldn't let go.

"Let go of me," I said to Roger in the hallway outside the court-room.

"If you'd done what I told you," he said, "we wouldn't be in this mess right now."

"Don't," said Eve, putting her hand on his arm. "They have enough to worry about."

Roger walked away from us and paced the hall, his hands in his pockets. He acted like it was my fault the cops had been lying about Claudia on the stand that morning.

"He doesn't mean it, Sam," said Eve. "We know you did the best you could."

"No, he didn't," said Roger.

"What could we have done different?" I said.

"Don't take the bait, Sam."

"Name one thing you did right."

"Hush, Roger, someone's going to hear you."

"You know so much," I said, "you tell me what we did wrong."

"For starters, how about turning evidence over to the police?"

"He didn't turn anything over to the police, Roger, and you know it," said Eve.

"He left it for them to find."

"What evidence?"

"The plastic bag. The prescription bottles."

Eve stepped between us fast, her hands on our chests.

"I don't think you should be discussing this here," she said.

"Go ahead, Roger. Tell me you think your own sister is a murderer."

"For all I know, buddy," he said, "you're the guilty one."

"You son of a —"

"At least I didn't talk to the cops about her."

"What about that monkey business with the evidence?"

"I never touched the evidence."

"Then how come a cop doesn't know his sister's going to get arrested?"

"I knew. I told her. In plenty of time. Just because she didn't tell you . . ."

When I grabbed his finger and twisted it out of my way, he shoved me, so I pushed him back. He caught hold of my jacket and shirt, I swung at him, and Eve got smashed between us. Then things got worse from there.

"Roger, Sam, stop it. Stop it, you two. My God, people are watching. What'll they think? Stop it, both of you. Roger, let go of his tie. Let go, I said. Sam, go stand over there. Go on, before somebody sees you. Think of Claudia, for heaven's sake. Think of the baby."

Roger and I went to the opposite sides of the hall, both of us breathing pretty heavy. A few people looked over at us, but I don't think anybody noticed anything. Eve's face was red as she stood in front of Roger, shaking her finger at him, and he didn't have a chance to answer, her mouth was moving so fast. I wished I was still smoking, so I could have a cigarette, but I'd promised Claudia I'd quit. Roger didn't mean what he said, though. It was the stress of the trial that made him say those things. The stress of not knowing what would happen to our family. It made us hurt each other. It made us cruel.

"What happened, Sam? Tell me, for heaven's sake. Did you get her there in time?" said Mom.

I closed the front door and walked past Mom to the dining room.

"Oh, no. It was too late, wasn't it, Sam?"

I yanked opened the bottom door of the hutch and got out Dad's bottle of scotch. Mom was right behind me.

"Poor Claudia. She must be heartbroken," she said. "To carry it this long and then lose it. You both wanted this baby so much. It's all my fault. If she didn't have to help me all the time . . ."

I poured a glass of the scotch and drank it down, then poured myself another. Mom tried to hug me or something. I moved away fast.

"I was just going to take your coat. It's wet, Sam. Don't drop it on the floor."

"Don't tell me what to do in my own house."

She gave me a look just like the one she used to give me when I was growing up, and that made everything worse. When she leaned over to pick up the coat, I put my foot on it.

"Leave it."

"It's getting the rug all wet. And that rug belonged to Grandmother Rose. . . ."

The glass broke in my hand. I pressed my finger to the cut edge of the glass so blood went into the scotch. Then I threw the glass. Blood and scotch went all over the dining room table before the glass shattered on the wall. I picked up another glass and threw it, too. They weren't really mine and Claudia's — they'd been an anniversary present from Dad to Mom — but I didn't care. Glass after glass hit the wall and exploded. When there weren't any more glasses, I sat down on one of the dining room chairs and put my head on my arms. Mom stood in the corner, holding herself, crying.

I don't know what else I said, I was so mad. I probably sounded like Claudia when she cut up my videotapes of the trial. I had them up in the attic, but she found them. Man, was she ever furious. I'll bet everybody in the state heard her yelling. I thought she'd never stop. She didn't have to cut them up, though. I mean, it's not like I was sitting around watching them all the time. I don't yell at her and grab the scissors when she sits around looking at that memory book she made with Mom, do I? I don't throw a fit about all the money we're paying so she can sit in Dr. Daniels' office and talk about everything that happened. Just because I had those videotapes, it didn't mean I was stuck in the past. Didn't I sell the old house and auction off my parents' furniture? Doesn't that prove I'm not stuck in the past? I told everybody I sold the house to pay the legal bills, and the bills did swallow up most of the money we got, even though Tracey took out some of her fees in trade at Claudia's bookstore. But I really sold the house because I didn't want to live there anymore. I didn't want to live with what happened in that house. I wanted to get free of it all.

"When this is all over, when you're free . . ."

"Tell me now, Roger," said Claudia when we went to see her at the jail. "Otherwise I'll imagine the most horrible —"

"He resigned."

"Damn it, Eve."

Roger twisted around in his chair to look at her, but Eve turned away. The visiting room was almost deserted. The only other visitors that day were on the far side of the room, huddled close together over their table, holding hands. Claudia sat across from me and Roger. Eve was behind us, her arms crossed over her chest, a scowl on her face.

"Why did you resign?" said Claudia.

"I took early retirement."

"He resigned."

"Why?"

"I had my time in. Let's just leave it at that. I've been wanting another job anyway."

The guard strolled past the table, swinging his baton around by its wrist strap. He nodded toward us.

"What did you do, Roger?" said Claudia. "Did you resign because of me?"

"You're not the center of the universe, Claudia. Not everything happens because of you."

"Stop it, Eve," said Roger.

"Why is she the only one anybody worries about? All of our lives got turned upside down by this trial, not just hers. We've been hurt just as much as she has."

"She's the only one in jail."

"We're every goddamned one of us in jail. She's just the only one who can see the bars."

"For Christ's sake, stop it, Eve. Don't say anything else."

"Go ahead," said Claudia. "I want to hear it."

"You'll regret it," said Roger.

"I regret it already," said Eve. "Reporters calling the house all day long, strangers taunting the kids by calling you Aunt Lizzie Borden, cranks phoning the house all night long then hanging up . . ."

"All that's really happening?" said Claudia.

"Are you calling me a liar?"

"Roger, why didn't you tell me?"

"I'm telling you," said Eve.

"She's exaggerating," said Roger.

"Don't you dare take her side. Don't you dare."

"Let's talk about this later. At home."

"I'm your wife, the mother of your kids. She's only your sister, and an adopted sister at that."

"Sam, take Eve out to the car, will you?"

"Hey, I've got an idea," she said. "Why don't you go ahead and tell them what you did, Roger? Go ahead: tell them what you did for Claudia. Then they'll put you in jail with her. Maybe they'll even give you a family discount."

"Sam . . ."

"Christ, Roger, what the hell do you expect me to do?"

"Don't worry. I'm leaving," said Eve, snatching her sweater off the back of one of the chairs. "For good."

As she was shoving her arms into her sweater, she glared at Claudia. The look on Eve's face was so terrible, I thought she was going to hit Claudia. Or Roger. Or somebody. Eve slapped her hands on the table and leaned so close she could have spit on Claudia when she looked up at her. Roger stood up and tried to pull Eve away, but it was too late.

"It's all your fault, Claudia," said Eve. "You're the one who destroyed our family."

CHAPTER NINE

$\mathcal{A}$LZHEIMER'S DESTROYS ENTIRE FAMILIES, doesn't it, Dr. Barnett?" said Tracey after the physician settled himself in the witness chair.

"It can," said Dr. Barnett.

"With all that tension in the home, don't you worry about your Alzheimer's patients committing suicide?"

"That depends on the individual patient."

"Did you worry about Eleanor Sloane committing suicide?"

"Objection."

"Sustained," said the judge.

The high school newspaper was doing a series of articles on the trial, so the front two rows of the courtroom on Claudia's side were filled with high school girls: Roger's twins and other girls who'd worked for Claudia and Eve in the bookstore. I didn't remember half their names, but it meant a lot to Claudia to have them there. Whenever she looked at them, some of her old beauty came back to her face.

"You prescribed quite a few drugs for Eleanor Sloane," said Tracey. "Do you usually prescribe so many drugs for your Alzheimer's patients?"

"It depends on the individual," said Dr. Barnett.

"So not all Alzheimer's patients need these drugs?"

"That's correct."

"But Eleanor Sloane was one of those patients who needed them, correct?"

"That's correct."

The high school reporters jotted down the testimony in their notebooks. Across the aisle from them, the professional reporters did the same.

"Why would you prescribe a sleeping pill for an Alzheimer's patient?" said Tracey.

"If the patient is up all night wandering around, trying to get out of the house, a sleeping pill will allow everyone to get some rest at night," said Dr. Barnett.

"Was Eleanor Sloane wandering at night?"

"Every night," he said, nodding toward the jury. "Till I gave her the sleeping pills."

"What about the anxiolytic: the antianxiety agent?"

"Eleanor was having panic attacks."

"Is that usual for Alzheimer's patients?"

"It's not rare."

"What did the anxiolytic do for Eleanor?"

"It decreased her anxiety and paranoia," said Dr. Barnett.

"So the drug improved the quality of Eleanor's life?"

"Yes, and, in turn, it improved the quality of Claudia's and Sam's life."

Tracey went over to the poster that listed all the prescriptions we'd ever had in our house, even the antibiotics I'd taken for my sinus infection. With the pointer, she indicated several of them listed at the top of the chart. The girl reporters leaned sideways to get a better view.

"Did you prescribe all of these medications for Eleanor Sloane?" said Tracey.

"Yes, I did."

"To be taken concurrently?"

"That's correct."

"And it wasn't dangerous for her to take all of these drugs concurrently?"

"Not as long as the instructions were followed," said Dr. Barnett.

"Can Alzheimer's patients follow instructions for medications?"

"Not beyond the earlier stages of the disease. Claudia gave the medications to Eleanor."

"Didn't you worry about Claudia's making a mistake when she gave Eleanor the pills?"

"If I had, I wouldn't have prescribed them."

Tracey stood beside the jury box, resting her hand on the wood railing.

"Dr. Barnett, why didn't you request an autopsy after Eleanor's death?"

"There wasn't any reason for one. She was terminally ill, in the final stages of her disease. And she had pneumonia."

"So you don't think Claudia helped Eleanor commit suicide?"

"No, I do not," said Dr. Barnett. "Claudia would never hurt anyone."

Instead, it was Mom's illness and death that hurt Claudia. She was so depressed, she couldn't sleep. Unless she slept in Mom's bed. If I woke up in the night and Claudia was gone, I knew where to find her. I didn't mind. At least, not till the night I found her sleeping with the silver box of cremains. That's when I decided to do something. I had to. I slipped the box out from under her right arm, but she didn't wake up. I carried the cremains up to the attic, to the baby dresser. I lifted the blanket draped over it, opened the top drawer, and placed the box inside. Then I took it right back out. It wasn't a good hiding place. In the basement, the bare bulb threw my shadow around the walls like some horror movie. A couple of times, I thought I heard Claudia, but I was all by myself. I looked for hiding places under the workbench, behind the washer and dryer, under the top drawer of my toolbox. I couldn't find any place in the house or the garage where she wouldn't have been able to find them, so I took the ashes out to the garden. It was so cold that night, the air burned, and the ground was frozen in ridges. At the far edge of the backyard, beside the overturned garden, I opened the silver box and dumped out the ashes. It didn't take long. Then I went in the house, up to the attic, and put the emptied box in the top drawer of the baby dresser. Claudia was still asleep when I went back to the bedroom. Mom would've understood. Besides, I did it for Claudia. I would've done anything for her. Anything at all.

"What would you do if you were sick, or dying anyway?" said Mom as we sat at the picnic table in the backyard.

"I still wouldn't do it," said Dad. "Too much to live for."

"Not even if you were in unbearable pain?"

"Nope."

"I don't believe it," she said, shaking her head. "You'd never commit suicide?"

"Wouldn't even consider it."

"Neither would I," said Roger. "It's gruesome."

"Of course it's gruesome when they use guns or knives," said Mom. "But I meant —"

"Hey, do you remember the Robinsons, over on Minster?" said Dad, salting his potato salad. "Their son shot himself."

"Jesus, you mean Eddie? He was just a kid."

"Roger's the one who had to go down to the basement where he was."

"When did that happen?" I said.

"Oh, please, let's not talk about it," said Eve, putting down her fork.

"He wasn't sick either," said Dad.

"He might've been suffering," said Mom. "You never know what kind of pain people are in."

"There's no kind of pain that would make me kill myself," said Dad, his mouth full.

"It's a sin," I said.

"Sam, you don't even go to church unless Claudia drags you there."

"That doesn't make it any less of a sin."

"Right," said Dad, reaching for another dill pickle.

"Oh, what do you know, Harold? You don't go to church either."

"I wouldn't kill myself," I said. "I'd pray for a cure."

"I'd have a few beers," said Dad, belching.

"I'd have a lot of beers," said Roger. "Then I'd pray."

"Don't make fun," said Eve.

"I don't know if I'd pray or not," said Mom. "I might be too angry at God to pray."

"How'd we ever get onto such a morbid topic on a day like this?" I said.

"Your mother's in one of those moods again," said Dad. "Has been for weeks. I told you."

"I'm not in any mood," said Mom.

I stood up and took another hamburger off the grill. After I slipped the patty onto a bun, I gave it to Dad, and Eve passed him the ketchup. When Roger held his plate up, I piled a few more bratwurst on it. The sun was warm on my back as I stood at the grill. Claudia pulled the bowl of potato salad closer and put some on her plate. She offered some to Eve, but Eve shook her head.

"Claudia, would you help someone you know kill himself?"

"I wouldn't," I said.

"We know you wouldn't, dear," said Mom, "but I was asking Claudia."

"How well do I know this person?"

"Claude, you wouldn't help anybody commit suicide, and you know it," I said.

"If the person were dying anyway . . ."

"You still wouldn't," I said.

Claudia looked at the trees in the backyard and at the flowers around the patio. She waved a bee away from the potato salad. She ran her fingers over the picnic table where the cloth didn't reach, and over the condensation on her glass of lemonade.

"I don't know," she said. "I might help someone commit suicide."

"Not if you wanted to stay married to me," I said, and everyone laughed.

"You want her dead, don't you, Sam? You left it here on purpose."

Claudia stomped into the living room and slapped the newspaper I was reading. When I lowered it to look at her, she held out one of my pistols.

"Where'd you get that?" I said.

"Where do you think I got it? From your mother."

"Where'd she get it?"

I reached for the gun, but Claudia yanked it away.

"She could've shot herself, Sam."

"She doesn't know how to use it."

"What's so hard about pulling the trigger?"

"You worry too much."

"What if she'd pointed it at Roger or Eve or one of their kids?"

I dropped the newspaper on the floor, stood up, and went over to Claudia. She held the gun away from me, but I managed to get it.

"What if she'd pointed it at me, Sam? What if she'd shot me?"

"It's not even loaded, Claude. See?"

I took the gun, flipped open the cylinder, and showed it to her. Her mouth opened a little before she pressed her lips together hard. I looked down at the gun. No, it wasn't possible. It couldn't be true. But there it was. Right there. In the very next chamber. A bullet.

I swear I took all the guns over to Roger's. I don't know how that one got left behind, and I definitely don't know how Mom found it. I never kept loaded guns in the house, so Mom would've had to load it herself, but she couldn't have done that. I didn't want her to shoot herself. Christ, if I'd wanted Mom to die, I could've packed her in the car some night when it was snowing like hell, driven her out to the boonies, and left her there. She couldn't have found her way back. She would've fallen asleep out there and died. Leaving that gun there wasn't wishful thinking or a Freudian slip or anything else like that. It was an accident, and that's all it was. My conscience is clear.

"I didn't do it," said Claudia.

Mom looked over at me for about half a second, then went back to dicing the tomatoes.

"So the garden hose just walked around to the back of the car and wrapped itself around the tailpipe?"

Claudia slid the chopped onions from the cutting board to the large bowl on the table.

"You and Eleanor are the gardeners," she said. "What would I be doing with the hose this time of year?"

She picked up one of the green peppers and began cutting it as Mom hunched herself over the tomatoes, chopping them smaller and smaller. Then Claudia started to talk about something that had happened at the bookstore, like I wasn't even there. God, it made me crazy when she did that. I never thought marriage was going to be all champagne and roses, but after Mom moved in with us, everything changed. It was like Claudia and Mom became the married couple, and I was just some houseboy who cut the grass and took out the garbage and paid the bills. After Claudia started chattering to Mom like I wasn't there, I grabbed the nozzle off the counter and dumped it into the trash as loud as I could. But it didn't matter. Claudia never even looked at me.

"Officer Burke, could you tell by looking at them who started it?" said Harlan Graham, straightening his red tie as he approached the witness stand.

"They were both pretty messed up when I got there," said the cop.

"The defendant and her husband were both injured?"

"Yes."

"In what way was Mrs. Sloane injured?"

The cop glanced down at his notes and read from them.

"She had a cut mouth and some bruises on her face. The emergency room X-rays showed she had a couple of broken ribs."

"And Mr. Sloane, what were his injuries?" said Graham.

"His face and neck were all scratched up," said the cop, flipping the page in his notebook. "He had a couple of broken fingers."

"Did either Mr. Sloane or his wife indicate how they sustained these injuries?" said Graham.

"He said she jumped him. She said he attacked her."

"Which one do you think started the altercation?"

"Objection."

"I'll rephrase. After interviewing them, were you able to ascertain which of the two started the altercation?"

"Mr. Sloane told me his wife started it," said the cop. "It had something to do with drugs."

"Can you be more specific?"

"He said the fight started when he was trying to stop Mrs. Sloane."

"Stop her from what?"

"From killing his mother."

CHAPTER TEN

$\mathcal{S}$HE SAID HER HUSBAND WAS TRYING TO KILL HIS MOTHER," said Simms, the second cop on the stand about the domestic dispute.

"Are you sure it wasn't the other way around?" said Tracey, frowning. "Officer Burke testified that Mr. Sloane claimed that Claudia was the one trying to kill his mother."

"I didn't talk to Mr. Sloane. I only talked to the defendant."

Graham's assistant leaned closer and whispered something, but Graham didn't respond. Tracey leaned back against the rail in front of the jury.

"Were Claudia and her husband in the same room when you and Officer Burke talked to them?" she said.

"No, the defendant and I went into the house. Her husband and my partner were out in the driveway."

"And you're sure that Claudia said it was her husband who was trying to kill his own mother?"

"Yes, those were her exact words."

The newspaper artist turned in her seat so that she was facing my direction, changed pencils, and started drawing me. I used to have all those clippings about the trial, including the one with my picture, but Claudia found them and threw them away. The same time she cut up the videotapes.

"Had you ever been called to the Sloanes' address on a domestic dispute before?" said Tracey.

"No."

"Had anybody else been called to that address on a domestic?"

"Not that I know of."

"Do you know which of the Sloanes called the police?"

"As far as I know, it was one of the neighbors who called 9-1-1."

"One of the neighbors?" said Tracey.

"The Sloanes were fighting out in the driveway when we got there."

I crossed my arms over my chest, then uncrossed them and put my hands on my knees.

"So the dispute started because Claudia was trying to stop her husband from harming his mother, correct?" said Tracey.

"That's what she told me, yes."

"Did Claudia tell you how her husband was trying to kill his mother?"

"Objection," said Graham.

"Overruled. You may answer the question."

"She said he was flushing his mother's prescription medicines down the toilet."

"How is that trying to kill her?"

"As the defendant explained it to me," said the cop, "several of the drugs her husband's mother was taking couldn't be abruptly discontinued without harming her. His mother could go into convulsions or have a heart attack or something if the medicine was stopped all the sudden."

One of Graham's assistants passed him a folder, which he opened and read. Then Graham leaned his chin on his hand, his lips pressed together.

"So, when Claudia said her husband was trying to kill his mother," said Tracey, "what she meant was that her husband was throwing all the medicine away, and if his mother were abruptly taken off that medicine, she might go into convulsions and die. Is that correct, Officer Simms?"

"That's what she said."

"In other words, Claudia was trying to protect Eleanor Sloane, wasn't she?"

"As far as I could tell," said the cop, "she was trying to do just that."

Of course Claudia protected her. Even after that illness swallowed Mom. Even after she didn't know us anymore. Even though she was dead before she died. The cops and the prosecutor thought that just because her lungs still inhaled and exhaled, or because her heart still pumped blood, my mom was alive. But that body Claudia found wasn't my mom. It was just a body. Nothing more.

"Mr. Bradshaw, what do you do for your terminally ill clients?" said Prosecutor Graham.

"I draw up advance directives," said the witness.

My back, chest, and shoulders felt as if there was a tight band around them, getting tighter with every breath I took. It was warm enough to go outside without a jacket, but the radiators were still blasting out heat. It was sweltering in the courtroom. I loosened my tie to unbutton my shirt collar.

"Could you explain to the court exactly what advance directives are?" said Graham to the attorney.

"Advance directives are legal documents — contracts, if you will — that allow the terminally ill to put their health care wishes in writing, and to appoint someone to act as their agent in case they become unable to communicate their wishes themselves."

I tried to slip off my jacket, but the bench was too crowded. If I'd gotten up and left in the middle of session, it would've looked bad for Claudia, so I had to stay there. It hurt to breathe, and my left arm ached all the way down to my hand.

"Are you all right?" said Roger under his breath.

"Was Eleanor Sloane one of your clients?" said Graham to the witness.

"Yes, she was."

"Did you draw up advance directives for her?"

"Yes, I did."

"Could you tell us what kind of advance directives you drew up for Eleanor Sloane?"

"A living will, a durable power of attorney for health care, and a declaration."

"In those documents, whom did Eleanor Sloane designate as her agent?"

"Her daughter-in-law, Claudia Sloane."

Tracey covered the microphone on the defense table with her hand and said something to Claudia as her assistants frantically shuffled through the papers in their briefcases. Then Claudia looked back at me.

"Tell us what areas the living will covers," said Graham.

"It covers life-support systems," said Bradshaw.

"Could you read aloud the paragraph I've indicated here?"

The attorney put on his glasses and read.

I, Eleanor Rose Sloane, being of sound mind and not under or subject to duress, fraud, or undue influence, do voluntarily make known my desire that my dying shall not be artificially prolonged. If I am unable to give directions regarding the use of life-sustaining treatment when I am in a terminal condition or a permanently unconscious state, it is my intention that this living will shall be honored by my family and physicians as the final expression of my legal right to refuse medical treatment.

Tracey sat so rigid in her chair she didn't even look like she was breathing. I took my tie all the way off, but my throat still felt like fishing line was twisted around it.

"Could you read this next paragraph aloud?" said Graham.

This statement is made after careful consideration and is in accordance with my strong convictions and beliefs. I want the wishes and directions here expressed carried out to the extent permitted by law. To the extent that the provisions of this Living Will are not legally enforceable, I hope that those to whom this Will is addressed will regard themselves as morally bound by them.

"In other words, this document is requesting that Claudia Sloane be morally obligated to let Eleanor Sloane die?"

"Yes, that's exactly what it's saying."

And still, Claudia kept looking at me. There were so many people jammed in that courtroom, and it was so hot. My chest and jaw were aching. I opened my mouth, but no words came out. Tracey pulled on Claudia's sleeve till she turned away from me. The room closed in around us.

Nobody said it was going to be easy. As a matter of fact, Roger and Eve both tried to talk me out of doing it. They wanted me to wait until the trial was over, but I didn't want Claudia to come back to the house where it all happened. I sold the old house while the trial was in session and got a new one, as far away from our old neighborhood as possible. Sometimes in the new house, I thought I was crazy, too. Some nights, lying awake in bed, with nobody there but Spike, who was just a kitten then, I wondered what the hell I'd done. I wondered what made me think a new place would make any difference. Other nights, I slept so hard that I missed the alarm and had to break all the speed limits to make it to Glenview by morning session. One night, when I couldn't sleep and was working on the living room floor, I found rotted subflooring. I started laughing and couldn't stop. There I was, in the middle of the night, in the middle of torn-up, rotted flooring, laughing like an idiot. Laughing till I cried. Till my side hurt. Till I fell backwards on the floor and Spike came over to look at me. And still, I kept on laughing.

"Will you stop looking at everybody else in the place and look at me?" said the woman at my table in the bar as she leaned closer, her red lips pursed. "You wanna kiss me? You can if you want."

"Do you want another beer?" I said. "Let's get some more beer."

It took me a few seconds to find our waitress in the crowd. I raised my hand and waved her over.

"Could we get a couple more here? And some pretzels?"

The waitress put our empty mugs and the pretzel basket on her tray before she went back to the bar. The woman at the table with me sighed loudly.

"Is this what we're gonna do all night?" she said. "Eat pretzels and drink beer?"

"Aren't you having a good time, Carla?" I said, tapping my fingers to the music.

"Sharla," she said, scooting her chair closer and touching my leg.

"Let's dance," I said, standing up.

"How're we gonna dance? The band ain't back from break yet."

"There's the jukebox."

"I don't like any of those songs."

"I'll put on some different ones. Damn. I'm out of quarters. Charlotte, do you have any?"

"Sharla," she said.

"Sorry. Hey, excuse me, buddy — you got any quarters? Thanks, man. So, Darla, what kind of music do you want to hear?"

"D'you ever think about getting one of them hair transplants?"

"What?"

"You'd look a whole helluva lot younger with more hair."

I pulled my chair around to the other side of the small table before I sat down again. She waved to a couple of guys in suits, and they raised their beer mugs to her. When the jukebox finished playing, the crowd's noise was a roar. I picked up my mug and gulped down half my beer. The carbonation burned the back of my throat. It felt good. Somebody at the jukebox selected a country song.

"So, where d'you live, Sam? Is it Sam or Sammy?"

"Samuel," I said.

"Samuel? Geez, that sounds like some Bible name. You ain't no Bible-thumper, are you?"

"What's a Bible-thumper?"

"Never mind. I guess you ain't. So, Mister Sam Samuel," she said, her long fingernails tracing a pattern on the back of my hand, "you wanna go back to my place or not?"

"I want to have a couple of beers," I said.

"You had a couple already."

"So, keep me company while I have a couple more."

"Whatsa matter? I look too much like your wife or something?"

"My wife?"

"You're still wearing the ring, Sammy. Her picture's in your wallet. I saw it when you paid for the drinks."

"You don't look anything like my wife. She has red hair."

She opened her compact and started redoing her lipstick, pursing her lips several times at her reflection in the mirror before she put it away. I stood up. Before I made it to the jukebox, the band members went back onstage and picked up their instruments. I returned to the table and drank more of my beer. When the woman smiled at me, she wasn't too bad looking.

"Do you want to dance?" I said. "Or go get something to eat?"

"Do you wanna go home?" she said. "Or call your pretty little wife?"

CHAPTER ELEVEN

$\mathcal{L}$ET ME CALL YOUR ATTENTION TO THIS DOCUMENT," said Harlan Graham as he handed another set of legal papers to the witness. "Could you tell the court what it is?"

"It's a durable power of attorney for health care," said Mr. Bradshaw. "It gives the designated agent the legal authority to make health care decisions for someone else."

"Does this durable power of attorney for health care designate Claudia Sloane as the agent to make health care decisions for Eleanor Sloane?"

"Yes, it does," said Attorney Bradshaw.

"Tell the court the difference between a standard power of attorney and this document."

"Technically, the durable power of attorney has no expiration date."

"That means it doesn't have to be periodically renewed or updated, does it?"

"Not unless the designated agent is changed."

Graham walked around to the side of the witness box and pointed to the document.

"At the bottom of the page, there's a box checked: could you read the paragraph next to that?"

I do not want my life to be prolonged nor do I want life-sustaining or death-delaying treatment to be provided or continued if my agent believes the burdens of the treatment outweigh the expected benefits.

"Now, on the next page, could you read the paragraph typed in all capital letters?"

If at any time I should become unable to communicate my instructions, and the application of artificial life-sustaining procedures shall serve only to prolong artificially the moment of my death, I direct such procedures be withheld or withdrawn, including withdrawal of the administration of nutrition and hydration.

"Why is that paragraph in all capital letters?" said Graham.

"For emphasis."

"What's written beside that paragraph?"

"Eleanor's Sloane's initials, indicating that she specifically authorized the instructions contained in that paragraph."

Graham took the paper from the witness and held it up in front of the jury.

"So this document gave Claudia Sloane the ability to make decisions concerning life-sustaining or death-delaying treatment, did it not?"

"Yes, it gave her that authority."

"In other words," said Graham, motioning toward Claudia, "this document gave Claudia Sloane the legal authority to make life-and-death decisions for Eleanor Sloane."

Even if Claudia had known about those documents, she never would've made a decision like that on her own. After all, it was my mother, not hers. Besides, Claudia and I discussed everything concerning Mom. We made all those decisions together. Always. Together.

"I didn't make that decision, so it must've been an accident," I said to the funeral director over the phone. "Well, then it's a mistake."

Claudia came into the kitchen. She poured herself some coffee and sat down at the table.

"But we already have the plot," I said, still on the phone. "No, I wouldn't expect you to know that, but . . . well, who was it that changed the arrangements? Mrs. Sloane? Which one?"

Claudia buttered her toast and dipped it into her coffee. After I hung up the phone, I stood there without moving. Claudia didn't look at me until I sat down at the table. Even then, she didn't ask me anything. She just sat there, dipping her toast into her coffee and eating it, like it was just another day.

"They cremated the body," I said, but she never said a thing.

"I'm not asking you to lie to Claudia, Sam."

"You're asking me to keep something from her."

"Just don't tell her during the trial, that's all I'm asking."

"She's my wife, Roger."

"And I'm your best friend. For over thirty years. Come on, Sam. You don't tell her everything."

"Yes, I do."

"You didn't tell her about Carla."

"Darla. And nothing happened."

"Not for lack of trying."

"What's that supposed to mean?"

"Listen, Sam, all I'm asking is that you not tell Claudia I got fired till after the trial."

"Fired? Did you just say 'fired'? I thought you retired."

All I could hear on the other end of the phone was his breathing. When one of the kids came into the room and asked him something, his voice got muffled, like he'd put his hand over the mouthpiece, then he came back on the line.

"Did you take early retirement or did you get fired, Roger?"

He was so quiet I could've sworn I heard his kids arguing downstairs. In our kitchen, the clock ticked loud. I watched the second hand move around the face while I waited for Roger to answer.

"If I hadn't retired," he finally said, "Internal Affairs would've investigated."

"Christ, Roger, what did you do?"

"Nothing."

"They fired you for nothing? Come on, Roger."

"I didn't do anything, Sam. I swear."

"Does Eve know?"

"What do you think?"

"Jesus," I said. "So you want me to lie to Eve, too?"

In the background, I heard knocking and a muffled voice. The phone clattered as Roger put it down. After he opened the bedroom door and yelled, I heard whining. Roger shouted louder, then slammed the bedroom door. He was breathing heavily when he picked up the receiver again.

"I don't know why the hell anyone wants kids," he said. "Little monsters, that's all they are."

"Claudia will never believe you took early retirement."

"I'll tell her the truth after she's had the baby."

"Like that's going to make a difference."

"Sam, if she loses this baby because of what happened to me, I won't be able to live with . . . Wait a minute. I think Eve just pulled into the garage. I've got to go."

Did he tamper with evidence or was he just trying to get a look at the case against Claudia? Even I don't know. He never told me. And if he told Eve, she never let the rest of us know what he'd done. Whatever it was, he did it for Claudia. He would've done anything for her. Anything at all.

"After everything I've done for you," said Claudia. "After everything I've done for your damned mother."

"I didn't say I wouldn't have married you. We were already living together, weren't we? We'd already talked about getting married. Jesus, I wish you'd stop twisting things around. All I said was, things might've turned out different, that's all."

"You bastard."

"You're the one that brought this up. You said you wanted me to tell you the truth, so I did. If you'd told me you'd started —"

"I did tell you."

"Two days before."

"That's telling you. That was enough time to call off the wedding if you didn't want to marry me."

"You weren't bleeding on the honeymoon. Pretty convenient, huh?"

"Oh, my God," she said. "You think I would've lied about something like that? To you? How could you think that, Sam? And how could you accuse me of that? After everything I've done for you? After everything I've sacrificed?"

"Yeah, well, why don't you get down off that cross once in a while and give your arms a rest?"

I saw Claudia out in the driveway, her arm held out to the side like somebody was out there with her. She dribbled the ball across the driveway, her free arm fending off invisible opponents. Each time she shot, she made a clean basket, the ball never touching the rim. After she caught it and ran back to the other side of the driveway, she turned and shot again. Her hair, black with rain, almost hid her eyes, but she didn't move it away. Her bare legs were already splattered with mud, and each time she landed, the puddles splashed her again. Her chest was heaving. Her shoulder blades and ribs poked out against the flimsy, wet T-shirt. Dribble and shoot, dribble and shoot. Over and over and over. I turned around once to look at Mom, curled up in bed like a newborn, her fists clenched in sleep against her face. Rain pounded the roof. Thunder rattled the windows. Claudia shot the ball. Over and over and over.

"Could you read that again, please?" said Graham.

I hope that those to whom this living will is addressed will regard themselves as morally bound by its provisions.

"'Morally bound by them,'" said Graham. "That phrase is requesting that the appointed agent respect Eleanor Sloane's wish to end her life, is it not?"

"Objection."

"Withdrawn. Doesn't that phrase request the agent to feel morally obligated regarding life and death issues?"

"Regarding life-sustaining and death-delaying treatment, yes," said Attorney Bradshaw.

"So this document asks Claudia Sloane, as the designated agent, to feel morally obligated to carry out Eleanor Sloane's death wish, doesn't it?"

"Objection, Your Honor."

"Sustained. Mr. Graham . . ."

"I'll withdraw that question, Your Honor. No further questions."

He did that all the time during the trial. Lied and misled the jury. But that wasn't the worst part of it. No, the worst part was how everybody else in the courtroom acted like it was all legal and ethical and fair.

"Be fair, Sam," said Eve. "Just listen to her."

I got up from the spare bed in their son Matthew's room as Roger closed the door.

"We wouldn't ask if it weren't important," he said.

"I can't see Claudia right now," I said as I began making the bed.

"Listen, Sam, you can stay here as long as you need to," said Roger. "No questions asked."

"But just talk to her," said Eve. "That's all."

"Is she here?"

"No. She called."

I picked up the phone next to their son's bed. There was a dial tone.

"She's not on the phone now. She needs to talk to you in person. Please, Sam."

"You can come back here afterward if you want," said Roger.

"There's nothing Claudia can say that will change my mind about us," I said, reaching under the bed and grabbing my tennis shoes.

"You still love each other," said Eve.

"Nobody said we didn't."

I stood and tucked my T-shirt into my jeans. After I put on my belt, I ran my fingers through my hair.

"It doesn't matter what you think Claudia did," said Eve.

"Or what she thinks you did," said Roger.

"It doesn't matter what happened," said Eve. "You love each other, and when you hear what she has to tell you . . . well, see how things work out."

We would've worked things out whether or not I'd gone over that day. By then, we'd been together so long, I couldn't imagine my life without her. You can't live with somebody that long and then just let go. You've got to give each other at least one more chance.

"Why the hell didn't you tell me Sam left you?" said Tracey as she slammed the door of the small conference room.

"I just went over to Roger's for a few days," I said.

She looked at me like I just got off a spaceship or something. Then she made a kind of screaming noise as she grabbed her own hair in her fists. She even stamped her feet. Like a kid.

"You left her," she said.

"You don't have to scream at me."

"Don't you realize how that's going to look to the jury?"

"What difference does it make to them?"

"How many times do I have to say this before it gets into your stubborn heads? I can't defend Claudia unless you tell me everything."

"We told you everything," said Claudia.

"You didn't tell me he moved out."

"I didn't move out."

"Don't play bullshit semantic games with me, Sam Sloane. Whatever the hell the two of you want to call it, you didn't tell me."

Claudia lowered herself into the chair by the small table in the center of the room. I stood over by the window. Though we were on the second floor, the window wouldn't open, and it was covered with elaborate ironwork, the bars too thick for decoration. I closed the blinds.

"Why did you leave after your mother's death? Sam? Claudia? Why did Sam leave you? Did he leave you, or did you ask him to go? Claudia? God damn it, don't do this to me."

"It's private," said Claudia. "Between me and Sam."

"Private? Private? Is that what you consider the advance directives, too? Something private?"

"I didn't know about them, Tracey. I swear."

"You know what the jury's going to think, don't you, Claudia? They're going to think you knew about those directives and felt morally obligated to help Eleanor kill herself. They're going to think that's why Sam left you."

"She didn't know about the advance directives. I never showed them to her, Tracey."

"You're her goddamned husband — you'd say anything to get her off."

"I wouldn't lie. Jesus, what kind of a person do you think I am?"

"I think you're the kind of person who doesn't tell his wife's lawyer everything she needs to know to put up a good defense. God damn it, my husband told me not to take this case, and not just because he went to school with Harlan Graham," said Tracey, digging a pack of cigarettes out of her briefcase. "I'm going outside to have a smoke. If there's anything else the two of you have forgotten to tell me, you sure as hell better remember it before I get back. I don't want any more surprises from Harlan Graham."

She slammed the door behind her. When I opened the blinds, sunlight streamed into the room, making bars of light across the floor, across the tabletop, across Claudia and her belly. When I saw Tracey outside, down on the sidewalk, dragging furiously on her cigarette, I closed the blinds and sat down. I reached my hand across the table toward Claudia's. She looked up at me as my fingers touched hers.

"I did what I had to."

"I know."

CHAPTER TWELVE

$\mathcal{H}$ow do you know your clients are telling the truth, Mr. Bradshaw?" said Tracey. "What if they're just saying they understand the advance directives, but they really don't?"

"I make them explain the documents to me in their own words," he said.

"And that's sufficient for you to determine their mental competence?"

"Yes."

"Were you the one who determined Eleanor Sloane's mental competence when she had these directives drawn up?"

"Yes," said Attorney Bradshaw, nodding.

"You didn't have any of your assistants do it?"

"No."

"So you don't send your clients into a room alone with your assistants while they're signing these directives?"

"Objection."

"Withdrawn. Were you in the room with Eleanor Sloane when she was proving her mental competence?"

"Objection, Your Honor. How many times does the witness have to answer the same question?" said Graham.

"Withdrawn," said Tracey before the judge could answer. "Exactly how did you assess Eleanor Sloane's mental competency, Mr. Brad-shaw?"

"I believe I've already answered that question, Ms. Garner," he said. "I had her explain the documents to me in her own words."

"Where were the documents while she was doing that?"

"Where were they?" he said, frowning.

"Were they on the desk, in her hands, in your hands, in your assistant's hands? Where?"

"I can't recall their exact location."

"So she could have been holding them."

"It's possible."

"She could have been reading from them."

"She explained it in her own words, Ms. Garner. She wasn't reading."

"But she was holding the documents. . . ."

"That's not an established fact," said Mr. Bradshaw.

"Do you specifically remember that she was not holding them?"

"No."

"So she could have been holding them."

"It's possible."

"She could have been simply repeating what was on the page in front of her, couldn't she?"

"I don't think so, Ms. Garner."

"But that's what satisfied you that Eleanor Sloane was mentally competent when she had those directives drawn up, isn't it? Her holding the documents and parroting back what she was reading?"

"She was mentally competent at the time I drew up the advance directives for her, Ms. Garner. I can assure you of that," said the attorney. "Otherwise, I wouldn't have allowed the document to be signed and notarized."

"It's pretty easy money, isn't it, drawing up advance directives, especially when your assistants do most of the work?"

"Your Honor," said Graham. "Objection."

"Withdrawn," said Tracey.

The judge glared at her over the top of his glasses, but she was just playing by the same rules as Graham. He didn't like it when Tracey used his own tactics against him, but we had to get the truth to the jury in some way. My mom couldn't have been competent when she drew up those papers. If she had been, she would've named me as her designated agent. I'm her son, after all. Those later directives were nothing more than pieces of paper. They didn't mean a thing.

"You don't mean that, Sam," said Eve.

"Don't tell me you haven't noticed."

"They aren't keeping anything from us, Sam. It's the police making you think this."

"She was there, Eve. All alone."

"You don't mean that."

"If she thought it was going to happen soon anyway . . ."

Eve shook her head.

"Why would she tell Roger?"

"He's her brother."

"He's a cop."

"Exactly. He'd know how to protect her."

Eve folded the towels and stacked them in the laundry basket. Through the laundry room windows, I could see Roger in the backyard at the grill. The twins were playing badminton. When one of them hit the birdie near the grill, Roger caught it and tossed it back. The twins clapped. Eve put the next load of wash into the machine. With the cup of soap in her hand, she turned to me.

"He wouldn't protect her if she'd done that," she said, pouring the soap in the machine.

"You know how he feels about her."

"Even Roger wouldn't do that," she said, closing the lid.

"I'd leave her. . . . If I thought that she . . . I couldn't live with her anymore. . . ."

Eve came up behind me. After I calmed down, she handed me one of the clean dishtowels so I could wipe my face. Roger waved the twins over as he piled the meat on the platter, and the three of them came in from the yard. Eve patted me on the back before she went out to the kitchen, leaving me standing there. All alone.

She was alone, lying in the bathtub, her head back, her eyes closed. She didn't hear me come to the doorway. Slowly, so slowly, her hands brushed her breasts till the nipples rose. She breathed through her open mouth, her eyes shut, as her hands disappeared between her legs. There was a light slapping sound against the water, slow at first, then quicker, and her tongue passed over her lips. She arched her back slightly from the steamy water before she shuddered and eased back. After a few minutes, she moved her hand up out of the water and lifted the wet washcloth. She folded it and laid it over her closed eyes. She sighed. I slipped away from the bathroom door.

Tracey sighed as she put her briefcase on the table in the small conference room.

"There's no reason to put Claudia on the stand," she said.

"She could tell them what happened," I said.

Claudia sat down, her rounded belly pressing against the table.

"It's not a good idea, Sam," said Tracey, taking a folder out of her briefcase.

"Why not?"

"Graham would bring up the polygraph test."

"You didn't agree to admit that."

"If he puts her on the stand, he can ask her about it."

"What's wrong with that?"

Tracey rubbed her forehead before she answered.

"She failed the polygraph," she said.

"She didn't fail."

"She didn't pass," said Tracey.

"Same thing."

"No, Sam, it's not, and I don't even know why we're having this conversation again. I'm telling you, it's too big a risk putting Claudia on the stand."

"If she doesn't testify, they'll think she has something to hide."

"That's a risk we'll have to take."

"But if the jury could hear what happened — from Claudia — they'd know she was telling the truth."

"The police didn't believe her."

"They're assholes."

"Oh, really?" said Tracey, slamming the folder shut. "And what if we've got some assholes on the jury? What then, Sam?"

"All the evidence is circumstantial, Tracey, and you know it. Claudia can straighten everything out if you put her on the stand."

"Like she straightened everything out for the police?"

"Sarcasm isn't going to help, Tracey."

"You're the one who's not helping, Sam. I'm her lawyer. . . ."

"I'm her husband. . . ."

"Will you please stop talking about me like I'm not even here?" said Claudia, standing up, her face flushed red. "You've been doing it ever since this trial started. You argue about how I should do my hair, what clothes I should wear, how much makeup I should put on. You act like I'm invisible or deaf. It makes me so mad I want to throw something or pull my hair out or scream or . . . or . . . oh, my God . . ."

Claudia sat down suddenly, so pale and trembling that I went over to her. She pushed me away.

"Now I know exactly how Eleanor felt," she said.

"Mr. Bradshaw, if you felt a client were not capable of understanding a living will," said Tracey, "or if a client weren't mentally competent to execute a living will or a durable power of attorney, would you draw one up anyway?"

"No ethical attorney would do that."

"After someone has Alzheimer's, she's not competent to draw up advance directives, correct?"

"Early in the disease, she would still be competent enough to draw up such documents."

"If there were documented evidence of her mental deterioration, any durable power of attorney or living will drawn up after that documented deterioration would be legally invalid, correct?"

Mr. Bradshaw looked at Tracey over the top of his reading glasses.

"As you well know, Ms. Garner, a mentally incompetent individual cannot legally execute a durable power of attorney."

Tracey walked over to the defense table and picked something up, carrying it with her as she went back to the witness stand.

"If someone had been diagnosed with Alzheimer's and with documented mental deterioration — oh, let's say, a year before drawing up a durable power of attorney — that durable power of attorney would not be legally binding, is that right?"

"Objection, Your Honor."

"Overruled."

"It would not be legally binding under those conditions," said Bradshaw.

"Could you tell the court what this document is?" said Tracey.

"It's the attending physician's follow-up report for Eleanor Sloane."

"Could you read this paragraph?"

" 'Mrs. Sloane's test performance clearly indicates significant deterioration of cognitive abilities since the last testing one year ago when she was diagnosed with Alzheimer's disease.' "

"Could you look on the last page of this document?" said Tracey. "Could you read that date aloud for the court?"

"That date's not correct," he said, looking up at her. "There's been a mistake."

"Could you read the date, please, Mr. Bradshaw?"

"But . . . there's been a mistake."

"Mr. Bradshaw, what's the date? I'm sorry, I didn't hear you. Could you repeat that for the court?"

"October 15, 1987."

"Thank you," said Tracey, taking it from him and handing him another. "Could you please read the date on the advance directives you drew up for Eleanor Sloane? Mr. Bradshaw?"

"May 3, 1989."

"Do you realize, Mr. Bradshaw, that your client, Eleanor Sloane, signed your durable power of attorney almost eighteen months after she'd been diagnosed with Alzheimer's and shown verifiable mental deterioration?"

"It must be wrong."

"Are you telling us that's not the date Eleanor Sloane signed the document?"

"I'm telling you that Mrs. Sloane was not mentally impaired when I drew up this document."

"You just told us the date on these documents," said Tracey. "Dr. Barnett has already testified about the date of diagnosis, and he'll testify as to the date of his follow-up examinations."

"I didn't draw up a power of attorney for a mentally incompetent client."

"She'd already been through an extensive battery of medical and psychological tests, Mr. Bradshaw, the results of which indicated that Eleanor Sloane was suffering from impaired mental function more than a year before she came to see you," said Tracey as the witness put the documents down and removed his glasses.

"Obviously, someone made a mistake," he said.

"Aren't you the one who made that mistake, Mr. Bradshaw?" said Tracey, but he never answered her.

CHAPTER THIRTEEN

"MR. BRADSHAW, COULD YOU READ TO US PARAGRAPH THREE of the notice attached to the living will?" said Tracey after she'd handed the document to the witness.

> *Even if the designated agent has the general authority to make health care decisions for you under this document, the agent NEVER will be authorized to refuse or withdraw informed consent to health care necessary to maintain your life (unless you are suffering from an illness or injury that is likely to result in imminent death, regardless of the type, nature, and amount of health care provided).*

"As I understand it," said Tracey, "that paragraph means Claudia Sloane, as the designated agent, would never be given the authority to refuse treatment that might have maintained Eleanor's Sloane's life if she weren't about to die anyway, correct?"

"That's correct. This document deals most specifically with life-support issues."

"It does not give Claudia Sloane the authority to end Eleanor Sloane's life, does it?"

"It gives her the authority to refuse medical treatment only if Eleanor Sloane's death is already imminent."

"Could you look at the declaration you drew up for Eleanor

Sloane?" said Tracey, taking the living will from the witness and giving him another document. "Read the third from the last paragraph, please, Mr. Bradshaw."

Death resulting from the withholding or withdrawal of life-sustaining treatment in accordance with this declaration does not constitute, for any purpose, a suicide or homicide.

"Is this document requesting that Claudia Sloane murder Eleanor Sloane?"

"No, it's not."

"Is it requesting that she assist Eleanor Sloane in committing suicide?"

"No."

"Read the final paragraph, Mr. Bradshaw."

This declaration does not condone, authorize, or approve mercy-killing or euthanasia.

"Does this document authorize Claudia Sloane to perform euthanasia on Eleanor Sloane?"

"No."

"Do any of the documents you drew up for Eleanor Sloane authorize Claudia Sloane to commit any illegal activity?"

"No, of course they don't. Claudia Sloane is only asked to be morally obligated with respect to life-support systems and other health care decisions."

"Is she morally obligated to commit a crime, Mr. Bradshaw?" said Tracey.

"No one can draw up a document like that," he said.

"It doesn't matter if you can't, Sam," she said, pulling on her sweater.

I was sitting on the bed, and I turned away from her, my head in my hands.

"It happens to everybody," she said.

I didn't say anything. She tugged up her jeans, then went over to the mirror to put on her lipstick. She smiled at herself, then wiped some lipstick off her teeth. When she looked at me in the mirror, it made everything worse.

"It's no big deal, Sammy."

She came back over, sat next to me on the bed, and patted me on the leg.

"I never saw a grown man act like this."

The bed creaked when she got up. She went over to the sink and turned on the water. When she came back to the bed, she lifted my chin and wiped my face with a damp cloth. Then she stroked my hair.

"You know what I think, Mr. Sam Samuel? I think you like me," she said. "But you still love your wife."

It was supposed to be a surprise. Like when we first got married. Breakfast in bed. Scrambled eggs, bacon, sausage, toast, orange juice, coffee. I put it all on the bed tray, along with one of Claudia's magazines, and carried it upstairs. The door to Mom's room wasn't completely closed, so I opened it by pushing with my foot. It was the first time I'd made her breakfast in bed since before Mom moved in with us. I felt like we were newlyweds again. As soon as the door opened, I realized what a jerk I was. Things could never go back to the way they used to be. I just stood there in the doorway, the tray getting heavier and the food getting colder. Claudia lay in the bed. Playing with the empty cremains box. She opened the lid, closed it, opened it again. Each time she opened and closed that empty silver box, the sunlight glared on the lid. Blinding me.

"I can't believe you're asking me to watch that movie."

"I thought it might cheer us up."

"How many times have we seen it together, Sam? About a million? You know I cry every time."

"Oh, come on, Claude."

"Don't call me that."

"I always do."

"You know I don't like it."

She threw the newspaper sections off the chair onto the floor.

"It's too bad the sofa bed's down at the bookstore," I said.

"Why?"

"We could pull it out to watch the movie. You know, like we used to do when we had the apartment."

She stood there, next to the chair, just looking at me. Mom was asleep upstairs, so the house was quiet. I patted the couch beside me. Claudia frowned and crossed her arms over her chest.

"I made popcorn," I said. "With extra butter and extra salt."

"When are you going to grow up?" she said.

She turned and went out of the room, stomping up the stairs. She woke Mom up when she slammed the bedroom door. I sat on the couch, the bowl of popcorn in my lap. On the television screen, chickens pecked at the dirt yard as Dorothy leaned against the hay, gazing up at the cloudy sky as she sang. Upstairs in our bedroom, something heavy hit the floor. Still singing, Dorothy walked over to the wheel and rested her arms on it. Toto wagged his tail. Upstairs, Mom called Claudia, and Claudia screamed at her. Toto jumped up on the tractor seat, and Dorothy pressed her cheek against the top of his head. I threw the bowl of popcorn at the screen.

Fitting the glass eyes into the horse's head was the last job I had to do before varnishing it. I put the soft filler into the drilled-out eye recess, then gently pushed in the glass eye, smoothing off the excess filler with the palette knife and damp rag. Before the filler dried, I fashioned it into an upper eyelid. Once the horse was varnished, I could nail on the saddlecloths, thread the stirrup leathers, and nail on the leather saddle. The bit and reins were already attached to the bridle, so I'd just have to buckle it on. I could feel that horse's life as strong as the baby's kick when I put my hand on Claudia's belly. I had to finish the horse soon. After the baby was born, I didn't want Claudia to think of anything but life.

Claudia gripped her belly with each contraction, her cheek wet with tears. The paramedics lifted her onto the gurney as the rest of the people in the courtroom watched.

"How early is it?" said the judge, hovering behind us.

"Two months," said Tracey.

"I'll pray for her," he said.

Everybody hurried out of the paramedics' way. I ran along beside them, holding Claudia's hand the whole way to the ambulance. She clutched her belly again and closed her eyes as the siren and lights went on. The back doors slammed and the ambulance rocked toward the hospital. Between contractions, Claudia looked up at me.

"It's all my fault," she said.

"Breathe, honey. Come on. Do your breathing."

"It's too early. He won't make it."

"The doctor's been called," said the paramedic. "He'll be waiting."

"He stopped the labor before," I said. "He'll do it again."

Claudia kept shaking her head, sweat beading at her hairline.

"I should've done more."

"Don't think about that now."

"It's better not to talk, Mrs. Sloane."

"Breathe, honey, breathe."

"I wanted Eleanor to die," she said. "Now I'm paying for it."

CHAPTER FOURTEEN

SHE DIDN'T MEAN IT LIKE THAT. She was just scared. That was our last chance to have a baby of our own. And she had the trial to worry about, too. That's one of the reasons I can't forgive Graham. He had no right to do those things to Claudia. She loved my mom more than anyone else in the world.

She loved Mom so much, she even tasted Mom's food. I saw her doing it once. I came home from work early — some electrician hadn't shown up on the site or something — and Claudia was at the kitchen table. Bowls, measuring cups, and spoons were spread out in front of her. There was a cookbook open in front of her. She closed it before I could see what it was. It's not like it was *Final Exit* or any-thing — it was just a cookbook. Claudia put the book between her arm and body, picked up the bowl in front of her, and went to the sink. I opened the refrigerator, got out the juice, and drank some.

"I wish you'd use a glass, Sam," said Claudia as she emptied the bowl and turned on the disposal.

"Why are you throwing that applesauce away?"

"It's bad."

"How can applesauce go bad?"

I put a spoonful into my mouth, then spit it back out.

"Goddamn."

"I told you it was bad."

"How'd it get so bitter?"

"What was that noise? Is that your Mom?"

"God, not even the juice is taking that taste out of my mouth."

"Please, use a glass. God, Sam, don't . . . That's disgusting."

"I've got to get that taste out of my mouth."

"Your mom's going to start screaming unless one of us gets up there," said Claudia as I went out of the room. "And neither of us can survive another weekend of her tantrums and fits."

I fit the drawer into the dresser, then pulled it out slightly. It was a smooth fit. As I picked up the next drawer, Claudia came in. She stood beside me, watching.

"You like it?" I said.

"It's beautiful, Sam," she said, her fingers brushing its top. "You do such good work."

"Do you like the color?"

"It's nice," she said. "What kind of wood is it?"

"Maple."

"I don't think I've ever seen a nightstand that big."

"It's a dresser, Claude."

"Oh. A dresser. It's kind of small for a dresser, isn't it?"

"It's a baby dresser."

"Oh. A baby dresser. That makes sense. I guess I should've known. Who hired you to make that?"

"Nobody hired me."

"Then why are you making it?"

"I'm making it for us, Claude. For our baby."

She put her hand over her belly, just starting to get round under her sweater. Her mouth opened a little bit, but no sound came out. I was kneeling on the floor, beside the unfinished dresser. When I reached out for her hand, she went fast out of the room, leaving me alone.

"Dr. Barnett, was anyone else present in your office when you first diagnosed Eleanor Sloane as having dementia of the Alzheimer's type?" said Tracey.

"Claudia was there. So were Sam and Harold, the late Mr. Sloane."

"What about when the two specialists were consulted? Did Claudia know of their diagnosis?"

"Objection."

"Sustained."

"How do you know those specialists corroborated your diagnosis of Alzheimer's?"

"I have letters from the specialists," said Dr. Barnett. "They confirmed my diagnosis. And I showed those letters to Claudia myself."

"So, Claudia knew that Eleanor was mentally incompetent, correct?" said Tracey.

"She was aware that Eleanor had lost some of her mental functioning and that she would continue to deteriorate, yes."

"Dr. Barnett, earlier you testified as to the date of Eleanor's diagnosis," said Tracey. "Are you confident that's the correct date?"

"Yes. I verified that date before I came to court."

"How did you verify the date?"

"With Eleanor's chart and with my appointment records."

Roger's daughter, Sarah, sitting next to me, put her hand on my arm. Beside Sarah, Laura took shorthand in her stenographer's notebook. The woman in the jury who always wore her pearl necklace dug around in her purse until she pulled out a tissue.

"Were you aware that Eleanor Sloane had made advance directives?" said Tracey.

"When I informed the family of the diagnosis, I advised them to get those documents drawn up," said Dr. Barnett.

"And did they?"

"Yes. I have copies of them in Eleanor's file."

"Is Claudia Sloane listed as the agent in those advance directives?"

"No, Harold Sloane is listed as the agent. Sam is listed as the alternate, in case of Harold's death."

"Is Claudia also listed as an alternate?"

"Not in the documents that I have on file," said Dr. Barnett.

After Tracey showed the papers to Harlan Graham and to the judge, the documents were entered into evidence. Laura flipped through the pages of her notebook. She was wearing dark-framed, round glasses, just like her brother Matthew, and they both looked exactly like Roger. Tracey handed the papers to the court clerk and returned to the witness box.

"At the time Eleanor Sloane executed the advance directives that you have on file, would you say that she was mentally competent enough to understand what she was doing?"

"I would say that, at that time, she was competent enough to fully understand the import of those advance directives, yes," said Dr. Barnett.

"What about the second group of advance directives?"

"I didn't know about those until you told me about them," he said.

"Don't you have copies of those documents in Eleanor's medical file?"

"No, she never gave them to me."

"This is a copy of the later living will," said Tracey. "Is the date it was signed before or after your diagnosis of Alzheimer's?"

"It's significantly later than my diagnosis."

"Did Eleanor Sloane's mental competence continue to deteriorate after your initial diagnosis?"

"Yes, it did."

"Was Claudia Sloane aware of Eleanor's continued mental deterioration?"

"Objection."

"Sustained. Rephrase the question."

"Did you continue to inform Claudia of Eleanor's condition as the disease progressed?"

"Yes, I was continually in contact with both Sam and Claudia."

"So you know for a fact that Claudia was well aware of Eleanor's mental deterioration?"

"Since she was the one who spent the most time with Eleanor, I would say that Claudia was the most informed member of the family."

"Since she knew that Eleanor was mentally incompetent, Claudia wouldn't have felt morally obligated to abide by the wishes expressed in this later set of advance directives, would she?"

"Given what she knew about Eleanor's mental competence," said Dr. Barnett, "I don't believe Claudia would have felt obliged to honor those later directives."

If I'd known how the jury would look at those directives, I might've done things different. Hell, if I'd known Claudia was going to be prosecuted for murder, I know I'd have done things different. But it was too late to do anything then. Except talk to Graham. After Claudia went into labor and was in the hospital, I decided to go see Graham. To get it all over with. Even if it ruined my life. Even if it meant I'd never see Claudia again. I had to protect her and the baby. God, it was a terrible gamble. The greatest gamble of my life.

"You didn't want to gamble on the jury's verdict, huh?" said Tracey after she got to the hospital room. "I don't think Harlan's going to be real happy that you decided to release yourself on your own recognizance. There you go — that's the smile we like to see. What'd the doctor say?"

"She's stabilized right now," I said. "But he said we have to minimize the stress in her life."

"I'm not sure he knows about the trial," said Claudia as Tracey took her hand.

"Everybody knows about the trial, honey," said Eve, standing beside Roger.

Claudia closed her eyes tight as another wave of pain started. After the contraction passed, the baby's heart rate, displayed on the fetal monitor, increased again.

"Maybe I should just confess," said Claudia.

"You can't confess if you're innocent," said Roger.

"That would end the trial, wouldn't it?"

"Christ, Claudia, you can't confess to something you didn't do," said Tracey.

"You're getting yourself all worked up again," said Eve. "Think of the baby."

"Put me on the stand, Tracey. Nothing will happen if I tell them I didn't do it."

"First you want to confess, then you want to declare your innocence. . . ."

"I can't lose this baby."

"Putting you on the stand isn't going to reduce your stress, honey," said Tracey.

Beside the bed, the fetal heart monitor beeped steadily, its red numbers flashing. Another contraction started, and the heart rate dropped. Claudia whimpered and squeezed my hand. As if I could stop what was happening. As if I could change things. As if I could save her.

"I could always say I did it," I said, looking over at Tracey.

"Did what?"

"Helped my mother commit suicide."

CHAPTER FIFTEEN

And when Jesus was come into Peter's house, he saw his wife's mother lying there, sick of a fever. Then he touched her hand, and the fever left her, and she rose and served him.

THE SANCTUARY LIGHT GLOWED. The stained-glass windows threw colored shadows on the floor. Incense filled the air with its smoke. Hundreds of candles blurred into one blinding light. But none of it meant a thing. I tried to feel something. Anything. But each time I looked at Mom, sitting in the pew beside me, there was nothing there.

Mom took my hand and held it, with both of hers, in her lap. She bent my fingers under, one at a time, then all at once. She closed my fingers over my thumb. She pressed my thumb over my fingers. She stared at the back of my hand. Then at the palm. Up in the pulpit, the priest droned on.

When the evening was come, they brought unto him many that were possessed with devils, and he cast out the spirits with his word, and healed all that were sick.

Mom let go of my hand and opened her purse. She took out the empty lipstick tube, put it on the pew between us, then put her tissues beside the lipstick. She laid the play money out, each bill touching another, the neon colors bright against the dark brown wood of the pew. She put a button on each play-money bill, on each tissue, and on the lipstick case. Then she sat there, her emptied purse open on her lap, and stared up at the stained-glass windows like she'd never seen them before.

And another of his disciples said unto him, "Lord, suffer me first to go and bury my father." But Jesus said unto him, "Let the dead bury their dead."

My mom was dead before she died. That body lived in the same house with us, but it wasn't my mom. The lungs kept working, the heart kept beating, and the blood kept moving through the veins — that's what bodies do. But it wasn't my mom. It was a body without a brain. Without a soul. When I sat beside that body in the dark, my fingers on the barrel of the gun in my lap, I knew it wasn't Mom anymore. And all I had to do was wait.

"All we can do now is wait," said Tracey.

"How long does it usually take?"

"There's no way to predict how long it'll take them to reach a verdict, Sam."

"What about Claudia?" I said.

"She can stay here in the hospital until the verdict comes down or until she has the baby, whichever comes first."

"Do you think it'll take that long, Tracey, I mean, till the baby's due?"

"Do you really think they can delay the labor till the due date, Sam?"

I paced the hall, my hands in my pockets. When I reached the end of the corridor, I saw Roger getting out of the elevator, so I waited for him. We drank some of our coffee by the elevator, so Tracey could make her calls. She was just hanging up the pay phone when we got back. She wrote something down in her calendar before she took her coffee from Roger.

"If only we didn't have to wait like this."

"I wish there were some way to make this easier, Sam."

"No matter what the verdict is," said Roger, "Tracey did the best she could."

"And we can always appeal," said Tracey. "I mean, we still have other options."

I tossed my empty coffee cup into the trash, then went to the chapel and tried to pray. I stayed there a long time. So long, my knees ached. I said every prayer I could remember from when I was a kid, then made up some of my own, but it felt like the words were falling down around me, instead of going up to God. Claudia says God hears you even if it seems like rocks are tied to your prayers. But she's always had more faith than I have. I know there's a God, I'm sure of that. But what if He never answers? What if all He does — no matter what you say — is listen?

"You're not listening, Sam."

"I thought you wanted my help, Claudia."

"If we don't do things exactly the same way every time . . ."

"You're the reason she overreacts in the first place, Claudia. You make everything so damned predictable that she goes crazy if we change things. What she needs is some variety. . . ."

"That's the very thing she doesn't need, Sam. You need to take her hands, like this, and then tell her what to do, like this: Get in the car, Eleanor."

"No," said Mom.

"Here, I'll do it."

As soon as I touched her, Mom grabbed the doorframe again.

"Mom, stop it. Let go. Claudia, don't just stand there. Help me."

"Don't hold her arms like that," said Claudia.

"Stop telling me what to do and help me."

"Ow. Shit. Why doesn't she ever hit you?"

"Here, get her legs. Claudia, will you get her legs? She's not going to kick you. Okay, move your head. Claudia, get out of the way. Push. Push, God damn it."

We slammed the back car door. Mom slapped her hands against the windows, shrieking as loud as she could. Then she rocked back and forth, holding onto the front seat. Claudia bent over and grabbed her purse.

"Shit," she said, looking down at herself. "There's blood on my sweater. What's bleeding?"

"Your lip. And your nose."

"I told you not to say 'doctor' around the car."

"I didn't. When did I say 'doctor'?"

"God, Sam, you can be so stupid sometimes."

"I thought you told me it made her worse when you yelled."

"You're the one who's yelling."

"Nobody's having problems hearing your voice either."

She kicked the leaves all over the driveway.

"What'd she do with the goddamned keys? Are you going to help me find them, Sam, or are you just going to stand there? Shut up, Eleanor. Will you shut the hell up?"

"Oh, that's good, Claudia. Hit the car roof harder next time. Let's get her a little more hysterical."

Claudia pounded her fists on the car roof, and her lip started bleeding again. She pounded it so hard, we couldn't hear Mom's screams. She pounded and pounded, then put her head down against the car's roof.

"Why don't you just die?" she said. "Why don't you just die and leave us in peace?"

Here is the moment of parting,
I can feel all the fear in your hand,

Leaving a home full of memories
On the verge of a strange new land.

Each time the song finished, I rewound the tape and played it again. I moved the medicine bottles on the nightstand so I could put the empty pudding bowl there. After I settled Mom in bed, I sat beside her till she fell asleep. I brushed her hair away from her face, then kissed her on the forehead.

And the stories I tell to my children
Are the ones that you told me before,
But the story now slowly unfolding
Is the saddest story of all.

After the tape finished, the room was quiet except for Mom's breathing. I closed the bedroom door and went downstairs. Claudia was standing in the entry hall, next to my suitcase. She'd opened the blinds by the front door. The sky was dark with clouds. Snow-clouds.

"I got her to eat some pudding," I said. "She's sleeping now, so you don't have to do anything."

I put my arms around her from behind. She'd lost so much weight, she felt like a ghost.

"Why don't you try to get some rest?"

"Did you leave me the number where you'll be?" she said.

"It's upstairs. I'll get it for you."

The note with the motel's phone number wasn't on my dresser or on our bed. Then I remembered carrying it into Mom's room. I found it on her nightstand. I stood there another minute after I picked up the slip of paper, looking at her. As I bent down to kiss her on the forehead once more, my hand hit something in the bed beside her. It was one of the prescription bottles. It was empty. I put the cap back on and set the bottle on the table. As I stepped away from the bed, two more prescription bottles rolled away from my feet. They were empty, too. I put them on the nightstand with the others. I closed the door, went back downstairs, and handed Claudia the motel's phone number. She slipped the number into her pocket.

"I wish you didn't have to go," she said.

"Well, if I hadn't lost Dad's company, I wouldn't have to go out of town on this job," I said. "Oh, sorry, I forgot. I didn't *lose* Dad's company. I *chose* to sell it. I keep forgetting it was something I wanted to do."

"Oh, please, don't be bitter," said Claudia.

"Who's bitter? Just another day in the barrel."

Claudia hugged me tight, her face against mine.

"Please, don't," she said. "I couldn't bear it if I lost you, too."

"We're here, aren't we?" I said as I closed my book and put it on the nightstand.

"But look at all the things we lost," said Claudia.

"In all the important ways, everything's the same. With us, I mean."

I took my reading glasses off and put them in the nightstand drawer. Claudia turned her pillow over and punched it a few times. When she bumped the cat with her leg, he jumped off the bed and went over to the basket of blankets near the dresser.

"You're depressed," I said.

"I'm not depressed."

"The doctor said that's normal."

"I'm not depressed."

I got my book off the nightstand and offered it to her, but she didn't take it.

"I'm almost done," I said. "You can start reading it if you want."

"I'm tired of scary stories."

"You used to love them."

"Not anymore."

"You must be depressed."

"Will you please stop saying that? Can't things be different without my being depressed?"

"If it's the house, we can move, you know."

"It's not the house, Sam."

"If you need me to help out more, just say so."

"It's not that either."

"You can't do the bookstore and the house and . . ."

Claudia sighed loud. I put the book down. Claudia looked at me. She was so beautiful, lying there in the faint light, her hair around her face and on the pillow. The shadows under her eyes were gone, and her cheeks had their old color. But she looked so sad. So lost.

"If you'd tell me what's wrong . . ."

"It's nothing you can fix, Sam."

"Then what's the matter?"

"It's just . . . different, that's all."

"Now that Roger's a cop again? And now that Roger and Eve got that house just a few streets from us?"

"Don't you feel any different, Sam? Not even a little?"

I slid closer to her under the covers and put my arms around her. I kissed her.

"Does this feel different?"

She pushed me away.

"I'm going to start seeing Dr. Daniels again," she said.

I didn't understand it. We finally had everything we'd ever wanted, yet nothing seemed right. Every night, lying there next to her, I wanted to reach out and hold her against me. Tight and hard. But she didn't want me to. I must've missed something, somewhere, yet I don't know what or when or how I missed it. And she won't tell me. She says if she has to explain it, then I'll never understand. I understand this, though — after everything we'd gone through, we were further away from each other than ever.

"Did I miss much?" said Claudia. "It took longer than I thought to do the dishes. What's the score?"

"Fourteen-seven. Cowboys."

"Go, Cowboys," said Mom.

Claudia laughed.

"Are you a Cowboys fan now, too, Eleanor?"

"The Cowboys are best," said Mom.

"Not the Buffalo Bills?" said Claudia.

"Cowboys."

"Sounds like somebody's been brainwashing you," said Claudia, settling down on the couch next to me.

"The Boys are the best," I said, passing her the popcorn. "Mom has good taste."

"You just like the cheerleaders," said Claudia.

"Nothing wrong with the cheerleaders," I said. "But Troy's my man."

"What about Michael and Ken?"

"Ken and Michael, too. But Troy's gonna be MVP."

"Go, Troy," said Mom, and Claudia laughed again.

Just then, a Dallas safety cut in front of the Bills' tight end and intercepted the pass. I jumped up and cheered. Mom did, too. Then she looked at Claudia.

"Go, Cowboys," said Claudia.

Later, a Dallas defensive lineman stripped the ball and Dallas recovered. Michael made a leaping grab for it near the goal line, then leaned into the end zone for another score. I cheered so loud Claudia covered her ears with her hands. When I spiked my foam football, Mom clapped.

"Who's gonna win Super Bowl XXVII?" I said.

"Cowboys," said Mom.

"Cowboys," said Claudia.

"Come on, Claude. You gotta do better than that. Who's gonna win this Bowl?"

"Cowboys," Mom and Claudia said together.

In the second half, when the Bills fumbled a high snap in the shotgun, Ken picked it up and ran it in for a touchdown. I strutted around the room with my football, making noise like a cheering crowd. Mom bounced up and down on the couch. Claudia did cheers like a cheerleader. Then Mom jumped up to do a cheer and knocked over the bowl of popcorn. I picked some of it up and tossed it at Claudia. She threw some back at me. Then Mom started to laugh and threw handfuls up in the air. Popcorn rained down on us. We laughed and laughed. Everything was so simple. So easy.

It wasn't easy getting the hoof notches done by myself — I had to lift the horse on and off its rockers quite a few times before I got it right. If Dad had been there, it would've been easier. But eventually I got the horse fitted on the rockers. Then I could drill the bolt holes. After all the bolts and nuts were secure, I stepped back and looked at the rocking horse. His cotton forelock swept over his head between his ears, and the matching tail hung in back. After I stepped closer to the horse and pressed down on his head, he rocked smoothly on the kitchen floor. Spike jumped when the horse first moved, then started grabbing at its tail. Dad and I had made a beautiful rocking horse. If only I could see my son ride it when the trial was over.

I knew I had to get it over with. I lost count of how many times I went up to the door, how many times I went back out to the car. Lawyers in three-piece suits and cops passed me as I stood there outside his door, but none of them even looked at me. Finally, I buttoned my jacket, took a deep breath, and opened the door. After the secretary saw me, her expression changed.

"You're not going to leave after I buzz him again, are you?" she said as she pushed the button on the intercom. "Mr. Graham? You were right. He's back."

Within a few seconds, the inner office door opened behind her. Harlan Graham stood there in the doorway. Without a word, he motioned me inside. The door closed with a heavy thud behind us.

When you've been accused of murder, things never get back to normal. No matter what the jury's verdict is. People never look at you in the same way. Strangers in the bank stare at you like you're a freak. Clerks in the post office whisper behind your back. And if you confess to murder, then people are even more unforgiving. No matter what the circumstances are surrounding the death, no matter how much you've suffered yourself, no matter how much you've lost or had stolen from you, people never forget.

And they never, ever forgive.

CHAPTER SIXTEEN

*H*OW COULD YOU FORGET ALREADY, MOM? I just told you. It's eight o'clock."

"It's not dark."

"It's not dark because of daylight savings time."

She knelt on the couch and pressed her face to the window screen.

"Where's Claudia?"

"She's at the bookstore."

Mom looked at me.

"This is her vacation. Remember? I'm taking care of you this weekend. We told you all about it, Mom."

"What time is it?"

"One minute later than the last time you asked me."

"Where's Claudia?"

"I just told you."

Mom got off the couch and went to the kitchen. She walked over to the phone, picked up the receiver, and pushed the button for the bookstore.

"No, Mom, put it down. Give me the phone. I promised Claudia we wouldn't bother her."

"Where's Claudia?"

"She'll be home after work on Tuesday."

"What time is it?"

"Eight o'clock."

"Where's Claudia?"

"Jesus, Mom, I've already told you that fifty times."

She ran over to the corner, near the windows, and huddled down with her arms up over her head. When I walked over there, she ran out the kitchen to the entry hall. The front door was locked at the top, above her head, so she couldn't get out, but she pulled at the doorknob anyway. When I finally got hold of her, she dug her nails into the back of my hand. She was just about to launch into one of her famous screams when I had an idea.

"Hey, Mom, let's go see Claudia."

She looked at me, her mouth open, but quiet.

"Claudia's upstairs. Yes, she is. You can go see her, but not if you scream, okay? And no scratching or biting either. Come on, Mom. You want to see Claudia, don't you?"

I coaxed her up the stairs and down the hall to her bedroom, wondering why I'd never thought of that before. After I closed the door behind us and Mom looked around her room, her body went rigid. She threw herself onto the bed. She grabbed her doll and hugged it to her chest. She rocked back and forth on the bed, screaming the whole time. I pushed the doll away to unbutton Mom's blouse, but Mom jerked away from me. When I took hold of her foot to get her shoe off, she kicked and swung the doll at me.

"Where's Claudia?"

"At the bookstore."

"Where's Claudia?"

"Jesus, Mom, are you going deaf, too? Don't you see my damn mouth moving? I just told you where Claudia is. Why don't you listen for a change? Jesus, I don't know how Claudia puts up with you all the time. Get your shoes off the bed, Mom. Get them off the bed. Don't hit me with that. Cut it out. Give me that doll. If you're going to hit me with it, you can't hold it while I'm in the room. God damn it, I said give it —"

I tried to take the doll away from her, but she wouldn't let go. So I only got part of it — its head. I knew I was in for it then.

"Oh, shit, Mom, I'm sorry. Here, I'll fix it."

She screamed as loud as a tornado siren.

"Christ, Mom, will you please stop that? Come on, give me the body. Give it to me. Well, do you want me to put the head back on or not?"

I held out my hand for the doll's body. Instead of handing it to me, Mom grabbed my hand and bit me. Hard. She was holding on to my arm with both hands, biting like she was going to break bones, and I was shouting and cursing and trying to get her off me.

Then I hit her.

She let go. But I hit her again. And again.

I don't remember anything else. I didn't mean it. I loved her. She was my mother. If Claudia'd been there, it never would've happened. I'll never forgive myself. Ever. Jesus Christ, I hit her. I hit my own mother.

I've never told anyone. I never will.

"Why did you wait till now to tell me?" said Harlan Graham, his hands folded together on the conference table. "Why wait till the jury was deliberating?"

His office was lined with mahogany shelves from floor to ceiling. The desk and the conference table were of the same wood. All of it was so highly polished, it gleamed. The chairs were dark, soft leather. Graham and his assistant were the only ones there with me. Sitting in that closed space with them, having both of them stare at me like that — it was terrible. Anyone would feel guilty. Even an innocent man.

"Claudia's gone into labor," I said.

"Again? When I checked this morning, they told me she was resting comfortably," said Graham.

"That was the situation a half hour ago," said his assistant. "That's the last time I called."

"Put me in jail," I said. "And let her go."

"I'm afraid it doesn't work that way, Mr. Sloane."

"She didn't do anything."

"There's no reason to raise your voice," said Graham.

"You're not listening."

"On the contrary. I'm simply wondering why you never said this to anyone before."

"I did."

"To whom?"

"The cops. Troy and that detective. Mitchum or Mitchell or something. They didn't listen either."

"You told them you murdered your mother?" said Graham's assistant.

"I didn't murder her."

"Then, what did you do?"

"I . . . I . . . helped her."

"Helped her what?"

"Commit suicide."

"That's murder in this state, Mr. Sloane," said the assistant.

"You don't believe me, do you?"

"Keep talking," said Graham. "I'm listening."

"Roger told me, but I didn't believe him," said Eve as she stood in the entry hall of the house, her hands on her hips. "You did rob a nursery, didn't you, Sam? That was a joke. You're supposed to laugh."

"Are there any left out there?" I said.

"This is the last one," said Roger, kicking the front door closed behind him.

"You got one hell of a lot of flowers," said Eve, shaking her head.

"Where do you want these, Sam?"

"How about in the living room?"

"Where in the living room?"

"Anywhere."

Roger carried the flowers to the coffee table. He set them down in the middle, next to the others. Then we went into the kitchen. A basket of daffodils, hyacinths, tulips, and crocuses was in the center of the table.

"Where'd you find spring flowers at this time of year?" said Eve.

"It wasn't easy."

"Do you have as many upstairs as you got down here?"

"Why? Too many?"

"I didn't say that."

"You think it's too many. It looks like a funeral, doesn't it?"

"No. Not at all. They're fine."

"It looks like a funeral," I said. "Damn."

"Don't worry about it, Sam. It'll be fine, really."

"Are you scared?" said Roger.

"Scared?"

"Nervous, I mean."

"Why would I be nervous?"

"You know, Sam, there's still a chance . . ."

"No, don't say it, Eve. There's no way they're going to do that."

Roger went over to the refrigerator and got us something to drink. We stood in the kitchen, drinking the beer, the bottles cold in our hands. Eve moved the flowers on the table to the counter, and moved the flowers on the counter to the table. Then she moved them back to where they'd been originally. When the phone rang, we all jumped.

"I hope this is the last time we ever have to do this," said Eve.

CHAPTER SEVENTEEN

$\mathcal{T}$HIS IS THE LAST TIME," said the nurse. "Come on. You remember what I told you."

"You're almost there," said the doctor. "One more push, and he'll be out. You've made it this far. Don't give up now. Help her out, Mr. Sloane."

I lifted Claudia's back and shoulders again. Her hair was wet when I pressed my cheek against hers. She held my hand hard. I don't remember what I said to her, but none of it was real. Not after so many disappointments. I was almost afraid to hope. Something could still go wrong. As the doctor and nurse urged Claudia, she strained forward. I put my arm around her. The doctor reached up. Claudia pushed. Then she fell back against me.

"There's his head. It's out," said the doctor. "Come down here, Mr. Sloane. Yes, come on. You want to see this, don't you?"

I eased my arms out from under Claudia and moved to the other end of the bed. The doctor turned the baby's head to clean his nose and mouth. The baby's eyes were puffy and closed. His hair was dark, like mine, but curly, like Claudia's. My throat was so tight I couldn't breathe.

"Okay, now one more push, and you're done," said the doctor. "Come on. This is the last one. Come on. You've already done the hardest part. Okay, here he comes. Here he comes. There he is. You did it."

With one movement, the doctor had my son in his hands. He turned the baby over and put him on Claudia's belly. He was covered with something whitish. The nurse put the identification bracelet on the baby's wrist. Claudia sobbed as she touched his head, his shoulders, his back. I reached out my hand. Her fingers brushed mine.

"Okay, Mr. Sloane, time to cut the cord," said the doctor.

He turned the baby and held him up in front of me. He was so small. There was still blood on him.

"Go on. Cut right here. Go ahead."

I cut the cord. The baby drew in a sharp breath. His eyes opened, but just for a second. The front of my clothes got wet and warm. I looked down. The stain turned the scrub suit darker. The nurse laughed.

"Sometimes they do that when you cut the cord," she said. "Here, I'll get you something."

She handed me a towel to wipe myself with. Then she took the baby and cleaned him up. I watched her. She made cooing noises to him. After she wrapped him in a blanket, she put him in Claudia's arms.

"He's not crying," I said.

"That's because he's a happy little boy," said the nurse. "Aren't you a happy little boy, hmmm?

"Isn't he supposed to cry?"

"His mother's doing enough crying for the both of them," said the doctor.

"But is he all right? I mean, if he doesn't cry?"

"New fathers," said the nurse, smiling. "They're all the same."

"He's fine, Mr. Sloane," said the doctor. "He's breathing. His color's good."

"He's strong," said the nurse. "See how he grips my finger?"

"He's got all his parts," said the doctor. "And judging by that stain on the front of your scrub suit, all his parts are in working order. He's a fine, healthy boy."

"I lost my bet," said the nurse. "Doctor and I had a bet. I was sure Baby would get Mommy's red hair."

"But he got Dad's coloring, it looks like."

"Now I owe Doctor lunch."

"At any place I want," he said.

The baby was so small, smaller than anything I'd ever seen. When I touched his cheek with my finger, he turned his face, his mouth open wide. I moved the blanket aside. Two arms, two legs, ten fingers, ten toes, tiny fingernails, a belly button, everything. God, he was so beautiful. He was absolutely perfect. And he was my son.

"Did you decide on a name yet?" said the nurse, and I looked at Claudia.

"Zachary," she said.

"Now, that's an old-fashioned name," said the nurse. "I haven't heard that one in a while."

"It means 'remembered by God,'" said Claudia.

After all those years. After all those tests and sacrifices. After all those trials and tribulations. God finally remembered us. Claudia believed all along. But that day, for the first time in years, I believed, too.

"You don't believe me," I said.

"I believe you love your wife," said Harlan Graham. "Whether or not you helped your mother commit suicide is another matter."

"I've told you everything that happened."

"You haven't told us anything you didn't hear in court," said his assistant, putting down his pen.

"But I'm telling you the truth."

"Does Tracey know you're here, Mr. Sloane?" said Graham. "Well, does she?"

"No."

"I didn't think so."

"Didn't she believe you either?" said his assistant.

"You'll have to have an attorney to enter a plea."

"A plea?"

"That's what you want, isn't it, Mr. Sloane, to enter a guilty plea? Then you need a lawyer so we can discuss the specifics of the charge and the sentence."

"Aren't you going to arrest me?"

"Go get a lawyer," said Graham, standing up and buttoning his jacket. "Then we'll talk."

But we never talked again. He didn't believe me. Hell, I could've brought in a copy of *Final Exit* with passages highlighted and he wouldn't have believed me. He was a pretty big man by then — he probably had a direct line to God Himself — so he didn't have to listen to some little guy like me. No, I wasn't important enough to get his attention. I was just a worm or a bug. Something to annoy him. Something for him to squash.

"Was I ever that little?" said Tommy.

"You were just the same," said Roger. "Maybe a little smaller."

"No, I wasn't," said Tommy.

Roger's son Matthew, standing with us at the hospital's nursery window, elbowed me.

"Look: he laughed."

"It looked like a yawn to me."

"No, that's a smile. Hey, he smiled at me," said Roger. "Hey, little Zach. It's me — Uncle Rodge."

"Oh, God, Dad, you're not going to let him call you that, are you?" said Sarah.

"Why not?"

"It's stupid," said Sarah.

"Totally stupid," said Laura.

Roger laughed. The twins leaned so close to the nursery window, their breath fogged the glass.

"Isn't he the sweetest little baby you've ever seen?" said Sarah. "He's so teeny."

"Like a doll baby," said Laura.

The twins tapped on the glass, calling to the baby.

"Can we hold him the next time they take him to Aunt Claudia's room?" said Sarah.

"Of course, you can."

"Aunt Claudia," said Sarah, turning around. "I get to hold Zach next time —"

"Claudia, what are you doing down here?" I said.

"I thought you were resting," said Roger.

"Are you supposed to be walking around this soon?"

"What's the matter? Are you all right?"

Roger went over to Claudia. Eve was standing beside her, and both of them were pale. Matthew, Tommy, and the twins moved closer to each other. Claudia took my hands in hers.

"The jury's come in," she said.

It was the longest hour in my life. Getting Claudia dressed. Driving to the courthouse. Cars behind us honked because I was going so slow. Roger and Eve and the kids followed us in their car. As we got closer to the courthouse, I thought of pulling off the interstate, circling back around to get the baby from the hospital, and taking off. I don't know where we would've gone. Anywhere. Nowhere. It wouldn't have mattered as long as we were together. It'd be just like the government's witness protection program. No one would ever find us. But Claudia wouldn't run. She said she wouldn't spend the rest of her life looking over her shoulder. So there was only one thing left to do. We had to go back. We had to face everything. No matter what.

"Sam, you can't tell the verdict by looking at them."

"What about that one, Eve?"

"No, I can't tell."

"The one in green? Didn't you just see the way she looked at Claudia?"

"Sam, don't do this," said Roger.

"What about that one there? What do you think that look means?"

"Will you stop it?" said Eve. "You're making me even more nervous than I already am."

"Will the defendant please rise?" said the judge.

Tracey squeezed Claudia's hand under the table before the two of them stood up.

"Madame Foreman, have you reached a verdict?"

"We have, Your Honor."

She passed it to the bailiff, who crossed the court and handed it to the judge. He opened it, read it, closed it, and handed it back to the bailiff — all without changing the look on his face. Eve was breathing fast. Sarah and Laura had their arms around each other. I was clenching my teeth so hard, my jaw ached. Roger's fists were on his knees. Claudia didn't turn around to look at us. Tracey put her hand on Claudia's back. I wanted to be on the other side of her, in case she needed me. But I couldn't move.

"On the first count of the indictment against Claudia Page Sloane, murder in the first degree, how do you find?"

"Not guilty."

Roger jumped to his feet. The judge pounded his gavel.

"On the second count of the indictment, criminal assistance at a suicide, how do you find?"

"Not guilty."

Roger hugged me.

"So say you all?" said the judge.

"We do."

Tracy hugged Claudia. Eve wept. Matthew reached over the bar and shook Tracey's hand. The twins squealed and hugged each other.

Tommy asked if Claudia got to come home. When Claudia turned around, I pulled her close to me, though the bar was still between us. I kissed her over and over. Roger and Eve hugged Tracey, then Claudia. The twins laughed and cried at the same time. The woman in the jury who wore a different hat every day wiped her eyes with a tissue. Graham put his notepads and folders into his briefcase and closed it. His assistant looked over at us. When Tracey led Claudia from the table, Graham nodded at them. Tommy hugged Claudia around the legs.

"We get to take you home," he said.

Home. Family. You don't realize how precious life is until something takes those things away. Life's made up of so many things we take for granted. Things that make the difference between happiness and grief. Between living and being buried alive. Without family, a man's nothing. Without a home, he's got nothing to fight for. I don't expect anyone who hasn't gone through it to understand. That's why I don't talk to people about it. What would be the point?

Claudia didn't say anything when we got to the new place. We sat in the car, just looking at the house. Then, finally, she opened the car door and got out. She looked up at the shade trees while I got Zach out of the backseat. After we went to the porch, I unlocked the front door and picked up the baby carrier. Claudia came up the steps. Spike was in the entry hall, waiting. He meowed when we came in.

"Hey, Spike, this is the mom. Remember? I told you she was coming home today. What do you think, Claudia? He's prettier than the picture, isn't he? And he's not really all black: he's got some white on his chest and his belly. Come here, Spike. Come on. Say hi to Mom. This is the mom. And this is Zach. How d'you like him, huh? He's your baby brother."

When Claudia leaned down to pet him, Spike licked her hand. I showed him the baby, and Spike touched his nose to the baby's hand. I unbuckled the restraint on the carrier. Holding Zach, I led Claudia through the house. It was the first time she'd ever been there. Spike followed us, jumping up to smell the flowers in each new room. When he meowed, I petted him and kissed him on the top of the head. Claudia petted him, too, but he didn't give her any kisses. All the curtains and blinds in the house were open. There was plenty of sunlight.

Claudia went ahead of me up the stairs. First I took her to our bedroom. She looked at the wallpaper — covered with roses, the design she'd always wanted — and at the ceiling fan. When Spike stood on the bed, the fan stirred his fur coat. In Zach's room, Claudia looked at the pale blue walls, at the wallpaper border, covered with baseballs and mitts and bats. I laid Zach down in my old cradle, on top of the sheets. The new blanket from Roger and Eve was folded at his feet. Claudia went over to the window. Spike put his nose to the bars of the cradle, looked at Zach with wide eyes, then looked up at me and meowed.

At the window, Claudia touched the rocking horse. He rocked slow and smooth. She touched his knotted mane, his saddle, his tail. Then she came back over to me. She put her head against my shoulder. Spike licked Zach's hand through the bars of the cradle. The wooden horse rocked slower and slower, until he finally stopped.

I put my arms around Claudia and held her.

As long and tight as I could.

Permissions

Adaptations of Living Will, Durable Power of Attorney, Uniform Rights of the Terminally Ill Act, and Declaration from *The Living Will and the Durable Power of Attorney for Health Care Book, with Forms,* by Phillip G. Williams. *Contemporary Public Health Issues, Volume 1* (Oak Park, Ill.: P. Gaines, 1991). Used with permission of P. Gaines Co.

Criteria for Alzheimer-patient hospice admission taken from "Feasible Criteria for Enrolling End-Stage Dementia Patients in Home Hospice Care," by Patricia Hanrahan and Daniel J. Luchins. *The Hospice Journal: Physical, Psychosocial, and Pastoral Care of the Dying,* 10,3 (1995): 47–54. Used with permission.

Excerpts from "Good-bye, Love, There's No One Leaving," by Tommy Sands (published by Elm Grove Music [PRS] on Green Linnet Records, 1994). Used with permission.

Excerpt from "King Kong Kitchie Kitchie Ki-Me-O." Traditional arranged by Peter Stanley. © Copyright 1976 Durham Music Ltd., London, England. TRO–Cheshire Music, Inc., New York, controls all publication rights for the U.S.A. and Canada. Used with permission.

Excerpt from "Out of Tears" by Mick Jagger and Keith Richards (*Voodoo Lounge,* Virgin Records, 1994). Published by PromoPub BV. Used with permission.

Memory Box and Memory Book activities adapted from *Failure-Free Activities for the Alzheimer's Patient: A Guidebook for Caregivers,* by Carmel

Author's Note

Acknowledgment is made to the following sources, which provided some of the details that appear in this book.

Alzheimer's: A Caregiver's Guide and Sourcebook, by Howard Gruetzner (New York: Wiley, 1988).

The Alzheimer's Cope Book: The Complete Care Manual for Patients and Their Families, by R. E. Markin (New York: Carol, 1992).

The Basics of Daily Care, by Lynn Adams and Mardi Richmond. *Tips for Caregivers Series: Helping You Help Others — Practical Ways of Helping You Better Care for a Person with Memory Loss and Confusion* (Santa Cruz, Calif.: Journeyman, 1993).

Bathing and Personal Care, by Lynn Adams and Mardi Richmond. *Tips for Caregivers Series: Helping You Help Others — Practical Ways of Helping You Better Care for a Person with Memory Loss and Confusion* (Santa Cruz, Calif.: Journeyman, 1993).

Care of Alzheimer's Patients: A Manual for Nursing Home Staff, by Lisa P. Gwyther (nc: American Health Care Association and Alzheimer's Disease and Related Disorders Association, 1985).

Choosing a Nursing Home, by Seth B. Goldsmith (New York: Prentice Hall, 1990).

The Consumer's Legal Guide to Today's Health Care: Your Medical Rights and How to Assert Them, by Stephen L. Isaacs and Ava C. Swartz (Boston: Houghton Mifflin, 1992).

Dealing with Anger, by Mardi Richmond. *Tips for Caregivers Series: Helping You Help Others — Practical Ways of Helping You Better Care for a Person with Memory Loss and Confusion* (Santa Cruz, Calif.: Journeyman, 1993).

Enjoying Everyday Activities, by Mardi Richmond. *Tips for Caregivers Series: Helping You Help Others — Practical Ways of Helping You Better Care for a Person with Memory Loss and Confusion* (Santa Cruz, Calif.: Journeyman, 1993).

The Essential Guide to a Living Will: How to Protect Your Right to Refuse Medical Treatment, by B. D. Colen (New York: Prentice Hall, 1991).

The Essential Guide to Prescription Drugs, 1995, by James W. Long and James J. Rybacki (New York: HarperPerennial, 1994).

Failure-Free Activities for the Alzheimer's Patient: A Guidebook for Caregivers, by Carmel Sheridan (Forest Knolls, Calif.: Elder Books, 1987). 1-800-909-2673

"Feasible Criteria for Enrolling End-Stage Dementia Patients in Home Hospice Care," by Patricia Hanrahan and Daniel J. Luchins. *The Hospice Journal: Physical, Psychosocial, and Pastoral Care of the Dying* 10,3 (1995): 47–54.

Final Exit: The Practicalities of Self-Deliverance and Assisted Suicide for the Dying, by Derek Humphry (New York: Bantam Doubleday Dell, 1991).

How to Care for Your Parents: A Handbook for Adult Children, by Nora Jean Levin (Washington, D.C.: Storm King Press, 1987).

Let Me Die Before I Wake: How Dying People End Their Suffering, by Derek Humphry (1991; rev. ed., Eugene, Oreg.: Hemlock Society, 1991).

The Living Will and the Durable Power of Attorney for Health Care Book, with Forms: Contemporary Public Health Issues, by Phillip G. Williams (Oak Park, Ill.: P. Gaines, 1991).

The Living Will Handbook, by Alan D. Lieberson (Mamaroneck, N.Y.: Hastings House, 1991).

Making Communication Easier, by Lynn Adams and Mardi Richmond. *Tips for Caregivers Series: Helping You Help Others — Practical Ways of Helping You Better Care for a Person with Memory Loss and Confusion* (Santa Cruz, Calif.: Journeyman, 1993).

Making Mealtime Easier, by Lynn Adams and Mardi Richmond. *Tips for Caregivers Series: Helping You Help Others — Practical Ways of Helping You Better Care for a Person with Memory Loss and Confusion* (Santa Cruz, Calif.: Journeyman, 1993).

On Death and Dying, Questions and Answers on Death and Dying, On Life After Death, by Elisabeth Kübler-Ross (New York: QPBC, 1992).

The Power of Attorney Book, by Denis Clifford, and edited by Lisa Goldortas (Berkeley, Calif.: Nolo Press, 1990).

Prepare Your Own Last Will and Testament without a Lawyer, by Daniel Sitarz (Wheaton, Ill.: Nova, 1988).

Reducing Restlessness and Anxiety, by Lynn Adams and Mardi Richmond. *Tips for Caregivers Series: Helping You Help Others — Practical Ways of Helping You Better Care for a Person with Memory Loss and Confusion* (Santa Cruz, Calif.: Journeyman, 1993).

Sleeping Through the Night, by Lynn Adams and Mardi Richmond. *Tips for Caregivers Series: Helping You Help Others — Practical Ways of Helping You Better Care for a Person with Memory Loss and Confusion* (Santa Cruz, Calif.: Journeyman, 1993).

The 36-Hour Day: A Family Guide to Caring for Persons with Alzheimer's Disease, Related Dementing Illnesses, and Memory Loss in Later Life, by Nancy L. Mace and Peter V. Rabins (New York: Warner, 1981).

Understanding Alzheimer's Disease, by Alzheimer's Disease and Related Disorders Association, edited by Miriam K. Aronson (New York: Scribner's, 1988).

Understanding Difficult Behaviors: Some Practical Suggestions for Coping with Alzheimer's Disease and Related Illnesses, by Anne Robinson, Beth Spencer, and Laurie White (Ypsilanti, Mich.: Eastern Michigan University and Geriatric Education Center of Michigan, 1989).

When Someone You Love Has a Mental Illness: A Handbook for Family, Friends, and Caregivers, by Rebecca Woolis (New York: Putnam, 1992).

Your Guide to Living Wills and Durable Powers of Attorney for Health Care in Ohio, by Gere B. Fulton (Holland, Ohio: Health Law Press, 1991).